BLIND EYE

Stuart MacBride is the author of several bestselling novels featuring DS Logan McRae. With *Cold Granite* he won the Barry Award for best first novel, and was shortlisted for the International Thriller Writers' best debut novel award. He has also won the CWA Dagger in the Library, awarded for a body of work, and Best Breakthrough Author at the ITV3 crime thriller awards. His work has been shortlisted for the Theakston's Old Peculier Crime novel of the Year Award three times.

Stuart lives in north-east Scotland with his wife Fiona, cat Grendel, and a vegetable plot full of weeds.

Visit Stuart MacBride's website at: www.stuartmacbride.com

Praise for Stuart MacBride:

'Hard-hitting prose with a bone-dry humour and characters you can genuinely believe in, Stuart MacBride's Logan McRae series of novels are a real treat' SIMON KERNICK

'Fierce, unflinching and shot through with the blackest of humour; this is crime fiction of the highest order by a writer whose dark star is most definitely on the rise'
MARK BILLINGHAM

'If you're looking for taut narrative, gut-churning incident, strong characterisation, all shot through with savagely dark humour, then look no further' REGINALD HILL

'If you're looking for taut narrative, gut-churning incident, strong characterisation, all shot through with savagely dark humour, then look no further' REGINALD HILL

'Ferocious and funny' VAL MCDERMID

'Makes Ian Rankin's noir seem blanc' *Observer*

'McRae makes John Rebus seem like a compliant wimp . . . bodies abound, blood flows freely and McRae is a delight' *The Times*

'Tartan noir's greatest exponent' *The Daily Mirror*

'Riveting and gruesome' *Daily Telegraph*

'The novel rattles along like a bolting horse and the dialogue crackles like a firework display . . . DI Steel should be declared a national treasure' ANDREW TAYLOR, *Spectator*

'Grim, gritty and great fun' *Daily Sport*

'Stuart MacBride goes straight for the jugular with a tight, thrilling novel' *Glasgow Herald*

'Cracking dialogue . . . a standout crime novel' *Metro*

By Stuart MacBride

Cold Granite
Dying Light
Broken Skin
Flesh House
Blind Eye
Dark Blood

Writing as Stuart B. MacBride

Halfhead

STUART MACBRIDE

Blind Eye

HARPER

This is a work of fiction. Any references to real people, living or dead, real events, businesses, organizations and localities are intended only to give the fiction a sense of reality and authenticity. All names, characters, places and incidents are either the product of the author's imagination or are used fictitiously, and their resemblance, if any, to real-life counterparts is entirely coincidental. The only exception to this are the characters Hilary Brander, Alexander (Zander) Clark, and Dave Goulding, who have given their express permission to be fictionalized in this volume. All behaviour, history, and character traits assigned to these individuals have been designed to serve the needs of the narrative and do not necessarily bear any resemblance to the real people.

Harper
An imprint of HarperCollins*Publishers*
77–85 Fulham Palace Road,
Hammersmith, London W6 8JB

www.harpercollins.co.uk

This paperback edition 2010
4

First published in Great Britain by
HarperCollins*Publishers* 2009

A catalogue record for this book is
available from the British Library

ISBN: 978 0 00 734257 0

Typeset in Meridien by Palimpsest Book Production Limited,
Grangemouth, Stirlingshire

Printed and bound in Great Britain by
Clays Ltd, St Ives plc

For Scott and Christopher

Without Whom . . .

In writing this book I *will* have got some stuff wrong. Sometimes it's on purpose, because I think it works better for the story, other times . . . well, nobody's perfect are they? But anything I did get right is down to the following people:

Superintendent Jim Bilsland and everyone at Grampian Police who helped, but wanted to remain anonymous; Andrzej Jastrzebski from the Old Warsaw Bakery; Mark 'Rentboy' McHardy and Michelle Brady; Father Keith Herrera; Eryk Grasela of Crazy Tours, Krakow; Przemyslaw Biernat, who fixed a lot of my Polish; Antoni Cybulski for teaching me to swear; and the ever wonderful Ishbel Gall who knows everything there is to know about death, and isn't afraid to share. Thanks guys.

I also want to thank my agent Phil Patterson and everyone at Marjacq; my editorial ninja Sarah Hodgson (who had to put up with an awful lot to get this book finished); Jane Johnson and the rest of the team at HarperCollins; James Oswald and Allan Guthrie for their input; Hilary Brander, who appears as a character in this book because she and her husband donated a vast sum of money to Grampian Police's Diced Cap Charity (www.dicedcap.org); everyone at Aberdeen

Royal Infirmary, especially the nurses and support staff in the A&E Ward and Ward 49 who looked after me during my little 'health scare'; and Fiona and Grendel for keeping me supplied with dead rodents and cups of tea.

Oh, and the next book's getting set in January/February – sod the tourist board, writing about all this sunshine's making me queasy.

See How They Run . . .

1

Waiting was the worst bit: hunkered back against the wall, eyes squinting in the setting sun, waiting for the nod. A disused business unit in Torry – not exactly the most affluent area of Aberdeen – downwind of a fish factory, and a collection of huge yellow bins overflowing with heads, bones and innards that festered in the hot June evening.

Half a dozen armed police officers – three teams of two, all dressed in black, sweating and trying not to breathe through their noses – listened for sounds of movement over the raucous screams of Jurassic-Park seagulls.

Nothing.

A big man, nose and mouth covered by a black scarf, held up a hand. The firearms officers tensed.

And three, two, one. . .

BOOM – the handheld battering ram smashed into the lock and the door exploded inwards in a shower of wooden splinters.

'GO! GO! GO!'

Into a gloomy corridor: grey walls, grubby blue carpet tiles.

Team One took the workshop at the back, Team Two

took the front offices, and both members of Team Three hammered up the stairs. Detective Sergeant Logan McRae slithered to a halt at the top: there was a dust-encrusted desk upended on the landing; a dead pot plant; dark rectangles on the walls where pictures used to hang; four open doors. 'Clear.'

PC Guthrie – the other half of Team Three – crept over to the nearest doorway, MP5 machine pistol at the ready, and peered inside. 'Clear.' He backed up and tried the next one in line. 'This is such a waste of time. How many of these things have we done this week?'

'Just keep your eyes open.'

'There's no bugger here,' he said, stepping over the threshold, 'it's a complete—'

His head snapped backwards – a spray of blood erupting from his nose. Guthrie hit the floor hard, helmet bouncing off the grimy carpet tiles. There was a harsh CRACK as his Heckler & Koch went off, tearing a hole through the plasterboard at waist height.

And then the screaming started. High-pitched and painful, coming from inside the room: '*Proszę, nie zabijaj mnie!*'

Logan snapped the safety off his weapon and charged through the door. Office: broken typist chair, rusty filing cabinet, telephone directory . . . woman. She was slumped back against the wall, one hand clutching at the large stain of dark red spreading out from the hole in her side. And in her other hand she had a heavy-duty stapler, holding it like a club. There was blood on the end.

Logan pointed his machine pistol at her head. 'On the floor, now!'

'*Proszę, nie zabijaj mnie!*' The woman was filthy, her long dark hair plastered to her head. She was sobbing, trembling. '*Proszę, nie zabijaj mnie!*'

Something about 'please' and 'not hurt'?

'Policja,' said Logan, doing his best to pronounce it right, 'I'm a *Policja*. Understand? *Policja*? Police officer?' Sodding hell . . . this was what he got for not paying more attention during Polish lessons back at the station.

'Proszę. . .' She slid further down the wall, leaving a thick streak of red on the wallpaper, saying 'please' over and over: *'Proszę, proszę. . .'*

Logan could hear footsteps clattering up the stairs, then someone reached the landing and swore. 'Control, this is zero-three-one-one: we have a man down; repeat, we have a man down! I need an ambulance here, *now*!'

'Proszę. . .' The stapler fell from her fingers.

A firearms officer burst into the room, gun pointing everywhere at once. He froze as soon as he saw the woman slumped against the wall, legs akimbo and covered in blood.

'Jesus, Sarge, what did you do to her?'

'I didn't do anything: it was Guthrie. And it was an accident.'

'Bloody hell.' The newcomer grabbed his Airwave handset and called in again, demanding an update on that ambulance while Logan tried to calm the woman down with pidgin Polish and lots of hand gestures.

It wasn't working.

The other half of Team Two stuck his head round the doorframe and said, 'We've got another one.'

Logan looked up from the woman's bloodshot eyes. 'Another one what?'

'You'd better come see.'

It was a slightly bigger office, the roof sloping off into the building's eaves. A dusty Velux window let in the golden glow of a dying sun. The only item of furniture was a battered desk, with a missing leg. The air was thick with the smell of burning meat, and human waste.

The reason was lying on the floor behind the broken desk: a man, curled up in the foetal position, not moving.

'Oh Jesus. . .' Logan looked at the PC. 'Is he. . .?'

'Yup. Just like all the others.'

Logan squatted down and felt for a pulse, double checking. Still alive.

He placed a hand on the man's shoulder and rolled him over onto his back.

The man groaned. And Logan's stomach tried to evict the macaroni cheese he'd had for lunch.

Someone had beaten the living hell out of the guy – broken his nose, knocked out a few teeth, but that was nothing. That barely merited a band-aid compared with what had happened to his eyes.

Just like all the others.

2

'All right, that's enough.' Detective Chief Inspector Finnie slammed his hand down on the table at the front of the little briefing room, then glared at the assembled officers, waiting for quiet. With his floppy hair, jowls, and wide rubbery lips he looked like a frog caught in the act of turning into a not particularly attractive prince.

'Thanks to last night's *sterling* work by Team Three,' he said, 'the press have somehow got the idea that we're all a bunch of bloody idiots.' He held up a copy of that morning's *Aberdeen Examiner*, the headline 'POLICE SHOOT UNARMED WOMAN IN BUNGLED RAID' was stretched across the front page.

Sitting at the back of the room, Logan shifted uneasily in his chair. The first operation he'd been involved in for six months and it was 'Bungled'. A cock-up. Fiasco. Complete and utter sodding disaster. It didn't matter that it wasn't his fault – he wasn't even the Lead Firearms Officer.

He let his eyes drift to the clock on the wall behind DCI Finnie. Twenty to eight. He'd spent half the night up at the hospital, and the other half filling in paperwork: trying to explain how they'd accidentally managed to shoot a civilian.

Right now he was operating on two hours' sleep and three cups of coffee.

Finnie slapped the newspaper down on the desk. 'I had the Chief Constable on the phone for two hours this morning, wanting to know why my *oh-so-professional* officers are incapable of carrying out a *simple* forced entry without casualties.' He paused for an unpleasant smile. 'Was I too vague at the briefing? Did I have a senior moment and say you could shoot anyone you felt like? Did I? Because the only *other* alternative I can think of is that you're all a bunch of useless morons, and that *can't* be right, can it?'

No one answered.

Finnie nodded. 'Thought so. Well, you'll all be *delighted* to know that we'll be getting an internal enquiry from Professional Standards. Starting soon as we've finished here.'

That got a collective groan from the whole team, all twelve of them.

'Oh shut up. You think you've got it bad? What about the poor woman lying in intensive care with a bullet in her?' He glanced in Logan's direction. 'DS McRae: Superintendent Napier wants you first. *Please,* do us all a favour and make-believe you're a policeman for once. OK? Can you do that for me? Pretty please?'

There was a moment's silence as everyone looked the other way. Logan could feel his face going pink. 'Yes, *sir*.'

'And when you're finished there, you're on chauffeur duty. Maybe that'll keep you out of trouble for a while. Next slide.' Finnie nodded at his sidekick – a stick-thin detective sergeant with ginger hair like rusty wire wool – and the image on screen changed. An unremarkable man's face: mid-twenties, grinning at the camera in a pub somewhere. 'This is victim number five: Lubomir Podwojski.'

Another nod and the photo changed. Nearly everyone in the room swore. The happy face was gone, replaced by the battered nightmare Logan had seen last night. The eyes just two tattered holes ringed with scorched tissue.

Someone said, 'Jesus. . .'

Finnie tapped the screen. 'Take a good, long look, ladies and gentlemen – because this is going to happen again, and again, until we catch the bastard doing it.' He left the man's ruined face up there for a whole minute. 'Next slide.'

Podwojski disappeared, replaced by a letter with lots of different fonts in lots of different colours. 'It arrived this morning.'

> **You let them in!!!** YOU let them in and they RUN WILD LIKE DOGS. These Polish **animals** take our jobs. They take our women. **They have even taken our God!** And you do nothing.
>
> Someone must fight for what is right.
>
> I will do what I have to. I will **BLIND** them all, like I **BLINDED** the last one**!** And **YOU** will **WADE** in the burning blood of ***wild dogs!!!***

Finnie held up a collection of clear plastic evidence bags, each one containing its own little laser-printed message of hate. 'Five victims; five phone calls; eight notes. I want you all to read the profile *again*. I've got Doctor Goulding coming in at three to update it with the new victim, and it *might* be nice if we can give him some input that makes us sound like we actually have a *clue* what we're doing. Don't you think?'

Meeting with Professional Standards was about as much fun as getting a tooth removed without anaesthetic. Superintendent Napier – the man in charge of screwing over his fellow officers the minute anything went wrong – droned on and on and on and on, letting Logan know exactly how half-baked and unprofessional Team Three had been during last night's raid. And somehow that was all Logan's fault . . . just because he was a Detective Sergeant and Guthrie was a mere Police Constable with a staple in his newly broken nose.

After two hours of having to explain every mistake he'd made for the last seven months, Logan was free to go. He stomped down the stairs, muttering and swearing his way out through the back doors and into the morning. Going to pick up a car so he could enjoy the privilege of ferrying DCI Finnie about.

The rear podium car park behind FHQ was a little sun-trap full of banished smokers sucking enough nicotine into their lungs to keep them going for another half hour. Logan worked his way through the crowd, making for the fleet of CID pool cars.

Bloody Finnie.

Bloody Finnie and Bloody Superintendent Napier.

And Bloody Grampian Bloody Police.

Maybe Napier was right? Maybe it was time to 'consider alternative career options'. Anything had to be better than this.

'Hoy, Laz, where do you think you're going?'

Damn.

He turned to find Detective Inspector Steel slouched against the Chief Constable's brand-new Audi, cigarette dangling from the corner of her mouth, big wax-paper cup of coffee resting on the car's bonnet. Her hair looked as if it had been styled by a drunken gorilla – which was an improvement on yesterday. She tilted her face to the sun, letting her wrinkles bask in the glow of a glorious summer's morning. 'Hear you had a spot of bother last night. . .?'

'Don't start, OK? I got enough of that from Napier this morning.'

'And how is everyone's favourite champion of Professional Standards?'

'He's a ginger-haired cock.' Logan stared at the shiny blue Audi. 'Chief Constable's going to kill you if he finds out you're using his pride and joy as a coffee table.'

'Don't change the subject. What did Napier say?'

'The usual: I'm crap. My performance is crap. And everything I touch turns to crap.'

DI Steel took a long draw on her cigarette and produced her own private smokescreen. 'Have to admit he's got a point with the "turning to crap" thing. No offence, like.'

'Thanks. Thanks a lot. That's really nice.'

'Ah, don't be so sensitive. You're having a bad patch, it happens. No' the end of the world, is it?'

'Seven months isn't a "bad patch", it's a—'

'Anyway,' she said, 'it's your lucky day: you get to accompany me on a tour of local primary schools. Some dirty old git's been trying to lure kiddies into his car with the promise of puppies and assorted sweeties.'

'Can't today,' said Logan, backing away, 'got to go visit the hospital and speak to our latest Oedipus victim, and that woman we—'

'Shot?'

'It was an accident, OK?'

'Aye, aye, Mr Tetchy-Trousers. Maybe I'll tag along? Show you how a real police officer questions witnesses.'

'Fine, you can ride in the back with Finnie.'

Steel clamped her mouth shut, sending a small cascade of ash spiralling down the front of her blouse. 'I'd rather have cystitis.'

'You're going to have to work with him eventually.'

'My sharny arse.' She took the last inch of her cigarette

and ground it out against the Chief Constable's wing mirror. 'You have fun with DCI Frog-Face, I'll give someone else the benefit of my brilliance. Where's Rennie?'

'Not back till Friday.'

'Oh for God's . . . Fine. I'll take Beattie, you happy now?' She turned and stomped her way back through the rear doors, swearing all the way.

Aberdeen Royal Infirmary wasn't a pretty building. A collection of slab-like granite lumps – connected with corridors, walkways and chock-a-block car parks – it had all the charm of a kick in the bollocks.

DCI Finnie hadn't said a word all the way over, he'd just sat in the back, fiddling with his BlackBerry. Probably sending bitchy emails to the Detective Chief Superintendent in charge of CID.

'If you don't mind me asking, sir,' said Logan, taking them on their second lap of the car park, looking for somewhere to abandon the shiny new Vauxhall, 'why didn't you take DS Pirie?'

'Believe me, you weren't my first choice. Pirie's got a court appearance this morning; soon as he's free you hand this over to him, understand? That way we might actually get a result.' Finnie watched as yet another row of badly parked vehicles went by. 'Well, *much* as I'm enjoying your magical mystery tour, I haven't got time. Drop me off at the main entrance, you can catch up later. Think you can handle that without screwing it up?'

Logan kept his mouth shut and did as he was told.

Fifteen minutes later he slouched along the corridor to the intensive care ward, following an overweight nurse with tree-trunk ankles.

'Don't get me wrong,' she said, 'it's not their fault, but

still: if you're going to move to a country, the least you can do is learn the bloody language.' She took a right, following the coloured lines set into the linoleum. 'Soon as they get a drink in them they forget how to speak English. Mind you, my husband's the same, but he's from Ellon, so what do you expect? . . . Here we are.'

She pointed to a private room at the end of the corridor. A uniformed PC sat by the door, reading a lurid gossip magazine with 'CELEBRITY CELLULITE!' plastered all over the cover.

'Right,' said the nurse, 'if you'll excuse me, I've got a two-hour presentation on the importance of washing my hands to go to. God save us from bloody politicians. . .'

Logan watched her squeak and grumble away, then wandered over to the constable and peered over his shoulder at a photograph of a bikini-clad woman with lumpy thighs. 'Who the hell is that?'

The constable shrugged. 'No idea. Nice tits though.'

'Finnie inside?'

'Aye, looks like someone shat in his shoe.'

Logan harrumphed. 'Need I remind you, Constable, that you're talking about our superior officer?'

'Doesn't stop him being a sarcastic dickhead.'

Which was true.

Logan pushed the door open and stepped into a brightly lit hospital room. Lubomir Podwojski was slumped in bed, his eyes covered with white gauze, a morphine drip hooked up to the back of his left hand. Finnie and a police interpreter had pulled up chairs on either side, the DCI sitting with his arms crossed as the female officer finished translating something into Polish.

After a long pause, Podwojski mumbled a reply. The interpreter leaned in close, putting her ear an inch from the blind man's lips. And then she frowned. 'He says he can't remember.'

Finnie tightened his mouth into a mean little line. 'Ask – him – again.'

The interpreter sighed. 'I've been asking him since—'

'I *said,* ask him again.'

'Fine. Whatever.' She went back to speaking Polish.

The DCI looked up and saw Logan standing in the doorway. 'Where have you been?'

'Had to park miles away. Do you want me to—'

'No. Go speak to the woman. Remember her? The one you somehow managed to put a bullet in? It might be nice to know *why* she was there and exactly *what* she saw.'

'But—'

'*Today,* Sergeant.'

'Yes sir.'

She looked as if she was made of porcelain, her pale skin marred by livid purple bruises. But you could still tell she'd been pretty, before all this. . .

A rats' nest of wires and tubes anchored her to a bank of machinery in the mixed high-dependency ward, just the gentle rise and fall of her chest – powered by the ventilator next to her bed – marring the stillness.

Logan flagged down a nurse and asked how the patient was getting on.

'Not that good.' The nurse checked the chart at the foot of the bed. 'Bullet went through the colon and small intestine, nicked the bottom of her spleen. . . Didn't stop till it hit her spine. They're going to wait to see if she gets a bit stronger before they try removing it. She lost a lot of blood.'

'Any idea who she is?'

'Never regained consciousness.' The nurse clipped the chart back on the bed. 'All I can tell you is she's in her early twenties. Other than that she's a Jane Doe.'

'Damn. . .' Logan pointed at the plastic pitcher of water on the bedside cabinet. 'Can I borrow one of the glasses?'

'Why?'

'Didn't bring a fingerprint kit with me.' Logan snapped on a pair of latex gloves, picked up a glass and wiped it clean with a corner of the bed-sheet. Then opened the woman's right hand and rolled the glass carefully across the fingertips.

He stood there, staring at her wrist. It was circled with a thin line of purple bruises, about a centimetre wide. The left one was the same. 'Bloody hell. . .'

Logan put the glass back where he'd got it. 'Help me untuck the sheets. I want to check her ankles.'

'Oh no you don't. I'll just have to make the bed again. I do have other patients to look after, you know.'

But Logan wasn't listening, he was pulling the sheets out, exposing a pair of pale legs. The ankles had the same ring of bruises. 'Has she had a rape test?'

'What? No, why would we—'

'The bruises round her wrists and ankles – she's been tied up and beaten. Pretty girl like that, do you think they just stopped there?'

'I'll get a doctor.'

3

'And what *exactly* did you think you were doing?' DCI Finnie stood in the hospital corridor, scowling at Logan as the nurse drew the curtain around their mystery woman's bed. 'Did I miss a memo? Did you *suddenly* get promoted to Senior Investigating Officer on this case?'

'I just thought it would save—'

Finnie poked Logan in the chest. 'You run everything through me *before* you do it. Understand?'

'But—'

'Do you secretly *yearn* to spend every day from now till you retire giving road safety lectures to sticky little children? Is that it?'

'No, sir. I just—'

'I don't know what kind of slapdash methods you're used to, but when you work for me you *will* follow the chain of command, or so help me I'll send you right back where I found you.'

'But—'

'After your performance last year, you're *lucky* to still have a job, never mind be involved in a major enquiry. What, did you think the magic *career* pixies put you on the Oedipus case? Because they didn't.' Finnie poked him again. 'You had experience with serial weirdoes and I thought, I *actually* thought you might take this opportunity to get your head out your backside and turn your train-wreck life around. Was I wrong? Are you the complete cock-up everyone says you are?'

Logan ground his teeth, took a deep breath, and said, 'No, sir. Thank you, sir.'

'And?'

'It won't happen again?'

'That's not what I meant – when are they going to get the results back from the rape kit. . .' He stopped and frowned at the evidence bag in Logan's hand. 'Is that a glass?' Finnie grabbed the bag and held it up to the light. 'Why have you got a glass?'

'We don't have an ID for the victim, and I didn't have a fingerprint kit with me, so I thought—'

'You see? That's *exactly* the kind of nonsense I'm talking about. We have officers posted here twenty-four-seven, do you think they might – *just* – have a fingerprint kit? Hmm? Do you think?' He stared at Logan for a beat. 'Well, go get it then.' He held out the evidence bag. 'And take your Junior Detective Set with you.'

By the time the fingerprint results came back from the lab, it was nearly half past two and Logan was back at his desk in CID, crunching on an indigestion tablet. That's what he got for microwaving vegetable curry for lunch. And now he had to go tell Finnie they still had no idea who the woman was. He'd love that.

Frog-faced git.

No wonder Logan had indigestion.

It took a while to track Finnie down, but he finally found the DCI in one of the small incident rooms – just big enough for two cluttered desks, three seats, and a strange eggy smell. He was sitting on the edge of a desk, deep in conversation with a gangly admin officer.

Logan settled back to wait.

Finnie didn't even look round. 'Did you want something, Sergeant, or are you just worried that wall's going to fall down with out you leaning on it?'

'We couldn't find her prints in the database.'

'And?'

'And nothing.'

'Have you told the Media Office to make up "have you seen this woman" posters?'

'Well . . . no.'

And at that, Finnie did turn round. 'Why not? Use your initiative, for goodness sake.'

'You told me not to do anything without clearing it through you first.'

'What are you, twelve? You sound like my niece.' The DCI held his hand out. 'Photograph.'

Logan handed over the eight-by-ten glossy showing their Jane Doe lying in her hospital bed, complete with ventilation tube and drips. It wasn't exactly the best head-and-shoulders shot in the world.

Finnie threw it back. 'This is useless. Get it up to Photographic. Tell them to edit out all the tubes and lines, give her skin a bit of colour, lose the panda eyes. . . Make her look like a person someone might actually recognize.'

'Yes sir.'

'Sometime *today* would be nice, Sergeant. You know, if you're not *too* busy?'

The technician in the 'BARNEY THE DINOSAUR FOR PRESIDENT' T-shirt made some disparaging comments about the quality of the photograph, then said she'd see what she could do. No promises though.

Logan left her to it and headed back down to the CID office for a cup of tea and a bit of a skive. Not that he got any peace there – his in-box was overflowing with new directives, memos, reminders about getting paperwork completed on time, and right at the top – marked with a little red exclamation mark – yet another summons from Professional Standards. Apparently there were some discrepancies between his version of events and PC Guthrie's – would he care to discuss them at half ten tomorrow morning?

No he wouldn't. But he didn't exactly have any choice, did he?

There was a little fridge in the corner of the CID office. Logan helped himself to the carton marked 'DUNCAN'S MILK ~ HANDS OFF YOU THIEVING BASTARDS!' and made himself a cup of tea, taking it back to his desk, where he sat staring out of the window: watching a pair of seagulls rip the windscreen wiper blades off a Porsche parked on the street below. Wishing he'd been able to dig up a couple of biscuits.

'. . .the labs yet?'

'Hmm?' Logan swivelled his seat round till he was facing the newcomer – Detective Sergeant Pirie, back from the Sheriff Court, swaggered across the room.

'I said, "do you have that photo back from the labs yet"?'

'What's with the smug face?'

'Richard Banks got eight years. Bastard tried to plea-bargain it down, but the PF stuck him with the whole thing.'

'Congratulations.'

'Photo?'

'They're still working on it.'

'Rape kit?'

'Same answer.'

'Ah. . .' Pirie ran a hand through his ginger, Brillo-Pad hair. 'The boss isn't going to like that.'

'Really? *That*'ll make a change.'

'Yes, well . . . email me everything you've got on our Jane Doe then you can go back to running about after that wrinkly disaster area Steel.'

Logan stared at him. 'Do you *really* want a "whose DI is the biggest arsehole" competition?'

'Fair point.' Pirie settled onto the edge of Logan's desk. 'Finnie tells me you tried to take our victim's prints with a water glass. . .' His eyes roved across the piles of paperwork and then locked onto the plastic evidence bag with the glass in it. 'And here it is! I thought he was just taking the piss.' He picked up the bag and grinned. 'What are you, Nancy Drew?'

'Ha bloody ha.' Logan snatched it back and stuffed it into his bottom drawer, burying it under a pile of *Police Review* magazines, then slammed the drawer shut.

'I don't get it: why's he got it in for me? All he ever does is . . . *moan*.'

'That's easy,' Pirie stood, turned, and sauntered out the door, 'he doesn't like you.'

The phone on Logan's desk started ringing, cutting off his opinion on what DS Pirie could do with his foreskin and a cheese grater.

'McRae?'

'You still working for Frog-Face Finnie?' DI Steel, sounding out of breath.

'Not any more, Pirie's taken over the—'

'Then get your arse downstairs. We've got a riot on our hands!'

* * *

The Turf 'n Track wasn't the sort of place you'd put on a tourist map. Unless it was accompanied by a big sticker saying, 'Avoid Like The Plague!' It sat in a small row of four grubby shops in the heart of Sandilands, surrounded by suicidally depressed council flats. A pockmarked car park sulked in front of the little retail compound, complete with burnt-out litter bin, the vitrified plastic oozing out across the greying tarmac. There was a grocers on one side, the dusty corpse of a video store on the other – its windows boarded up with plywood – and a kebab shop on the end. Everything was covered in layer upon layer of graffiti, except for the Turf 'n Track. Its blacked-out windows and green-and-yellow signage were pristine. Nobody messed with the McLeods. Not more than once, anyway.

The whole area had a rundown, neglected air to it, even the handful of kids clustered on the borders of the car park, watching the fight.

Logan screeched the pool car up onto the kerb and leapt out into the warm afternoon, shouting, 'POLICE!'

No one paid the slightest bit of attention.

DI Steel hauled herself from the passenger seat and sparked up a cigarette, blowing out a long plume of smoke as she surveyed the scene. Six men were busy trying to beat the crap out of one other. 'You recognize anyone?' she asked.

They were dressed in jeans and T-shirts, all swinging punches and kicks with wild abandon. Someone would rush in, throw a fist at someone else, then retreat fast. Amateurs.

The inspector pointed at one of the combatants – an acne-riddled baboon with a bloody lip – as he took a swing at a fat bloke with a bowl haircut. 'Him: Spotty. I'm sure I've done him for dealing.'

Logan tried again: 'POLICE! BREAK IT UP!'

Someone managed to land a punch and a ragged cheer went up from the spectators.

'I SAID BREAK IT UP!'

Steel laid a hand on Logan's arm. 'No' really working, is it: the shouting?'

Logan took two steps towards the mass of flying fists and trainers. The inspector tightened her grip. 'Don't be an idiot – they might be a bunch of Jessies, but they'd tear *you* apart.'

'We can't just sit back and—'

'Yes we can.' Steel hoiked herself up onto the bonnet of the pool car, her shoes dangling a foot off the ground. 'Come on: none of them's got any weapons. Sit your backside down and enjoy the show. Uniform will be here soon enough with their Freudian truncheons and batter the lot of them.' She flicked an inch of ash onto the tatty tarmac. 'You eat that curry yet?'

'Yeah. . . Had it for lunch.'

'And?'

'Tell Susan it was very nice. Bit spicy, but nice.'

'You're *such* a wimp. Next time I'll get her to make you a nice girly korma.'

Another fist hit its target and this time DI Steel joined in the celebration, clapping her hands and shouting, 'Jolly good! Well done that man! Now kick him in the goolies!' She checked her watch. 'Where the hell's Uniform got to? Bunch of lazy—'

Right on cue a siren wailed in the distance, getting closer.

'Ahoy, hoy,' the inspector pointed across the car park at the front door of the Turf 'n Track. A large man stood on the threshold, half in shadow: mid-thirties, face like a bowl of porridge, missing a chunk of one ear, huge shoulders, a lot of muscle just starting to turn into fat. 'Looks like the guvnor's in. Shall we go say hello, perchance to partake in a cup of tea and a garibaldi?'

'You'll be lucky. Last thing Simon McLeod offered me was a stiff kicking.'

'Watch and learn. . .' She wiggled her way down from the car bonnet, then sauntered around the punch-up, hands in her pockets, whistling a jolly tune, right up to the betting shop's front door. 'Afternoon, Simon, how they hanging?'

He wrinkled his nose. 'Do I smell bacon?'

'No, Chanel Number Five.' Steel smiled sweetly. 'Anyway, from the look of things, you smell pies.' She stopped and poked him in the stomach. 'Lots and lots of pies.' She nodded back towards the brawl. 'These your boyfriends then? Fighting over who gets to take you to the dance?'

'Fuck you.'

'Lovely offer,' she said, holding up her left hand with its sparkly wedding ring, 'but my wife doesn't like me playing with podgy gangsters.'

The first of the patrol cars appeared, slithering to a halt on the hot tarmac. Simon McLeod uncrossed his huge arms and took a couple of steps forward, shouting, 'Get out of it, you stupid bastards: police are here!'

Spotty the Baboon turned someone's nose from flesh and bone to blood and meat paste. The man sat down hard, and got a kick in the head for his trouble. But as soon as the first uniformed officer jumped out – extending her truncheon with a flick of the wrist – the fight started to break up.

The bright ones ran for it: Bowl Haircut and Hippy with a Limp made for the council housing estate. Tattooed Gimp sprinted back towards the roundabout. And Low-Budget Porn Star scarpered down the road, a uniformed officer chasing after him, shouting, 'Come back here!'

Mr Meat Paste for a Nose lay on the ground, curled up in a ball with his arms protecting his head as Spotty the

Baboon tried to kick him to death. The other officer from Alpha One Four waded in with her truncheon.

Logan watched Spotty fight back, before being battered into submission. Steel was right: Uniform could look after themselves.

He turned back to the doorway, expecting to see Simon McLeod still arguing with the inspector, but there was no sign of either of them. Right now McLeod was probably turning DI Steel into lesbian tartare. Logan swore, dug out his little canister of pepper-spray and hurried through the door.

Out of the sunshine and into the heart of darkness.

Inside, the Turf 'n Track was shabbier than it looked from the car park. The only natural light oozed in through the door, and even that was too scared to go more than a couple of feet over the threshold. The woodwork was black as a smoker's lung, coated in the accumulated tar from countless cigarettes. A pair of televisions were bolted to the wall at either end of the counter, flickering away to themselves: a race meeting in Perthshire, with the sound turned off. The door to the back office was open.

Maybe Simon McLeod had dragged the inspector back there and put her out of everyone's misery?

The linoleum floor stuck to Logan's feet as he hurried round behind the counter and – WHAT THE HELL WAS THAT?

He froze.

A deep bass growl rumbled up from somewhere to his left. The kind of growl that came with lots of teeth and ripping and tearing and running for your life. Logan turned around slowly, until he was facing an ancient-looking Alsatian, lying in a tartan dog bed. 'Nice doggy. . .' Logan frowned. 'Wait a minute, is that. . .?'

Simon's voice blared out from the back office, 'Winchester: fuck's sake, shut up!'

Winchester – Jesus, surely the thing was dead by now? It'd been ancient when Desperate Doug MacDuff had owned it. The dog looked in the vague direction of his new master's voice, eyes white and rheumy. Then Winchester yawned – showing off a lot of big brown teeth – and rested his grey muzzle back down on his paws.

It wasn't quite the scene of carnage in the back office that Logan had been expecting. A large desk sat opposite the door, beneath the mounted head of a two-tonne Rottweiler called Killer, the last known resting place of Simon McLeod's missing half ear. A collection of girly calendars dotted the walls, some going back as far as 1987. DI Steel was flicking through them while Simon McLeod made two mugs of tea.

'Bloody hell,' she said, peering at Miss March 1996, 'this one's got nipples like champagne corks. Could hang your coat on those.'

Simon handed her a mug. 'Milk, two sugars.'

'Ooh, ta.' She took an experimental sip. 'So, Simon . . . why are a bunch of drug dealers having a barney outside your shop?'

'No idea what you're talking about.'

'No?' Steel scratched her head. 'What a strange coincidence. You see, a little birdie told me there was a gang of Eastern Europeans trying to muscle in on your territory.'

'I don't have a "territory", I'm a legitimate businessman.'

'Aye, aye, and Miss Stiff Nipples here is a brain surgeon. I'm no' having a turf war in my city, Simon.'

'You're not listening, Inspector. I don't know anything about it.'

Steel nodded. 'Well, hypothetically speaking, if you or your brother *did* know anything about it – say you were both into protection, loan sharking, prostitution, supplying class A drugs . . . *hypothetically* speaking, would you tell your Auntie Roberta who these Eastern Europeans were?'

There was a pause.

'Like I said, *Inspector*, I'm a legitimate businessman. Now if you've finished your tea, you can fuck off. I've got work to do.'

4

'That went well,' said Steel, sauntering back out into the sunshine. 'No biscuits though. . . You'd think a "legitimate businessman" could rustle up a chocolate digestive, wouldn't you?'

Logan looked back in through the Turf 'n Track's front door at the dark interior. 'How the hell did you manage that? I thought he hated the police?'

'The McLeod brothers like to think they're old-school gangsters. . . Well, Simon does, Colin's just a bloody thug. You ever met their mum? She'd tan their arses if she found out they'd hit a woman.'

'You remembering what happened to Gabrielle Christie? Broken jaw, cracked ribs, fractured leg—'

'Aye, but she wasn't a woman, was she? She was a hoor.' Out came the inspector's cigarettes, the smoke spiralling up into the bright blue sky. 'It's no' the same to these people. Prostitutes aren't women, they're property. And before you say anything, I know, OK? It's just the way they think.'

Outside the bookmakers, the pre-pubescent mob had dispersed. Now there was just a single grubby child, watching as Mr Meat Paste for a Nose was loaded into Alpha One Four.

Another two patrol cars had arrived, their white paintwork sparkling in the sunshine. Spotty the Baboon was in the back of one, looking woozy and bruised from all that resisting arrest.

The other officer from Alpha One Four was limping back up the road, his black uniform trousers all torn at the knee. It looked as if Low Budget Porn Star had got away.

'Two out of six,' said Steel, leaning on the roof of the empty patrol car, 'no' exactly a brilliant arrest rate.' She smoked in silence for a moment, staring at Spotty and his swollen face. 'Right,' she said at last, pinging her fag end away, 'let's go see what the Clearasil Kid has to say for himself.'

Logan dragged out his phone. 'I'll get them to set up an interview room, we can—'

'Don't be so wet. Here,' the inspector dug into her pocket and pulled out a handful of change, 'go get some ice-lollies.'

By the time Logan returned from the little grocers, Steel was lounging in the back of Alpha One Six with Spotty. Logan clambered in on the other side, sandwiching him in.

Steel leaned across the prisoner and looked at Logan. 'What did you get?'

'Strawberry Mivvi, Orange Maid, and a Chocolate Cornetto.'

She stuck her hand out. 'Cornetto – gimmie.' She unwrapped it and took a happy bite, talking with her mouth full, 'What about you, Derek? Fancy an orange lolly? Nah, better no' it'd clash with your ginger hair. Strawberry Mivvi for Derek here, Laz.'

Logan held it out, but Spotty the Baboon, AKA: Derek, didn't take it. Which wasn't that surprising, his hands were cuffed behind his back.

'Give it here,' said Steel. She took the lolly and held it against Derek's cheek. 'There you go, that'll keep the swelling down a bit.'

Derek's voice was a high-pitched croak, 'It's cold. . .'

'Aye, well, that's what you get for being stupid. When someone yells, "Police", you either give up like a good boy, or you run like buggery.' She took a bite out of her Cornetto. 'Mmmph mmmf mnn mmnnfmmmmph fmmmnnnt?'

'Think that bloody copper broke my jaw. . .'

'Then you wouldn't be able to talk, you moron. I said, "who were you fighting with?"'

'I'm in pain!'

'You'll be in a lot more if you don't start talking.' She tossed the lolly back to Logan. 'My sergeant here likes to slam people's hands in car doors. It's his hobby. You want me to take a wee walk and see if you've still got all your fingers when I get back?'

'It was . . . a . . .' Spotty licked his top lip. 'They were Rangers supporters; said the Dons were shite. Couldn't let them get away with that. . .'

'Bollocks.' Steel cracked the door open. 'Start with his wanking hand, Laz, I'm going for a walk.'

Derek peered at Logan. 'You can't—'

'Can I break his thumbs as well?'

The inspector nodded. 'Fine by me.'

'It was just a fight! That's all. Football. You know what it's—'

'Do his toes too.' Steel levered herself out into the sunshine, licked a runaway dribble of chocolate ice-cream off the back of her hand, and slammed the car door.

Derek flinched.

'NO, WAIT! I didn't . . . I . . .' He closed his eyes and shuddered as Steel climbed back into the car.

'Make it fast, Derek, my Cornetto's melting.'

'They was trying to tell us we had to . . . sell stuff for them. You know . . . instead of . . . who we usually sell it for.'

'Uh-huh, and who would that be?'

'Don't remember.' Derek scowled out of the car window at the man in the back of Alpha One Four: Mr Meat Paste for a Nose. 'Fucking Polish bastards. Come over here, taking our jobs, screwing our women. . .'

Logan poked him in the shoulder. 'Ever sent anonymous letters, Derek? You know, lots of different fonts and exclamation marks?'

'Eh?'

'Where were you last night?'

'Went round Harry Jordan's and got wasted. Ask him. We had a party with his . . . we had a party.'

Steel tutted. 'Hope you wore protection, Derek: you'll get all sorts of nasty diseases partying with Harry Jordan's girls.' She slapped the Strawberry Mivvi back against his cheek. 'So, you going to come clean about who you're selling for? Like I couldn't already guess.' She pointed at the green-and-yellow Turf 'n Track sign. 'Come on, Derek, play it smart for once.'

But Derek had no intention of changing the habit of a lifetime.

Mr Meat Paste for a Nose sat on the other side of the interview room table, repeating for the umpteenth time, *'Nie mówię po angielsku.'*

It was all he'd say, over and over again: I don't speak English.

Lying sod.

Steel yawned, checked her watch, and told Logan to switch off the tapes. 'Hell with this.' She stood, then leant on the table, doing her best to loom over the prisoner.

'Listen up, Sunshine, I know fine well you speak English: I've got witnesses who heard you do it. But if you want to play silly buggers we'll get you an interpreter, and then we'll bang you up for obstruction. And public disorder. And anything else I can think of. We've got a whole pile of unsolved burglaries on the books, fancy getting fitted up for some of them?'

'Nie mówię po angielsku.'

'Blah, blah, blah.' She headed for the door. 'Chuck him back in his cell, Laz. We'll have another crack with a translator in the morning. You and me are going to knock off early and go find somewhere with a beer garden.'

It was the best idea Logan had heard all day.

Half past seven Wednesday morning and interview room three was like a sauna – the battered radiator in the corner pinged and clanked away to itself, even though the sun was blazing down outside. Logan and Steel sat at the chipped table, both of them sporting the rosy glow of a mild sunburn from three hours sitting at a picnic table outside Triple Kirks drinking lager and white wine.

The interpreter was slumped on the other side of the table, sweat darkening the armpits of her blouse as she repeated yet another phrase Logan was getting sick of.

'He says he doesn't know anything.'

Steel slammed her fist down on the chipped Formica tabletop. 'Stop sodding about – I want to know who he's working for!'

The interpreter sighed and tried again, *'Zapytać: dla kogo pracujesz?'*

The thickset man with the flattened nose shrugged and replied in bunged-up Polish. His face was one big bruise today, crisscrossed with sticking plasters. It wasn't a good look.

'He's not working for anyone. He's in Aberdeen visiting his cousin.'

'Then why did we catch him brawling outside a known hangout for lowlife scumbags? Why have I got a drug dealer downstairs in the cells telling me Lumpy here tried to recruit him? Who – is – he – working – for?'

'Which question do you want to ask first?'

'Oh for God's sake. We know the bastard can speak English—'

A knock at the door.

DCI Finnie marched into the room without waiting for an invitation. 'Inspector, a word please.'

The interpreter waited until Steel was out of the room before asking Logan if she was always this bad. 'Doesn't she like Polish people?'

'Not when they lie to her, no.'

'You've got to understand it from their point of view,' the interpreter nodded at the prisoner. 'Polish police were a nightmare under the Communists. They were enforcers for the regime, they'd make people disappear. And they weren't much better after independence: corrupt and lazy. So no one trusts the police anymore, and you can't really blame them, can you?'

'I can when they. . .' Logan trailed off into silence, listening to the raised voices coming through the door.

The interpreter looked puzzled. 'What?'

'Shhhhhhh!' He held his hand up for silence. It was Steel and DCI Finnie, having a stand-up row in the corridor outside.

Steel: 'No way! I am not—'

Finnie: 'That wasn't a *request*, Inspector, it was an *order*.'

Steel: 'I'm in the middle of—'

Finnie: 'You're interfering with an ongoing investigation.'

Steel: 'I'm doing my bloody job!'

Finnie: 'Not any more you're not. And if you've got a problem with that you can take it up with the DCS.'

An angry silence.

Steel: 'Fine. Laughing Boy in there's *all* yours.' She yanked the door open and glowered at Logan. 'Pack it up. We've been pulled off the case.'

Two Days Later

5

Logan shifted in the driver's seat, ruffled his copy of the *Aberdeen Examiner*, and said, 'Four across: "Forbid forever, like." "B", something, something, "I", something, something.'

Steel looked up from an in-depth analysis of her own cleavage. 'You know what,' she said, flicking a tiny avalanche of cigarette ash out of the passenger window, 'I think I've finally found one of these damn things that fits.' She tugged at her bra strap, making the contents jiggle.

Logan went back to his paper – there was no way he was getting drawn into another conversation about the Detective Inspector's underwear. Five minutes to eleven on a Friday morning and the sun was dappling its way through the trees, sending little flecks of light dancing across the speed-bumps outside Sunnybank Primary School. 'How long do we have to keep doing this?'

'Till we catch the bastard.' Steel gave up on her boobs and lounged back in her seat. 'Anyway, what you whinging about? Three days sitting on your arse in the sunshine, reading the paper and eating ice-lollies. You rather be running around after DCI Frog-Face?'

She had a point.

'No, we lounge about here till four, sod off home for the weekend and back again on Monday for another glorious week of doing bugger all.' The inspector took a long drag on her cigarette and blew, fogging the windscreen with second-hand smoke. 'Not like we got anything better to do, is it? Bloody Finnie. . .'

Here we go again.

'I mean, who the hell does he think he is? "Stop interviewing that prisoner,"' she said, doing a less than flattering impersonation of the Detective Chief Inspector, '"You're interfering with an ongoing investigation." Ongoing investigation my sharny arse. Bastard just wants all the sodding glory for himself.'

She snorted. 'And can you *believe* he let Derek McSpotty walk with a caution? We caught the wee bastard red-handed kicking the crap out of someone, resisting arrest, and being a lying junky tosspot. "You have to see the bigger picture, Inspector."' She smoked furiously for a moment. 'I'll show Finnie the bigger picture with the toe of my bloody boot.'

'What do you want to do for lunch today? We could grab a sandwich, or—'

'Kebab.' The inspector finished her cigarette and dumped the stub into an open can of Pepsi, swirling it around in the warm, flat liquid. 'That place in Sandilands. And while we're there we can accidentally nip next door to the Turf 'n Track. Have another wee chat with Simon McLeod.'

'But Finnie—'

'Finnie can pucker up and kiss my perky bumhole. Since that wee riot on Tuesday we've had five Polish blokes in A&E with their kneecaps smashed. Someone took a claw hammer to them.' She struck a pose, tapping the side of her forehead. 'Now who do we know with form for battering people with a claw hammer? Think, think, think. . .'

'OK, OK, I get it: Colin McLeod. But Finnie—'

'What is he, your boyfriend or something?'

'Why do you have to make everything—'

The school bell jangled through the warm, lazy air – eleven o'clock on the dot. Time for morning break.

'We're on.'

Screams and shouts echoed out of the school, then a stampede of five-to-seven-year-olds dressed in the standard grey-and-blue primary uniform burst out into the sunshine, hell bent on cramming as much fun as possible into their fifteen minutes of freedom.

'Anything?' asked Steel.

Logan checked the street. 'Nope. Looks like. . . wait a minute. . . Blue Toyota Yaris: there, just pulling up. You see it?'

The inspector shuffled forward in her seat, peering through the windscreen at the little mud-spattered car. The driver got out and wandered over to the playground fence. Beige cardigan, grey hair, feral moustache.

'About sodding time.' Steel clambered her way into the warm morning, and sauntered down the road with her hands in her pockets.

Logan locked up and followed her, nipping across the road at the last minute so he could come round on the guy's blind side.

Not that the man in the beige cardigan would have noticed, he was far too busy smiling at a little girl through the railings. Blonde hair, pigtails, big blue eyes.

'You know,' said the man, hands rummaging in his trouser pockets, 'my doggie's very sick and can't look after her puppies. Isn't that sad?'

The little girl nodded.

'Would you like to see them? Maybe you could take one home? Would you like that?' And all the time the trouser rummaging was getting faster. Sweat beaded on his forehead. 'Would you like to see my. . . oh God. . . puppies?'

'Jesus, Rory,' said Steel, slouching back against the man's car, 'could you *be* any more of a cliché?'

Rory stood up fast, and hurled a handful of little paper wrappers over the playground fence. 'I never did anything! You can't prove I did anything, I—'

Logan placed a hand on his shoulder. 'Rory Simpson, I'm arresting you under section five point one of the Criminal Justice Scotland Act—'

'No – I didn't do anything! I was just— mmmph!'

Steel had clamped a hand over his mouth. 'Wee kiddies, Rory: let's no' corrupt their innocent little ears with your filthy lies. Now, you want to go quietly this time, or kicking and screaming like a girl?'

Rory bit his bottom lip, frowned, then said, 'I think I'll go quietly this time.'

'Good choice, much more dignified.' The inspector nodded at Logan, 'Pick up whatever he threw to the lions.' Then she marched Rory Simpson along the road to the CID pool car.

Ten minutes later, Logan climbed in behind the wheel of the shiny new Vauxhall he'd signed for that morning. Rory and the inspector were sitting in the back, like a pair of elderly relatives waiting to go for a nice Sunday drive.

'Here,' Logan passed a clear evidence pouch back between the seats – a small handful of white paper wrappers sat in the bottom, about the size of pound coins, 'that was all I could find. There's probably more, but the little buggers weren't talking.'

DI Steel opened the bag and sniffed the contents. 'Come on then, Rory, what we going to find when we send this lot to the lab: icing sugar? Washing powder? Crack cocaine?'

Rory shrugged. 'You know how it is, Inspector, kids these days. . .'

'Yeah, yeah: six-year-olds are all Playstations, tattoos, and gang-rape. Spit it out.'

'It's not like it was in our day, is it? Then they'd get in your car for a Sherbet Dib-Dab. Now they all want drugs, booze and cash.' Rory shook his head. 'They look like butter wouldn't melt. . .' A soft smile flitted across his face.

'Rory, if you're thinking about melting butter on wee kiddies, I'm going to have my sergeant here drive us out to the middle of nowhere and kick the shite out of you.'

'Just an expression. . . I mean look at that little tease back there,' he said, pointing at the troupe of uniformed monkeys screeching their way back to class, 'she knew exactly what she was doing, didn't she? Wasn't going to give me anything for free. It's depressing really.'

A tinny Banff and Buchan accent jangled out of the radio: *'Alpha Three Sivin, from Control—'*

'Oh buggering hell.' DI Steel fumbled for the handset. 'We. . . with . . . non . . . over?' Then she went into an Oscar-winning hissing noise: 'Kshhhhhhhhhhhhhhhhhhhhh. . .'

'Aye, nice try. Incident: Primrosehill Drive. Sounds like a domestic disturbance. I've no' got any patrol cars free and yer closest so—'

Steel grimaced. 'Sorry, Dougie, but we're in Altens, miles away, you'll just have to find someone else.'

'You do know these new cars have GPS in them, don't you? I can see you right here on the screen: Sunnybank Road.'

Pause.

'Bugger.'

'Aye, so: Primrosehill Drive. And get a shift on – neighbour reported screams coming from the hoose opposite.'

Steel gave it one last try, 'But I've got prisoner in tow—'

'Some poor sod's probably getting murdered, and you're buggering about wasting time!'

Steel took her thumb off the transmit button and indulged in the kind of language that would make a social worker blush. 'Fine, we're on our way. You happy now?'

Logan started the car, drowning out the sarcastic response.

Primrosehill Drive was a curving line of large, semidetached houses with big gardens and four-by-fours in the driveways, sweltering beneath the hot sun. Logan killed the siren, and asked Steel for the address again.

She squinted out at the street. 'There, on the left: that one. Looks like a building site.'

Two storeys of grey granite, almost invisible behind a forest of scaffolding and tarpaulins. The garden was home to a cement mixer, a JCB digger, a pile of rubble, and a bright blue porta-potty. A battered green skip sat on the road outside, orange cones and planks of wood blocking anyone from parking in front of the house. Logan pulled up as close as possible.

'What now?'

Steel smacked him on the arm. 'What do you think? We charge in and save the day. Picture in the paper. Medals. Dancing girls.' She turned in her seat and poked at Rory. 'You stay here. Don't move. If I think you've so much as farted while we're gone I'm going to take your goolies off with a potato peeler. Understand?'

She took out a pair of handcuffs and slapped one side on Rory's right wrist, then dragged him forwards until he was bent double in the foot well.

'Hey!'

'Oh don't be such a whinge.' She poked the cuffs through the metal struts securing the driver's seat to the car floor, then fixed Rory's other wrist in place. He was well and truly stuck.

'Surely there's no need for this, Inspector, you know I won't—'

'Shut up before I change my mind and lock you in the bloody boot.'

She smacked Logan again. 'What you waiting for?'

They climbed out into the sunshine.

The only sound was the distant drone and rumble of traffic on Great Northern Road. No screams.

They picked their way through the churned-up dirt, skirting a stack of breezeblocks. The front door was poking out of the skip at the kerb, leaving the hallway a gaping black hole.

Logan pulled out his Airwave handset. 'DS McRae to Control, I need backup to Primrosehill Drive—'

'You are *such* a bloody Jessie. . .' Steel took another look at the dark hallway. 'Come on then,' she said, pushing Logan ahead of her, 'you go first.'

Logan swore and pulled out his little canister of pepper-spray. According to Control there still weren't any patrol cars free. They were on their own.

Steel gave him another shove and he stumbled over the threshold.

Gloom.

The builders had ripped everything back to the bare granite, and started again from scratch. Wooden stud-frames had been fixed in place with enormous masonry screws, lining the walls. Stiff ribbons of grey mains wiring were laced through holes in the joists, stretching out in hanging loops across the ceiling.

The chipboard flooring creaked beneath Logan's feet as he crept inside.

First left: the living room was empty. A green tarpaulin had been stretched over the glassless window, shrouding everything in mouldy shadows. No sign of anyone. Dining room: empty. Downstairs toilet: empty, just the hole where a WC was supposed to go and a couple of plastic pipes poking out through the floor. The kitchen was little more than a storeroom for piles of wood, boxes of tiles, bags of concrete, thick rolls of Rockwool insulation, and sheets of plaster-board.

Logan worked his way back to the stairs and started to climb. If anything it was even darker up here. It looked as if the builders had started their renovating job on this floor: the granite walls were already clad; doors hung; double glazing in; architrave, windowsills and skirting nailed in place. Logan froze on the top step and whispered, 'Did you hear that?'

'What. . .?' Steel frowned. 'Why the hell are we creeping about?' She took a deep breath, 'POLICE! Come out with your hands up and no one has to get hurt!'

A voice sounded in one of the bedrooms: *'Kurwa!'*

A figure exploded out of the open bedroom door – large, male, it was difficult to tell much more than that in the dark. He had something in his hand. Something long, that glinted in a rogue sliver of light. Crowbar.

He tried to take Logan's head off with it, swinging the thing like a broadsword.

Logan ducked and it whistled by close enough to ruffle his hair before embedding itself in the plasterboard. Logan slammed his fist into the man's stomach.

He didn't collapse and roll about on the floor in agony, he just grunted and yanked the crowbar out of the wall, taking a puffball of Rockwool with it.

Oh God. . .

Logan flipped the cap off his pepper-spray and gave him a liberal dose in the eyes.

'Aaaaghh. . . *Matkojebca!'*

It was close quarters. Too close. The jet hit and spattered back off the man's face, a mist of stinging liquid that coated everything within a three-foot radius. Including Logan.

'Ah, Jesus!' It was like being sandpapered with dried chillies, his eyes were on fire, he could barely breathe.

The crowbar smashed into the balustrade, bounced, and went spiralling down the stairwell.

Steel swore.

Clang, crash, bang, wallop.

When Logan peeled his eyes open again, the man at the top of the stairs was just a blurry figure: on his knees, swearing and panting.

God that stuff *stung*. . .

Steel shoved past Logan shouting, 'POLICE! Get your arse—' She smashed backwards into the balusters with a splintering crack.

Logan staggered against the wall, trying to peer through the pain and tears as a second figure loomed at the top of the stairs. Logan dragged up the canister of pepper-spray. 'You! Face down on the ground!'

The man stepped forwards, right arm whipping out, grabbing Logan's spraying hand and twisting it back on itself.

Logan swung a left hook, but the man blocked it, took hold of the sleeve and yanked him off balance.

'Let go you bas—'

A knee slammed into Logan's stomach, and his world went from bad to worse. The pepper-spray was painful, but this was agony, tearing across his scarred abdomen. His legs gave way.

A hand wrapped itself into his hair, pulling his face up.

Even through pepper-spray blur the silhouette was unmistakeable: a semiautomatic pistol. The man pressed the barrel against Logan's forehead, cold metal on hot skin.

At this range the bullet would leave a little burnt halo around the entry wound as superheated gas forced the chunk of copper-jacketed lead out of the barrel and into Logan's skull. The hole would be about the same size as a garden pea on the way in, bigger than a grapefruit on the way out, spreading grey and pink and red all over the nice new plasterboard walls.

Logan closed his stinging eyes.

And then the Airwave handset in his pocket went off, the voice of Control announcing that backup was on its way.

The man let go of Logan's hair and patted him on the cheek.

'You are lucky boy today,' he said in a heavy Eastern European accent. 'I let you live. You remember this.'

Then he was gone, dragging his fallen friend with him.

6

Logan knelt on the floor with his forehead resting against the cool chipboard. He was still alive. . . Oh thank God.

He could hear the gunman and his friend thumping down the stairs; Steel groaning; a magpie cackling somewhere outside; the blood singing in his ears. Fear-induced adrenaline made his whole body tremble.

Maybe now would be a good time to be sick?

A crash sounded from downstairs and Logan struggled to his feet, forcing his wobbly legs to take him to the big window at the far end of the hall. It was double-glazed, the glass covered in blue plastic to keep it clean and scratch free while it was being installed. He twisted the handle and wrenched it open. The world was a blurry haze. Logan wiped his eyes with the back of his sleeve and squinted through the tears.

The gunman had made it out of the front door – he was half dragging, half carrying his friend across the dry mud of the drive.

Logan scrubbed at his eyes again, but the two men wouldn't stay in focus. And then they were on the pavement and the tarpaulin-draped scaffolding that covered the house hid them from view.

He clambered out of the window and onto the little walkway of boards outside. They bounced beneath his feet as he staggered to the outer edge, yanking back a green tarpaulin sheet. Logan took a deep breath and yelled: 'STOP POLICE!'

They didn't even turn around. The two blurry figures hurried along the pavement towards the CID pool car: the one with Rory Simpson handcuffed in the back.

For a brief moment Logan caught sight of a pale blob – Rory's face, peering up from the gap between the front and back seats – and then the gunman and his friend were past.

They disappeared from view, and the sound of a car starting echoed up from the street below. The engine roared, the wheels spun, and it accelerated away: getting out of there before the sound of distant sirens got any closer.

They were gone.

Logan staggered back to the landing, where Steel was lying slouched against the cracked woodwork of the banisters, head lolling, making incoherent mumbling noises.

'Inspector? Are you OK?'

'Nnnffff . . . can't find my hat . . . mphhhh. . .'

Logan dug out his Airwave handset and called Control, telling them to get an ambulance over here ASAP. He slumped back against the banisters next to Steel, listening to the background chatter of the control room as it got everything organized.

His stomach ached, the initial biting pain settling down to a dull throb. His face wasn't much better. No doubt about it – they came, they saw, and they got their arses kicked.

Logan stared through the open doorway into the darkness of the bedroom the gunman had burst out of. There was something lying on the floor.

He grunted his way to his feet and wobbled into the room.

It was a large bedroom, complete with ensuite shower, he could just make out the tiles glittering in the gloom. The whole place smelled of scorched meat.

The something lying on the floor was a man, smoke curling up from the holes where his eyes used to be.

He was large, heavily built, muscle just starting to turn to fat. Half of his left ear was missing. Simon McLeod.

Logan didn't think it was possible, but today had just got even worse.

The ambulance sat on the road beside the skip, flanked by a pair of patrol cars. Half a dozen uniformed officers were already going door-to-door. Logan watched their fuzzy, out-of-focus figures from the tailgate of the ambulance, while a paramedic rummaged about in the back.

'Right,' said the man, dressed in a wrinkly green jump-suit, 'head back and we'll wash that crap out your eyes.'

Logan did as he was told, and instantly regretted it. The stinging pain had been easing off a little, but now it was back at full strength. 'Ahh, Jesus!'

'Hold still. . .'

And gradually it began to subside. He could actually see by the time they were walking DI Steel out of the house. They helped her into one of the ambulance beds. She sat there swaying back and forth as they checked Simon McLeod was securely strapped into the other bed. Unconscious and hooked up to a heart monitor.

'OK,' said the paramedic who'd washed out Logan's eyes, 'we've got to get going.' He shouted through to the driver. 'Lights and music, Charlie!'

Logan hopped down off the tailgate, said, 'I'll follow you up there,' then marched over to the CID pool car. Trying to pretend he wasn't still in pain. He climbed in behind the wheel, starting the engine as the ambulance pulled away – lights and sirens blazing in the sunny afternoon.

Rory's voice sounded from the back, 'What happened?' He was still handcuffed to the seat support.

'You saw them, didn't you? You must have been looking right at them when they passed.' Logan stuck the car in gear, accelerating after the ambulance as it turned right onto Leslie Road.

'I. . . What did they do? We—'

'I want a description.'

The speedometer hit fifty as they screamed through the roundabout and onto Westburn Drive.

'Aaaagh! Slow down! I haven't got a seatbelt on!'

'Did you see them or not?'

Right again, onto Cornhill Road, the grey and brown concrete mass of the old children's hospital whipping past as they made for Accident and Emergency.

'Slow down!'

'Hold on tight – speed bump.'

'AAAAAAAGH! OK, OK: I saw them, I saw them!'

Logan pulled the car into the closest A&E parking spot and jumped out.

Rory shouted from the back, 'Wait! You can't leave me like this!'

'Oh for God's sake.' Logan opened the door and uncuffed one of Rory's hands.

'Ow. . .' Rory creaked upright, groaning, rubbing at the small of his back. 'That wasn't funny.'

There was a uniformed PC standing by the automatic doors; Logan called him over. The officer looked as if he was about twelve, his badge number marking him out as one of the newest batch of recruits – probably only been on the force for a couple of months. Logan steered him towards the pool car.

'Keep an eye on Captain Cardigan, here. And if he offers you any sweeties, don't take them.'

As the young constable got into the back, Rory Simpson smiled, patted him on the knee, and asked him if he liked puppies.

Accident and Emergency looked as depressing as it always did. This wasn't a place people came to have fun, it was where they went when something had gone spectacularly wrong, and after all these years a little bit of that suffering had seeped into the room's magnolia walls and green lino floor. A couple of women sat at opposite ends of the grimy seating area, one of them breastfeeding a small child and swearing quietly to herself. The other was sitting next to a little boy who kept screaming, 'Mummy, it hurts! It hurts!'

'Well you shouldn't have fallen down the bloody stairs, should you?'

Logan flashed his warrant card at the desk and asked what had happened to DI Steel and Simon McLeod. One of the admin staff looked up from her computer, sighed, then said, 'Are you a relative? Because—'

A cry of, 'HELP!' came from the direction of the examination rooms, then, 'LIE STILL, DAMN IT!'

Someone screamed.

Logan lurched into a run, following the sounds down the corridor, towards a row of cubicles. He burst through the curtain: a nurse and a female doctor were struggling with Simon McLeod, trying to keep him on the examination table. A second doctor was crunched up against the far wall, clutching his groin and moaning.

The nurse glared at Logan. 'Don't just bloody stand there!'

He grabbed one of Simon's flailing arms, putting a lock on the wrist. The huge man roared and tried to break free, feet flying in random directions. One caught the nurse on the side of the hip and she staggered back, swearing.

The doctor let go of Simon McLeod's waist and grabbed his ankles, trying to pin them to the table and failing – he was just too big for her.

'Bugger this!' Logan tightened his grip on Simon's wrist and yanked, pulling Simon off the examination table and onto the floor. He crashed into the linoleum, and Logan twisted, forcing him over onto his ruined face.

The doctor tried to drag Logan off. 'What the hell are you doing? He's been seriously injured!'

Logan stuck a foot on Simon McLeod's shoulder and shoved, keeping the arm fully stretched out and twisted round. 'You want me to let him go?'

She paused for a second. 'No. Stay there!' She hurried out through the curtain and was back thirty seconds later with a hypodermic syringe and a small glass vial of clear liquid.

She threw the syringe cover onto the floor, drew a hefty measure from the vial, then stepped in close to Logan. 'Hold him still. . .' She yanked Simon's shirt sleeve back, smacked his wrist a couple of times, and slid the needle in.

Slowly the struggling began to fade. One kick. Two. The fingers clenched and unclenched. And then Simon McLeod went limp.

Which was when three burly men in hospital security uniforms burst in through the curtains.

The doctor dropped the used syringe in a yellow sharps bin, then gave the new arrivals a slow handclap. 'Oh yes, well done. Very good. We could all be *dead* by now.'

One of the guards shrugged. 'Fight in the maternity ward – some bloke turned up to see his kid. The mother's husband wasn't very happy about it.'

'You think Doctor Patel's happy about the state of his goolies?' She pointed at her groaning colleague. 'You're lucky

I was next door, or he'd be a eunuch by now.' Then she asked Logan to help her get Simon McLeod's unconscious body back onto the examination table.

'Is he going to be OK?'

'I doubt it.' The doctor peeled back the gauze dressing they'd put on in the ambulance, exposing the top half of Simon's face. Then winced. 'Both eyes are gone and the optic nerve's been burnt. He's blind. Probably in a great deal of pain. All we can do is clean his wounds, keep him sedated, and hope he doesn't get an infection.'

Five minutes later, Logan followed the doctor through to the next cubicle, where DI Steel was sitting up on the examination table, wobbling slightly. The doctor pulled out a tiny torch and shone it in Steel's eyes, flicking the light away, then back again. 'OK,' she said, 'can you tell me who the Prime Minister is?'

'Is it. . .? I can picture him. . .' Steel scrunched her face up, lips moving silently for a moment. 'Whatsisname – slimy, lying tosspot. . .?' As if that narrowed it down.

'Well, you've definitely got a concussion.' The doctor felt around the back of Steel's head with a latex-gloved hand. 'Probably going to have one hell of a lump tomorrow, but nothing's broken. We'll keep you in overnight for observation, OK?'

Steel frowned again. 'Is it Margaret Thatcher?'

'I'll give you something for the headache.' She turned to Logan, 'Do you want to contact her next of kin? Let them know where she is.'

'I'll give Susan a call. Get her to bring in some—'

'Next of kin!' Steel hopped down from the table. 'We—oops!' Her legs gave way and the doctor grabbed her. Steel kissed her on the cheek. 'Is that a stethoscope in your pocket, or are you just pleased to see me?'

'Maybe we should sedate you?'

The inspector tugged at Logan's sleeve. 'We need to tell McLeod's next of kin.'

'I'll get someone on it when I get back to the station.'

She shook her head, and nearly collapsed again. 'You do it. I'm no' trusting one of Finnie's monkeys: they'll screw it up.' She snapped her fingers. 'Tony Blair!'

The doctor steered her towards the wheelchair in the corner. 'Nice try, but no cigar. Come on, we'll get you into bed.'

'Ooh, saucy. I love a woman in uniform.'

Logan held the curtain open for them, watching as the doctor wheeled Steel away. The inspector flapped her arms and tried to turn around in her seat. 'Laz! Laz – look after my car, OK? It's parked round the back of . . . thingy. You know: the place we work?' And then she was round the corner and out of sight, laughing like something out of a Carry On film.

But Logan didn't have anything to laugh about – not if he had to tell Colin McLeod someone had mutilated his brother.

7

'Ah. . .' Rory Simpson looked up at the camera bolted to the wall of the interview room. 'That wasn't what I meant.'

Logan sat back in his seat and folded his arms. 'You *said* you saw them!'

'Heat of the moment. I got caught up in all the excitement: high-speed chase, the sirens. . . Being handcuffed bent double like that, blood must have rushed to my head.'

Rory had developed amnesia the moment he'd overheard some idiot talking about what had happened to Simon McLeod and the other victims.

'Do you have any idea how important this is? People are being—'

'Suppose I *had* seen them – and I'm not saying I did – but suppose I had. What do you think they'd do to me if they found out I'd identified them?' He ran a hand across his bushy grey moustache. 'I'm rather attached to my eyes. I need them for looking at stuff.'

'Rory, we can stop them. But we need to know what they look like.'

'Can't you. . .' He waved his hands around. 'You know, DNA, fingerprints, that kind of thing.'

'They were wearing gloves.' Logan scooted his chair closer to the interview table. 'We can protect you. Make sure they can't lay a hand on you.'

Silence.

'Hmmm. . .' Rory pursed his lips and stared at the camera again. 'And would it make you forget all about our little . . . *misunderstanding* at the school this morning?'

'You mean when you were trying to coax little kids into your car with drugs?'

Rory actually blushed. 'Well, it might have looked like that, but—'

'Were you shopping for yourself, or someone else?'

This time the awkward pause stretched out for almost a minute. 'I . . . I don't know what you mean.'

'Don't play dumb, Rory. We know someone's in the market for young "livestock" – we've been hearing rumours for years. Was the little girl for you, or were you snatching to order?'

He shifted in his seat, licked his top lip, fidgeted. 'About those men this afternoon . . . I *may* have seen them after all.'

'You know what happens to people who abduct children, don't you Rory?'

'I was looking right at them as they went past.'

'How much was that little girl worth? How much was someone going to pay you for her?'

'I. . . If I tell you about those men, can you make all this . . . go away?'

Logan doubted it. 'The Chief Constable doesn't like it when we let paedophiles go: says it doesn't look good in the papers. But. . .' He glanced over his shoulder at the uniformed PC standing against the wall, then dropped his voice to a whisper, 'I could have a word with the Procurator Fiscal. Let her know you're helping with a major investigation. It'd be up to her whether we prosecute or not.'

Rory wiped a hand across his sweaty forehead, and said, 'OK, let's do it.'

By the time four o'clock arrived, Logan had reasonable e-fits for the men who'd blinded Simon McLeod and concussed DI Steel. He'd just finished signing Rory back into custody when DS Pirie appeared. 'The boss wants to see you.'

Which was lucky, because Logan wanted to see him too.

Detective Chief Inspector Finnie's office was one of the bigger ones on the fourth floor, with a view of the rear podium car park and the back of a row of granite buildings. DS Pirie sat back against the windowsill, flicking through a forensics report, a smug smile on his face. A couple of Eric Auld prints graced the walls above Finnie's desk, their cheerful summery colours in complete contrast with the DCI's expression as he put the phone down and glowered at Logan.

'How many times do we have to have this discussion, Sergeant?'

'Sir?'

'Did I imagine it, or did I tell you to run everything by me *before* you did it?'

'But you said—'

'So imagine my *disappointment* when I found out that you interviewed the only witness we've got to the Oedipus attacks, without even telling me he existed.'

'We caught him trying to lure children—'

'I have six people with their eyes gouged out, Sergeant McRae: six. And not only did you *spectacularly* fail to arrest the man who did it – don't interrupt – you also concealed a witness!' He started a slow round of applause. 'Good job. Well done. You must be *so* proud. I can't *imagine* why you haven't made DI yet.'

He held out his hand, and Logan had a sudden urge to spit in it.

'Well,' said Finnie, 'let's see these e-fits then.'

Logan gave him the printouts, and the DCI examined the two identikit faces. One was in his mid-thirties: heavy eyebrows, thickset features, broken nose, and little piggy eyes. The other looked like an ageing movie star – the kind who was still playing the hero in action films: grey hair, steely eyes.

'And do we believe these are accurate?'

'Simpson's done time in Peterhead before, he knows what'll happen to him if he gets sent down again.'

'You're cutting him a deal?'

'He thinks I am.'

'I see. . .' Finnie settled back in his chair, fingers steepled together as he considered the ceiling for a moment. 'Pirie?'

His sidekick barely glanced at the printouts. 'I don't like it. The profile says we're looking for a single white male in his mid-twenties.'

Logan said, 'Well, the profile's wrong then, isn't it?'

Pirie held up the e-fit of the older man. 'Are you *positive* this is what he looked like?'

Logan opened his mouth. Then closed it again. Coughed. 'Technically I didn't actually *see* either of them – well, I did, but it was dark and I had a face full of pepper-spray – but Rory Simpson—'

'Is a paedophile looking at some serious jail-time for breaking his parole conditions. I wouldn't trust him as far as I could spit him: he's just telling you what you want to hear.' Pirie smiled – patronizing sod. 'The profile clearly says our boy's local and he works on his own. So this—'

'Don't be an idiot, Pirie.' Finnie pursed his rubbery lips, and swivelled back and forth on his seat a couple of times. 'We're not ignoring evidence just because it *disagrees* with the profile. Email those faces to Dr Goulding, tell him I need an update ASAP. And get some posters made up: I want them all over Aberdeen by close of play. "Have you seen these men?" etcetera.' He looked at Logan. 'Anything else?'

'The older one had an Eastern European accent. He definitely wasn't local.'

Pirie curled his top lip. 'Every time there's a new victim we get an anonymous phone call. Usually on the victim's own mobile. Voice is muffled, Slavic accent. We're pretty sure it's a put on: he sounds like Mr Chekov from *Star Trek*. Dr Goulding thinks our boy's either mocking his victims, or using them as a cipher.'

Finnie waved a hand at him. 'Oh, thank you, that's *very* helpful. A "cipher": that's really going to help us catch the bastard.' He snatched the printouts from Pirie and stuck them in the middle of the desk. 'DS McRae, I want you to set up a meeting with Dr Goulding. Go through everything that happened today.'

Logan groaned. 'But, sir—'

'As soon as possible, Sergeant.' He stared off into the distance for a moment. Then smiled. 'Has anyone spoken to Simon McLeod's next of kin yet?'

'Ah. . .' Logan could feel the blush rising in his cheeks – he'd been putting that particular task off since getting back from the hospital. 'Actually I thought that would be better . . . coming from someone more senior.'

'Excellent.' Finnie levered himself to his feet. 'I think it's time for us to indulge in some *real* police work, don't you gentlemen? Pirie, get a pool car sorted. We're going to pay our respects.'

The traffic was dreadful, a stop-start procession of people trying to beat the rush hour and failing miserably. 'Lazy bastards,' said DS Pirie from the driver's seat. 'Look at them all. Why does no one work till five o'clock any more?'

Logan sat in the back, watching the sunshine glinting off a pale white blob in skinny jeans and an 'UP THE DONS!'

T-shirt. Her arms were already starting to go lobster-red. Aberdonians just weren't designed for the sun.

Finnie turned round in the passenger seat and handed Logan a clear plastic evidence pouch with a sheet of paper in it. 'We received this in the morning post.'

> **You still will not do anything!!** You are CORRUPT. You sit there in your tower of SIN and you let THEM run around ***free from consequence.*** *You complain* when the **SHEEP** do not behave themselves, but **you do nothing about the foreign wolves!**
>
> The last one *screamed like a woman* when I cut out his eyes. **The next one will too!!!**
>
> You will wade in the **blood** of dogs!!!

'Fingerprints?'

'Same as all the others.' Pirie's voice was clipped, his face an ugly shade of pink that clashed with his hair. Still sulking – it probably didn't help that Finnie had made him drive, instead of Logan. 'No prints on the letter or the envelope, and no fibres either.'

Finnie handed over a second evidence bag. This one had the envelope in it. 'Posted day before yesterday in Aberdeen.'

Logan read through the letter again. 'So are the Polish people supposed to be dogs or wolves now?'

DS Pirie glanced over his shoulder. 'I think the fact this guy has a tendency to mix his metaphors is the *least* of our problems, don't you?'

Finnie smirked. 'So, tell me: does the great Detective Sergeant Logan "Lazarus" McRae have any *startling* insights to share with the class? Come on, this is why I brought you on board, remember? Chance to redeem yourself?'

'Well. . . He's definitely unhinged. No sane person uses that many exclamation marks.'

'That's your startling insight? The man who gouges people's eyes out and burns the sockets is "unhinged"? Pirie, call the *Press and Journal*: tell them to hold the front page.'

Bastard.

'OK. . . Postage dates. This was posted day before yesterday, right? What about the others? Is there a pattern?'

'Pirie?'

Finnie's ginger-haired sidekick shrugged. He was tailgating a Renault Megane with a 'HONK IF YOU'RE HORNY' sticker in the back window. 'The letters arrive pretty much at random. Dr Goulding thinks they're a coping mechanism, by writing to us he makes us complicit in his acts. That's why he keeps telling us it's our fault: if we didn't want him to keep on blinding people we'd have caught him by now.'

'I suppose. . .' Logan handed the evidence bags back to Finnie. 'Then why attack Simon McLeod? He's not Polish.'

The DS leant on the horn: BREEEEEEEEEEEP! 'Come on: move it!' The Megane lurched forward and Pirie accelerated up behind it again. 'Who knows with whack-jobs? The McLeods run a stable of hoors, maybe our boy was after a nice piece of local ass and ended up with a Polish bird instead? Doesn't like them mucking up our good Aberdonian gene pool with their filthy foreign ways. Or maybe Simon McLeod was just in the wrong place at the wrong time?'

Finnie smiled again. 'Serves him bloody right too – whole family's been a pain in my arse for years.'

Twenty minutes later, DS Pirie parked outside a rose-encrusted bungalow in Garthdee. Not really the kind of place you'd expect a criminal mastermind to operate out of, but for forty years that's exactly what Tony McLeod did. Right up until his third heart attack. CID sent a wreath, then threw a party.

'Right,' said Finnie, climbing out into the warm afternoon, 'Sergeant McRae, do you *think* you could keep your eyes open and your mouth shut in there? Hmmm? Just for me?'

Logan sighed. 'Yes, sir.'

They opened the gate and marched up the path, bathed in the scent of roses. A little old woman answered the door on the second ring, smiling up at them. She had a pair of bright-yellow Marigold gloves on and smelt of furniture polish.

'Can I help you?'

'Morning, Doris.' Finnie showed her his warrant card, and the smile disappeared from her face. 'Agnes about?'

She turned and shouted back into the house, 'Mrs McLeod, the pigs are here! *Again*.'

Simon McLeod's mother appeared: a hard-faced woman with short blonde hair, dressed in black cashmere and white silk. She was clarted in gold jewellery, every finger encrusted with rings of bling: diamonds and sapphires and rubies and sovereigns. A magpie with a credit card.

She took one look at Finnie and said, 'What the hell do you want?'

'Mrs McLeod, can we come in please?'

'You got a warrant?'

Finnie tried on a smile. 'Wouldn't be asking if I did.'

'Then you can bugger off back where you came from.' She let her eyes drift from the Chief Inspector to Logan and Pirie. 'Aye, and you can take your pet poofs with you.'

'It's about Simon, Mrs McLeod.'

She folded her arms, hoisting her bosoms up a notch. 'You should be ashamed of yourself – there's perverts out there walking the street and you're round here harassing us. My Simon's a legitimate businessman, and he's—'

'He was attacked this morning.'

'Don't be stupid, who would be daft enough to—'

'Simon's up at A&E. He's been blinded.'

All the colour drained from her face. 'But. . . We. . .'

'Someone gouged his eyes out.'

'Oh God. . .' Mrs McLeod stumbled and the old woman rushed to her side, holding her up.

Finnie's voice softened. 'Can you think of anyone who'd want to harm your son?'

Doris pulled Mrs McLeod gently back into the house, turning her back on the policemen on the doorstep. 'Go away. Can't you see she's had a terrible shock?' And then she slammed the door.

8

Logan unlocked the front door to his flat and slumped inside. He should have been home an hour and a half ago, but sodding Finnie had insisted on following Mrs McLeod up to the hospital. Just to let her know he was watching her. Dickhead.

Taking one look at the lounge – dust sheets over the sofa, carpets ripped up, bare light bulb, the smell of paint – Logan decided he really couldn't be bothered with the decorating. So five minutes later he was sitting in Archibald Simpson, a converted bank on the corner of Union Street and King Street. The pub was busy, full of off-duty police officers and assorted locals, numbing the memory of another week with beer, wine, and spirits.

Logan sat at his usual table, nursing a pint of Stella and waiting for his mushroom stroganoff. He had the whole weekend to commit DIY, one night off wasn't going to hurt.

Someone said, 'Hey, Billy No Mates, where's your wrinkly old girlfriend then?' and Logan looked up from his pint.

Samantha – the Identification Bureau's only Goth – was

standing over him, holding a pitcher of something evil and alcoholic-looking. She had those strange tribal tube things in her earlobes, stretching them beneath half a dozen sparkly piercings. Another ring in her bottom lip. Scarlet lipstick, black eye makeup, Marilyn Manson T-shirt, black leather jeans, pixie boots. . . But it was the top of her head that made Logan stare.

'New hairdo?'

'You like? It's called "flame red".'

'Thought you Goths were into black, black and more black.'

'You're *such* an old man.'

'Your arse.'

'You wish.' She winked. 'Anyway, got to go, it's Bruce's birthday and we're going to get him completely weaselled. Vodka and Red Bull to the rescue— Ow!' Someone had wrapped her up in a bear hug. 'Get off me you moron!'

Detective Constable Rennie – tanned and grinning – kissed her on the cheek. 'Hey beautiful, love the hair. Miss me?'

'No.' Samantha struggled her way free and pulled up the sleeve of her T-shirt, exposing a pad of white gauze bandage. 'If you've buggered my new tattoo, I'll bloody kill you!'

'Sorry, I didn't know.' Rennie fluttered his eyelashes. 'Forgive me?'

'You are *such* an arsehole!' She stormed off.

The constable watched her go. And when she was safely out of earshot, said, 'Phwoar. . . I would. Wouldn't you? Bet she's filthy in the bedroom. . .' He gave himself a small shake. 'Anyway, drinkies: the prodigal Rennie has returned!'

Three minutes later he was back from the bar with two pints of Stella and a packet of cheese and onion. 'Seriously,' he said, handing over Logan's drink, 'you should go to Thailand. It was *brilliant*. . .' and that started a half-hour monologue on how great it was to get out into the real country and meet real locals and eat real Thai food and see real orang-utans and have a real massage. 'And,' he leaned forward, 'I met someone.'

'What, in Thailand? Got yourself a mail-order bride?'

'Cheeky bugger. No, she's from Inverness, a lecturer.' The constable held up a hand. 'And before you say anything: I checked her passport. She's older than I am.'

Logan smiled. 'How much older?'

Shrug. 'Couple of years.'

'Ten, fifteen, twenty?'

'Hey, at least I've got a girlfriend. Unlike *some* sad bastards.'

'Touché.'

Two pints later and Rennie was in full whinge – going on about how it wasn't fair that he'd been assigned to DI McPherson. 'I mean the man's a bloody jinx, isn't he? "Accident prone" doesn't even come close. And you know what we did today? Went looking for a bunch of stolen shotguns. *Shotguns*. It's a disaster waiting to happen.' He drained his pint. 'Want another one?'

'I've got the day off tomorrow: what do you think?'

'Come on, it'll be . . . it'll be fun.' Rennie was a little unsteady on his feet as they wound their way up Union Street. The place was buzzing – people staggering from pub to club. Lots of happy faces and quite a few miserable ones too.

Somewhere up ahead a group of drunken men were singing *Sto Lat,* a traditional Polish folk song borne on the wings of lager and vodka. A ramshackle chorus of *Flower Of Scotland* started up in competition.

At least the Poles were in tune.

'No it won't. It'll be bloody horrible,' said Logan as they

crossed the road and made their way down Belmont Street, past Café Drummond and its little knot of banished smokers.

'You wouldn't be there on your own, we could . . . could set you up with one of Emma's friends. She's *bound* to know someone who's desperate—'

'I'm not going to a dinner party.'

They joined the queue for the kebab shop.

'Please? I don't really have any other growed-up friends.'

A lanky man near the front of the queue was swearing loudly into his mobile phone, 'No, you fuckin' listen to me – you tell him he gets over here with the stuff now, or I'm gonnae kill his ma and fuck the corpse!' Denim jacket, ripped jeans, hair down to the middle of his back, cheek-bones sharp enough to slice cheese. Heroin: the ultimate slimming aid.

'Anyway,' said Rennie, 'what's wrong with dinner parties? It's what civil. . .' Belch. 'Civilized adults do.'

The man on the phone was still going strong. 'I don't fuckin' care if he's havin' a fuckin' heart attack! You tell him to get his arse over here!'

'What makes you think I need you to fix me up with anyone? What am I, a charity case. . .' Logan trailed off. Four men had just marched round the corner from Union Street. Not meandered, or staggered, but marched. They were dressed in the standard CCTV-avoidance costume: hoodies and baseball caps, their faces hidden in the shadows.

Logan nudged Rennie. 'Look left. . . Your *other* left. Four IC-One males.'

'Uh-huh. And?'

'Don't you ever read the day book? Someone got stabbed last night on Thistle Street. They got four hoodies on camera, running from the scene.'

'No, I don't want to fuckin' speak to him! You tell him

I'm no' fuckin' around anymore. . . Aye. . . Don't be fuckin' stupid. . .'

The four hoodies were less than a dozen feet away now, making for the front of the kebab queue and the swearing man.

Hoodie Number One pulled something out of his pocket. 'Oi, you, *Retard*! Kevin Fookin' Murray!' He had a face like streaky bacon, with a big prominent nose. The accent was pure Manchester. 'What did I fookin' tell yeh?'

Kevin Murray ignored him. 'Naw, I'm no' gonnae give him another week, I want it *now*!'

'You fookin' deaf, Murray?' One flick of the wrist and the thing in his hand unfolded into a butterfly knife.

Logan swore. So much for a quiet night out – he should have stayed at home with a paintbrush. He grabbed Rennie and stepped forward, getting an outraged, 'This is a queue here, you know?' from the person in front of them.

Hoodie Number One shoved Murray. He staggered, scowled. Then told the person on the other end he'd call them back. 'Fuck's your problem?'

Hoodies Two through Four were fanning out, getting ready.

Bloody hell. . . Logan glanced up the street, looking for the familiar fluorescent yellow and white police jackets of night-shift. Eleven o'clock on a Friday night, there should have been uniformed officers all over the place, but there was no sign of them. Probably breaking up a fight somewhere.

'I fookin' told yeh, Murray, but you wouldn't fookin' listen, would yeh? Had to act the cunt?' He was trembling, spittle flying from his mouth.

Logan dug about in his jacket for his warrant card. 'OK, let's all calm down.' He snapped his ID open and held it up. 'No need for anyone to get—'

Murray took a swing at Hoodie Number One. The punch went wide.

The hoodie's blade didn't.

'AAAGGHH!' Kevin Murray fell to his knees, hands clasped over his face. Blood spilling out between his fingers to spatter on the cobbled street.

The queue disintegrated, everyone retreating to a safe distance to watch the fight. Not one of them stepped in to help break it up. So much for community spirit.

Logan shouted, 'POLICE! You're all under arrest!' And then wished he hadn't.

The three back-up hoodies pulled their weapons out – a cleaver, a combat knife and a machete. All Logan had was a drunk Detective Constable Rennie.

'OK, everyone's in enough trouble as it is, don't make it any worse.'

Hoodie Number One laughed. 'You think you're so fookin' big, don't yer? Well you know wha'? I eat pigs like you for breakfast. . .' He snaked his knife through the air in front of Logan's face. Back and forth in curving loops, his hand covered in blue DIY prison tattoos.

Logan felt his stomach clench. Why did it have to be a knife? Why did it *always* have to be a knife?

Well, Logan had a nasty surprise for him: pepper-spray beat a knife any day of the week. He felt in his pocket, then remembered it was sitting on his desk back at FHQ, waiting to be refilled.

Damn.

He held up his hands, trying to keep his voice level: sound as if he was in control. 'Come on, it doesn't have to be like this. . .'

Murray was sobbing, lying curled up on the ground between them. 'My face!'

Hoodie Number One grinned, wiped his blade clean on a KFC napkin, then flipped the butterfly knife shut. 'See you round, Mr Pig.' He bounced back a couple of steps, then he and his cohorts were off, bounding down Belmont Street, whooping and laughing.

Logan pulled out his mobile phone and called Control – telling them to get the CCTV team to look out for four white males in hooded tops and baseball caps running onto Schoolhill.

And send an ambulance.

Logan scowled at Rennie. 'You were a lot of bloody help!'

The constable shrugged. 'I'm actually quite pished.' He staggered on the blood-slicked cobbles. 'Aren't we going . . . going to chase them?'

'Two of us against four armed men? That's a *great* idea.' Logan pulled a handkerchief from his pocket, folded it into a square, and handed it to Kevin Murray, telling him to keep the pressure on.

Dark red seeped through the white material, saturating it.

Logan sent Rennie to fetch some napkins from the kebab shop, then squatted down beside the injured man.

'You want to tell me what that was all about?'

'Ma fuckin' face!'

Logan snapped on a pair of latex gloves, and pulled Murray's hands away. His nose was split in two, the lower half hanging loose. A deep gash stretched across his right cheek with bone glinting away in the depths, and then it all disappeared in a wash of dark scarlet.

'Is it bad? It's bad, isn't it? Fuckin' tell me!'

'It's . . . just a scratch. Couple of stitches and you'll be fine.' Lie. Lie. Lie. 'Who were they?'

But Murray just clutched his nose back together and started to cry, tears mingling with the blood of his slashed face.

Rennie reappeared with a big stack of napkins. They were

better than nothing, but it didn't take long before all they had left was a pile of sticky red papier-mâché.

By the time an ambulance arrived their patient had passed out on the cobblestones.

9

The phone sounded like an aluminium hedgehog trapped in a tumble-drier. Logan groaned, rolled over onto his side and checked the alarm clock – nearly half past nine. He flopped an arm across his eyes and waited for the answering machine to kick in.

Blessed silence.

And then his mobile got in on the act – the 'Danse Macabre' warbling out from somewhere on the other side of the room.

'Bloody hell. . .' He struggled out of bed, padded across the bare floorboards, and rummaged through the pile of clothes dumped on the chair in the corner. His suit jacket was at the very bottom, all crumpled and wrinkly. He pulled his phone out of the pocket, checked the display, and swore. It was DI Steel.

'Hello?'

'Aye, Laz, where the hell are you?'

He pulled the bedroom curtains back, blinking out at the sparkling granite buildings and the perfect sapphire sky. 'It's Saturday morning. . .' He yawned, and sank down on the edge of the bed. 'I'm knackered. Watching CCTV tapes till God knows when o'clock this morning.'

'Get your arse in gear. They're discharging me, I need a lift.'

He groaned, fell back on the rumpled duvet, and stared at the freshly painted ceiling. He'd missed a bit. 'Get Susan to do it.'

'Susan has a . . . she has a thing this morning.' Steel's voice dropped to a hoarse whisper, *'And the nurses are acting all weird, like I'm a serial killer or something.'*

'But it's—'

'You can pick up my car from the station. Keys are in my desk.'

Logan rubbed his eyes with the ball of one hand, enjoying a fleeting fantasy of feeding the inspector through a wood-chipper. 'OK,' he said at last, 'twenty minutes.'

The ward was nearly empty, just a grey-haired old woman in the corner, babbling on about Aberdeen Royal Infirmary being a front for the IRA. And people with bird heads trying to steal her biscuits.

The inspector was stuffing yesterday's clothes into a little pink suitcase, muttering away to herself.

Logan called out from halfway across the ward, 'Madame, your carriage awaits.'

She scowled up at him. 'You're late.'

'You're not even packed yet.'

'Can't find my bloody wedding ring.' Then she started stripping the bed. 'Got to be here somewhere. . .'

She was still at it five minutes later, when a young woman appeared with a trolley laden with tea and coffee. The lady in the corner got fussed over for a bit, but Steel was totally ignored, the trolley making a pointed detour around where the inspector scrabbled on the floor beneath the bed.

Logan pulled on his best smile and asked if there was any chance of a cuppa.

The trolley's guardian looked him up and down, then

asked if he was taking *that* – she pointed at DI Steel's waggling bum – home?

'Problem?'

'She's been a nightmare: they had to check her every two hours last night, because of the concussion, and everyone got their arse pinched or their breasts groped. And the *language*!'

'Ah. . .' He watched the inspector as she started to take the little bedside cabinet apart. 'If it's any consolation, I get that every day. Well, except for the groping.'

That got him a look of sympathy, a cup of milky tea, and a digestive biscuit.

By quarter past ten, DI Steel was rummaging through the bins.

Logan left her to it, and went for a wander through the hospital, treading the familiar corridors, looking at the familiar paintings, feeling the familiar depression. Drifting towards the small ward where Simon McLeod was being kept under observation.

The big man was slumped back against a mountain of scratchy hospital pillows. White bandages kept a pair of thick gauze pads in place over his eyes. . . Well, where his eyes used to be.

A woman sat in the chair beside the bed, holding Simon's hand and sniffling into a handkerchief. Early thirties, blonde, smudged makeup, with bright-red nail varnish and lots of gold jewellery, Hilary Brander – Simon's bidie-in – was basically a younger version of his mum. Which raised some disturbing questions about their sex life. But would explain why Hilary and Simon's two kids turned out the way they had.

She wasn't the only visitor: Simon's brother was there too, pacing back and forth, mouth working soundlessly. As if he was chewing on something bitter.

Colin McLeod had all of his father's rough looks, but none of the charm. Five foot four of aggressive muscle, hair cut short to disguise the fact he was going bald. Tattoos twisted up and down his furry arms: skulls, daggers, thistles, 'MOTHER', 'FREEDOM', and 'KYLIE'.

Logan stopped at the bottom of the bed. 'How is he?'

Colin McLeod glowered at him. 'Fuck is it to you?'

'Hey, I was just—'

'Someone cut his eyes out, how the fuck you think he is?'

Hilary looked up from her bedside vigil, her Essex accent wobbling. 'Why can't you leave us alone?'

Logan held up his hands. 'I didn't mean to intrude: just wanted to make sure he was OK. We're going to do everything we can to catch the men who did this.'

Colin McLeod stormed across the room, only just stopping at the last moment, inches from Logan; teeth gritted, neck muscles standing out like guy-ropes, a thick vein throbbing on his forehead. 'You fucking leave this to me, understand?' He poked Logan in the chest with a finger, the word 'HATE' tattooed across the knuckles. 'This is none of your fucking business.'

'You know we can't do that, Colin.'

The finger made another poke. 'Get in my way and you'll be fucking sorry. Understand? He's *my* brother.'

Logan took a step back. 'Don't do anything daft, OK?'

Simon groaned, shifting painfully in his hospital bed. Hilary squeezed his hand, a fat tear rolling down her cheek, taking the last sliver of mascara with it. She wiped it away. 'Please, just leave us alone.'

Outside in the corridor, Logan bumped into the nurse from yesterday. She had heavy black bags under her eyes, and a bedpan in her hands. 'Watch out!' she said, trying not to spill the contents. 'Charging about like an. . . Oh, it's you.' She straightened the cover on whatever was slopping about in there. 'You don't hang about, do you? I only phoned five minutes ago.'

'Phoned?'

'That woman who got shot: she woke up.'

The blinds in the small ward were down, shutting out the sunshine and the outside world. A young couple were sitting by one of the other beds, the woman crying, the man looking as if he didn't really know where he was. The small child hooked up to the ventilator didn't move.

Only one other bed was occupied – the shooting victim. She didn't look that much better than she had five days ago, still connected to a bank of machinery that pinged and gurgled. Her eyes were shut, but they flickered open as Logan dragged a chair over. He pulled the curtains around the bed, giving the young couple some privacy.

'How are you feeling?'

She looked at him for a while in silence.

Logan tried again, going for the simplest Polish phrase he knew. *'Dzień dobry?'*

'Thirsty. . .' it was barely a croak.

He poured a small glass of water from the jug by her bedside. 'Here. Take small sips.'

'Dziękuję.'

Logan smiled. 'I can't remember what's Polish for "you're welcome".' She emptied the glass and Logan gave her a little more. 'Too much at once and you'll be sick. Trust me, the last thing you want to do is throw up when you've got stitches in your stomach. Hurts like hell.'

'Please not to deport me. . .' Her English was a damn sight better than Logan's Polish, but he had to strain to hear the words.

'Why would we do that?'

'The . . . the man who make me do films, he say he tell police I am prostitute they send me to prison. Deport me. I am sorry. . .' Her lips trembled, tears welling up in her eyes. 'Please. . .' She clutched onto Logan's hand – her fingers were cold and pale.

'Trust me, no one's going to deport. . .' Frown. 'What films?'

'Please, I will being good!' The heart monitor was starting to beep faster and faster.

'Calm down, shh. . . It's OK, no one's going to deport you. What films?'

'Dirty films. Horrible. I have to make . . . with men . . . is. . .' She was sobbing now, great heaving sobs.

The heart monitor sounded as if it was about to explode.

Logan grabbed the nurse call button and stabbed it repeatedly with his thumb. 'Come on, come on.'

He could hear the ward door slam open, the squeak of rubber-soled shoes on linoleum, then the curtains were flung open and a nurse stormed up to the bed. 'I told you not to upset her!'

The bleeping was getting erratic.

Logan stood. 'I didn't, I was just—'

'Out! *Now*!' She ran a hand across the woman's forehead. 'Shhhhh, it's OK. You're all right. He's not going to hurt you.'

Logan stumbled out into the corridor, lurching out of the way as a doctor hurried into the ward. Then the door closed and Logan was alone.

Brilliant job. First class. Way to go. His one chance to find out if she knew anything about who blinded Simon McLeod and he blew it. When Finnie found out. . .

He groaned and let his head thunk gently into the wall. A woman was lying in there, seriously ill, and here he was worrying about bloody Finnie.

Someone tapped him on the shoulder. 'Excuse please?'

Logan turned to find a small, round woman standing behind him, dressed like a retired schoolteacher.

'She is to be OK, yes? Krystka?'

Oh . . . crap. 'You know her? The young Polish woman?'

'My *siostrzenica*. How you say this? Brother's daughter?'

'Niece.'

'Niece? Yes, niece. She come over here to get better job. Stay with me and Fryderyk. Send money home to her family. Now look. . .' She sniffed.

Logan tried to sound reassuring. 'I'm sure she'll be fine. The doctors here are very good.' They'd better be: he didn't need any more guilt.

'I see her in newspaper as unknown person: my brother's daughter is unknown person. I am so ashamed.'

At least Finnie's appeal for information had been good for something.

'Do you know who she was working for?'

The little woman shrugged. 'She never want to speak about it. Back home she is model for clothes. Very beautiful. Look . . .' The woman went rummaging in a handbag the size of a small country, and produced an envelope with 'PHOTOGRAPHS DO NOT BEND' printed on it. She pulled out a glossy eight-by-ten of a young woman posing in a studio somewhere, wearing nothing but her underwear and a smile. She was stunning. Hard to believe it was the same person lying in the hospital bed.

'Wow.'

'She was most beautiful girl in Włoszczowski. . . Look what they have done to her.'

Logan turned the photo over, there was something scrawled on the back: 'KRYSTKA GORZAŁKOWSKA' and a mobile phone number. 'Can I keep this?' Adding a hasty, 'I'm a police officer,' just in case she thought he was a pervert.

The little woman looked him up and down. 'You can keep.'

'And you're *sure* you don't know who she worked for?'

'All she say is she work for crocodile man.'

'Crocodile. . .' Logan closed his eyes and swore.

Steel was waiting for him back in the ward. The old lady in the corner bed had fallen asleep – lying starfish-spread under the covers, snoring.

'Where the hell you been?'

'Find your ring?'

The inspector held up her hand and there it was. 'Must've been off my head last night. Found it stuffed inside a tub of anti-wrinkle cream.'

From the look of things, it wasn't working.

Logan hooked a thumb over his shoulder. 'Got a small detour to make on the way home.'

'Oh, you're kidding me! First you bugger off for half an hour, and now you want to—'

'Got to see a man about a porn film.'

And with that, Steel's face blossomed into a smile. 'Well why didn't you say so?' She hurried past, pulling her Barbie-pink suitcase behind her. 'There's *always* time for pornography!'

10

ClarkRig Training Systems Ltd was an industrial unit hidden away down a little alleyway off Hutcheon Street. Logan parked the inspector's Mazda at the front door, next to a battered Volvo Estate, and Steel climbed out into the sunshine, still clutching Krystka Gorzałkowska's photograph.

Logan locked the car. 'You finished drooling over that yet?'

'I'm no' drooling, I'm assessing the evidence. And you can talk, had to prise it out of your hands with a bloody crowbar.' She stopped and stared up at the ClarkRig sign. 'You sure she was getting forced to make porn films?'

'That's what she told me. Said they'd get her deported if she refused.'

The inspector blew a long wet raspberry. 'Silly cow. She's Polish – a member of our glorious European Union, how are we going to deport her? We can't even deport convicted bloody terrorists.'

'Well, obviously she didn't know that.'

'You know what I think? I think Gorza-le-kowska—'

'"Gorzałkowska". You pronounce an L with a line through it like a W.'

'Aye, thank you professor. If I want a bloody language lesson I'll show up to the ones at the station.' Steel hitched her trousers up. 'As I was *saying*: she's been making porn films and now she's scared her family's going to find out. So what does she do – admit she's in it for the money, or say a bad man made her do it?'

'If she's telling the truth—'

'I'll buy you a big sodding T-shirt with "I told you so" printed on it. That make you happy?' Steel was already heading for the front door. 'Come on. Less talk, more porn.'

Reception was an airy room, the walls covered with safety industry awards and framed DVDs. A pair of ancient film projectors sat in the middle of the polished wooden floor, in matching glass cases. Leather couches, steel coffee tables. Everything gleamed and sparkled. No sign of naked flesh anywhere.

DI Steel marched straight up to the long mahogany reception desk, banged on it with her fist and shouted, 'SHOP!'

A round face appeared from one of the doors behind the desk, bringing with it a cheery smile. 'Can I help you?' She was in her late sixties with dyed brown hair, arms like sides of ham, and as she wobbled towards her chair it looked as if her stomach was giving them a Mexican wave.

Steel stood entranced. 'Bloody hell, it's like—'

Logan took over before the inspector got them thrown out. 'Is Mr Clark about?'

'*Whom* shall I say is calling?'

'Detective Sergeant McRae. We met a couple of—'

'Oh aye! I remember you fine!' She dropped the posh accent and beamed at him. 'You just go straight through, he's in the editing suite.'

Steel raised her eyebrows. 'No' a safety film is it?'

'Oh no.' She winked. 'It's one of our *special* ones.'

* * *

The editing suite was a bank of keyboards, dials, sliders and switches, dominated by a dozen flat-screen monitors. All of them full of naked people inserting things into each other. And for some strange reason, everyone was singing. Every time the cameras moved there was a flash of bright blue or green scenery.

Steel paused in the doorway, looking up at the wall of flickering flesh. 'Bleeding heck . . .'

'Hmmmph?' The man sitting in the room's only chair swivelled round. He was huge – tall and fat – with little rectangular glasses, a greying goatee, and a trendy haircut that made him look as if he'd dried it sideways in a wind tunnel. He was drinking soup from a mug, leaving little bits of minestrone sticking to his moustache.

He took one look at Logan and a huge smile creased his face. 'Sergeant McRae! It's so *great* to see you!'

Steel stuck her hand out for shaking. 'Hi, Mr Clark, I don't know if you remember me, but we met last year and it was, well, you know, and I wasn't, but then I watched all your films properly and they were, you probably hear this all the time, *really* brilliant, and I must sound like an absolute idiot, but they're just so great.'

He frowned at her. 'Aren't you the—'

'Yes, well, sorry about that, I'm a big fan, Mr Clark. Huge.'

The frown became a smile. 'Then all is forgiven. And please, call me Zander. With a "Z". I'm always delighted to meet someone who appreciates—'

Logan cut straight across him. 'Mr Clark, do you recognize this woman?' He pulled out the photograph.

'Of course I do: Krystka Gorzałkowska.' His pronunciation was perfect. 'Such a shame, she was gorgeous – terrible actress though. Couldn't carry a tune in a rucksack.'

'So you don't deny that she worked for you?'

'More that she *didn't* work for me. She just didn't have

that . . . spark. You know? People don't have sex in my films, they make love. They have to look happy, joyful, as if this is the best thing that ever happened to them. Poor Krystka always looked like someone just crapped in her borscht.' He sank back into his chair. 'Tried her for a couple of scenes, but it just wasn't working. I had to let her go.'

'She claims she was forced to make porn films.'

'Not by me she wasn't!' He spun round and fiddled with some buttons. All the screens went blank, then blue, a single image stretched to fill them all: the Crocodildo Productions logo, and then a caption, 'SCENE 174B'.

It was Krystka, on her knees on a bright blue floor, marked out with a grid of little white Ping-Pong balls. An identical blue surface acted as a backdrop. She and another pneumatic blonde were 'entertaining' a man dressed in a top hat and frock coat. The camera swooped in.

Zander's eyes sparkled with reflected flesh. 'This is going to be my masterpiece. The whole set's digital; I've got a stack of blade servers, a brand-new rendering farm, and half a dozen top geeks. 3D modelling, animation, the whole thing. You should see some of the results we're getting. *Spectacular.*' He took another slurp of soup. 'I'm going to do for Aberdeen what Peter Jackson did for New Zealand.'

And then it was time for the money shot. A look of utter horror spread across Krystka Gorzałkowska's face, just moments after the other stuff.

'Cut!' Zander appeared on the screen, marching into shot. *'Krystka, darling, you know I love you, but you can't keep doing this. It's only sperm, it's perfectly natural and it's not going to hurt you. Kurt's medicals are all up to date. Aren't they Kurt?'*

Kurt grimaced. *'Please tell me we don't have to go* again!*'*

Krystka burst into tears and Zander wrapped her up in a big hug, careful not to get any perfectly natural sperm on his jumper. *'Come on, sweetheart.* Napij się herbaty. *Would you like that? Nice cup of tea?'* Then he led her out of shot.

Three beeps and the screen went blank.

'See?' The director leaned back in his chair. 'Does that look like I'm forcing anyone to do *anything* they don't want to?' Another slurp. 'We tried putting a happy face on her with the computers, but to be honest it's going to be cheaper just reshooting her scenes with someone else.'

'Well. . .' Logan put the photo back in his pocket. 'Maybe she was working for another outfit? Who else makes porn films up here?'

'We're the only professional studio in the North East, so it's probably just some gonzo operation. Amateurs. I can ask around if you like?'

Steel coughed. 'Can you put the first lot of humping back on again?'

The director shrugged, hit some buttons, and the screens filled up with pink. 'I. . .' He cleared his throat. 'I was *so* sorry to hear about Inspector Insch. It was a terrible shame.'

And one Logan really didn't want to talk about. 'Yes, well. . .'

'Is he doing OK? My dear old dad had a heart attack and it knocked the stuffing right out of him. Pretty much gave up after that.'

'We need to—'

'Only, I was thinking: if Insch wanted something to keep him busy, I could always use him here?'

DI Steel shuddered. 'No' in a porn film! Jesus, who'd want to see all that blubber humping about?'

'I *meant* as a production assistant.' Zander stuck the topmost of his chins in the air, the others stretching out behind it. 'And some people *like* larger men, thank you very much!'

'I was only—'

'Actually,' said Logan, 'if we could get back to Krystka Gorzałkowska? How did you get hold of her?'

'Kostchey International Holdings Limited, it's an agency: they specialize in Polish actresses for adult films. Absolute Godsend. Their girls look fabulous, most of them can sing, they remember their lines, and they can act too. I can't get local girls who look anywhere *near* as good – all the attractive ones want to be on crap like *Big Brother* or the *X-Factor*.' Sigh. 'No one wants to be a porn star anymore.'

DI Steel was disturbingly happy on the drive back to her house, staring at the pair of brand-new DVDs the director had given her as a parting gift: *Harriet Potter and the Gobbler of Firemen* and *Indiana Jane and the Temple of Dildos*. The covers were surprisingly classy. 'Bet these are packed with girl-on-girl actiony goodness.'

'I want to check with the agency, see if they hired Krystka out to another outfit.'

'Supposed to be having the weekend off, remember? Phone the station, tell them to get some idiot to do it. If Rennie's back, he'll do.'

She turned in her seat, staring out at the sunshine as they slogged their way towards the Bridge of Don. 'Susan couldn't pick me up today because she's. . .' Steel fidgeted with the DVDs some more. 'She had an interview with the adoption and fostering people.'

'Thought she liked being an accountant?'

'Not a job interview, you moron. For a kid.' She cracked her window open and lit a cigarette, blowing a mouthful of smoke at a passing cyclist. 'Susan wants a kid. She's always wanted a kid.'

'Ah.'

'It really matters to her and I'm. . . Well, I'm no' exactly *Mother of the Year* material, am I? Got to go see some social working cock-weasel on Tuesday, convince them I'm the sort of person you'd want to give a wee baby to.'

Logan followed the queue of traffic across the bridge, listening to the plaintive wail of seagulls in the background. 'You're a shoo-in. They'll love you.'

'I'm no' good with children! I'm a forty-three-year-old lesbian chain-smoker who swears like a fucking sailor and boozes it up every night.'

Logan couldn't believe that. 'Forty-three?'

'Oh, shut up.' She spent a couple of minutes smoking and scowling. 'Any fuckwit under the sun can get his girlfriend knocked up and bang: he's a dad. Doesn't matter if he's a junkie, a wino, or a pervert, as long as he's got a working dick he gets to make babies. No one from the Social interviews *him*, do they? How fair is that?' She smacked her hand on the dashboard, sending an avalanche of ash all over the black plastic. 'Aw shite. . .' She swept the worst of it up and turfed it out of the window, leaving a grey smear behind. 'No fags, no drink, and no swearing. That sound like me to you?'

'Maybe it won't be as bad as—'

'You know what? Sod it. If I've got to be someone else for the rest of my life, I'm bloody well giving the old me a good send off.' Steel flicked the last of her cigarette out into the beautiful afternoon, where it ricocheted off the side of an electrician's van. 'Call the gang, Laz: seven o'clock tonight we're getting blootered and hitting a titty bar.'

Classy.

But never let it be said that Logan wasn't a team player.

11

The Monday morning briefing had a carnival atmosphere to it, everyone lounging in their chairs, talking about where they were going on holiday. DC Rennie – tanned and smug – handed out a mound of bacon butties, the tinfoil packages releasing their savoury-scented steam into the crowded room. Logan's stomach growled, then lurched as Rennie stuck one under his nose, saying, 'Don't say I'm never good to you.'

'Urgh . . . get that bloody thing away from me!'

The constable sank into the next seat. 'God, you're not *still* on that vegetarian nonsense are you? Been seven months: get over it.'

'You know what you can do with your bacon buttie? You can shove it right up your—'

The door opened and everyone sat up, shut up, and prepared to pay attention. Only it wasn't DCI Finnie standing in the doorway – hauling his bra up with one hand, and carrying a plastic bag from Tesco in the other – it was DI Steel. She paused and stared at them all. 'Don't tell me he's *still* no' here!'

She finished rearranging herself, then took the seat on

the other side of Rennie. The constable smiled and offered her Logan's rejected buttie. 'Got an extra one for you.'

She took it without a word, ripped a huge bite out of it, then sat chewing in scowly silence.

Rennie sniffed. 'You're welcome.'

'Oh don't be such a whinge.' The inspector's words were muffled by a cheek-straining mouthful. 'Is this going to take long? Only I've got a date with a rapist called Norman.'

'You know, when I was in Thailand—'

Steel made a little naked sock puppet out of her left hand and went, 'Blah, blah, blah. Look at me, I'm Defective Constable Rennie, and I went to the Far East with Gary Glitter Tours.'

The constable blushed. 'That's not funny.'

'Aye it is. Isn't it Laz?'

Logan shook his head. 'Didn't you hear? Rennie's got himself a grown-up lady friend. About twenty years older than he is.'

'Is it his mum?'

Rennie scowled. 'That's the last time I get a round of bacon butties in. Ungrateful bastards.'

'Does she make you a packed lunch in the morning and tell you not to talk to strange men?'

'Just—'

'Read you a bedtime story?'

'We—'

'Bet she gives your arse a good spanking when you've been naughty.'

And at that, Rennie's blush got even redder.

'She does!' Steel laughed, spraying out a claggy mush of half-chewed bread and bacon. 'Oh, you are such a pervert!' Five minutes later she was obviously getting bored of winding the constable up, because she shouted across the room: 'Hoy, Pirie – where's your lord and master?'

DCI Finnie's sidekick looked at his watch. 'Supposed to be here.'

'I know where he's *supposed* to be, what I want to know is where he actually is!'

'Em. . .'

'Oh for God's sake.' Steel marched down to the front of the room. 'Right, we're none of us getting any younger, so: briefing. Everyone who's on an active case, stand up.'

Tumbleweed.

'Aunty Roberta says, on your feet, you lazy bastards!'

Reluctantly, they did as they were told, the sound of rubber-soled chair legs squeaking on the green terrazzo floor.

'Better.' Steel crossed her arms. 'Right, if you can see someone else on your case who outranks you, sit your arse down.'

That left half a dozen Detective Constables and Detective Sergeants. The inspector made them all give a little report on their investigations: background, current status, and estimated chances of not cocking the whole thing up. The last one standing was DS Pirie.

He ran a hand through his wiry ginger hair, straightened his suit jacket on his skeletal frame, and brought everyone up to date on Operation Oedipus. The slideshow was set up ready for the absent DCI Finnie, and Pirie started at the beginning. The very first victim's tattered face filled the screen. 'Tolek Dobrowski, twenty-three, electrician, originally from Gdańsk.'

Steel scrunched up the tinfoil her bacon buttie came in and lobbed it at the detective sergeant. 'Don't sod about, we've been over this already. Tell us something we don't know.'

Pirie flushed, filling in the space between his freckles. 'Fine. . .' He went scrabbling through his notes. 'The . . . here we are: the only thing our victims had in common, is that they're all Polish nationals, except for Simon McLeod. And none of them will tell us anything about what happened, or why.' He turned and poked the projection screen. 'Someone does *that* to you, and you don't talk to the police?'

Steel snorted. 'They're scared, you idiot. What do you think our eye-gouger would do to them if he found out they talked: bake them a cake? Move on!'

'Ah, yes, well. . .'

Rennie stuck up his hand. 'Why are we calling him Oedipus?'

Pirie squared his shoulders, scowling at the interruption. 'If you'd been paying attention *Constable*, you'd know why. Now—'

'Yeah, but Oedipus slept with his mum, murdered his dad, then gouged his own eyes out. He didn't blind anyone else.'

Steel snorted. 'And if anyone knows about sleeping with his mum, it's Rennie.'

Laughter.

The constable blushed. 'If you want a proper name we should call him Cornwall – he's the one who blinds the Earl of Gloucester in King Lear. You know, Shakespeare?'

Pirie just stared at him. 'If you don't have anything constructive to add, *Constable*: shut up.'

Rennie put his hand down and Finnie's sidekick nodded. 'Now, does anyone else have any stupid comments. . .?' Silence. 'Good. We got Dr Goulding to update the profile following the attack on DS McRae and DI Steel on Friday. I've got copies here at the front – make sure you take one and *read* it. Dr Goulding believes we're now looking for two men.' The e-fits appeared on the screen. 'You'll have seen these faces on posters all over town, but bear in mind they're probably wrong. No offence to DS McRae, but his source is highly questionable. Posters went up Friday evening and we've not had a single positive identification yet. So forget the e-fits: we're looking at a pair of men in their *mid to late twenties*. One will be older than the other – probably very charismatic – the younger man is following him and may be mentally subnormal.'

Steel made another Rennie joke.

Pirie carried on, ignoring the laughter: 'We need to start looking at the usual care-in-the-community jobs. Find out if any of them have recently fallen in with an older man.' The DS fiddled his paperwork into a neat pile. 'I would have expected the Polish community to come out in force on this one, given the fact it's them being targeted, but I get the feeling they wouldn't talk to us even if they knew. It's a conspiracy of silence out there. Keep that in mind when you're interviewing them – they don't trust us.'

The inspector let Pirie finish his briefing before she handed out the day's assignments. 'One last thing,' she said, before anyone could escape, 'the language in this department is fucking shocking. We're going to do something about that.' She grabbed her carrier bag from the floor and dragged out a big tin of Quality Street.

An excited murmur went around the room.

'Don't get your hopes up, I've eaten them all.' The tin went on the desk at the front of the room, then Steel put on a sing-song voice, as if she was speaking to very small, very thick children, 'This is our new swear box, isn't that *exciting*! And every time you rude bastards come out with some verbal filth, you have to put money in it.'

Everyone groaned.

'Oh shut up. When it's full the money either goes to charity or we stick it behind the bar and get blootered.'

She crumpled up the empty carrier bag and stuck it in

her pocket. 'And before I forget: since his brother got blinded it looks like Creepy Colin McLeod's been doing a world tour of the local lowlife with his pet claw hammer. Harry Jordan got his kneecaps done last night – that makes six. Now I know drug dealers and affiliated scumbags aren't as cute as puppies and kittens, but that doesn't mean Creepy gets to cripple them. Eyes and ears open, people.'

She sniffed, then stared at them for a moment. No Questions. 'Right, we're done. One quick chorus of "We are not at home to Mr Fuck-Up" then you can all go catch some bloody crooks for a change.'

By half past eight Logan was on the phone to the hospital, checking up on Kevin Murray – the man who'd got his nose cut in half on Friday night. Apparently he'd been given lots of stitches, lots of painkillers and was back on the street within twenty-four hours.

There was no sign of the four hoodies who'd attacked him.

'It's like a bloody jungle out there most weekends,' said the inspector in charge of the CCTV room, covering the front of his white shirt with cake crumbs. 'We've got the four little sods on tape, but there's no way to make an ID.' He called up the footage, letting it play across one of the monitors that dominated the wall opposite the control desk. 'See? They never even look at a camera. Keep their faces hidden the whole time.'

Logan helped himself to a slice of coconut sponge. 'They had Manchester accents, if that helps?'

'It doesn't.' The inspector spooled the tape forward a bit, and Logan watched Kevin Murray go down in a spray of blood. Hoodie Number One bounced in front of Logan, then he and his fellow thugs were off and running. The picture tilted to follow them, then jumped to another camera. Then another one. . . And then they were gone, vanishing into one of the little side roads off George Street. Swallowed by granite and shadow.

Logan finished his mouthful. 'Thought Britain had more CCTV cameras per head of population than anywhere in the world?'

'Don't you bloody start – I get enough of that from the wife.' The inspector pointed at a stack of VHS videos in their black cases. 'Got about forty hours' worth of drug-related stabbings and fights there, if you want it?'

Logan patted him on the shoulder and said he'd think about it.

DI Steel was slumped in her office with her feet up on the desk, a cup of coffee sitting in front of her, while she fiddled about in her cleavage. Logan settled down into the only visitor chair that didn't look as if it was covered in pee-stains. 'Is it just me,' he said, 'or is Pirie a total wanker?'

'Yup. . .' The inspector kept on rummaging.

'I mean, can you believe all that rubbish? "The profile says this, the profile says that." Idiot.' There were copies of the e-fits on the inspector's desk, Logan picked them up, staring at the two faces. 'We know Oedipus isn't in his early twenties – Rory saw him – he had grey hair. . . And what kind of serial nut-job goes after Simon McLeod?'

'Suicidal one?' She managed to get two hands down the front of her shirt.

'Would you stop doing that?'

'Lost a bit of nicotine gum. . .'

Logan took another good long look at the e-fit of the older man. Short grey hair, chiselled jaw, stern eyes. . . 'Does he not look a bit . . . familiar to you?'

Steel snatched it off him, one hand still well and truly

rammed down her cleavage as she squinted at the composite photo. 'No.' She handed it back. 'Susan and me watched that *Indiana Jane and the Temple of Dildos* last night. Brilliant. Tell you, she can raid my forbidden palace any time she likes.' Steel gave up on the rummaging, stood, and untucked her grey blouse.

'If you're getting naked, I'm leaving the room.'

'Don't flatter yourself. . .' She jiggled up and down until a small white rectangle of gum fell out onto the carpet. 'Aha! Knew it was in there somewhere.' She bent to retrieve her spoils.

'What if Rory screwed us over?'

'Nah,' said Steel, brushing the fluff off her nicotine gum, before popping it in her mouth, 'the wee shite only likes little girls.'

'No – I mean what if this isn't the guy who attacked us in the house? Rory didn't want to ID them in the first place, was scared in case they found out. What if Rory fiddled the description so he'd be in the clear?'

'I'll bloody kill him!'

'Maybe that's why no one's recognized the pictures yet?'

Steel grabbed her coat and tucked her blouse back into her trousers. 'Well, come on then: let's go pay Mr Rory Simpson a visit. Dirty wee bastard should still be in the cells.'

'And that's one pound fifty you owe the swear box.'

'No I don't.'

'Yes you do. One "bloody" one "bastard" and a "shite". Fifty pence each.'

The inspector opened her mouth, then closed it again. 'You are such a. . .' Scowl. 'Well, *you* called Pirie a wanker!'

She had him there.

* * *

Down in the cell blocks, the sound of someone yelling echoed around the concrete and breezeblock walls. 'POLICE BRUTALITY! HELP! SOMEONE CALL A LAWYER! FUCKING BASTARD FUCKERS! HELP!'

Steel stopped on the stairs. 'Maybe we should come back when things are a bit less shouty?'

'You want me to do it?' asked Logan, one hand on the stairwell door.

'Oh aye, and take all the credit? No thank you.' She pushed past him into the depressing grey corridor.

'POLICE BRUTALITY!'

One of the Police Custody and Security Officers was standing in the middle of the cellblock, grinding her teeth.

'What's all this then?' said Steel. 'You been beating up our prisoners again? How often do I have to tell you that's CID's job?'

'POLICE FUCKING BRUTALITY!'

The PCSO gave cell number six a filthy look. 'Says he found a pubic hair in his tea. As if! Lucky we give the bastards breakfast at all. Next time he's brought in I'm farting on his rowie.'

'Come on then, Celebrity MasterChef, which one's Rory Simpson in?'

'He's not—'

'WHAT ABOUT MY BLOODY HUMAN RIGHTS?'

The PCSO banged on the cell door with the palm of her hand. 'WILL YOU SHUT UP!' There was a moment of blessed silence. 'Rory Simpson's been here since Friday afternoon so he got dibs on an early court hearing. They took him first thing. Got released on bail – trial date's been set for three weeks.'

'Oh for fff. . .' Steel ground to a halt. 'I mean, oh dear.' She turned and marched back towards the rear doors. 'Rory's a creature of habit: he'll go straight home from court, pausing only to pick up a wee bottle of brandy and a packet of custard creams to make himself feel better. We'll pick him up there. Not a problem.'

Wrong.

12

According to the Police National Computer, Rory Simpson rented a top-floor flat in a seventies development in Ruthrieston – not too far from Great Western Road, but just far enough from the local primary school to avoid breaching the exclusion zone required by his registered sex-offender status. The block was three storeys of bland, white-painted concrete – about two dozen flats in total – the walls streaked with grey and patches of green mould.

Logan abandoned their CID Vauxhall in the empty car park out back, then they worked their way round to the front of the building, avoiding the collection of broken wheely bins. The contents were being artistically spread all over the tarmac by a pair of cackling magpies.

'So,' said Logan, 'why the sudden desire for a swear box?'

'Told you, language in the department is appalling. Supposed to be professionals. . .' The inspector drifted to a halt. They'd reached the building's front door. The lock had been ripped right out of the wooden frame. She placed a hand against the door and pushed – it swung open on a tatty stairwell.

DI Steel peered inside. 'You thinking what I'm thinking?'

Logan reached out a hand and pressed the buzzer marked 'R SIMPSON'. An electronic grinding noise sounded from somewhere above.

No answer.

'Maybe we should call for backup?'

'You *always* want backup.'

'Yeah? Well look what happened last time.'

She stepped across the threshold and started up the stairs. 'We'll just take a quick peek.'

Logan watched her disappear into the gloomy hallway. Swore. Then followed her. 'Still say this is a bad idea. . .'

Whoever the landlord was he hadn't wasted any money making the block of flats look homely. The stairwell and landings were bare concrete, the walls a cheap shade of builder's magnolia.

Rory's flat was right where the computer said it would be. The front door was hanging from a single hinge, wide open, exposing a hallway cluttered with broken furniture and crockery.

'That's it,' Logan dragged out his phone, 'I'm calling for backup.'

But Steel was already heading inside.

'Damn it.' He snuck in after her, mobile clamped to his ear, waiting for Control to pick up.

The hallway led onto a lounge that looked like a bomb-site. Everything was smashed. The small bedroom was the same, drawers torn from the bedside cabinets, their contents scattered about the place. A loose mosaic of Polaroids spilled from the upturned bed onto the floor – all little girls in their school uniforms. Albyn School, Robert Gordon's, Springbank Primary, Victoria Road, Hamilton. . . All these and many more. Rory seemed to like it best when they were running around the playground, especially if he could capture a flash of white pants.

Steel picked her way through the devastation to the window, looking out at the magpies and their collage of nappies and takeaway food containers. 'You know what I think? I think our Rory's nasty little habits finally caught up with him. Some outraged parent finds out there's a paedophile living next door and decides to do something about it.' She looked down at the Polaroids. 'Can't say I blame them.'

They searched the rest of the flat, but there was no sign of its owner. Or his battered body. The inspector found a brand-new half bottle of supermarket brandy lying on the carpet behind the broken front door. 'It's no' been touched. . . Better get a couple of uniforms over here sharpish. I want everyone in the building given the full Spanish Inquisition, and don't spare the thumbscrews.'

Logan took another look around the lounge. 'You'd think there'd be signs of a struggle.'

Steel pointed at the broken picture frames, the upturned sofa, the smashed CDs, the television set with a coffee table embedded in it. 'You're kidding, right?'

'No. You attack someone, they fight back, a couple of things get knocked over; broken. This place has been trashed. If they had Rory, why do all this? And why isn't there any blood?'

Shrug. 'Maybe. . . Well. . . How the hell am I supposed to know?'

'I think they broke in, but he wasn't here, so they took it out on the furniture. He comes home, sees the mess and does a runner.'

Steel groaned, rubbing at her eyes with nicotine-yellowed fingers. 'So now we've got a paedophile on the run. The sodding media are going to have a field day.'

'Look on the bright side, maybe he's lying dead in a ditch somewhere.'

* * *

BANG – the incident room door bounced off the wall and Finnie stormed in, face like a bad day in Chernobyl. 'Is this some sort of joke to you? Is it? Do you think it's *funny*, Inspector? Rory Simpson was a key witness in the Oedipus case, and you thought it'd be a giggle to let him get away!'

Steel didn't even look up from her copy of that morning's *Aberdeen Examiner*: 'DRUG VIOLENCE AT AN ALL-TIME HIGH'.

'Morning, Andy.'

'Don't you "morning Andy" me.' Finnie thrust a finger in Logan's direction. 'And you: why haven't you been to see Dr Goulding yet?'

'Tomorrow afternoon, sir. He's been away at a conference in Birmingham.'

Steel put her paper down on the desk. 'Laz, why don't you go get the teas in, eh? Milk and two for the DCI here. Go on, run along like a good wee boy.'

Logan didn't need to be told twice; if there was going to be an explosion he wanted to be as far away as possible.

As soon as the door was closed behind him, the shouting started. He stood there for a minute, listening to Steel and Finnie having a go at each other, then sloped off somewhere safer.

He was up in CID, working his way through a pile of incident reports, when Steel finally put in an appearance. She didn't say anything, just marched straight over to the swear box and stuck a pile of cash in it.

Everyone in the room looked up to watch her feed in the coins.

Clatter, clang, clink, clink, clatter, clink – sounded like about a fiver's worth.

And then she turned on her heel and marched back out again, pausing only to tell Logan to get his backside in gear, they were going out.

* * *

'You want to talk about it?' Logan inched the pool car forward. Mounthooly roundabout looked more like a huge bronze-age burial mound than a roundabout, and it was just starting to get busy as people sneaked out for an early lunch.

'What the hell do you think?' Steel folded her arms, and sat there like a wrinkled gargoyle, while Logan waited for a break in the traffic.

The inspector shoogled in her seat. 'I hate these new pool cars. What the hell was wrong with the old ones?'

'Falling to bits, remember?'

'Well . . . the new ones don't smell right.'

'That's because they've not been used as rubbish tips for years. Anyway, it's nice not having to worry about rats hiding under the seats for a change. . .'

Steel scowled at him. 'Are you planning on sitting here all day, or should I just get out and bloody walk?'

He put his foot down and they joined the rush, all the way round to the other side. 'There's no point taking it out on me, OK?'

'You know what that sanctimonious, cock-faced, fuck-weasel said to me – and if you tell me that's another quid I owe the swear box I'm going to batter you one – he said it was my fault Rory Simpson walked. Like I had any sodding choice in the matter?' She put on her best DCI Finnie impersonation. '"He was a key witness in the Oedipus case, *Inspector*." "Why did you let him go, *Inspector*?" "Why can't you do anything right, *Inspector*?"'

Logan kept his mouth shut. No point throwing petrol on a burning building.

'And Oedipus is *his* bloody case!' she said. 'If anyone should've been keeping an eye on Rory Simpson, it was him.' She slammed her hand down on the dashboard. 'Pull over at that wee shop. Sod the "new me" I want a packet of fags.'

Logan didn't stop, just kept on going.

'Hoy!'

'You'll thank me later.'

'I'll bloody murder you now!' She watched the little shop slide past, then thumped back in her seat as they drove deep into darkest Froghall.

Two minutes later, Logan pointed through the windshield. 'That's it up there, second from the end.'

The street was all council owned, a pair of matching terraces running down both sides. They were broken up into blocks of six flats, three on each floor, arranged around a communal door and stairway. White harling walls shone in the noonday sun, but there were no mad dogs or Englishmen about, just a couple of evil-looking children jumping up and down on an old brown sofa someone had hauled to the kerb.

Steel stared at the scenery. 'No' exactly Butlins, is it?'

Logan climbed out into the sunshine, leant on the roof of the car, and watched the bouncing children watching him. Then one – a snottery-faced girl of six or seven – stuck her middle finger up at him and shouted, 'Fuck you lookin' at, pervert?'

The inspector slammed her door, and yelled back, 'Bugger off you ugly wee shite, or I'll come over there and ram my boot so far up your arse the Tooth Fairy will be picking up your molars for weeks!'

The little girl froze for a moment. Then ran off crying.

And Steel thought she wasn't good with children. . .

The shared hallway didn't stink of old urine and disinfectant, which made a nice change. Logan stepped up to the steel-vault-style front door of Flat C and knocked. The sound echoed down the stairwell. Second floor: must have been a sod for Harry Jordan to get up here with two smashed kneecaps.

Steel was still grumbling away, 'Bloody Finnie; not his sodding messenger boy; I'll give him "no' competent"; frog-faced, arsehole-licking spunk-bucket. . .'

Logan tried the door again. 'Maybe no one's in?'

'Aye, typical Finnie: send us all the way over here on a wild bloody goose chase. "Make yourself useful, *Inspector*, go check on Harry Jordan, *Inspector*."' She made the universal hand-gesture for 'wanker'. 'Give it one more try then we're sodding off for lunch.'

Logan did, and a voice sounded on the other side – female, afraid, 'Who is it?'

'Police. Can you open the door please?'

'I. . . I'm not. . . What's it about?'

Steel stopped swearing and kicked the door, making the whole thing rattle. 'Tell Harry to get his crippled arse out here. I'm having a shitty day and I'm in no mood to piss about!'

Two minutes later they were standing in the living room. Inside, the place was surprisingly spacious – three bedrooms, one bathroom, kitchen, and the heart of Harry Jordan's little criminal empire.

The lounge was shrouded in darkness, curtains closed against the sunshine, just a tatty standard lamp to break the gloom. Three painfully thin women in various stages of undress hovered in the background. Dark circles lurked beneath their eyes; it was about the only colour on their emaciated frames. Can't be a pimp without merchandise.

Harry Jordan sat in a wheelchair in the middle of the room, both legs sticking straight out: encased in fibreglass casts from hip to ankle. The rest of him didn't look much better – his nose looked like a squashed prune, and the purple-yellow stain of fresh bruises covered the whole left-hand side of his face. According to his police record he was only twenty-nine, but with the lank hair and spreading bald spot he looked at least forty.

'Harry!' Steel beamed at him. 'A wee birdy tells me you had a falling out with Creepy Colin McLeod.'

A joint smouldered between Harry's lips, the smell filling the lounge: a cross between sweat, herbs, and chocolate. He squinted, then let out a huge lungful of smoke. His pupils were dark and wide. 'It's medicinal, OK? I'm in a lot of pain. . .'

'Serves you right.' Steel settled herself down on the huge grey couch, and stuck her feet up on the coffee table.

Logan got the feeling it was his turn to play 'Good Cop' again. 'We need to speak to you about Colin McLeod.'

The joint fell from Harry's lips. 'Aye. . . W. . .' He looked down at the hand-rolled parcel, smouldering away on the burgundy carpet, then up at one of the stick-thin women. 'Fuck's wrong with you? PICK IT UP!'

She hurried forward, track marks standing out against the pale skin on her arms as she grabbed the joint and returned it to its rightful place in Harry's trembling fingers.

Steel tutted. 'Can't even pick up your own spliff, Harry. Creepy really did you over, didn't he?'

Another deep drag. Harry closed his eyes, letting the delta-9-tetrahydrocannabinol ooze its way into his bloodstream. 'Girls,' he said, on a wave of sweet-smelling smoke, 'leave us. . .'

Steel grinned. 'What's the matter, Harry, scared the poor cows'll find out you're no' invincible after all?' She pointed at the wheelchair. 'Bit late for that, isn't it?'

Harry slammed his hand down on the armrest. 'I SAID LEAVE!'

The girls hurried out and closed the door behind them. Now the only sound was Harry's laboured breathing and some halfwit playing *Whitney Houston's Greatest Hits* in the flat downstairs.

'So,' the inspector stretched out, knocking a pile of hardcore

Swedish pornography off the coffee table with her feet, 'Colin McLeod came round and battered the crap out your knees with a claw hammer last night? That's *gotta* hurt!'

Harry just went on nursing his joint, so Logan had a go: 'You should be in hospital where they can look after you.'

'Fucking hospitals do my head in, Man. Checked myself out.' Another toke. ''Sides, got me some painkillers and vodka, know what I mean?' He scowled at the closed door. 'Bitches think I'm not up to it any more. Fucking showed them though, didn't I? Nobody screws with Harry Jordan.'

'Except Creepy Colin McLeod.' Steel smiled at him. 'Why'd he do it? That tart of yours give him a dose of something? Path of true love, and all that.'

'You want to know what happened?' Harry finished the joint and crushed the remains out with his fingers. 'OK. . . Here's what happened. Creepy barges in here, acting the big man, ranting on about his brother's eyes. Like I'm supposed to know something about it—'

'Do you?'

'Do I fuck, but try telling Creepy that. Bastard starts screaming at me and my bitches, like.' Harry jerked his chin up, bruised face pulled into a defiant pout. 'Couldn't have that, could I? So I twat him one. Bang!' He threw a right hook at thin air, then followed it up with a left. 'Bang! Creepy goes down and he's begging me to let him be, you know? So I says to him, I says, "You learn your lesson, Man, you don't disrespect a guy in his own home."' Sniff. 'That's just bad manners.'

Steel applauded. 'Bravo! God, that was better than Harry Potter that was.'

Harry shifted in his wheelchair, the whole thing squeaking as he moved. 'You calling me a liar?'

'Hurrah! Got it in one! You're on fire today, Harry.' She stuck her feet on the floor, rested her elbows on her knees, then her chin in her hands. 'So come on then, dazzle me with your fictional prowess. If you gave Colin McLeod a spanking, how come you're the one with two smashed knees?'

'Gave as good as I got, OK?' But Harry wouldn't look at them.

'Shhhhhure you did.'

Logan pulled a sheet of paper from his pocket – faxed over from Aberdeen Royal Infirmary that morning. 'The orthopaedic surgeon who put your legs back together says you're never going to be able to walk properly again. Even if they give you a pair of artificial knees, you're always going to limp.'

Shrug. 'Fucking doctors, what do they know?'

Steel picked up one of the fallen porno mags, flicking through it. 'Here's the deal, Harry: my governor's a sarcastic frog-faced tit, with a serious stiffy for putting the McLeods behind bars. So I want you to press charges against—'

'No!' Harry sat bolt-upright in his wheelchair. 'No! I'm not pressing anything!' A shudder ran through his battered body. 'It was an accident. I fell down the stairs. Told you – I gave Creepy a hiding, then we had a drink. Yeah, a drink. And I got wankered, fell right down the stairs.'

'He took a hammer to your knees, Harry. Crippled you for life.'

'I told you, it was a fucking accident.' Harry fumbled a little metal tin from his pocket – rolling papers, loose tobacco, and a chunk of resin as big as his thumb. 'That's all it was, an accident.' His fingers wouldn't stay still long enough – a thin sheet of Rizla wafted to the carpet, little shreds of brown going everywhere as the tobacco refused to cooperate. 'Fucking thing. . .'

'Here,' Steel stood and took the tin from him, balancing it on her knee as she laid out a couple of papers, put down a line of Old Virginia, then took a lighter to the lump of resin. A tiny curl of black smoke made its way into the expectant silence. 'I want you to have a good hard think about who your friends are, Harry.'

She crumbled in the little dark flakes, then rolled the whole thing up, sealing the papers with her yellowy tongue. 'Creepy Colin McLeod's no' your mate, he's a borderline psychopath. Today it's your knees, what's he going to break tomorrow? Your arms? Back? Skull?' The inspector levered herself to her feet. 'Maybe next time you'll wind up a vegetable in a hospital bed, eating through a tube till someone comes along and switches you off.'

She lit the joint, drawing in a lungful of smoke, then stood there in silence with her eyes closed. It oozed out with a sigh. 'Good shit. . .'

Steel popped the spliff into Harry's mouth. 'Think about it. We'll let ourselves out.'

13

Someone was waiting for them in the hallway. She probably wasn't much more than eighteen, but looked a lot older. Her face was pinched, prematurely lined, with matching purple bags under her eyes. Hair like deep-fried string. Spots. Wearing a silky negligee that had dried egg down the front. At least Logan hoped it was dried egg.

She waited for him to close the door. 'Did Harry. . .' She coughed, wrapped her arms around herself, fidgeted from one foot to the other. Then glanced back at the lounge, and whispered, 'Kylie's sick.'

Steel didn't stop on her way to the front door. 'What do we look like, the clap clinic? Use a bloody condom.'

'No . . . it's. . .' Another cough. She grabbed Logan's sleeve. 'Please?'

'We—'

'Please!' She dragged him towards a door opposite the kitchen.

Steel marched out of the flat. 'I'll be in the car.'

It was a small, brightly lit bedroom – the open window letting the sunshine in. Kylie was lying in bed, curled up on her side, a cigarette smouldering away between her cracked and swollen lips.

It looked as if a herd of elephants had trampled across her head, leaving black eyes and bruises behind.

Her friend let go of Logan's sleeve and wobbled into the room. 'Kylie? Kylie, there's a policeman here. He's going to help you, OK?'

It might have started out as a sarcastic laugh, but it ended up as a wheeze and a grimace – Kylie's face creased up in pain. Ash tumbled across her pillow.

Logan sank down on the end of the bed. 'Who did this?'

She closed her blackened eyes and shook her head. 'Fell down. . .' Her voice was soft and wet, the sort of sound you get when someone knocks out a couple of teeth.

The girl in the eggy negligee produced a bottle of vodka from God knows where and glugged a hefty measure into a chipped china mug. It had 'WORLDS GREATEST DAUGHTER' printed on the side, along with faded red hearts and teddy bears. Then she helped Kylie to sit up, fussing around, making sure she was all tucked in.

'Thanks. . .'

'Hey, what are big sisters for?'

Kylie took a deep drink and shuddered. Then had another one.

Logan waited for her to surface. 'A lot of people seem to be falling down in this flat, Kylie. First Harry, now you?'

This time the laugh turned into a painful coughing fit. She lay back in her pillows, sweat covering her bruised face. 'He . . . he didn't fall down shite.' Pant, groan, mouthful of vodka. 'Creepy comes round and he's shouting his head off. Never seen him so angry. . . Usually he's nice, you know? Well . . . he's nice to me. He's always nice to me.'

Logan frowned at her. 'Wait: Kylie? Like the tattoo on his arm?'

Her sister nodded. 'He's always saying he's going to take

her away . . . but his mum won't have it. You know? Like Kylie's not good enough for her ugly bastard son.'

'We're like that Romeo and Juliet. . .' Kylie closed her eyes and smiled – the liquid anaesthetic obviously starting to work.

The silence drew out for nearly a minute, until Logan was beginning to think she'd fallen asleep.

And then Kylie sighed. 'But he was *so* mad, coz of Simon getting blinded, you know? Real pissed. He's screaming at Harry and Harry's all "yes Colin, no Colin", but Colin wants to know who did it. And Harry says he doesn't know. . . So he gets a kicking. And I'm hiding behind the sofa watching Colin do it.' She drained the last of the vodka. Then stared into the depths of the empty mug. 'Harry's on the ground and he's crying and his face is all bloody, and Colin . . . Colin takes this claw hammer from his jacket, you know? And it looks fucking huge.'

She shuddered again and her sister topped up the mug.

'He smashes it right into Harry's knee. And Harry *screams*. Then he does it again and again and again, and Harry's wriggling on the floor, only he can't get away, coz Colin's sitting on him. Battering away. And by now Harry's all quiet and he's not moving or nothing, but Colin just keeps on going. The hammer makes this horrible noise, wet thuds and squelching, and there's bits of blood and bone and stuff going everywhere. . . And then he saw me. . .'

The girl in the eggy nightie, took a swig straight from the bottle. 'You're going to help her, right? Get her a doctor or something?'

'Colin McLeod did this to you?'

Kylie shook her head, the motion sending a little vodka slopping onto the duvet cover. 'No. Colin loves me. . . He just wanted me to blow him, coz he's all . . . all hard after doing Harry over.' The words were becoming slurred. 'Harry's blood all up his arm and on his. . .' She waved a hand in front of her face. 'Freckles. You know? Just like freckles. . .'

'So who hit you?'

Kylie's sister spat. 'Who do you think?' She pointed back through the door towards the lounge. 'Harry comes back from the hospital, like, about three in the morning, and he hits the booze. Starts going on about how he's the man and Creepy's going to pay. How no bastard pushes Harry Jordan around. . .' She patted Kylie's hand. 'And this silly bitch starts laughing. Coz there he is, sitting in a wheelchair, telling us how nobody can push him around. And he grabs her hair, you know? So she can't get away. And he starts punching and shouting about how it's her fault Creepy's round here the whole time. . . We tried to help her, we did, but he was. . . I'm sorry Kylie.'

Kylie managed a smile. There were teeth missing. 'I know, Tracey, I know.'

Logan pulled out his notebook. 'Right, here's what we'll do: I'll call an ambulance. We can write up your statements while we wait.'

'No! No way! No statements.' Tracey was on her feet in an instant. 'And no ambulance; Harry'll go mad if he finds out. Can't you just get someone to come and fix her up or something?'

'You want him to *get away* with this?'

'I won't testify to nothing. You saw what he did to Kylie – I'm not stupid.'

'But—'

'Please.' Kylie started to cry. 'Please don't tell anyone! It wasn't Harry's fault. I made him do it. I shouldn't have laughed.'

'Kylie, we have to—'

'No!'

'Fine.' Logan dug a Grampian Police business card out of

his wallet, flipped it over and wrote his mobile number on the back. 'If you change your mind, give me a call.'

Tracey followed him out of the room, all the way to the front door. 'What about a doctor?'

'There's a GP who owes me a couple of favours. I'll give her a call, see if she can swing past.'

'Thanks.'

Logan stood in the doorway, looking down at the girl in the dirty nightie, with her needle-track arms and sunken cheeks. 'You don't have to live like this. We can get you and your sister into a rehabilitation programme, sheltered housing; off the drugs, off the streets, and away from bastards like Harry Jordan.'

'Aye,' she almost smiled, 'and maybe me and Kylie'll meet nice blokes, and get married, and we'll have kids, and live next door to each other in Cults, and no one'll give a toss we was hoors and drug addicts. Nice fucking dream.'

Steel was slouched against the pool car, smoking in the sunshine. 'Well,' she said, as Logan climbed back in behind the steering wheel, 'hope you used a condom. They looked a bit skanky to me.'

'Why the hell do we bother?' Logan started the car. 'I've just spent the last ten minutes listening to an eighteen-year-old girl called Kylie lying to protect the pimp who battered the living hell out of her.'

'What, Harry?' Steel scowled back at the flat. 'The little bastard. . .'

Logan pulled away from the kerb, heading back towards the station. 'She says it was definitely Colin McLeod who hammered Harry's knees; she watched him do it.'

'Good. Serves him right.'

'What do you want to do now?'

Steel puffed out her cheeks. 'Go to the pub and drink

myself into a happy haze. But I suppose we should report in to our great lord and master, Finnie the Unwashable.' She dug out her phone and did just that, flicking two fingers in the general direction of Force Headquarters whenever the DCI was speaking. And then she hung up and added a long, wet raspberry. 'Detective Chief Inspector Frog-Face is unimpressed with our lack of progress.' She dug about in her trouser pocket, coming out with a handful of loose change and a couple of crumpled notes. 'How much do I owe the swear box?'

'Four pound fifty.'

'Let's make it an even fiver. Finnie is a complete and utter, total WANKER!' And then Steel handed over a five pound note that looked as if it'd been lining the bottom of a birdcage for a month. 'He wants us to rush straight back to the station. So we're going in the opposite direction: Turf 'n Track, Laz, and don't spare the horses.'

The betting shop was alive with the sound of greyhounds. They pelted round on the two wall-mounted television screens, all teeth and tongues and flying legs. A pair of baggy old men sat watching the race, passing a half-bottle of Bells whisky back and forth.

Mrs McLeod sparkled away behind the counter – dripping with jewellery – face buried in a copy of the *Racing Post*. She looked up as the door bleeped, her face souring as she recognized Logan and DI Steel. 'What the hell do you Muppets want?'

Steel slapped her wallet on the counter. 'Fifteen quid on Mary Hinge: three thirty at Chepstow.'

'Why aren't you out there catching the bastard who blinded my Simon?'

The inspector slumped onto one of the cracked-leatherette barstools in front of the televisions. 'Where's Colin?'

'None of your damn business.'

'Come on, Agnes, you and I both know he should be here, looking after his dear old mum in her dotage, not out gallivanting with a claw hammer.'

'Who the hell are you calling "in her dotage"?'

'Leaving you here to run the shop while he's off cracking people's kneecaps, it's not right is it?'

Mrs McLeod threw her *Racing Post* across the counter. It smacked into Steel's chest and fell apart, riders and runners fluttering to the sticky linoleum. 'Get out.'

The inspector didn't budge. 'When he comes back, I want you to tell him it's over. This stops *now*. I don't care if he's only battering drug-dealing scumbags, I want him to hang up his hammer.'

'My Colin's a good—'

'Oh, give it a rest, Agnes. We've just spoken to one of the guys he crippled: Harry Jordan's prepared to finger him.' Wink. 'And I don't mean in a sexual way.' She stood and shambled her way to the door. 'No more kneecaps, Agnes. Understand?'

Mrs McLeod glowered, her pinched face almost white in the artificial light, golden earrings glinting, mouth a hard red line. 'Get the fuck out my shop!'

14

Archibald Simpson was packed with off-duty police officers. Quarter past five and nearly the entire day-shift was in there, getting themselves outside the first pint of the evening. Logan pushed his way through the throng to the bar, flashed his warrant card and got a free pint of Stella from the Polish barman.

The hubbub rose, and then someone shouted, 'As you know. . .' Then tried again: 'SHUT UP!' Silence settled into the crowded bar. 'That's better.'

Logan couldn't see who was speaking, but it sounded like Detective Chief Superintendent Bain, the baldy head of CID.

'As you know, we had a great result today, thanks to DI McPherson—'

Everyone cheered.

'—excellent job. He and his team have dealt a significant blow in the fight against gang violence in Aberdeen.' Bain raised his glass. 'Ladies, gentlemen, and Custody Assistants, a toast: DI McPherson, and his team.'

And they all drank to his health, honour, and the large stash of weapons he'd stumbled upon hidden in a caravan in Stoneywood.

'Right,' said, DCS Bain, before the noise could start again, 'there's three hundred quid left behind the bar. First come, first served!'

Logan sat at their usual table, under the television in the little alcove off the main bar, watching DC Rennie weaving his way through the crowds with a tray of drinks and crisps.

The constable sank into his seat and everyone helped themselves: pint of Stella for Logan, pint of Export for DS Beattie, pint of ice and a bottle of cider for Gary from fingerprints, and a lager for himself. 'Tell you,' said Rennie, popping open a packet of prawn cocktail, 'it was funny as hell. McPherson's just done this big motivational speech thing – all duty and public trust and stuff – then he turns to walk back to the car, slips, and goes arse over tit all the way down the hill! Right through a dozen gorse bushes and a pile of dog turds big as your house.' Rennie took a mouthful of lager, chasing it with a handful of crisps, crunching round the words. 'So he's lying there, spread-eagled, covered in scratches and jobbies, groaning away to himself, and we're all up at the top of the hill trying not to piss ourselves laughing.'

More lager disappeared. 'So I go down there to help him up and what do I see, but this manky looking caravan hidden away in the trees and bushes. "Oh-ho," I thinks, "this looks a bit fishy." And when we pop it open, guess what: it's full of bloody Kalashnikovs!'

Logan still couldn't believe it. 'So you're saying this was all down to you?'

Rennie posed, one hand on his chest, the other flopping about in the air. 'I am a detecting *machine*!'

DS Beattie scratched a hand through his beard, sending a dusting of dandruff fluttering down the front of his shirt.

'Is it just me, or is Aberdeen getting bloody scary? What do they need machine guns for?'

The constable snapped his fingers. 'Maybe it's Al-Qaeda? Eh? Maybe I just foiled some *huge* terrorist plot.'

'In Stoneywood?' Another little snowfall drifted from his chin.

'You want to know what I think?' said Rennie, scooting forward in his seat, 'I think—'

A voice cut him off. 'What happened to all the free drink?' Samantha, the IB's pet Goth, stood with a frown and a noxious looking pint of something dark purple. 'Had to pay for this myself!' She grabbed the only free chair and helped herself to Rennie's crisps.

The constable snatched the packet away. 'Your own fault for being late.'

'It's you greedy bastards in CID more like. First sniff of free booze and you drop everything.'

'I'll drop everything for you, Sam, especially trousers.' Rennie gave her what was probably meant to be a suave smile. 'Go on, show us your tattoos.'

Two hours later they'd vacated Archie's for the Pizza Express on Union Street. By which time Rennie was making even less sense than usual, and Beattie looked as if he'd emptied a carton of desiccated coconut all down his front.

Logan topped Samantha's glass up with the last of the wine, then ordered another bottle. 'Did it turn out OK? The tattoo Twit-Boy tried to ruin?'

She smiled and rolled up the sleeve of her skull-and-cross-bones T-shirt. It was a life-sized handprint in black ink, made up of little tribal squiggles, the skin still slightly red and inflamed around the design. 'What do you think?'

'That must have *hurt*.'

'Not as much as this one.' She turned her back on him

and pulled open the neck of her T-shirt. 'It's OK, you're allowed to look.'

Logan peered down inside – it was a Chinese dragon and it covered pretty much everything, the bright colours only broken by the black of her bra strap. 'Wow.'

Samantha grinned at him. 'You ain't seen nothing yet.'

They giggled their way into the flat and tumbled through to the bedroom. Kissing and groping and stumbling over a cardboard box in the gloom. Logan flicked on the bedside light. 'I want you to know,' he said, trying to sound serious, 'that I don't usually do this. . .' He frowned. 'Come to think of it, I've not done it for. . .' Counting backwards on his fingers – June, May, April, March. . . 'Nine months!'

Sam whistled. 'Nine months? Hope you can still remember where everything goes. I better get you started.' She pulled her T-shirt up over her head, exposing even more tattoos. A pair of skeletons stretched a banner across her chest above the bra-line with, 'QUOTH THE RAVEN, "NEVERMORE"' on it, and a spiky tribal thing poked out from the waistband of her black leather trousers, as if a really big spider was trying to escape from her pants. Both arms had a collection of skulls and hearts and swirly things.

She looked him up and down. 'Well, don't just stand there, get your kit off.'

As Logan fumbled his way out of his shirt, Sam stripped off her stripy socks and black leather trousers, until she was kneeling on the bed in nothing but her underwear. Which was a lot more impressive than Logan's slightly baggy pair of blue Marks & Spencer briefs.

'Oh *very* sexy!'

He shrugged. 'Didn't think anyone would see them.'

The spidery tribal tattoo reached all the way down to her left knee, thick spikes of black ink forever ingrained into her skin. It was disturbing and strangely erotic at the same time. She unhooked her bra, lay back on the bed and said, 'Well, don't just stand there. . .'

He didn't need to be told twice.

They lay side by side, catching their breath. Samantha ran a finger across Logan's stomach – the little worms of scar tissue shining in the soft glow of the bedside light. 'Did it hurt?'

'No, you were very gentle with me.'

She hit him. 'Getting stabbed, you idiot. Did it hurt?'

'The first six or seven times are the worst. After that they all kind of blend into one another.'

She counted her way across his stomach. 'Twenty-three.'

'Think I chipped a tooth on your nipple ring.'

'Is it true you died on the operating table?'

Logan slid out of bed. Changing the subject hadn't worked, but leaving the room would. 'I'm going to get a glass of water, you want one?'

She smiled. 'Man of mystery, eh? I'll have a Coke. And then you can get your sexy scarred arse back in bed. I've still got two condoms left.'

15

Torry sat just south of the River Dee, its whorl of old granite tenements and concrete council housing making a three-quarter-mile-long fingerprint in shades of grey. The scene was a two-bedroom flat halfway along Victoria Road, with views out across the fish factories and storage sheds to the harbour. Sun sparkled off the mud and fuel storage tanks in the middle distance, a collection of huge, neon-orange supply boats lolling in the blue-grey water beyond. It was almost pretty.

A pair of white gulls circled in the clear blue sky, squawking obscenities at each other.

FLASH – and the small bedroom lit up. Green patterned wallpaper. Brown carpet. Double bed. MFI wardrobe. Dead body.

FLASH.

Three figures in breathing masks and white SOC cover-alls. A cloud of bluebottles frozen mid-flight.

FLASH.

'And one more for luck. . .' The Identification Bureau photographer hunkered down for a close-up.

FLASH.

'Right, that's me. You can shift the body if you like.'

Logan shook his head. 'Better leave it till Doc Fraser gets here.'

'Okey-doke.' The photographer dug in the pocket of his white paper oversuit, pulled out a business card and handed it to Logan. 'Listen, if you know anyone getting married, I'm doing homers, OK? Wedding albums, family gatherings, that kind of thing.'

Logan looked down at the body oozing out into the carpet and said he'd think about it.

Lubosław Frankowski lay on his front, head turned to face the open door. He was swollen: bloated with internal gasses fermented over the week and a half he'd lain there undisturbed. His skin was mottled purple and black with flecks of white mould. Crawling with fat, black flies.

The whole room stank – the sickly sour-sweet odour of rotting meat.

'Bloody hell!'

Logan looked up to see DCI Finnie standing in the doorway, one hand clamped over his nose and mouth.

'Morning, sir.'

Finnie gagged. 'Open a window!'

Logan did as he was told, but it didn't make any difference to the smell.

The Chief Inspector stared down at the corpse. 'Is it him?'

'Far as we can tell.' Logan pulled a photo from the folder he'd dumped on the bed earlier: Lubosław Frankowski sitting up in a hospital bed, the bandages removed from his ravaged face. Not a pretty sight, but the way he looked now was a damn sight worse. 'We'll take fingerprints soon as Doc Fraser's been.'

'You taking my name in vain again?'

The elderly pathologist was peering around the door frame. He was swamped by his SOC oversuit, the crinkly white paper covering everything except the tired circle of his face – large nose, lined cheeks, watery eyes. Eyebrows like elderly toothbrushes, their bristles pointing in random directions. 'Come on then – everybody out, give a man some space to work.'

They did as they were asked, Finnie grabbing the excuse to get away from the smell. But he was nice enough to tell Logan to stay behind and help.

Doc Fraser levered himself slowly down beside the body. 'Death been declared?'

Logan nodded. 'Any idea what killed him?'

'Give us a chance. Only just got here.' He ran his fingers over the body's head. 'No sign of blunt trauma, no blood on the clothes. . . Help us turn him over, eh?'

Logan grabbed the man's stained sweatshirt and heaved. The body came away from the carpet with a sticky sound and a fresh eruption of flies – buzzing into the air like a pall of smoke. Logan let go and the body flopped down on his back with a wet belch of escaping gas. 'Ah . . . God's sake!'

Doc Fraser waved a hand in front of his face. 'At least it wasn't me this time.' More prodding. And then the pathologist stood and snapped off his gloves. 'Right, no obvious signs of external trauma—'

'Except for the eyes.'

'—but we'll have to get him on the slab to tell for sure. Can't rule out foul play *yet*, but as a wild guess,' the Doc pointed at an empty litre bottle of supermarket whisky lying on the floor by the bed, 'it was drink related.'

'Oh. . .' Logan stared at that bloated face again. 'Any chance you could take a look at the eyes, you know, while you're here?'

'I've taken off my gloves.'

'Quick look. Two minutes tops. We haven't got a clue

what he's using to gouge their eyes out. Or burn them. We need to know what we're looking for.'

Doc Fraser furrowed his hairy eyebrows. 'I'm not a detective or anything, but I would have thought the obvious answer would be to ask the victims who're still alive.'

'They won't talk to us. Terrified of reprisals.'

He shifted from foot to foot. 'All right,' he said at last, 'two minutes.' Doc Fraser pulled on a fresh pair of gloves and went back to the body again. He peered at the flesh around the eyes. 'Skin's been cut away and stitched back . . . most of the upper and lower lids missing . . . presumably that was the hospital getting rid of any burnt tissue. Can't see inside.'

He stuck his finger in one of the eye sockets and started flicking out little wiggly things. 'Off you go. . .' More followed. Then Fraser pulled out a pen-sized torch, shone it in the hole, and hummed and hawed for a bit. 'No,' he said at last, 'this is totally pointless. Any evidence was erased by the surgical team. The whole site's been cleaned and sterilized.'

He tried to stand, but didn't manage. 'Little help please?'

Logan hauled him to his feet.

'Thanks.' Fraser clicked off his torch and slid it back into the pocket of his SOC oversuit. 'If you had a fresh victim, I mean *before* they wheeched him off to A&E, I might be able to tell you something. . .' Shrug. 'Get this one back to the mortuary, post mortem will be half twelve, one-ish? Depends what's for lunch.'

Logan watched the IB roll the bloated, stinking remains of Lubosław Frankowski into a body-bag. Somehow lunch had lost its appeal.

His appetite still hadn't returned by the time he made it back to Force Headquarters. Half eleven and the canteen was gearing up for service; the smell of sausage, beans and chips wafting through the building just made him feel even more queasy.

Steel was sitting in her office, rummaging through a stack of printouts.

Logan slumped back against the wall. 'You seen Finnie?'

The inspector didn't look up. 'If I had I'd be bankrupt by now. That flipping swear box is costing me a fortune.'

'Did you just say, "flipping"?'

'Oh shut up.' She stuffed the printouts back in her in-tray. 'What do you want that . . . Finnie for?'

'We found one of the old Oedipus victims dead this morning. Doc Fraser thinks he probably drank himself to death.'

'Can't say I blame him. If some bast. . . If someone gouged *your* eyes out, would you no' want a wee bit of alcoholic oblivion?'

'Poor sod was face-down on the carpet for a week and a half before anyone found him.'

'In this heat?' She stared at Logan, then at his clothes. 'Thought I smelled something rank, but I was too polite to mention it. Might have been your new aftershave.' She sniffed. 'What is it with you and mouldy corpses?'

'Well, at least I'm not at the post mortem this time. Got an appointment with that criminal psychologist, Dr Goulding. Finnie's orders.'

'Yeah? Think I'd rather go to the PM myself.' She stood. Sat down again. Picked the pile of printouts back out of her in-tray. Shuffled through them. Put them down on her desk. 'Any chance of a cuppa?'

Logan stared. 'Are you wearing a *skirt*?'

'Milk two sugars.'

'You are, aren't you? You're actually wearing a skirt.' It was blue with little yellow dots.

Steel yanked open one of her desk drawers and pulled

out an Airwave handset. 'Can you believe Finnie wants everyone in CID to carry one of these damn things now? Aye, and no' just the plebs: DIs as well!'

'Stop avoiding the subject. What's got into you today?'

She produced a moth-eaten handbag and dropped the handset inside. 'Like carting a brick round with you.'

And that was when it clicked. 'Ahhhh. You've got your adoption social work interview thing this afternoon. I told you: don't sweat it, you'll be fine.'

Steel laughed, but it wasn't a happy sound. 'Bollocks I will. I've no' had a fag for two days, I'm off the booze, I'm wearing a skirt, and I'm no' allowed to swear. You got *any* idea how unnatural that is?' She fidgeted with the collar of her blouse. 'Feel like somebody's mum.'

'Thought that was the idea.'

'If you've got nothing better to do than get up my nose, you can go chase up that lookout request on Rory Simpson.'

'Already did: no sign of him. Even been on to Dundee, Glasgow, Fraserburgh and Inverness. He's vanished.'

Steel screwed her eyes tightly shut, bared her teeth, clenched and unclenched her hands. 'I'm no' going to swear, I'm no' going to swear. . .'

'Oh, and I checked out Kostchey International Holdings as well.'

'What?' She peeled open one eye. 'Who the hell are they?'

'That company supplying Polish actresses for porn films, remember? They aren't on the register at Companies House. They don't exist.'

'Oh for God's sake. I – Don't – Care. OK? I *really* don't. Let it go.'

'But Krystka Gorzałkowska—'

'Was a silly tart in the wrong place at the wrong time. You saw the footage – no one was getting forced to do anything. The Crocodildo girls are happy making dirty films,

I'm happy *watching* them, and Zander with a "Z" is happy paying for them. Ergo, leave it the hell alone.' She sighed. 'Oh don't look at me like that. You know it's true.'

Logan didn't say anything.

'OK, OK, *fine*.' Steel banged her handbag down on the desk. 'Quit it with the puppy-dog eyes: we'll look into it, even though it's a *vast* waste of police time. Go see that idiot McPherson, he's supposed to be the official liaison with the Polish police. Get them to chase up Kissing International Whatever-it-is, maybe they're registered over there.'

'Yes, ma'am.'

'But if Finnie finds out and goes mental, I'm telling him it was all your idea.'

Logan gave her a little salute and left the room, trying to pretend he couldn't hear Steel's parting shot: 'And don't forget: milk, two sugars!'

Detective Inspector McPherson had taken over the medium-sized incident room at the back of the building, with a lacklustre view of the mortuary. There had to be nearly a hundred firearms in here, piled up on every available surface: machine guns, shotguns, handguns, rifles, each one sealed in a transparent evidence pouch.

DC Rennie was sitting behind a desk covered with semi-automatic pistols, tongue sticking out of the side of his mouth as he filled in a form.

Logan picked an AK-47 from the next desk, turning it over in his hands. It was surprisingly heavy. 'Where's McPherson?'

'Eh? Oh. . . Didn't you hear?' The constable went back to his forms. 'He got totally pished last night. Staggered out into the middle of the road.'

Logan winced. 'Car or bus?'

'Neither. The daft sod was sick on someone's girlfriend

and the bloke twatted him one. Punch didn't do much damage, but hitting the tarmac did. Broken wrist and a concussion. Should be back in on Friday.'

'Who's doing the Polish liaison stuff till then?'

'Don't know, don't care.'

Fair enough. Logan put the machine gun to his shoulder and sighted along the barrel at the constable's head. 'So . . . you got any idea what all this stuff's for?'

Rennie scowled. 'Not my job to wonder, that's what *sergeants* and *inspectors* are for. Constables like me are for knocking on doors and filling in bloody forms. The thickest thickies in Thick Town. And don't point that bloody thing at me! Don't even know if it's loaded.'

Logan lowered the gun. 'Who rattled your cage?'

'Who the hell do you think: Finnie. Waltzed in this morning and said he was taking over till McPherson got back.' He chucked his pen down on the desktop. 'If it wasn't for me, we wouldn't have found *any* of this. And do I get the credit? Do I get mentioned in dispatches and showered with nubile young women? Do I buggery.'

Logan let him rabbit on, not really listening as the constable moaned about how unfair the world was, how genius was never appreciated in its lifetime, and how Detective Chief Inspector Finnie could take one of these machine guns, ram it up his own backside, and pull the trigger.

Rant over, the constable picked up the pen again and jabbed it at his stack of forms. 'And I'm sick of cataloguing all this crap.'

'Anyone been in touch with SCDEA yet?'

'Yeah, like *that's* going to happen. We can't have the Scottish Crime and Drug Enforcement Agency grabbing the glory from Darth Finnie, can we? Heaven forefend!' He leaned back in his chair and groaned. 'Fancy going out for lunch?'

'Can't. Got to see a man about a psychological profile.' Logan took another look around the room. 'You know, you could start a major drug war with this lot.' He put the AK-47 back on the desk. 'And if you're a terrorist there's worse places to blow up than Aberdeen. BP, Shell, Total: all the major oil companies. . . You could seriously screw up the whole North Sea in one easy move.'

Rennie gathered up the array of handguns on his desk and dumped them in a blue plastic box in the corner. 'Whatever it is, I should be getting the pat on the back for stopping it.'

Logan wished him luck with that.

16

A woman with nervous hands and pink-rimmed eyes looked up from her desk and gave a little smile. 'Dr Goulding will see you now.'

Goulding's office was part of Aberdeen University's Psychology Department, a grotesque three-storey concrete and glass sandwich stuck onto the equally unattractive Arts Lecture Theatre. A pair of Seventies-style ugly sisters playing against the fifteenth-century grandeur of King's College.

The room wasn't huge, and wasn't designed for comfort either. Clean lines and chrome-plated furniture dominated: a black leather chair and a matching couch; a glass-topped desk covered in piles of paper and Post-it notes. One wall was solid books, the others peppered with framed diplomas and newspaper clippings.

Dr Goulding was behind the desk, poking away at a computer keyboard and peering at a pair of flat-screen monitors. He didn't look up as Logan entered, just said, 'If you'd like to take a seat I'll be with you in a minute. . .' in a flat Liverpudlian accent.

Logan squeaked down on the couch and looked out of

the small, high window, getting a view of yet another ugly concrete building.

Eventually the psychologist stopped what he was doing and stood. 'Sorry about that.' He stuck out his hand, 'Doctor Dave Goulding.' He had a nose like a can opener, and short, dark, animal-pelt hair.

Logan took the hand and shook it, trying not to stare at the lurid green tie with two huge red dice embroidered on it. 'I know, we met last year? On the Flesher case?'

'We did?' Frown. 'Ah of course, I remember you: Sergeant McRae. The poor chap who had to eat human flesh. Well, we all might have eaten it I suppose, difficult to tell, isn't it? But at least we can pretend we didn't – you *know* you did.' He let go of Logan's hand. 'How did it taste?'

'It. . . I. . .' Cough. 'DCI Finnie wants me to talk to you about the men we saw when Simon McLeod was blinded.'

'Are you seeing anyone?'

Logan moved a little further away. 'Sorry? I mean, I'm flattered, but—'

'I don't mean *romantically*, I mean therapy.' Goulding settled into the couch's matching black leather chair, crossed his legs and folded his hands over his middle-aged paunch. 'It can't be easy coming to terms with what you went through last year. All that death and blood.'

'Erm. . . Look, I appreciate the—'

'Do you suffer from insomnia? Interrupted sleep? Nightmares? Maybe a bit depressed?'

'Well—'

'It's "Logan", isn't it?'

'Yes, but—'

'I can help you, Logan. I *want* to help you. It's not healthy to keep this kind of thing bottled up inside.'

'Look, Dr Goulding—'

The psychologist smiled. 'Please, call me Dave.'

'I just want to go over the Oedipus attack, OK? I don't need my head shrunk. I'm fine.'

The psychologist sat and stared at him, expression completely blank. 'How's your relationship with your mother?'

'DI Steel and I were attacked by two men, one of them had an Eastern European accent.'

'Yes. . .' Goulding played with the lumpy little mole on his cheek. 'I'm a little uncomfortable about that.' He stood and crossed the room to a large whiteboard covered in black scribbled notes, all linked by a dense web of coloured lines. It was flanked by a pair of corkboards, full of Post-its, print-outs, and articles clipped from the newspapers. He unpinned one of the sheets of A4, frowned at it for a moment, then handed it to Logan.

It was a photocopy of an early Oedipus note, the writer banging on about how the Polish incomers were stealing God.

'You see,' said Goulding, 'these messages definitely aren't a joint project, they're one man's very personal obsession. Full of rage. The blindings are too. It's *possible* the eyes are gouged out by two people working together, but when he burns the sockets it's. . .' Goulding waved a hand about, 'excessive. It's not necessary – they're already blind. It means something to him.'

'Maybe it's a warning?'

'Perhaps. Would you say you feel tired: all the time, often, sometimes, rarely, or almost never?'

'What? Erm, often, it's the shift work. Anyway, we know couples do horrible stuff all the time: Ian Brady and Myra Hindley, Rose and Fred West . . . Richard and Judy.'

'Not really the same thing, is it? Do you ever keep yourself awake at night, going over things that happen in your life?'

'Can we just stick to the Oedipus case?'

'Looking at the notes and the previous victims, the pattern's clear: we're looking for a single male, probably works in construction, or hotel services, that kind of thing. Mid twenties. Recently unemployed.'

'Yes, but—'

'He blames the turn his life's taken on the Polish workforce coming over and stealing his job. He's likely to have a very harsh super-ego: he's externalizing his own guilt and projecting it onto the people he blinds. His actions are an attempt to redeem himself in the eyes of an absent father figure. Possibly deceased.'

'That's lovely, but it doesn't help us, does it? There were definitely two of them: I *saw* them. We have a witness.'

'Ah yes . . . your paedophile.' Goulding crossed his arms and leant back against the cork board. 'Your colleagues would never need to know, if that's what you're worried about? I really think therapy could help you.'

Logan shifted forward in his seat. 'What if Simon McLeod wasn't anything to do with Oedipus? He's not Polish – he's a mid-level gangster. What if it was someone using the attacks as a cover? Someone getting their own back and blaming it on the nut-job in the papers?'

'Ah yes, that well-known psychological term: "nut-job".'

'You know what I mean.'

'It *would* explain why Simon McLeod doesn't fit my victim profile.' Goulding turned and faced the scribble-covered whiteboard. 'And if we take him out of the picture, it means we're still looking for that white male, early to mid twenties, who lost his father. Probably still lives at home with his mother. But she's emotionally distant. . .'

The psychologist ran his fingers across the board, just above the surface, as if feeling his web for vibrations. A Liverpudlian spider in a nasty tie, waiting for its prey to reveal itself. 'He's a local lad, we know that from the disposal of the victims – each of them left in an unoccupied building. All in Torry. . . Did you know there are so many Polish people living in Torry now they're calling it Little Warsaw?'

Goulding traced a line of red boxes, each one detailing a different address. 'Our man knows the territory. He knows where to take them so he won't be disturbed while he carves out their eyes. All that "They're stealing God" stuff means he's very religious, or at least he believes he is. . .' There was a long pause. 'Fascinating.'

The psychologist stepped back from the board and smiled at Logan. 'Tea, coffee? Might even have some biscuits. Then we can have a chat about you coming to see me on a regular basis.'

'Liver failure.' Doc Fraser was standing in his office, wearing nothing but his vest and pants, skin so white it was almost fluorescent. He looked like a threadbare sock puppet. There wasn't any hair on top of his head, but he more than made up for that with the tufts growing out of his ears. 'Our friend Mr Frankowski drank and drank and drank and drank and died. Stomach contents reeked of whisky. Have to wait for the tox screen to come back, but I'll bet you a fiver his blood's about eighty percent proof. And he'd ingested a serious amount of painkillers and antidepressants.'

Logan stuck the kettle on. 'Suicide?'

'Maybe. Or an accident. Difficult to tell.' The pathologist paused for a good scratch. 'Can't say I'd blame him either way, after what happened to his eyes. . .'

The kettle rumbled to a boil, and Logan made the tea while Doc Fraser climbed back into his usual corduroy and cardigan ensemble.

'Anything else?'

The pathologist checked his notes. 'Some bruising to the

chest, knees, back and shins – not surprising if he's stumbling about blind for the first time in his life. Found a small tumour in his left lung. . . And you'll be disappointed to hear I couldn't get anything on how his eyes were removed. Like I said, I really need to see a fresh victim.'

Logan handed over the pathologist's tea. 'Soon as he kills one, you'll be the first to know. Otherwise they're all going to the hospital, not the mortuary.'

Doc Fraser sniffed. 'Shame. . . Still, hope springs eternal, eh?'

It was a cheery thought.

Rush hour was in full swing – the Esplanade nose-to-tail with cars trying to avoid King Street on their way to the Bridge of Don. Logan pulled the pool car up to the kerb, behind DI Steel's little open-topped sports car. Then sat there, looking out on a glorious June evening.

Aberdeen beach glowed beneath the summer sun, the North Sea sparkling with reflected highlights. Down on the sand, a couple meandered along behind a lumbering black Labrador; an old man and a young boy fought with a bright-red kite; a family played in the sand – two little girls shrieking to the water's edge and back again.

The beach was a good twenty foot lower than the road, down a steep grass embankment, across a wide tarmac path, and down another embankment made of big sloping concrete blocks. DI Steel was easy enough to spot. She'd commandeered a bench two hundred yards along the path, and sat there wobbling a bit, swigging from a bottle of eighteen-year-old Macallan.

Logan picked his way down the grass and sat next to her. 'Finnie's looking for you. He's throwing a strop about some progress report.'

She turned and squinted at him. 'Lazar . . . Laza . . . Logan!

How's my favourite. . .' she paused for a hiccup. 'Lovely day, eh?' Swinging an unsteady arm around at the scenery. 'Sposed to rain later. How crap is tha . . . is that?'

Logan picked up the bottle of whisky and gave it a little shake, just over a third left. 'You feeling OK?'

'I'm a bit . . . a bit drunked.' An ominous gurgling sound came from her stomach. 'Uh-ho. . . Don' . . . don' tell anyone, OK?'

'Are you going to be sick?'

'Car keys, car keys. . .' Steel went rummaging through her handbag, scattering the contents all over the bench. She squinted at the collection of receipts, combs, breath mints, lipstick, Airwave handset, loose change, nicotine gum, and fluff, then picked the keys out of the junk and handed them over. 'Friends don' let . . . don' let friends drive drunked.'

She hiccupped again. 'Is . . . how you find me?'

'Your Airwave handset. I got the control room to check the GPS on it.'

'Pfffffffffffff. . . Can't even . . . even dissspear no more. No' like old days. . . You wanna chip?' The inspector looked around her, frowned, then pointed at three fat seagulls squabbling over a discarded paper bag from Burger King. 'Oh. . . Have to fight for them.'

'You're absolutely blootered, aren't you?'

'I like seagulls. Everyone . . . everyone *hates* them. But they're only . . . only. . .' another hiccup, 'you know? What they're supposed to be.' She threw her arms wide, accidentally belting Logan in the chest. 'I am a seagull! SQUAAAAAAAAAAK!'

The three real ones paused in their squabble over the thin ribbons of deep-fried potato and glared at her with beady yellow eyes.

'SQUEEEEAAAAAK!' She took another swig of whisky, swallowed, and shuddered. 'You wan' some?'

'Why don't I take you home?'

She giggled and hit him again. 'No, you . . . I'm lesbian . . . but . . . but if I wasn't . . . eh?' Hiccup. 'Did I tell you I was a seagull?'

'You might have mentioned it.' He stuck out his hand. 'Come on, Susan will be worried.'

When the tears came, they appeared from nowhere, great hacking sobs accompanied by twin shiny streams from her nose.

Logan took the whisky and popped the cork back in, then hauled the inspector to her feet. He helped her stagger back up the embankment and over to the pool car, safe in the knowledge that she was probably going to be sick in it.

The radio blared into life as he manhandled her into the back: Control calling with an update on some fire in Sandilands. Fire engines in attendance, two unit cars, suspicious circumstances. It wasn't until they mentioned the address that Logan started to pay attention.

Someone had petrol-bombed the Turf 'n Track.

'Bloody hell.' He jumped in behind the wheel. 'Inspector?'

No reply.

He looked in the rear-view mirror. She was fast asleep, head lolling to one side, with the bottle of Macallan clutched to her breast like a little glass baby full of whisky.

Logan pointed the car in the direction of Sandilands, switched the siren on, and put his foot down. The Tuesday afternoon rush hour parted before them like sluggish custard.

The Turf 'n Track was surrounded by fluorescent orange and yellow fire engines, spraying thousands of gallons into the dying blaze. A thick pall of black smoke curdled its way into the bright blue sky, stinking of burning plastic and years of cigarette tar. The shops on either side had been evacuated, the patrons and owners loitering behind the police cordon, watching the betting shop burn.

An ambulance sat half on the pavement and half on the road, its blue lights spinning lazily as the paramedics fussed over someone in the back.

Logan abandoned the pool car as close as he could to the scene, checking that DI Steel wasn't going anywhere before locking her in. The rumble of diesel motors was almost deafening as he picked his way through the rivers and puddles covering the car park, past the fire engines, and over to the ambulance, where two uniformed officers were trying to take statements from the coughing witnesses.

Logan beckoned a PC over. 'What's the situation?'

The officer pointed at an old man in a soot-stained cardigan and flat cap. 'They're a bunch of lying bastards. The guys from the newsagents next door say they saw a man wearing a balaclava chuck a petrol bomb in through the front door. But the people *in* the bookies say that's rubbish. It was a faulty radiator.'

'Yeah?' Logan turned to give the betting shop's clientele another look. Two old men, and a filthy West Highland Terrier in a bright-pink raincoat with little yellow daisies on it. 'Who was running the shop – Mrs McLeod, or Creepy Colin?'

'The bidie-in, Hilary Brander.' The officer pointed again at the ambulance and a dishevelled figure sucking on an oxygen mask.

Up close she reeked of smoke, her clothes, face and hair blackened with a thin layer of burnt betting shop. Green eyes ringed with red.

Logan leant against the side of the ambulance. 'So . . . faulty radiator?'

Hilary didn't even look up. 'I already gave a statement.'

'What happened to Colin and Mrs McLeod?'

'Agnes is looking after the kids. I. . .' She coughed, wrinkled her nose, then spat something black into a handkerchief. 'What do you want?'

'I want to know who firebombed the shop.'

'I already told them: it was a faulty radiator.' Her Essex accent was getting stronger as she raised her voice. 'Don't you people ever *listen*?'

Logan turned to look back at the Turf 'n Track's smouldering remains. The blaze seemed to have finally died; the firemen were rolling their hoses up and hefting them back to the engines. 'You know what I think? I think someone's fed up with Colin running around hammering the hell out of people's knees.'

'You should be out there catching whoever blinded my Simon, not harassing his family.'

'I'm not harassing anyone, I'm trying to make sure no one else gets hurt!'

The ridiculous little Westie in the plastic Mac skittered up and started barking at him. Hilary scooped the thing up, called it 'Mummy's little angel', and held it tight. 'Did the nasty man frighten you?'

A big bloke in the standard padded, baggy brown fire fighter's uniform stepped out of the bookies' front door, carrying something in his gloved hands. One of the uniformed constables pointed him in Logan's direction.

'You in charge?' asked the fireman.

'Depends.'

He held out his hand, revealing the neck and top half of a glass bottle. 'Smell that. Found it just inside the shop.'

Logan did as he was told. The familiar sweet-acrid aroma of petrol. He turned to Hilary and the snarling dog. 'Still say it was a faulty radiator?'

'You calling me a liar?'

'Yes. We've got witnesses, we've got evidence, and with a bit of luck, we'll have fingerprints too. So why not give me a break and tell me what happened?'

She told him to go to hell instead.

17

For once luck was on Logan's side: DI Steel wasn't actually sick in the pool car. Instead she waited until she was being half-carried, half-dragged up the path to her house before painting the rose bushes in several shades of yuck.

Logan left her kneeling in front of the spattered red blossoms and rang the doorbell – no answer. The house was a big granite lump of a place on a leafy side street; bay windows showing off a lounge and a dining room both decorated in pastel shades. Logan cupped his hands to the glass and peered inside: fireplace, leather couches, upright piano, lots of bookshelves. No sign of life.

He tried the bell again and waited in the sunshine, trying not to listen to the inspector bringing up everything she'd eaten in the last seven years. On and on and on.

One more go. . .

The door rattled open and Steel's wife, Susan, peered out at him. Short, blonde, pretty in a Doris-Day-after-too-many-pies kind of way, and at least ten years younger than the inspector. Her nose and cheeks were red, her eyes pink and swollen. Freshly-applied mascara all clumpy on her lashes. She sniffed, then pulled her face into a smile. 'Logan, how nice to see you.' Which was probably a lie. 'If you're looking for Roberta, she won't be back till. . .'

Susan trailed off, staring past Logan to the vomit-sodden lump in the ugly dress, lying curled up on the garden path.

Logan tried a smile. 'I think she might've killed the roses.'

'I'm sorry about this,' said Susan, watching as Logan arranged Steel into the recovery position on the downstairs bathroom floor.

'Don't worry about it – if she's sick again at least the tiles will be easier to clean than the carpet.'

'I mean sorry about . . . well never mind. You've got some on your jacket.'

'Oh, you're kidding.' She was right: the outside of his sleeve was covered with vomit.

'Come on, take it off and I'll rinse it out for you.'

Susan made him a cup of tea, then sat him at the breakfast bar while she sponged his sleeve with lukewarm water. Standing at the sink, with her back to him.

Through the kitchen window Logan could see a big fluffy grey cat sprawling on the grass in the back garden. Legs akimbo as it soaked up the sun.

'They. . .' Susan cleared her throat and tried again. 'To be honest, things have been a bit strained lately.' She pulled the plug and let the foamy, sour-smelling water drain away. 'They won't let us have IVF.'

The cat rolled over onto its front as a white butterfly bobbed and weaved a drunken trail above a clump of yellow buttercups. The cat stared at it for a moment, then pounced. And missed.

Logan watched the cat tear around the garden after the butterfly. 'I'm sorry.'

'Apparently we're not a *priority*. There's nice heterosexual couples out there and they need babies much more than we do.' She twisted the taps back on again, filling the sink.

Susan dropped her head and sighed, and when she spoke again her voice was brittle with forced cheer: 'But listen to me, moaning away. Forgot to ask how *you* were. . . Ever think about hooking up with that Rachael woman from the Procurator Fiscal's office again?'

'Not really – think she's engaged now.' He actually blushed, even though Susan hadn't turned around the whole time. 'Don't tell Her Nibs, but I've . . . em . . . started seeing someone from work.'

'Good. Good for you. Yes. Very good. You deserve someone nice. Settle down, get married, start a family. Why not? After all *you're* not gay, why shouldn't *you* have bloody babies?' She hurled the sponge into the sink, and water splashed up the inside of the window. 'It's so bloody unfair!'

Logan couldn't argue with that.

Back home it was colder inside the flat than out, so Logan opened the lounge windows wide, letting in the noise of Aberdeen harbour: the drone of ship engines, the clang and clatter of loading and unloading, someone singing along to a crackling radio.

Sunlight bathed the buildings opposite, turning them from grey to gold as Logan cracked open a bottle of Belhaven beer. Maybe he should give Samantha a call? Tell her he'd had a nice time last night. Only that would sound desperate, wouldn't it? Much better to play it cool. Maybe bump into her at work tomorrow – accidentally on purpose. . .

The phone rang. He ignored it, letting the answering machine pick it up. Logan took another swig of beer and listened to his own voice telling whoever it was on the other end they could leave a message.

'Hi, Logan, it's me: Sam. Look, I wanted to say—'

Logan scrabbled through the lounge and grabbed the phone. 'Hello?'

Pause. *'Look, I was thinking about playing it cool, but you know what, I'm a grown up and you're a grown up and I had fun last night, so what's the point of playing daft games?'*

He stabbed the off button on the answering machine. 'I was just thinking the same thing.' Liar. 'You eaten yet?'

'Nope. Was hoping a certain Detective Sergeant would turn up unannounced with a takeaway.' And then she gave him the address of a static caravan on Mugiemoss Road.

'A caravan?'

'Yes, a caravan. I live in a caravan, OK? And you make one joke about trailer trash and you're not getting any, understand?'

'Wouldn't dream of it.'

Not long after eight, Logan pulled into a small knot of static caravans on the south bank of the River Don, opposite a steeply banked graveyard, and a hundred yards downwind of the Grampian Country Chickens processing factory. A bank of trees screened the caravan park from the sewage plant on the opposite river bank, but it wasn't thick enough to keep out the glare of the huge Tesco on the other side of the bridge.

Samantha's caravan was a big rectangular box of a thing – more like a Portakabin than something designed to grind traffic to a standstill on a bank holiday weekend – surrounded by trellis fencing plastered with climbing roses. At least no one had been sick on these ones. She was waiting at the door for him, watching as he unloaded the carryout from DI Steel's car.

'You took your time.'

'Meal deal.' Logan held up two white plastic bags and a big square cardboard box. 'Pizza, garlic bread, a litre of Coke and a tub of Mackies vanilla.'

'Oh aye. . .' She waited for him to lock up. 'Didn't think you were the sports car type.'

'Just looking after it while Steel's . . . not feeling well.' It was cheaper than getting a taxi, and it wasn't as if the inspector was going to be sober enough to drive anywhere for a while, was it? And she *had* given him her keys.

Inside, the static caravan wasn't that much smaller than Logan's flat. Sam gave him the quick tour: bedroom, lounge, kitchen, and bathroom, all decorated in various shades of dark red and purple. Every surface was jammed full of books, dragons, pewter skulls, goblets, and crystals. The whole place was festooned with flickering candles. Like a morbid Santa's grotto.

Logan stood in the middle of the lounge. 'It's very . . . Gothic.' The only thing that didn't seem to fit was an ancient-looking orange teddy bear, given pride of place on a throne of Stephen King novels.

'You were expecting little pink unicorns and Laura Ashley prints?'

'Do I get brownie points if I say it goes with your hair?'

'Make with the pizza, Sergeant, and we'll see what you get.'

They squeezed together on the couch, fumbling their way inside each other's clothes. Undoing buttons, zippers, pulling off shirts, T-shirts, trousers, underwear. Logan ran his tongue along the curves of her body, tracing the outline of that huge tribal spider tattoo. The skin was marked by little ridges, like stretch marks, on the inside of her thigh, buried beneath the blank ink. Logan kissed them and she arched her back, moaned . . . then swore as his mobile phone went into an epileptic fit of bleeps and whistles.

They lay in the candlelight, listening to the thing warble its asymmetric tune.

'Go on then,' she said, 'answer it.'

'No chance.'

'But it might be work.'

'I know.' Logan found his place again, kissing his way higher with every word. 'That's – why – I'm not – answering it.'

'Oh yes. . .' The phone went silent. 'Oh yes. . . Mmmm, oh God. . .' Then the ringing started again. 'Oh *bloody hell*!'

'One second.' Logan opened the lounge door, threw his jacket into the hall, then closed the door again. 'Now where were we?'

They lay in a heap on the caravan floor, listening to the first drops of rain pattering on the thin roof. The clock on the DVD player glowed '21:15' as Samantha ran her fingertips lightly over the paths of scar-tissue on Logan's stomach. Playing 'join the dots' with his knife wounds in the candle light.

It was a disconcerting feeling, but in the post-coital glow he was willing to put up with it.

Outside in the hall, the exiled mobile phone started ringing yet again.

Samantha stretched like a cat, showing off her tattoos to disturbing advantage. 'You're going to have to answer it eventually.'

Logan grunted.

She poked him in the ribs. 'Come on. You go do that, I'll get us a couple of beers, then we can crack open the ice cream.' She stood and disappeared into the hall. 'Think there's some garlic bread left too. . .'

Logan dragged himself up and through to where his jacket lay, just in time for it to go through to voicemail. Blessed silence. He dragged the thing out of his inside pocket. According to the readout he had twenty-two messages.

But before he could check them the phone blared into life one more time.

He flipped it open. Didn't recognize the number. Pressed the button. 'McRae?'

Silence.

'If you're not going to say anything, stop bloody calling! I'm—'

'Is this the. . .' Pause. *'Are you that policeman, Detective Sergeant McRae?'* It was a woman's voice, sounding young. Scared.

Logan wandered back into the lounge, where his clothes were strewn all over the carpet, stifling a yawn as he sank down, naked, on the sofa. 'What can I do for you?'

'You was round here yesterday. Harry Jordan's gaff? You said I could call. . .?'

He'd forgotten all about it. Yawn. 'Did Sheila turn up? The doctor?'

'Something's happened, you know? It's. . .' Her voice dropped to a whisper. *'You gotta come over. You gotta come right now, before it's—'*

'I can't, I'm off duty. I'll get them to send a patrol car and—'

'No! It's gotta be you! You gotta come! You got a doctor for Kylie. We don't trust no one else.' Another pause, and this time when her voice came back on the line there were tears in it. *'Please, you said!'*

'But—'

'Please!'

Logan looked up to see Samantha standing in the kitchen doorway, carrying two bottles of lager and a heaped bowl of vanilla ice cream. She pointed at the phone and mouthed the word, 'Work?'

He nodded. 'Sorry.'

'Fine, but if you're not back here before midnight, I'll have gone off the boil.'

Logan told the woman on the phone he'd be there in twenty minutes.

The flat was silent as the grave – which was kind of appropriate given what was lying on the living room floor. Harry Jordan's wheelchair was on its side in the corner, but the man himself was spread out on the carpet. It looked as if someone had put on a pair of stilettos then jumped up and down on his head – it wasn't even the right shape anymore.

His face was a mess of red and purple, the features all mashed up, bone reflecting dully in the dim light. A shiny slick of blood had oozed out into the carpet, making it sticky and wet.

Logan stood in the middle of the room and swore. So much for getting back before midnight.

Someone tugged on his sleeve and said, 'See, told you, didn't I tell you? I did, I told you. . .' It was Kylie's sister, Tracey, only now she wasn't wearing an eggy nightie, she was wearing the full-blown stockings, suspenders and basque outfit. Cheap, shiny black material edged with red lace. Pale skin, protruding ribs in the hollow between her small, hoiked-up breasts. Thin and sickly looking. Eyes like shiny black buttons. 'Told you.' She was chewing on her fingers. 'Told you, yeah, you know?'

'You didn't tell me he was dead!'

'You've got to get rid of him. Get him out of here.'

Logan pulled out his phone and called Control. 'This is DS McRae, I need to report a suspicious death. I want two patrol cars, the IB, Duty Doctor, and whatever pathologist's on call, to Flat C—'

Tracey snatched the phone off him. 'What are you *doing*? You can't tell the police!'

'I *am* the police.' He held out his hand. 'Give me the phone back.'

'You promised you'd help!'

'Who did it?'

'You promised!'

Logan grabbed her by the arms, trying not to touch the weeping sores where she'd injected herself. 'Who was it?'

'It. . .' She looked down at Harry's battered body, then quickly away again, staring at the blood-soaked carpet instead. 'Creepy. It was Creepy.'

18

Tracey sat on the arm of the sofa, a cigarette smouldering away between her fingers as she told Logan all about it. How Creepy Colin McLeod had burst in and battered Harry Jordan's head in with a claw hammer.

'He was screaming and swearing, you know? Someone told him what Harry did to Kylie, and he wasn't having none of it. And Harry's all, "Don't hit me!" and he's crying and that. . .' She shuddered, took a drag on her cigarette and went back to chewing her fingers again. 'And Creepy just keeps on hitting him. Blood flying everywhere, you know? Again and again and again. . .'

Logan squatted down beside the body. 'You expect me to believe Colin McLeod killed Harry Jordan, just because he beat up his favourite prostitute?'

Tracey scowled at him through a haze of cigarette smoke. 'Wasn't like that, OK? Was complicated. Creepy loves her. Got her name tattooed on his arm and everything. Been sweet on her since school.'

'And you're sure you saw him batter Harry?'

She bit her bottom lip and nodded. 'Uh-huh. So did Laura and Emma. He was like . . . *crazy* or something.'

'And where are they?'

Tracey stared at the carpet. 'Did a runner. Thought Creepy might come back, you know? Said fuck this, they was off to Edinburgh.'

'What about Kylie?'

'Never seen nothing.' Tracey pointed back towards the hallway, 'Barely been out of her room since Harry battered her, yeah?'

Logan looked down at the wreckage of Harry's head.

Better get it over with. He snapped on a pair of latex gloves, reached out and felt for a pulse. The duty doc, or the pathologist, would declare death when they turned up, but as First Attending Officer Logan had to check too. The skin was turning sticky as Harry's blood coagulated. There was no way he was alive. Not with his head looking like a burst haggis.

Something fluttered beneath Logan's fingertips.

Harry Jordan was still alive.

Alpha One Nine was first to arrive, closely followed by an ambulance. Logan got the uniformed officers to start going door to door taking statements while the paramedics strapped Harry's battered body onto a backboard.

By the time DCI Finnie turned up they were loading Harry into the ambulance, its blue and white lights sparkling in the rain. The Detective Chief Inspector gave them a cheery wave as they slammed the back doors and roared away.

Then he bounded up the path to where Logan was standing beneath the building's concrete portico. Every light in the tenement block was on, and in the surrounding buildings too; faces in the windows staring out at the little scene of tragedy on their doorstops. Probably wouldn't be too long before the first floral tribute appeared as the bandwagon of public-performance-grief started rolling.

Finnie clapped Logan on the shoulder and beamed at him. 'Any chance Harry Jordan's going to die?'

'That or severe brain damage.'

'To be honest, I'd rather get Creepy Colin McLeod for murder, but attempted will do at a push. Right.' He clapped his hands together. 'Let's see if you go to the top of the class, or have to sit in the corner wearing a dunces cap: door-to-doors?'

'Underway: Three teams of two. Every flat in the street.'

'Witnesses?'

'One: a prostitute working for Harry Jordan. There were two more, but they've legged it for Edinburgh. I've asked Lothian and Borders to keep an eye out for them.'

The DCI nodded. 'Lookout request on Creepy?'

'Already in hand: nothing so far.'

'Warrants?'

'I called the PF: she's sorting them out with Sheriff McNab. Arrest for Colin McLeod, search for his house, his car, and what's left of the Turf 'n Track.'

Finnie's smile slipped a little. 'What about his brother and his mum's houses?'

'PF says McNab won't give us warrants for them without probable cause. Lucky to get what we did without corroboration.'

The DCI seemed to think about it for a minute. 'In that case, I'll give you a B plus. Now I think it's time to go see a man about a claw hammer, don't you?'

The pool car drifted to a halt at the kerb, headlights making the rain look like glowing nails, pounding themselves into the road. DS Pirie turned off the engine, and they sat there in the sudden darkness, listening to the downpour.

A faint glow oozed out between the curtains of number fourteen. Colin McLeod's house.

Three cars down, a new-ish Vauxhall flashed its lights at them.

'Right,' Finnie checked his watch and picked up the radio, clicking it to transmit. 'Pay attention, the lot of you. All teams are to go in on my mark: simultaneous, both properties. This is the best chance we've ever had to get Colin McLeod off the streets, let's pretend we're all professionals and *try* not to screw it up, shall we? You've got three minutes to get into position.' Then he sat back and waited.

'Er. . .' Logan leaned through from the back seat. 'Don't you think we should have a firearms team?'

'I've got enough idiots to supervise without—'

'But McPherson found that huge stash of guns yesterday: we could be walking right into the middle of a drug war.'

DS Pirie joined in: 'He's right, Chief. Creepy Colin could be armed with God knows what.'

'Colin McLeod is a hands-on thug – claw hammers, screwdrivers, pliers, maybe a blowtorch. But if you're *scared*, you can both stay in the car. I'll get someone to bring you out a nice glass of warm milk and some cookies when we're done. Would you *like* that?'

'No, sir.'

They clambered out into the rain, Pirie making a quick detour to pick up the bright-red mini battering ram from the car boot. They hurried up the path to the front door, then Finnie gave the word.

'Time for the big red door key.'

Pirie yelled, 'POLICE!' and swung the battering ram. BOOM. Nothing happened, so he did it again. And again. And again. 'Bloody UPVC double-locking bastards. . .' Again. Three more times, and finally the heavy-duty plastic started to crack, but by then the sergeant was puffing and panting, sweat mingling with the rain. 'Come on you son-of-a-bitch!'

BANG, and the door fell apart, leaving the locking

mechanism intact. The harsh shriek of an alarm bit through the air, blue lights flashing on the box bolted high above the door.

They shouldered their way in, Finnie first, Logan second, Pirie hobbling along at the back, out of breath.

Team Two charged through from the kitchen. 'No one there.'

Finnie stood in the middle of the hall, shouting through the alarm's din, 'Colin McLeod, I have a warrant to search these premises: come out with your hands up!'

Logan checked the lounge. Expensive-looking leather couches, massive plasma TV bolted to the wall, framed Jack Vettriano prints on the walls, hand-carved oak coffee table. . .

Pirie stuck his head around the door. 'Wow. And they say crime doesn't pay.' He crossed to a fancy wall unit and opened the doors to reveal a vast array of spirits, glasses, and wine. 'Think we should take a couple bottles of malt into protective custody?'

Finnie was still bellowing away in the hall, 'SOMEBODY SHUT OFF THAT BLOODY ALARM!'

Pirie closed the door, shutting out most of the noise. 'Think McLeod's still here?'

'Not unless he sets the motion sensors before he goes to bed, no.'

'The guvnor's not going to be happy.'

'Shock horror – hold the front page.' Logan pulled on a pair of latex gloves and poked his way through Creepy's belongings. 'We should get the IB down here, have them take the dishwasher apart. If I had a blood-soaked hammer to clean up, that'd be a good start.'

'He's not as bad as you think.' Pirie settled down on the arm of a huge sofa and watched Logan search. 'Finnie's a pretty decent guy when you get to know him.'

'Yeah? That why everyone in the station hates him?' The lower part of the drinks cabinet was stuffed with shoeboxes. Logan dragged one out and opened it: hundreds of old photographs.

'You know I said he didn't like you? Well. . .' Shrug. 'I was yanking your chain. He thinks you've got a lot of potential.'

Logan riffled through the snapshots. A small, ugly child with a tall, ugly man. He had sideburns and a chunky-knit jumper on over a pair of blue shorts, the kid was in swimming trunks. Standing outside the open-air swimming pool at Stonehaven. 'TONY AND COLIN ~ SUMMER HOLS 1975' was written on the back in perfect biro copperplate.

'Well, he's got a funny way of showing it. . .' The box was full of McLeod family snaps. Birthdays, Christmases, holidays, school sporting events, the colours slowly fading to an orangey-grey.

'Come on, why do you think he keeps dragging you along to things? Thinks if he keeps you under his wing you'll turn out OK. You'd have a really good track record, if you didn't keep screwing it up.'

'Thanks a heap.' The next shoebox was full of wedding photographs: Simon McLeod getting married to an attractive redhead who disappeared three years later, never to be seen again. The reception pictures were a who's who of Aberdeen's criminal underbelly, everyone wearing their best suits – the ones they saved for weddings, funerals, and court appearances.

Logan stuffed the photos back in their box and wandered over to the answering machine. 'Think I can do without Finnie as a mentor, if it's all the same to you.'

'You've just got to tune him out when he goes off on one. That's what I do if—'

DCI Finnie barged through the door and glowered at the

open drinks cabinet. The alarm blared in from the hallway behind him and he had to shout to be heard: 'He's not home. So if you girls have *finished* your little cocktail party, do you think you could possibly do your jobs and help me find that bloody hammer?' He paused, watching Logan examine the answering machine. 'If it's not too much *trouble*, Sergeant.'

According to the display, Colin had three stored messages. Logan pressed play, then had to crank the volume up to full to make anything out over the burglar alarm.

'Message One: Kssssssssh. . . Col, it's Dunk, yeah? I need you to give us a call, OK? Do it 'fore six though, me and Shaz is going out.'

Beeeeeeep.

Finnie slammed the door, cutting off the screaming alarm. 'Oh I'm *sorry*, Sergeant, I didn't realize you were hard of *hearing*: find – that – hammer!'

'Message Two: Fucker!' A man's, voice the words slurred and blurry around the edges. *'I'm gonnae kill you . . . you hear me? Creepy? You hear me? Nobody fucks with Harry Jordan! Not you, not . . . not anyone!'*

Beeeeeeep.

'Message three: *Colin, it's Mum. Are you still coming over for your tea tonight? The doctors say Simon's getting home tomorrow; going to have a party to cheer him up. We'll talk about it when you get here, OK? Bye.'*

Beeeeeeep.

'End of messages.'

'There you go,' said Logan as the machine fell silent, 'we've got a threatening call from Harry Jordan before the attack, and thanks to Colin's mum, we now know where he is.'

Finnie scowled at him, held up a single finger, said, 'That's one,' then turned and marched out of the room.

19

By the time they'd made it across town to Mrs McLeod's rose-encrusted bungalow in Garthdee it was just after midnight and the rain looked as if it was settling in for the duration. The pool car's radio chattered away to itself, playing the symphony of Aberdeen after the pubs shut: drunk and disorderly, assault, theft, vandalism, more assaults. And then the voice of Team Two came through with a report on what was left of the Turf 'n Track.

Finnie picked up the handset and said, 'Nothing, you're sure?'

'Aye, place is deid. No sign of oanybiddie, just a burnt oot shell, like.'

The DCI switched the thing off, then climbed out of the car and into the downpour.

'Actually,' said Pirie, following him, 'we don't have a warrant to search the mother's house, so—'

'I'm not searching the mother's house; I'm here to inform her that her son's home has been broken into. And if I just so *happen* to spot the little sod while I'm here, I'll arrest him.' He stopped at the gate, looking up and down the street for something. 'Pirie, you stay out front. McRae, you're round the back in case Creepy Colin does a runner.' And then Finnie marched right up to the front door and started banging on it with his fist.

Logan had to scrabble up the path, across the front of the house, and round the side. . . He stopped at a six-foot fence with a wrought iron gate set into it, secured with a dirty big chain and padlock – as if anyone would be daft enough to steal from the McLeods' saintly mother.

Logan stuck one foot in the trellis nailed to the wall, and used it to scrabble over the fence, coming down in the pitch black of the back garden.

He stood in silence for a minute letting his eyes adjust to the dark as the rain soaked through his jacket and trickled its way down his back and into his underwear. There was a shed off to one side; a clump of fruit trees, already groaning under the weight of plums; a climbing frame and a plastic chute for the grandchildren; and a couple of sinister gnomes, lurking in the gloom. Rumour had it that good old Tony McLeod used to buy his wife a new gnome every time he personally introduced someone to the Grim Reaper. Logan could see at least ten from where he was standing.

He could hear Finnie's voice booming out from the front of the house, calling for someone to come open the door. Like that wasn't going to make Colin do a runner if he was inside.

'Come on Mrs McLeod, let's not mess around, shall we?'

Logan snuck along the wall, ducking down as he passed beneath the black hole of the kitchen window.

Rain bounced off the patio's paving slabs, soaking into Logan's shoes as he crept into position between the kitchen and the conservatory. Creep, creep, creep, SQUEEEEK!

He froze, one foot on top of a small rubbery lump.

Something shifted in the shadows.

Oh fff. . . Logan raised his foot slowly and the thing he was standing on went, *WheeeeEEEEEEEEeeeeeeeeEEEEEEK!*

The something in the shadows started growling. It wasn't the kind of noise a little terrier in a tartan raincoat made, it was a full-on Great-Big-Sodding-Monster growl. Winchester – the huge Alsatian from the Turf 'n Track.

'Nice doggy?' No it wasn't, he'd seen the mangy, vicious thing before. It was like a rabid mincing machine on legs.

And then the kitchen door burst open, slammed into the house wall, and a figure exploded into the back garden. Two security lights cracked into life, giving Creepy Colin McLeod a perfect view of his escape route as he sprinted for the side fence.

Round the front, Finnie shouted, 'COME BACK HERE!' but Colin kept going. So Logan went after him, praying to God they kept the Alsatian chained up.

They didn't.

Winchester was even more scary in the light than he'd been in the dark, foam flying from his grey muzzle as he charged through the downpour. Barking, snapping.

Colin made it to the fence and threw himself over.

Logan ran for it. Vaulted the plastic slide, and scrambled up the fence.

Too slow.

He came to a sudden stop, one leg already over the top, the other weighed down by a half-ton of angry wet Alsatian.

'GET OFF ME!' He kicked out, but it barely moved.

Winchester shook his head back and forth, and then a miracle happened. Logan's trouser-leg gave with a loud ripping sound, and the dog fell back into a rosebush. Crackle, whimper, snarl. Logan dragged his leg over and dropped into the neighbour's garden before the dog could have another go.

Just in time to see Colin McLeod charging through a wall of dark leylandii on the other side.

Logan ran after him – through the damp, scratchy hedge,

across an anonymous garden. Over a box hedge, through another garden, then a creaky panel fence into what looked like a huge vegetable plot. Yellow streetlight showed a trail of destruction across two dreels of tatties, a row of leeks, and a patch of broccoli. But it was the runner beans that had done for Colin McLeod; he was thrashing in the mud, trying to disentangle himself from a duvet-sized chunk of green plastic netting and bamboo canes.

Swearing, he dragged himself to his knees and slithered through the mud towards the next fence, but Logan got to him first. They crashed into a greenhouse, plastic glass splintering as the frame buckled. A clatter of tomato plants and pots. A rake, fork, and spade clanged onto the concrete path.

Light spilled across the garden, as someone threw open the kitchen door and shouted, 'Get out of it you little buggers! I've got a gun! Do you hear me? A gun!'

Logan opened his mouth to shout, 'Police!' but all that came out was a painful grunt as Colin McLeod's elbow slammed into his face. Blood.

Another elbow – right in the temple – making the world swim in and out of focus.

Logan let go, and Colin struggled to his feet, lurching off balance. The sound of police officers crashing through the back gardens was getting louder – shouting and swearing their way through hedges and over fences in the pouring rain.

Colin turned to face the noise. Then turned back to kick Logan in the head.

Only he never got that far. There was a soft *crack* and the big man froze, teeth gritted, eyes open wide. Then he clutched at his buttock and went, 'Aagh, FUCK!'

'I told you I had a gun, you little bastards! Get out of my garden!' Then came the sound of an air rifle being broken and racked again.

Colin turned and limped towards the householder in a barrage of foul language.

Crack – only this time the shot went wide, bouncing off the crumpled greenhouse.

The man said, 'Oh God. . .' then jumped back inside and slammed the door.

Logan scrabbled around in the sudden darkness, grabbing the rain-slicked handle of some fallen piece of garden equipment, then staggered upright. 'Colin McLeod, I'm arresting you on suspicion of attempted murder—'

Creepy Colin ignored him, hurpling towards the side gate and the road, one hand clamped to his backside.

'—you do not have to say anything . . . ah bugger it.' Logan raised his makeshift truncheon, the yellow streetlight glinting on the flat face of the spade, and swung it at the back of Colin's head.

CLUNK.

The big man went face-down in a patch of muddy strawberries and stayed there.

Logan dropped the spade and slumped against the fence. Spat out a mouthful of salty blood. And listened as DS Pirie struggled his way out of the last hedge, just as DCI Finnie was rattling through the gate. They both came to a halt, staring down at Colin McLeod's unconscious body.

Logan coughed, spat more blood, and probed the swollen lump above his left eyebrow. His head was pounding from the elbow in the forehead. His trousers were clarted in mud, one leg ripped to the knee. 'You took your time.'

Finnie nudged Colin in the ribs with his shoe, then scowled at Logan. Held up a pair of fingers. 'That's two.'

The householder was peering out at them from the safety of the kitchen window. 'I've called the police!'

'I wanted to *question* him!'

'Yeah, well . . . he wanted to kill me, so—'

'Oh, I'm *sorry*. Did I not make myself *clear*, Sergeant McRae? Were you *confused* by why we were after Colin McLeod? Or did you think it'd be easier to question him if he was *un-bloody-conscious*?'

'What? I stopped him, didn't—'

'Don't you *dare* answer back! When I tell you to—'

'No!' Logan pushed off the fence, lurching forwards till he was nose-to-nose with the DCI. 'You listen to me: I have had *enough* of your bloody sarcasm. You asked me to watch the back garden: I watched the back garden. And when Colin did a runner I chased him and I *stopped* him. If it wasn't for me, the bastard would've got away.' His voice getting louder and louder till he was shouting in Finnie's face. 'So I'll answer back if I bloody well like!'

Silence.

The Detective Chief Inspector took a step back, then held up another finger. 'That's three.' And a smile spread across his rubber-lipped features. 'About bloody time too!'

Logan opened his mouth, then shut it again. 'What?'

But Finnie had turned to DS Pirie. 'Was I right? Didn't I tell you?'

'Yup.'

'Tell him what?'

No answer. The DCI just sauntered from the garden, ordering Pirie to 'Escort *that* back to the station,' as he passed Colin McLeod. Pirie did as he was told, leaving Logan all alone in the ruined back garden. Soaking up the rain.

'What?'

20

'Bloody hell,' said Rennie, 'and I thought Steel looked bad.' Half past eight on Wednesday morning and the constable was making the first tea round of the day, carting a tray full of dirty mugs around the CID office.

Logan scowled up from his desk, and instantly regretted it. His face *hurt*. By the time he'd clocked in for work this morning, the whole left hand side was puffy and swollen, the bruised skin a psychedelic mixture of purple, blue and green.

'No, seriously,' Rennie grabbed the mug from Logan's desk and added it to the collection, 'you're like the Elephant Man on a bad day.'

'Didn't think Steel would be in this morning.'

'Oh aye. Smells like she's eaten a pickled skunk. Hungover isn't the *word*. Tell you, I've seen people look healthier after they've been post-mortemed.' He turned as someone slumped in through the door. 'Oops, speak of the Devil and *She* will appear.'

Rennie wasn't kidding – DI Steel looked dreadful. Her hair lay on top of her head like a ruptured ferret, black bags under her eyes, face a delicate shade of week-old roadkill, bringing with her a miasma of Chanel Nº 5, extra strong mints, and stale whisky.

Logan asked how she was feeling, but she just grunted and slouched past, making for the swear box. She picked it up off the little fridge in the corner and frowned. Shook it. Glowered. Opened it. Swore. Her voice was about two octaves lower than usual, marinated in gravel and razorblades. 'What thieving bastard. . .?' She turned the Quality Street tin upside down, but nothing fell out. It was empty.

Steel threw it to the ground, then kicked it the length of the CID office. 'I put forty quid in that!'

Everyone turned to stare at her.

Rennie winced. 'Maybe—'

'FORTY QUID!'

'We could—'

'WHAT'S THE POINT OF HAVING POLICE IF YOU BASTARDS JUST STEAL EVERYTHING?' She ground her eyes with the heels of her hands, then stormed off, muttering obscenities.

'Well, that was—'

But DC Rennie didn't get any further, because Steel stuck her head back round the door. 'McRae, my office, *now*. You,' she pointed at Rennie, 'coffee: milk, two sugars. And get me some bloody cigarettes.' Then she scowled at DS Beattie. 'And Beardy Boy, you're supposed to be a detective. Find out what thieving cock-weasel stole my swear money!'

And then she was gone.

Detective Sergeant Beattie brushed the biscuit crumbs from his beard and said, 'Well, it wasn't me.'

Logan sighed, clambered to his feet, and followed her.

Up close the inspector looked even worse. Her pupils were the size of pinheads, floating in a lake of spider-veined pink. She collapsed into the chair behind her desk and ran her hands through her hair. 'Mouth feels like a badger's arse. . .'

'Didn't think you'd be in this morning.'

She stared at him. 'You look like shite.' Then she rummaged through her in-tray. 'Where's Rennie with my sodding fags? And where's my car?'

'I moved it last night, it's parked out back. That all you wanted? Because I've got—'

'Nice try.' The rummaging produced a small stack of colour printouts; she tossed them across the desk. 'E-fits of a bloke who's been spreading his seed all over the city. Literally. Dirty bugger wipes his spunk on handrails and door handles. Shopping centres are a particular favourite.'

'Sounds like a class act. . .' According to the accompanying notes, the electronic identikit pictures were put together by three different witnesses, all women, who'd only noticed something was horribly wrong after it was all over their hands. The suspect had shoulder-length curly brown hair, long face, squint teeth, sunglasses. Late thirties or early forties.

'I don't see—'

'Get those circulated to the heads of security at every major supermarket in town. And the shopping centres too. The guy's smearing bucket-loads of DNA all over the place, all we need is someone to match it to. Tell them I want called the moment this skanky tosser shows his ugly face. And chase up that lookout request on Rory Simpson, little child-molesting sod's got to be somewhere.'

'Going to have to be tomorrow. Finnie wants me—'

'Oh for God's sake, tell the frog-faced git to take a run and jump. He's—'

'We arrested Colin McLeod last night: attempted murder. He paid a visit to Harry Jordan's head with a claw hammer.'

Steel actually smiled. 'He going to be OK?'

'Probably not.'

'Good.' She coughed, grimaced, then went potholing in her desk again. 'Why have I no' got any paracetamol. . .?'

'Anyway, I've got to sit in on the interview, and we'll have to make a formal ID, and—'

Bang, crash. DC Rennie backed into the room with a mug of coffee in one hand, a packet of biscuits in the other, and a manila folder tucked under his arm. 'Sorry.'

Steel scowled at him. 'Oh aye, that's right: destroy the bloody place. Where's my fags?'

'Got you three Silk Cut. Had to rob them off DS Griffiths, so if he goes on the rampage you don't know anything about it, OK?'

'Gimmie, gimmie, gimmie.' She held out her hand, and Rennie dropped the cigarettes into it. She lit one, sucking the smoke down, then letting it out in a long, contented sigh. 'Oh God, that's better.'

Logan told Rennie to close the door, while he opened the window. Outside, the city shone: all the dust of a long, hot summer washed away by the overnight rain, leaving everything sparkling clean. Not so much as a puddle of vomit on the pavements. Even the early morning fog had burned away.

Rennie dumped the manila folder on the inspector's desk. 'Got the initial forensics back on the fire.'

Steel didn't even look up, just stayed slumped in her chair, smoking at the ceiling. 'What fire?'

'At the Turf 'n Track? Arson? You're SIO?'

'I am?'

Rennie poked the folder. 'You were at the scene yesterday. DS McRae put you down as Senior Investigating Officer.'

And now she did sit up. 'I was there?'

'Technically.' Logan picked up the folder and flicked through the contents. The fire brigade were sticking with their first guess: fire started by a petrol bomb thrown in through the front door. 'Nothing from fingerprints?'

The constable shook his head. 'They're backed up doing all them guns we found. Say they might get round to it tomorrow, maybe Friday.'

Steel snatched the folder from Logan and grumbled through the contents. '*I'm* SIO, remember? I'll ask the bloody questions.'

'Good for you.' Logan stopped on the way to the door. 'You still want me to give you a hand tomorrow?'

'What do I need *you* for when I've got Defective Constable Rennie here?' She levered herself to her feet, pinged the last nub of her cigarette out of the open window, then handed the three e-fit printouts to the constable. 'Did you like Pugwash when you were a kid, Rennie? Coz you're going looking for Seaman Staines.'

'For the benefit of the tape,' said DCI Finnie, holding up a clear plastic evidence pouch, 'I am now showing Mr McLeod Exhibit A: a claw hammer. We found this in your garage, Colin. Want to tell us about it?'

Colin McLeod scowled back from the other side of the interview room table. Other than a couple of small scratches there wasn't a mark on him, not even a bruise where Logan had bounced the spade off his head.

Leaning back against the wall, watching proceedings, Logan didn't think that was exactly fair. Especially given the mess his own face was in today.

McLeod barely glanced at the contents of the evidence bag. 'It's a hammer. You use it for hammering in nails.'

'Yes, *I* would use it for nails, but *you* use it for kneecaps, don't you?'

'No comment.'

'And last night you used it on Harry Jordan's head.'

'Bollocks.'

'No, just his head.' Finnie handed Exhibit A back to DS Pirie. 'You might want to have a wee think about that one, Colin. You see,' and at this the DCI leant over the table and put on a theatrical whisper, 'we have what are known in the trade as *witnesses*.'

'I. . .' The big man shied back. 'I never touched him.'

'Three witnesses say different, Colin. Or can I call you Creepy?'

'No you fuckin' can't!' McLeod's face got even uglier. 'I want my lawyer, and I want him right now.'

'Don't be such a drama queen; you know how this works. You get a lawyer when *I* say so, not before.'

'I NEVER TOUCHED HIM!'

DS Pirie – silent up to this point – leant over and whispered something in Finnie's ear.

The DCI nodded. 'If you never touched him,' he said, 'then why did Forensics find traces of Harry Jordan's blood on your hammer?'

'Told you, it's not my hammer.'

'Did you?' Finnie put on a show of frowning and asking the room, 'Does anyone remember Mr McLeod saying this wasn't his hammer?'

'It's not my—'

Pirie checked his notes. 'Then why does it have your fingerprints all over it?'

'I. . . I didn't fuckin' *kill* him!'

'Oh dear,' the DCI had the kind of smile you only normally saw on grizzly bears. 'We've got forensics, we've got witnesses, and thanks to DS McRae,' he pointed over his shoulder at Logan, 'we've got a threatening phone call from the victim on your answering phone. And we all know Harry Jordan beat the crap out of that tart you're soft on. Not bad enough he's renting out the love of your life—'

A knock at the door.

'Oh for. . .' He glanced back, 'Get that would you, McRae?'

Logan opened the door to find an out-of-breath PC Karim standing in the corridor. The constable huffed and puffed for a second, then blurted out his news.

They'd found another victim with his eyes gouged out in an abandoned building. Oedipus strikes again.

21

An ambulance sat in the middle of the narrow strip of tarmac that ran between the rows of Lego-brick homes on Burnbank Place, its engine still running as a paramedic in a green jump-suit argued with the uniformed PC guarding the property. A skip sat by the front door, full of chunks of plaster, an old sink, and a pee-stained mattress.

'You've got to let us in: we need to get him to hospital!'

'I can't, OK? I've—' and then the constable spotted DCI Finnie, marching up the pavement, dragging Logan and DS Pirie in his wake. 'Chief Inspector! They really want to collect the victim and—'

Finnie pushed past him. 'No one in or out till the pathologist gets here.' And then they were inside.

It wasn't a big place, and about as boxy and featureless on the inside as it was on the outside. Like the house in Primrosehill Drive, it was in the process of being refurbished. The walls were stripped back to the bare breezeblocks, the concrete floor covered in dust and bits of plasterboard.

Another PC, presumably the partner of the one standing guard outside, stopped them at the bedroom door. 'We can't just leave the poor bastard here, it's not—'

Finnie waved him into silence. 'Why aren't you wearing an SOC suit? I said I want this treated as a murder scene.'

'He's in *pain*!'

The DCI stared at him for a moment, then rapped on the top of the PC's head with his knuckles. 'Hello? Hello? Is this thing on? Am I speaking too quickly for your little brain? Get – me – some – SOC – suits. I will *not* have the scene contaminated any further!'

For a moment, the constable looked as if he was about to introduce his truncheon to a private and internal portion of Finnie's anatomy. Then he gritted his teeth and forced out a, 'Yes, sir.' He was back two minutes later with a small stack of plastic-wrapped suits, a couple of facemasks and a collection of blue plastic overbooties. 'I still think—'

'When you make Sergeant you can think, till then it'd be nice if you could just do what you're bloody well told. Now go help your little friend guard the front door. And let me know the minute the pathologist gets here.'

The bedroom was getting crowded. It wasn't the biggest of spaces to begin with, but now that Doc Fraser had arrived, it was even smaller. The old man dumped his medical bag by the doorway and hunkered down next to the body.

'Death been declared?'

Finnie shook his head. 'You said you wanted to see a live one before the hospital got their hands on him.'

'You mean he's. . .' The pathologist felt for a pulse – and the body on the floor groaned. Doc Fraser stared up at Logan. 'You've got to get those paramedics in here now! This man's—'

'This man,' said the Chief Inspector, 'is the only physical evidence we have. I know it sounds harsh, but we can't afford to just throw that away. Now can you be a *team player* long enough to examine him, or do I have to get someone else out here?'

'But—'

'No, Doc, no buts. When he goes up to A&E they'll destroy anything we might be able to use. And when he wakes up he'll be too afraid to speak to us.'

'This isn't just unethical, it's—'

'It's all we've got! Do you want this to keep happening? Is *that* what you want? Because until we get some real evidence it's going to!'

Lying on the ground at their feet, the latest victim twitched and moaned.

Doc Fraser went quiet, face creased up in thought. 'First you get one of the ambulance crew to give this man a painkiller and a sedative, otherwise I'm out of here and on the phone to Professional Standards. Understand?'

Two minutes later a grim-faced paramedic pulled a needle from the victim's arm and taped a wad of cotton over the injection site. 'I don't like this.'

The pathologist grimaced. 'Believe me, you're not the only one.' Then he handed a Dictaphone to Logan, snapped on a pair of latex gloves, and gently cupped the victim's head, pulling it round. Then winced. 'Oh dear God, that's disgusting. . .' The eyes were completely gone, nothing left but dark slits, surrounded by angry red tissue, curls of crispy black skin, and drying blood.

'Come on, Doc,' said Pirie, obviously trying to lighten the mood, and failing miserably, 'you've seen worse than this.'

'Not on a living human being. . .' He took a deep breath and with both hands tried to pull the eye socket open. There was a crackling noise and some of the tissue crumbled into the hole. 'Oh. . .' He leaned in for a closer look.

'I can smell an accelerant of some kind. Give me a cotton swab from my bag.'

The paramedic did the honours and Fraser ran it around the socket, then dropped it in a small evidence vial. 'We can test it in the lab, but it's probably petrol or lighter fluid. He's lucky. . .'

'*That's* lucky?'

'The eyes are right next to the nasal passages and throat – all your major airways. Too much heat from the burning and they swell, close up. You'd suffocate.' He ran a gloved-fingertip gently around the ragged hole. 'There's scarring to what's left of the lower eyelid. Maybe a knife?' He peered even closer. 'Something with a hooked blade, no longer than your thumb. He's right handed too. Give me a torch.'

Click, and a bright LED light shone into the ravaged eye socket.

'Chemical reaction with the tissue at the back of the orbit. Ragged end to the optic nerve, so it was probably torn, not cut.' Doc Fraser sat back on his heels. 'I'd say the eyes were gouged out of the head with a small hooked knife, cutting the muscles. Then the assailant takes the eye in the palm of his hand like this—' he did a little mime, just to make sure everyone got the full picture '—with the optic nerve between the middle two fingers, and yanks like he's trying to start a chainsaw.'

Which was an image Logan *really* didn't want at this time of the morning.

'Then,' said the pathologist, 'once he's done the left and the right, he pours accelerant into the empty sockets and sets fire to it.' Fraser asked Logan to help him stand. 'Take some photos then get this man to hospital.' He turned and tottered from the room. 'I'm done here.'

Back at Force Headquarters, the IB technician took one look at the photo in Logan's hand and made a small gagging sound. 'You could've waited till I'd finished my sandwich!'

Today her T-shirt said, 'I've Seen Your Mum Naked.' If that was true, Logan pitied her.

He put the picture on the desk, next to a packet of smoky-bacon crisps. 'Finnie wants it touched up so the victim looks like they would . . . before.'

'Any idea what colour his eyes are?'

'He didn't have them on him at the time.'

'Not asking for much, are you?'

'And I need about a hundred appeal-for-information posters: Finnie wants them up all over Torry, see if we can get an ID.'

'I'm not promising anything.' She dropped the last of her sandwich in the bin. 'And next time you've got a photo of some poor bugger's gouged-up face, try waiting till *after* lunch.'

Two hours and a stack of paperwork later, Logan knocked on DI Steel's office door . . . waited a second . . . then walked in anyway. She was slumped across the desk, head on one side, cheek resting in a little puddle of fresh drool. Snoring gently. Very attractive.

He sank down into one of the visitor chairs and went for a sneaky rummage through Steel's in-tray. Mostly it was just expenses forms and witness statements, but right at the bottom was a memo from DCS Bain telling the senior officers that because DI Gray was resigning due to ill health, there was an opening for a new Detective Inspector. They were to think about suitable candidates.

The inspector gave a little grunt and shifted in her sleep. Logan froze. Then put everything back the way he'd found it.

He cleared his throat. 'Ahem?' No response. 'Inspector?' Still nothing. He leant forward and gave her shoulder a shake. 'Wakey, wakey!'

'Grnmmmmph?' Steel opened a bloodshot eye, then peeled her face off the desk, leaving a string of dribble behind. 'What time's it?'

'Back of two. We've got a shout: Polish grocery on Victoria Road's been turned over.'

She ran a hand over her face, pulling it all out of shape. 'Urgh . . . I feel awful.' She looked it too, but Logan was too polite to say anything.

'I've got us a pool car and—'

'Get stuffed, I'm no' going anywhere. You do it. Take that useless sack of skin Rennie with you.' She yawned, showing off a proper Scottish set of black metal fillings. 'Think I might've still been drunk this morning.'

'Finnie says he wants you to go. He's—'

Steel's voice went up into a squeaky Monty-Python-esque impersonation: '"Finnie says, Finnie says". Why don't you just bloody marry him?'

'Bit of fresh air might do you the world of good?'

'Oh don't be so—'

'And if you're not here, the Assistant Chief Constable can't walk in and find you snoring face-down on your desk.'

She dragged herself to her feet. 'I'll get my coat.'

Logan rolled down the windows to minimize the acrid smell. DI Steel moaned and groaned in the passenger seat, clutching a two-litre bottle of Irn-Bru from a petrol station. Where they'd had to make an emergency stop so she could be sick.

'Must've been something I ate.'

The Krakow General Store sat on Victoria Road, Torry, between a dry cleaners and an off-licence. Once upon a time it'd been a newsagents, but the days of top-shelf pornography and stale rowies were long gone. Now the place had been given a cheerful coat of bright-blue paint, the window filled with tempting foreign delicacies and posters of old buildings and winding streets.

Inside was a different matter. Someone had given the place a serious going over: the stands were smashed; the shelves broken; and the display cabinet lay on its back in the middle of the floor, surrounded by broken eggs, dented tins, crushed packets and broken bottles. A chiller cabinet full of meat and cheese was the final resting place for the cash register and the contents of three huge plastic bottles of bleach.

Logan surveyed the damage from the front door, while Steel stayed behind in the car to 'make some important phone calls'. Which seemed to involve locking the doors, rolling the windows up, reclining the passenger seat as far back as it would go, pulling her jacket over her face, and lying very still.

A middle-aged man stood beside the ruined display cabinet, mouth hanging open. He didn't say anything, so Logan had to repeat himself.

'Are you Mr Wojewódzki?'

The man just kept staring at his devastated shop. 'You have to come back later. We are . . . closed.'

Logan pulled out his warrant card. 'I'm a police officer, I'm here. . .' He drifted to a halt, watching the sudden look of fear and suspicion that stampeded across the shopkeeper's face. 'It's OK, I'm here to help. Can you tell me who did this?'

A snort. 'Animals. That is who did this. *Animals.*' He dropped his eyes to the food-covered linoleum. 'I do not know. I was not here. They must have broken in.'

'Right. . .' Logan picked his way between a bloody stain of smashed beetroot jars and what looked like carrot juice. 'You didn't call the police. We had to hear it from one of your customers. Any reason?'

'What can I say when people do this? I work hard to build this business and look at it.' He leaned back against the wall, running a hand through his close-cropped greying hair. 'First it is papers: *Aberdeen Examiner* telling everyone that Polish shopkeepers refuse to serve local people. Pah. Is hard enough to make living without turning good money away.' He kicked a carton of milk. 'Small-minded people telling lies. I make *everyone* welcome. I *want* local people to buy my things, is why I come here in first place.'

'So who ransacked your shop?'

'Pffff,' Wojewódzki threw his hands in the air, 'what do you care? You *Policja*. Leave me alone, I have nothing here for you.' He cleared away a small mound of tinned peas, then struggled with the fallen display cabinet.

Logan took hold of the other side and heaved. It weighed a ton, but they managed to get the thing upright. 'I meant what I said: all I want is to catch the people who did this.'

That got him a grunt. Then Wojewódzki began gathering up the unbroken bottles.

'Look, I know you've probably had some bad experiences with the police in Poland, but—'

'I was landlord. Owned nine buildings in Kraków, very nice places. And then big shot from Warsaw comes to say he has business opportunity for me. He has cousin who works in the parliament; big land deal being done, lots of money to be made. So I sell my buildings and invest.'

The shopkeeper picked up a jar of pickled peppers, turning it over in his hands. 'Pfffffff, cracked.' He dropped it to smash against the floor.

'Two months go by and nothing happen: no building, no contract, no land. I ask him, where is my money? And he tells me there is no money, go back to Kraków. Like I am a small child. Of course I go to *Policja*, but the man's cousin was big in Finance Ministry when Communists are in charge. *Policja* tell me to forget about my money. Is gone.' He unfurled a black plastic bag and started filling it with crushed loaves of garlic and onion bread. 'That is what *Policja* do. No one cares. Everyone corrupt.'

'Got any more bin bags?'

The shopkeeper shrugged and handed one over. 'Sometimes I wonder why I come to Aberdeen. Everyone so tight with money, afraid to try new things. Six years I try. . .'

They cleared up in silence for a while, picking up the shattered glass and sweeping up the breakfast cereal. Then they hauled the cash register out of the chiller cabinet. The drawer was lying open, and the contents were gone.

He sighed. 'You see? They break everything. They *take* everything. What can I do?'

'You can tell me who did it.'

'Four men, they come in here. Loud, shouting at each other, laughing. They throw bottles across shop, smash on the floor. Then they tell me I have to pay them for "damages". That if I don't, more things will get damaged.' The shopkeeper stuck out his chest. 'I tell them I am not afraid! And they show me knives.' He looked away, sliding the cash register drawer shut again. 'I tell them I already pay for shop to be safe. . .'

'So they trashed the place.'

'They say I have to pay them or I am never safe. Five hundred pounds every week.'

Logan pulled out his notebook. 'What did they look like?'

Shrug. 'Those tops with hoods. One have tattoo on his hand. Thin face, big nose? Fancy knife that folds up. Not sound Scottish.'

'English?' Logan pulled on his best Manchester accent, 'Did dey sound a bit like dis, den?'

Another shrug. 'All English sound the same to me.'

The shopkeeper produced a broom and pushed a chinking clump of broken glass across the linoleum. 'Everything is violence these days. Everyone want money, but no one want to work for it.'

Logan watched him sweeping up his broken merchandise, the pickle juice turning the spilled breakfast cereal into a brown vinegary mush. A red-top tabloid was pulled from the rack and thrown down to sop up the mess. The cover photo of a girl in an unfeasibly small bikini slowly disappeared into the saturated newsprint. Now they'd never find out what 'PERKY POLISH PETRA'S PARTY PIECE' was. It looked as if Zander Clark wasn't the only one importing attractive women.

There was a bottle of Polish brandy lying underneath a stack of soggy paperbacks. Logan pulled it out; it wasn't even broken. 'Ever heard of a company called Kostchey International Holdings?'

The man froze. 'No. Never.'

'You sure?'

'Yes. Now you have to leave, I have lot of cleaning to do.'

'But we were—'

'Please, I am very busy.'

Logan put the bottle back on the shelf. 'OK. . . One last thing before I go.' He unfolded three printouts from his pocket and held the first one up. It was the Oedipus victim they'd found that morning, the IB technician had done a pretty decent job painting in the eyes. 'Do you know this man?'

The shopkeeper took the printout, stared at it for a bit, then handed it back. 'No.'

'What about these two?' Logan showed him the e-fits he'd put together with Rory Simpson of the men who'd blinded Simon McLeod.

This time there was a flicker of recognition in the shop-keeper's eyes. 'This one,' he said, pointing at the old man's picture, 'I know him!'

Ha – Finnie would have to put him up for that DI's job now. 'Who is it?'

'Is Clint Eastwood.'

Logan turned the sheet around and stared at the face. The shopkeeper was right – it *was* Clint Bloody Eastwood.

If Logan ever got his hands on Rory Simpson, he was going to throttle him.

22

The pool car smelled horrible. Booze, bad breath, and BO, all underpinned by the eye-nipping odour of old vomit. Steel was snoring away beneath her makeshift blanket, the sleeves dangling down into the footwell.

Logan slammed the car door, and she shot up in her seat, jacket still draped over her head. 'Mmphhh? What? Eh?'

'Bloody Rory Bloody Simpson! He lied about the e-fit.'

Steel yawned, squinted, then ran a hand through the electrocuted mop on top of her head pretending to be hair. 'Why does my mouth taste of sick?'

'Clint Eastwood!' Logan dragged the car key out of his pocket and rammed it into the ignition.

'I'm thirsty. . .'

'That's what you get for drinking a whole bottle of whisky on your own.'

'No I didn't. . .' She closed her eyes and wrapped her arms around her head. 'Oh God, yes I did.'

'There's a big thing of Irn-Bru at your feet. I can't believe that tosser Simpson lied to me!'

'He's a kiddie fiddler, no' George Washington.' There was the distinctive *hissssss* of the top being unscrewed from a plastic bottle of fizzy juice, and then the distinctive swearing of it going all over someone's lap. 'Aaaagh! Rotten bastarding . . . it's everywhere!'

'Well, hold it out the window.'

'I'm all sticky!'

Logan turned in his seat. 'We have to find Rory. Make the lying little sod give us a proper description.'

The inspector took a deep swig from the bottle, then belched.

'Maybe,' said Logan, 'we should get onto Tayside and Edinburgh? If he's not here, he's got to be somewhere.'

'Give it a rest, would you?'

'He *lied* to us!'

'And stop bloody shouting. Head hurts bad enough as it is.'

'I'm just saying—'

Steel clamped her hands over her ears and screamed, 'SHUT UP! YOU'RE BREAKING MY HANGOVER!'

Outside, on the pavement, a small group of locals was staring at the car.

The inspector groaned, face creased up in pain. 'Why'd you make me *do* that?'

'Sorry. I'm just. . . I'm tired of letting the bad guys get away, OK?'

Steel squinted at him. 'I'll forgive you if you get us some paracetamol and a packet of fags.' There was a pause. 'And maybe a bacon buttie?'

The sweeping granite tenements of Victoria Road sparkled in the sunshine, but that didn't make much of a dent in Logan's mood. Why did it always have to come down to running sodding errands for sodding DIs? Bloody Steel. Just because she got hammered last night, why did he have to play nursemaid?

He got the paracetamol and a small pack of Lambert and Butler from a little corner shop that hadn't been trashed by hoodies, and the bacon buttie from the Torry Fish Bar, just down the road. It'd probably bounce as soon as it hit Steel's stomach, but Logan didn't care, as long as she wasn't sick in the car. And if she was, she could clean it up herself.

Logan got himself a portion of chips: thick fingers of crisp, golden potato slathered in salt and vinegar, in a little polystyrene tray. He ate them as he wandered back to the car, taking the long way round. Hoping that if he took long enough, Steel's bacon buttie would be cold.

He strolled down Walker Road, took a left just before the primary school, up a small lane, and out onto Grampian Road.

Maybe he could persuade Steel to put his name forward for that promotion? Ingratiate himself. . .

Damn.

Letting her bacon buttie go cold probably wasn't such a good idea after all. He felt it through the carrier bag they'd given him at the chip shop. It wasn't exactly hot, but it would still be edible.

He stuffed the last couple of chips into his mouth, and hurried down Grampian Road back towards the car.

And then stopped dead, staring up at the fortress-like hulk of Sacred Heart.

Torry's only Catholic church had a strangely Spanish look to it, even if it was built out of granite and the terracotta pantiles had a thick layer of green and grey moss. Sacred Heart sat on top of a small hill, looming over the surrounding streets like a drunken uncle. Threatening them all with eternal damnation.

A flimsy outer skin of scaffolding and tarpaulins covered the east side of the building, and the whole place was sealed off by an eight-foot-tall cordon of temporary fencing.

What was it Goulding had said? *'All that, "They're stealing God" stuff means he's very religious. . .'* And Oedipus was probably a local boy with an intimate knowledge of Torry.

Logan crossed the road.

A laminated sheet of A4 was fixed to the fence, with 'CLOSED FOR REFURBISHMENT. OPENING FOR THE LORD'S WORK IN OCTOBER!' printed on it, and 'IN CASE OF EMERGENCY CONTACT REV. J BURNETT.' Then what looked like the same message in Polish. And right at the bottom was an Aberdeen telephone number.

Logan dialled, let it ring for nearly a minute, then left a message after the beep.

There was a man in paint-stained overalls sitting on one of the scaffolding boards, twenty foot off the ground, legs hanging over the edge, drinking a can of coke and smoking a cigarette.

'Excuse me?'

The man looked down from his vantage point. 'Hello? I can help you?' Definitely Polish.

'How long has the church been shut?'

'Three month? Maybe more? I don't know. Is number on sign to call.'

'I tried: no one's answering.'

The man grinned. 'You want make confession? I have break time.'

'No thanks. I—'

'You go St Peter's, in Castlegate. Father Burnett there. Good man.' And then, cigarette finished, he went back to hauling filthy pantiles off the roof.

'Urgh. . .' DI Steel made a face, chewing around the words. 'This is cold.'

'Really?' Logan threaded the pool car around the roundabout and onto Market Street. 'It was hot when I bought it.'

'Well it's cold now.' The inspector chased her mouthful down with a swig of Irn-Bru. Then ripped another bite out of the bacon buttie. Munching away as she stared out of the passenger window. 'I failed the adoption interview. They said I'm too old. . .'

Logan pulled up at the traffic lights, beside a huge advertising billboard – 'McLennan Homes. Your Place Is Our Passion – 400 New Homes For NE Families!' – and waited for a convoy of eighteen-wheelers to rumble out from the harbour exit.

'Rubbish. I know a couple in their sixties and they're still fostering kids.'

'Fostering's no' the same. Susan wants a baby of her *own*. She's. . .' Steel sighed. 'Ah, you know what she's like.' The inspector snuck a glance at Logan, then went back to staring at the billboard. 'Only chance we've got is if Susan gets pregnant.'

'Artificial insemination? But I thought—'

'Yeah . . . *something* like that.' She coughed. Fidgeted. Sniffed. 'You . . . er. . . You don't fancy donating some sperm, do you?'

Logan almost stalled the car. 'What?'

'Come on, we're like family, aren't we?' A blush crept up from the neck of her blouse, turning her cheeks from unhealthy grey to embarrassed pink. 'We could . . . you know. . .' Her eyes never moved from the huge advert and Malcolm McLennan's crooked, smiling face. 'Turkey baster.'

Logan opened his mouth a couple of times, but nothing came out. He tried again, 'Well. . . I—'

The blare of a horn sounded behind them, accompanied by someone shouting, 'Light's green, Moron!'

Back at Force Headquarters, Logan ran for it, blaming a last-minute meeting with Professional Standards. It was a lie, but at least she might leave him alone if she thought he was in for a bollocking.

He had to find somewhere to lay low until he could sod off home. So Logan made his way down to the Operation Oedipus incident room.

Steel hated Finnie, this was the last place she'd look for him.

Finnie almost bowled him over on the way through the door. The DCI was hauling his suit jacket on over a crumpled pink shirt. 'Where have you been?' He wrinkled his nose. 'And what is that *smell*?'

'You told me to take DI Steel over to Torry for—'

'Never mind. Just got a call from the hospital: they've released Simon McLeod. Won't he be *pleased* when we pay him a little visit.'

Logan was about to complain – the dayshift was officially over in two minutes – but there was that DI's position coming up. And it wouldn't hurt to have Finnie on his side. 'What about DS Pirie?'

Finnie gave an evil grin. 'Let's just say that Pirie and the McLeods don't get along anymore. So chop-chop: pool car.'

Simon McLeod had done well for himself. His 'five-bedroom executive villa' was part of a small development on the very outskirts of Cults, backing onto woodland. Small garden out front, huge one out back. A shiny BMW four-by-four sat on the drive, next to a Porsche Boxster.

Logan reverse parked onto the driveway, blocking them both in.

'Right,' said Finnie, rubbing his hands, 'the McLeods aren't exactly known for cooperating with the police. So I want you to work the bidie-in while I give Simon a going over. We split them up and maybe he'll give us something, especially now his wee brother's looking at attempted murder.'

The doorbell was answered on the second go by Simon's common-law wife: Hilary Brander. The expectant look on her face died as soon as she saw Finnie.

She folded her arms across her chest and blocked the entrance. 'What do you want?'

'I hear the doctors let Simon out today; I need a quick word.'

'After what you did to our Colin?'

Logan stepped up. 'It's important, Ms Brander. We need to catch whoever blinded him.'

She looked at Logan. 'What happened to your face?'

He gave her a lopsided smile. 'Colin's elbow.'

Hilary's lips twitched up at the edges and she took a step back into the house. 'Five minutes, no more. His mum's coming over to help set up the party – you *really* don't want to be here when she does. And if you upset Simon I'll kill you.'

She led them through to the lounge, where that same daft-looking West Highland Terrier lounged in a tartan bed in front of the gas-effect fire. Today the dog was wearing a lime-green raincoat with sheep on it.

The lounge walls were speckled with tapestry artworks and holiday snaps: skiing in Aspen; a train trip through Alaska; Simon and Hilary on safari somewhere, posing with an elephant in the background; the Great Pyramid of Cheops.

Funny, Simon always seemed like more of a Costa del Sol kind of guy.

He was hunched in a large leather recliner, eyes hidden behind a swathe of white bandages, a half tumbler of whisky clutched in his trembling hands.

Hilary put a hand on his shoulder and he flinched, nearly spilling the drink.

'Sorry sweetheart, but there's someone here to see you.'

Simon scanned the room. 'Jesus, Hilary, I told you not to let anyone in! What if—'

'It's OK, it's OK. Shhhhh. . .' She stroked his hair. 'It's just the police. They want to know who did this to you.'

'Tell them to fuck off! No, you know what, I'll do it. . .' He struggled to his feet, dropping the glass. 'FUCK OFF! You hear me?' Whisky soaked into the oatmeal-coloured carpet.

In the tartan basket, the Westie in the raincoat started to growl.

Hilary grabbed hold of Simon's shirt and dragged him back into the chair. 'You listen to me, Simon Emerson McLeod, you will *sit* there and you will *calm down*!'

'But—'

'No! No buts. You do as you're told.' Then she turned and glowered at Finnie. 'Five minutes, not a second more.' She marched through into the kitchen, the little dog trotting happily after her.

Logan waited a beat, then followed the terrier, closing the kitchen door behind him, shutting Simon in with Finnie. 'You want some tea?'

'What is it with you coppers and tea?' She turned her back on him. 'Just walking clichés.'

'I'll take that as a no then.' He leant back against the worktop, trying to look casual. 'We found another victim this morning. Just like Simon. . .'

'That's not our problem, all right? We've got enough of our own.'

'Hilary, the person who did *that* to your husband is still out there. What are you going to do if he decides to come back and finish the job?'

She sank into one of the wooden chairs at the kitchen table. 'He told me he was going into work early. Something about a supplier playing silly sods with a delivery.'

'A delivery?'

'We run burger vans, not that it's any of your business. Every industrial estate in Aberdeen has one. Sometimes we get invoiced for stuff that doesn't turn up. Simon said he was going to get it sorted out.' She reached down and picked up the dog. 'Says he was in the office when someone starts banging on the back door; he goes to answer it; and the next thing he knows he's in hospital. . .'

'Does he know who did it?'

'If he did they'd be dead by now.'

Probably true.

'What about business rivals? We've heard rumours someone's trying to move in on his turf?'

'He doesn't have "turf", he's a—'

'Legitimate businessman. Yeah, that's what he told me.' Logan stared at her in silence for a while, until she started to fidget. 'We both know that's not true, Hilary. I think there's a major turf war brewing in Aberdeen and someone's made sure Simon can't fight back.'

'It was that serial nutter: the one in the papers! He—'

'No it wasn't. Simon doesn't fit the pattern: he's not Polish, he wasn't dumped in Torry, we didn't even get a phone call. Someone saw all the publicity and thought they could use it to cover their tracks. Now who's trying to move in on him? Polish mafia? Russians? We know Manchester's been sniffing around.'

She went back to stroking the dog. 'I can't, OK?'

'You have to.'

'I've never seen him so scared before.'

'Hilary, you can't let them get away with this. You tried it Colin's way and it didn't work, did it? Running around hammering people's knees at random? And after what he did to Harry Jordan—'

'He didn't!' She rubbed a hand across her eyes. 'It wasn't him. Those bitches are *lying*.'

'Even without their testimony we've got him on the forensics—'

'He wasn't even there.' Hilary pulled back the dog's hood and ruffled the hair between its ears. 'Poor little Skye has Cushing's disease, don't you sweetie? Her fur falls out in big clumps, leaves nasty raw patches, so she has to wear a silly coat.'

'Hilary, this is important.'

She glanced over her shoulder, back towards the lounge. 'There's nothing they can do for him. He's always going to be blind.' A fat tear rolled down her cheek, and dripped on the Westie's head.

'We—'

'He can't even get glass eyes: they won't stay in. . . Someone burnt off his eyelids. What sort of person *does* that?'

Logan reached across the kitchen table and took her hand. 'Then help me catch them.'

That got him a small, bitter laugh. 'You want them caught? These *bastards*? You want them to stop hurting people? Let Colin go.'

23

Samantha wasn't answering her home phone, or her mobile, so instead of heading straight home after signing out, Logan took the lift up to the Identification Bureau's lab on the third floor. Just in case.

Considering how much police work relied on forensic science the place was tiny. It wasn't much bigger than Logan's living room, and every available surface was piled high with plastic crates full of guns. A single white lab-coated figure was dusting an AK-47 for prints over by the vacuum table, the loud hum of the motor fighting against the radio – Northsound Two turned up full blast. The Chief Constable on the local news:

'. . . recent upswing in drug-related violence should give us all great cause for concern. Criminals seem to think Aberdeen is a soft target for their hard drugs, but I'm here to tell you that we are anything but. Officers recovered a substantial amount of heroin earlier this week, with a street value of over two hundred thousand pounds. . .'

Logan stopped at the central table. 'Hello?'

'. . . complacent. So if anyone sees anything suspicious, they can call our dedicated drugs hotline. . .'

Try again. 'HELLO?'

Samantha turned, pulled off her safety goggles and breathing mask, and shouted back at him, 'WHAT HAPPENED TO YOU LAST NIGHT THEN?'

'WHAT?'

Logan turned down the radio as the newsreader came on. *'And finally, jobs in the North East were given a boost today when McLennan Homes chairman Malcolm McLennan announced plans for yet another luxury golf course. . .'*

'You're all grubby.'

'Tell me about it. Bloody fingerprint powder gets everywhere. . .' Samantha switched off the vacuum table and the motor whined to a halt. 'You look like someone's battered you about the head with a sledgehammer.'

'Fancy doing something later?'

She pointed at the stacks of weapons. 'I wish. Roz is on holiday, Mark's got a dose of the squits, Davie's on a training course, and Tracy's in Glasgow giving evidence. So I'm on my lonesome.' She hefted the AK-47 onto a stand for photography. 'Could do with the overtime, anyway.'

'Oh.'

'Tell you what though. . .' She snapped off her blue nitrile gloves. 'Long as you're here, you can give us a hand in the store room.'

Not exactly the way Logan had planned on spending his evening, but it was probably better than going home to paint the lounge ceiling.

Ten minutes later someone shouted, the store room door flew open, and DI Steel appeared. 'Where the hell is every. . .' She stood there, staring as Logan and Sam straightened their clothes. 'No wonder the labs are backed up! Bloody IB spends all its time shagging CID.'

'We weren't *shagging.*' Sam's face went bright red. She

grabbed a random bit of equipment from the shelves that lined the walls, 'I was looking for this and got something in my eye—'

'Got something in your pants, more like.'

'It's not—'

'Oh, like I care. Just give us the results of that DNA test I sent up yesterday and you can go back to your bonking.'

'We weren't bonking!' Sam pushed past Steel back into the lab, marched over to the filing cabinet, and yanked out a drawer.

'And while you're there,' said Steel, 'see if there's anything on that fire at the Turf 'n Track.'

'We've not had time. We're up to our ears fingerprinting this lot.' She pointed at the piles of weapons.

'Too busy bumping uglies with Detective Sergeants, more like.'

Samantha glared at Logan. He cleared his throat. 'Erm. . . Why don't I chase these up and bring the results down to your office, ma'am?'

The inspector stood there for a moment, shrugged, then wandered out of the lab with her hands in her pockets, whistling the tune to *Lydia the Tattooed Lady*.

As soon as the door closed, Samantha slumped back against the wall and buried her head in her hands. 'Oh God . . . it's going to be all over the station by morning. . .'

Logan tried for a reassuring smile. 'Could be worse?'

'She's a nightmare. She's a card-carrying, cold-sweat-in-the-wee-small-hours, bed-wetting nightmare.'

'Don't let her get to you.' He stroked the back of Samantha's neck, feeling the soft downy hairs goosebump beneath his fingers. 'Anyway, so what if everyone knows about us?'

'Easy for you to say, you're not going to be "the tattooed slut who shags Detective Sergeants in the bloody store room", are you?'

'I'll have a word with her. She's not really as bad as everyone thinks. Besides. . .' he looked back at the door and suppressed a shudder. 'She wants me to do her a favour.'

They found the remains of the Turf 'n Track petrol bomb buried under a stack of evidence bags. It only took five minutes to bring up three good clear prints from the broken bottle.

Samantha took reference shots with the lab's digital camera, then transferred the prints off with lifting tape to an acetate sheet and handed them to Logan.

'Just promise me,' she said, filling in the paperwork, 'you won't tell anyone I rushed that through for you, OK? If it gets out I do favours for sex there'll be a line right round the bloody building. . .'

24

The sign on the door said, 'ABERDEEN BUREAU ~ SCOTTISH FINGERPRINT SERVICE', which was pretty grandiose, given it was just a couple of rooms at the end of the third-floor corridor. One wall was dominated by a huge rack of pine drawers, each one stuffed with hundreds of old-fashioned fingerprint files, the rest of the space taken up with cubicles and light-boxes.

Logan found someone in the computer room – little more than an alcove with a scanner, a desktop machine, and a laser printer. The fingerprint technician sagged in his typist's chair, groaned, rubbed at his eyes, then pulled a sheet of acetate from the scanner, replacing it with another one from the pile.

He clicked the mouse a couple of times then glanced at Logan. 'Whatever you want, the answer's no. I'm swamped.'

'Who says I want anything? Maybe I just popped up to say hello.'

'Yeah? Then how come you're holding a fingerprint sheet?'

Logan slipped it onto the top of the pile. 'Oh, come on, Bill. I only need—'

'No! I've got three million prints to run for Finnie as it

is. Supposed to be home having a romantic dinner with my wife. . .' All the time he was talking, the mouse was moving on the screen, clicking and dragging things.

Logan perched on the edge of the desk. 'Can't believe they left you here on your own to do all this. It's just not fair, is it?'

'Don't even try with the fake sympathy.' He clicked the button again, sending the print off to be evaluated against the database.

'Not even if I say "pretty please"?'

Bill gave an elaborate sigh, emptied the scanner, then started again with a new set of fingerprints. 'When I finish this one I'm going for a cup of coffee. While I'm away you can play on the machine to your heart's content. As long as you don't break anything.'

'But—'

'Final offer.'

'Done.'

How hard could it be?

It turned out to be a lot harder than it looked. Scanning the print in had been easy enough, but getting the contrast up without losing detail on the whorls, loops and deltas wasn't. After five minutes of fiddling, Logan finally had something that looked like it would do. Then he tried to follow the hastily-scrawled instructions Bill had left him: rotating the fingerprint so it was the right way up, then taking the mouse and marking up the distinguishing features. Find the end of a ridge, mark the tail with a pointer, then drag the mouse back along the line, then do it again, and again, and again.

Finally, when the screen was covered in little red circles and blue lines, Logan tried to get the machine to search for a match. Then did a lot of swearing when it wouldn't. He was poking away at random buttons when Bill reappeared with a huge wax-paper cup of coffee from the canteen.

'You not finished yet?'

Logan jabbed with the mouse again. 'Bloody thing doesn't work. . .'

'You didn't follow the instructions, did you?' Bill shouldered him out of the way, clicked twice, punched a couple of numbers into the keyboard, then hit 'PROCESS RESULTS'. 'See, piece of cake.'

'How long?'

'Depends. The machine doesn't actually compare prints, it compares the relative distance between points and the direction of the tails. Hundreds of different permutations analysed against every fingerprint we have in the database.' He pulled Logan's sheet out of the scanner and swapped it for the next one in line. 'Anything up to an hour.'

'I'll come back in the morning.' Logan stopped past the lab to say a final good night to Samantha – no tongues – and then wandered down to DI Steel's office.

She was sitting in one of the visitor's chairs, squinting her way through a stack of crime reports, scribbling indecipherable notes on them in red biro.

Logan dumped the DNA file Samantha had given him on the inspector's desk. 'You got a DNA match.'

'Eh?' She looked up from her forms. 'Oh . . . who is it?'

He flipped through the pages till he got to the conclusions at the back. 'Someone called Derek Allan?'

'Oh bloody hell, that's *all* I need.' Then she went rummaging in her trouser pocket and pulled out a fifty-pence piece. 'Here, stick that in the swear box. Bottom desk drawer.'

Logan popped the inspector's money into the Quality Street tin. 'Thought you said you were giving up on the whole "new you" thing?'

'Aye, well. . .' She sniffed, and buried her head in the reports again. 'You thought any more about . . . what we talked about?'

'Ah, about that: maybe you'd be better off with Rennie?'

'Rennie? No' exactly grade-A genetic material, is he?'

'I just think it'd be. . .' *Horrifying* was the first word that sprang to mind. 'It'd be awkward, you and me working together if you were the . . . mother of my child?'

'*Susan* would be the mother.'

'So what would you be, the father?'

'The . . . I don't know, do I? All I'm asking for is a turkey-baster's worth of sperm. You probably wasted that much up in the storeroom—'

Logan's phone started ringing and he grabbed at the excuse. 'McRae.' He listened in silence for a minute, a smile slowly spreading across his face. Then he thanked the man on the other end and hung up. 'That was Bill from fingerprints. We've got a match on the petrol bomb. Kevin Murray – he got slashed last Friday night, four hoodies nearly cut his nose off.'

Steel grabbed her jacket off the back of her chair. 'Right, get a car and we'll go see what he's got to say for himself.'

Logan backed away. 'Oh no you don't: my shift finished two and a half hours ago. I'm going home.'

'Oh, don't be such a wimp. Don't see me sneaking off when there's work to be done, do you?'

'You spent all day snoring off a hangover! At least I've *done* some work today.'

She squinted at him, and Logan could almost hear the evil little cogs working in her brain. 'Be a shame,' she said at last, 'if anyone found out you and our friendly neighbourhood Goth were going at it in the IB lab like a couple of horny teenagers.'

'Not going to work.'

'All that forensic evidence compromised by your dirty little urges. . .'

'Even you're not that much of a bitch. And everything was in evidence bags, thank you very much.'

Steel drummed her fingers against the desktop. 'I'll sign off on your overtime?'

'Still say we should've got a warrant.' Logan looked up at the two-bedroom semi and locked the car door.

'Wah, wah, wah; I want a warrant; I want backup; my shift's over – I want to go home; boo-hoo.' Steel lit a cigarette and blew a small plume of smoke into the evening sky. 'If we'd sodded about waiting for a warrant we'd still be here at midnight.' She started up the short path to the front door. 'Well, come on then, don't want to keep you from your red-haired semen thief.'

'Will you stop that?'

'No' as if you're using the bloody stuff, is it?'

Logan leant on the doorbell. 'This is sexual harassment.'

Brrrrrrrrrrrrrrrrrrrrrrrrrrring. . .

A muffled voice came from inside, 'Just a minute.' And then the door opened, revealing a short, older woman with a wide face and an ugly haircut. But she had a lovely smile. 'Can I help you?'

The inspector nodded, 'Aye, Kevin Murray about?'

The woman ran an eye over Steel, then did the same with Logan. 'What's he done now?'

'He's won the National Lottery,' said Steel, 'we're here to give him his big cardboard cheque.' She sooked the last gasp from her fag, then pinged the stub away into the gutter. 'He in?'

The woman's face hardened – eyes thin slits, mouth turned down at the edges. She walked back into the house, motioning for them to follow. The sound of something sickeningly cheerful blared out from the lounge. A little girl and boy sat on the rug in front of the television, gazing with rapt attention at a singing warthog and meerkat.

Kevin Murray was slumped on the settee, a tin of lager dangling from the fingers of one hand.

The woman stepped in front of him, blocking his view of the TV. 'Kevin, it's the police.'

Kevin looked up, frowned, tried to focus, then gave up and had another swig from his can. His nose was hidden behind a wodge of bandages, a gauze pad held in place over his nostrils by a couple of ties that went all the way around his emaciated head. Another clump of gauze had been taped over his cheek, the white fabric stained with yellow and dark red blobs. 'Told you no' to open the door, Ma.' It sounded as if he had a heavy cold. 'Could be anyone, like.'

'We had a deal, Kevin: you could stay here if you kept out of trouble.'

He shrugged. 'No trouble, Ma, no trouble at all. Keepin' myself to myself, like. You know?'

Steel looked at the little kids watching the television for a moment. Then said, 'Can we have a word in the kitchen, Kevin?'

Kevin drained the last of his lager and belched. 'I'm comfy here.'

'Let's no' do this in front of the kids, eh?'

'Hey, no one's forcin' you to do anythin'. I've got no secrets from my wee angels. You wanna arrest me? You do it right here.'

His mother slapped him on the shoulder. 'Kevin, you promised me!'

'I never did nothin'.'

Steel stuck her hands in her pockets. 'What do you think's going to screw your kids up more: the fact you got arrested, or the fact you made the poor little sods watch?'

Kevin's mum hit him again. 'What did he do this time?'

'Ow! I told you, I never did—'

'We've got a petrol bomb with his fingerprints all over it. Found it in the burnt-out remains of a betting shop.'

'Kevin!' His mother belted him across the back of the head, then dragged him out of the armchair by the ear.

'Aaagh! Let go! Ma, you're hurting—'

'Kevin Murray, you swore on your father's *grave* you'd behave if I took you in! What sort of example are you setting for Britney and Justin?'

Britney and Justin didn't even turn around as their grandmother hauled their father out into the hall and started battering the living hell out of him: raining slaps down on his head as he cowered in the corner by the front door. 'What –' slap '– did –' slap '– I –' slap '– tell –' slap '– you?'

Steel closed the lounge door, shutting out the singing animal noises. 'Actually, Mrs Murray, we kind of like to beat up our own suspects. So if you don't mind. . .?'

Kevin's mother delivered one last ringing slap. 'Go on, tell them what happened. The truth, or so help me I'll swing for you!'

'But I didnae—'

His mother raised her hand again.

'OK, OK! I did it.' He glanced up at Logan and Steel, then back to the floor. 'It wasnae. . . I didnae want to. But they said they knew where I lived and they'd come round and cut my kids and my Ma if I didn't torch the place.'

Logan pulled out his notebook. 'Who were they?'

Kevin kept his eyes on the carpet. 'Don't remember, do I.'

His mother hit him again.

'Stop it! It was the guys what did this. . .' He pointed at the mass of bandages covering his slashed nose. 'So yeah, I chucked a petrol bomb into the bookies.'

Steel whistled. 'They'd have to be pretty damn scary people, Kevin. Firebombing the Turf 'n Track? Did you no' think the McLeods would be a wee bit annoyed when they found out?'

'Aye, but the McLeods are old school. I do somethin' to them: they come after *me*, no' my kids. Or my Ma. What choice did I have? Eh?' He stood tall as his mother patted him on the arm. 'If you had kids, you'd understand.'

While DI Steel wrestled Kevin Murray into the back of the car, Logan phoned Finnie, telling him that they'd arrested the man responsible for firebombing the Turf 'n Track.

'Excellent.' The DCI demanded a blow-by-blow account then asked the big question: *'Is he going to give us the Manchester Muppets who put him up to it?'*

Logan watched Kevin Murray arguing with Steel.

'Probably not.'

There was a pause that went on and on and on and. . .

'Sir?'

'I want you to call me as soon as you get him back to FHQ. Understand? The minute you get him back here, you let me know.'

'OK, I'll—'

Steel stuck her head out of the car window. 'We haven't got all sodding day, Sergeant – move it!'

'I'll call you back.'

Logan parked the CID pool car by the back doors to FHQ. The rear podium lay beneath a veil of blue shadows, the security lights already on, even though it was only half past eight. Up above, the sky was the colour of varnished duck eggs, and down below, DI Steel was still arguing with Kevin Murray as she dragged him out of the back seat:

'Yes you bloody well will!'

Kevin shook his head. 'No. Nu-huh. No way. I'm no'

sayin' nothin'. I arsoned that place on my own. No one else involved.'

Logan pulled out his phone and called Finnie – as instructed – letting him know they were back.

'OK,' said Finnie, *'give me five minutes, then get him to number three.'*

Steel poked Kevin in the ribs as Logan hung up. 'Don't be such a moron. They'll throw the book at you. And when you get out . . . in about *four years,* the McLeods'll hammer your kneecaps into the middle of next week.'

'You deaf? I'm no' sayin' nothin'! The bastards'll come after my kids if I grass them up.'

'Don't be so melodramatic.' Steel gave him a shove towards the battered back doors, where a couple of support staff were eating crisps and smoking cigarettes.

'No! It never happened! I was lying, OK?' His voice was getting louder and louder. 'I burned the place down coz I was pissed at Creepy. You can't prove nothin'. . .'

'You really don't know me very well, do you?'

'I'm no' grassin' them up!'

He kept it up all the way through processing: while his photo was being taken, and his fingerprints – the only time he shut up was when Steel stuck the DNA swab in his mouth. Kevin was still complaining as Logan hauled him along the corridor to interview room three.

'I told you, *I* did it. Me. On me own. No one forced me to do bugger all.'

The inspector had another go. 'Protective custody: you, your mum and the kids. No one could touch you.'

'Aye, like I'd trust *you* lot. Protective custody? I seen what happened to Big Rob Barkley, and it's no' happenin' to me.'

Steel poked him in the arm. 'That was an accident.'

'Gets talked into grassin' up Malk the Knife and the next thing you know: splat, he's under an articulated lorry.' Kevin glanced up and down the corridor, and the next time he spoke it was in a whisper. 'Look, most of you bastards are on the take, right? I mean, everyone knows it. So how about you make this go away and I'll give you two . . . no, *three* grand. Eh?'

This time Steel did more than poke him in the arm, she shoved him up against the wall. 'I'm going to pretend you didn't say that, Kevin. Because no' even *you* could be thick enough to think you can buy me for three—' She bounced him off the wall. 'Lousy—' Again. 'Grand!'

'I was only saying.'

'I'm no' for sale, you manky sack of crap!'

The interview room door opened and there was DS Pirie, dragging a handcuffed man out into the corridor. Short spiky haircut, designer stubble goatee, eyebrow ring, a gauze pad taped over one ear, a dark red stain on the shoulder of his white T-shirt, broad Mancunian accent: 'Let go of us! You fookin' haggis-munchin' bastards is all the same. . .'

The man trailed off into silence, staring at Kevin Murray. 'You! You dirty *fooker!*'

Kevin scrambled backwards. 'No-no-no-no-no. . .'

The guy in the T-shirt lunged, but Pirie stopped him short.

'You fookin' told, didn't yez? You grassed us up.'

'I never said nothin', I promise! It—'

T-Shirt's left foot lashed out, probably aiming for Kevin's balls, but the trainer slammed into his thigh instead. 'Yer fookin' dead, you hear me? Dead. You and your whole fookin' family! Yer—'

DS Pirie twisted him round, and sent him crashing to the floor. *Accidentally* bouncing his head off the green terrazzo.

'Aaagh. . . dirty bastard. . .' And then Pirie was on top of him, knee pressed into the small of his back. 'Gerroff!'

'Shut up and hold still, you ugly wee shite.' Pirie grinned up at Logan and Steel. 'We caught this one battering the living hell out of a doorman on Bon Accord Street. Didn't take kindly to being chucked out.' He leant harder, getting a squeal of protest in return. 'Trying to flog heroin to a bunch of drunk girlies on a hen night, weren't you?'

Logan couldn't make out T-Shirt's response, but it sounded filthy.

Kevin Murray's interview didn't go very well. After running into the thug from Manchester, it was all he could do to confirm his name and address for the tape. After that it was nearly impossible to get anything out of him.

DI Steel gave it an hour before giving up, then told Logan to get him out of her sight.

Down in cell number six, Kevin Murray limped up and down the side of the bed – little more than a thin plastic mattress slapped down on a concrete platform built into the wall. 'You have to tell him,' he said as Logan pocketed the handcuffs, 'I didn't grass them up, yeah? You'll tell him?'

'Don't know if it'll do any good. Would you believe me, if you were him?'

Kevin collapsed onto the mattress, buried his head in his hands. 'They're gonnae kill my kids. . .'

Logan sat next to him. 'Tell me who they are and maybe I can help, OK?'

The thin man rolled onto his side, face to the wall, knees drawn up against his chest. 'I'm no' a clype.'

There was a knock on the cell door and Kevin flinched. 'It's them!'

'Don't be ridiculous. You're in a police station.'

Kevin backed away from the door. 'I know how it works! You're in on it – you're all in on it!'

The door opened and DCI Finnie was framed in the glow of a fluorescent tube. He clasped his hands together and nodded at Kevin. 'Just checking everything's in order with your room, Mr Murray. Bed comfortable? Enjoying the view?' There wasn't one. The room's single window was three rows of rippled-glass bricks, six foot off the floor. 'Would you like a newspaper, or an early morning wakeup call?'

Kevin just sat on the thin blue mattress. 'I never grassed them up.'

Finnie stepped into the cell. 'I've got this from here, Sergeant. Why don't you knock off? I understand DI Steel is organizing a trip to the pub, maybe you could have one for Kevin here. Would you like that Kevin?'

The thin man scowled, face all puckered up around his gauze-covered nose. 'You're a right bastard.'

Finnie loomed over him. 'Oh, you have *no* idea.'

25

'Got any spare change?'

Logan stopped in his tracks, and looked down at the figure huddled in the entrance to Lodge Walk – a little alley that ran between the Toll Booth museum and the pub on the corner, connecting Union Street to Force Headquarters. It was a shortcut in regular use by uniform and plainclothes officers. Not the usual place for beggars. And at five to seven on Thursday morning, it was a bit early too.

She was sitting cross-legged on a dirty orange Kenny-from-South-Park-style parka, gazing up at him with panda eyes. She'd done her best to make them match, but the left eye was all swollen, the bruising barely hidden by a thick layer of pancake makeup and too much eyeliner. Bright-red veins spidered their way across the white of her eye, making the pupil look like an emerald floating in a sea of Tabasco. It was Tracey – the girl who'd fingered Creepy Colin McLeod for battering Harry Jordan's head in with a hammer.

She was dressed in a short black skirt and a lacy top that still had the security tag hanging from the side, high-heeled ankle boots, and stockings with more ladders than your average fire station. Someone had broken her nose.

'Oh,' she said, 'it's you. . .' Tracey stuck out her hand and Logan pulled her to her feet, where she wobbled on four-inch heels. As she bent to grab the parka she'd been sitting on, he caught a flash of skin between her skirt and her top. It was a collage of bruises and welts.

'Been waiting, like, forever.' She ran a hand through her bleached blonde hair. 'Haven't got a fag, have you? I'm gasping.'

'Gave up years ago. What happened to your face?'

She turned and squinted across Union Street at a small flurry of pigeons fighting over a discarded kebab. 'I was wrong, you know? About what happened. It . . . it wasn't Colin McLeod battered Harry.'

'*What?*'

'It wasn't him. It was someone else. Colin didn't touch him.'

'You can't just change your statement—'

'I was wrong, must've been off my face or something, you know? Colin was nowhere near the place when Harry got his head caved in.'

'And all of a sudden he's "Colin", not "Creepy"? Tell me, Tracey, would this have anything to do with your new black eye?'

'I was wrong, OK? It wasn't Colin, you gotta let him go!'

'We found a claw hammer in Colin McLeod's garage with traces of Harry Jordan's blood on it.'

'It. . . We. . .' She rubbed at her arms. 'You must've planted it. You know? To fit him up, like.'

'You got a visit from Agnes McLeod last night, didn't you? That or a couple of her son's *associates*, and they helped change your mind about what happened.'

'No! I just remember it better now. It wasn't Colin. It wasn't. . .' She grabbed for Logan's hand. 'You've got to let him go.'

'We can't do that, it's—'

'How about a blowjob? Right now, on the house like? No? I got girlfriends, we could, you know, put on a show for you? Like an orgy or something? You could do *whatever you like*, we wouldn't tell no one. . .' She licked her chapped lips, leaving a smear of saliva behind. The effect wasn't exactly erotic. 'You know you want to. . .'

'No I bloody well don't.'

Logan got a cappuccino and a rowie with butter and jam from the canteen. And as a rowie was, more-or-less, just a croissant that had really let itself go, *technically* it counted as a continental breakfast. Chewing, he made his way to the morning briefing.

With any luck all that salt and saturated fat would kill him before he had to tell Finnie that Tracey was changing her story.

Halfway down the stairs Logan's phone started ringing. He juggled hot coffee and greasy pastry. 'Hello?'

'Hello? Yes?' A man's voice. *'Is this Detective Sergeant Mackie?'*

'McRae.'

'Is it? Oh, sorry. This is Father John Burnett, Sacred Heart. . . Well, Saint Peter's now I suppose. Erm . . . I know it's early, but you left a message asking me to call you back?'

Two minutes later Logan was hurrying out of the side door, dragging a moaning Constable Karim with him.

'But I'm supposed to be at the briefing; you *know* what Finnie's like!' Karim was dressed in the standard Grampian Police uniform: black T-shirt, black stab-proof vest, black peaked cap, black trousers, black boots, and a fluorescent yellow waistcoat with 'POLICE' across the back. Which kind of spoiled the whole ninja ensemble.

Logan punched the keycode into the gate that lead out onto Lodge Walk. 'We're only going to be fifteen minutes.'

'But—'

'You can blame me if it makes you feel any better.'

'Damn right I'm blaming you.' He followed Logan out of the shadowy alleyway and onto Union Street. The sunshine was blinding. 'Jesus!' Karim grabbed his hat and pulled it as far down as it would go, hiding in the shade of the brim – making his ears stick out at right angles. 'Like a sodding microwave out here. . .'

They crossed the road and headed into the Castlegate, a wide-open plaza of cobbles and pigeon droppings, with the Mercat Cross sitting in the middle like a dirty granite carousel. A pair of tramps were slouched against the hoarding that surrounded the Salvation Army Citadel, basking in the morning sun and sharing a breakfast of white spirit and cigarettes. They waved and cheered as PC Karim went past.

Logan waved back. 'Didn't know you had family in Aberdeen.'

'Oh ha, ha.' The constable sniffed. 'That's Dirty Bob and his mate Richard. Saved them from a kicking last year. They might stink, but at least they're grateful, unlike *some* people. Broke up a fight outside the McDonalds last night: rival hen parties. Matron of honour called me a Paki bastard and tried to take my head off with a plastic tray. Said I should go back where I bloody came from.'

'What: the exotic, sun-soaked shores of Fraserburgh?'

'Makes you proud to be Scottish, doesn't it?'

St Peter's Catholic Church was hidden away at the end of the Castlegate, between a card-shop-come-printers and a defunct hairdressers. A little recess led between the buildings into a tiny courtyard that stank of bleach and disinfectant.

A pair of big blue doors sat off to one side – beneath a lancet window of unstained-glass – posted with the standard welcome for this part of town: 'NOTICE ~ THESE PREMISES ARE PROTECTED BY CLOSED-CIRCUIT TELEVISION SECURITY SYSTEMS'.

Karim marched straight past them and up to the battered wooden door of the parochial house. It opened on a clean, but shabby hallway: primrose walls, white ceilings – the paint blistering and cracked, showing the grey plasterwork beneath. The whole place had an air of neglect Logan hadn't been expecting. It was a long, long way from the opulence of the Vatican. Like a dying relative no one wanted to talk about, let alone visit.

The constable opened a part-glazed door into the main building, and shouted, 'Anyone home?'

A disembodied voice replied, 'Hello? I'm in the kitchen.'

Logan followed Karim into a large room dominated by a big wooden table and units that had seen better days. Possibly during the Crimean War.

There was a man sitting at the table, in front of an open laptop. Early forties; bouffant hair starting to grey at the temples; thin, blue cardigan over a black priest shirt; glasses. 'Constable! How nice to see you again. Did you manage to catch him?'

He stuck out his hand, and Karim shook it, smiling.

'Not yet, Father.'

'Oh, that's a pity. . . Still, I'm sure you're all doing your best.' He half rose from his seat and offered Logan a handshake too. 'Have we met?'

'DS McRae. Are you Father Burnett?'

'Guilty as charged. Now why don't you both grab a pew and we can have a chat.'

Logan and PC Karim sat, listening to the kettle grumbling its way to a boil while Father Burnett went hunting through the fridge.

'Trouble is, we've got an open-door policy, and people

will insist on leaving the milk out. Ah, excellent. . .' The priest emerged with a plastic carton of semi-skimmed. 'Where was I?'

Logan pointed at a framed photo on the kitchen wall: it was Father Burnett, in full vestments, standing in front of Sacred Heart, Torry.

'Right, right. Well, it's been in pretty poor repair for years, but we've finally got the money together to have the place done up properly. So, while it's closed for refurbishment, I came down here to lend a hand. Be four months next Friday.'

Teabags, hot water, milk. He waggled a mug at Logan. 'That about the right colour for you?'

'Perfect. What about your congregation?'

'Ah, therein lies a tale. . .' He brought the teas back to the table, followed by a tin of Marks & Spencer fancy biscuits. 'Last year we started doing Mass in Polish, twice a week – thought it would make our European friends feel more at home, if they could attend services in their native language. Help them integrate. Trouble is, pretty soon they'd only go to the Polish Masses, so instead of helping them get to know the locals we ended up with a segregated Catholic community that didn't mix at all.'

He slurped his tea. 'Long story short, when we shut Sacred Heart for refurbishment, we thought we'd give it another go. We do the Mass half in English and half in Polish, four times a week.'

'Working?'

'So far. We're packed to the rafters. Literally. You'd think more people would go to the Cathedral, but . . . well, their loss is our gain.' Father Burnett helped himself to a chocolate biscuit. 'Parishioner of mine brings in a tin every week. Just between you and me, I think they're the spoils of shoplifting, but she's in her eighties, so what can you do?' He offered the tin around again. 'But I'm guessing you didn't come here to talk about Polish integration and pilfered biscuits?'

'Actually,' said Logan, 'we sort of did. Since the Poles started coming to Mass here, have you noticed anyone who's stopped turning up? Someone who used to go to Sacred Heart all the time?'

Frown. 'Can't say that I have.'

'Lives with his mother? Father's dead? Probably used to work in a bar, or a hotel, or on a building site?'

Father Burnett put his tea down. 'What's this about?'

'You've heard of Oedipus?'

'Greek tragedy: murdered his father and slept with his mum – a bit like Fraserburgh—'

Karim sat up in his chair. 'Hey!'

'No offence. Then he gouged his own eyes out with a spoon.'

Logan pulled out a set of photographs, laying them on the table. Each one showed a victim's face, the eyes hollow, scar-ringed sockets. 'I think whoever did this was an active member of Sacred Heart.'

The priest stared at the pictures, then crossed himself. 'Dear God. . .'

'Has anyone said anything. You know, in confession?'

That got Logan a stern stare. 'The confession is *sacrosanct*, Sergeant. I couldn't tell you, even if I wanted to.'

Logan picked up a photo at random. 'Lubosław Frankowski drank himself to death six weeks after this was taken. His health visitor was off sick for a fortnight. When she got back, Lubosław had been dead for nine days. Alone in his flat in the middle of June. . . The smell was unbelievable.'

Father Burnett winced. Then sighed. 'I know it's hard to accept, but I *can't* break the confidentiality of the confession.'

'So if someone came in here, told you he'd blinded seven people then set fire to the sockets . . . you'd give him what: three Hail Marys and absolve him of all blame?'

'Well,' the priest put the lid back on the biscuits, 'I'd do my best to convince them to go to the police and hand themselves in. But it's immaterial, because no one's confessed to anything like this. And while I couldn't tell you if they had, I *can* tell you that they haven't.'

A buzzing noise sounded in the hall and Father Burnett glanced up at the CCTV monitor sitting on top of the fridge – a view of the courtyard outside, slowly panning from left to right. 'We get a lot of people peeing in the courtyard after the pubs shut. . .'

The top of a bald head came into view, standing at the front door.

Father Burnett scraped his chair back and stood. 'Would you excuse me for a minute?'

Logan waited until he heard the front door open and the mumble of muffled conversation, then turned to PC Karim. 'You believe him?'

'Don't see why not. He's a nice enough bloke. Last time I was here, it was a break-in. Someone kicked in a connecting door from the choir loft and ransacked the place. Caught the Father in the bath. Poor sod had to talk his way out of it wearing nothing but bubbles and a smile. Anyway, he's a priest: you can trust him.'

'Thousands of choirboys might beg to differ on that one.' Logan wandered over to the window and looked out on a walled garden. Rose trees at the bottom, a baptismal font in the middle, and a snowdrift of empty carrier bags in the corner. 'If Oedipus really was a member of Sacred Heart, why doesn't Father Burnett recognize the description?'

'Too vague?'

'Sorry about that.' The priest was back, a brown paper bag in his hands. He unloaded a collection of glass jars and stacked them in one of the cupboards. '*Gołabki*: stuffed cabbage leaves. I love this stuff – got a taste for it when I worked in Krakow. Mr Wołoskowski brings me some every time his nephew comes to visit.'

Father Burnett closed the cupboard door. 'They're good people, Sergeant. They come over here looking for a better life for their families, they work hard – and yes, I know some of them like to get a bit drunk and rowdy – but deep down. . . Look if someone's targeting them I want to help. OK?'

'OK.'

Father Burnett gently shepherded them out into the hall. 'I'll put the word out at Mass this evening. See if we can't rustle up some information for you.'

He stopped at the threshold and shook both of their hands again. But he held on to Logan's. 'I know this probably isn't my place, but I do actually know who you are. I read about you and the Flesher case last year.'

Logan opened his mouth to protest, but the priest carried on regardless, 'And I know you probably don't want to hear it, and you're obviously not a Catholic, but if you ever want to talk, please: you have my number.'

By the time they got back to the station, the briefing room was empty, just a whiff of stale coffee and cheesy feet to show it had been packed with CID and uniform less than fifteen minutes before. Logan abandoned PC Karim at the main desk and headed up to Finnie's office. Might as well get it over with. . .

Pirie was there, scribbling things on a whiteboard already crowded with photos, diagrams, and notes: Operation Oedipus in all its going-nowhere glory.

Finnie looked up from a report as Logan closed the door. 'Ah,' he went back to his report, 'DS McRae, how *good* of you to join us today. Let me guess: you were too busy interrogating your duvet this morning to *bother* showing up at my morning briefing?'

Pirie sniggered. 'Heh, "Interrogating your duvet", that's—'

Finnie cut him off. 'If I wanted someone to repeat everything I said, I'd buy a parrot.'

The tips of Pirie's ears went bright pink. 'Sorry, sir.'

'Now, DS McRae, care to tell me what was so *important*?'

Here we go: 'Tracey Hamilton wants to retract her statement. Says it wasn't Colin McLeod who bashed Harry Jordan's head in after all.'

He filled them in on the details, but instead of shouting and swearing, Finnie just sat back in his seat, steepled his fingers and said, 'Excellent.'

'It is?'

The DCI pointed at Pirie. 'How long have I been after the McLeods? Five years, six?'

His sidekick nodded. 'At least.'

'And now it's all paying off. Sod the witnesses: we've got enough forensics on Creepy Colin to send him down for at least fourteen years. Simon's out of commission and blind as a bat. And if your pet tart's been forced to change her story – we've got a crack at the McLeods' mum for attempting to pervert the course of justice.' He played a little drum roll on his desk. 'This is going to be a good day, gentlemen!'

'Yeah, about that. . .' Pirie cleared his throat. 'Those paramedics from yesterday made a formal complaint. They say we obstructed—'

'Eggs and omelettes; eggs and omelettes.' The DCI spun his chair round and stared at the Oedipus board, then round to a smaller board with 'CARAVAN FULL OF GUNS ~ TERRORISTS?

~ DRUGS? ~ BANK JOB?' written on it. The word 'DRUGS' had been underlined three times.

'Pirie: I want you to get onto your contacts. Yardies, Triads, Northfield Massive, Kincorth Groove Brigade, and anyone else you can think of. I want to know who's trying to move in on the McLeods' territory. McRae: we picked up a tosspot from Manchester last night, trying to flog heroin to a hen night. Steve Preston. Get him in an interview room, and we'll see what he's got to say for himself.'

Logan didn't move. 'I thought Pirie interviewed him last night.'

'No, I had Pirie drag him into an interview room, so he could *accidentally* bump into your Kevin Murray. Wasn't that a *nice* surprise for everyone involved?'

'You did it on *purpose?*'

'Our friend Mr Preston has form for drugs and knife crime. You said Murray was being leant on by drug dealers from Manchester who cut his face.' Finnie held up both palms. 'Hardly rocket science is it?'

'But they threatened to kill Kevin Murray's kids!'

'You just get Steve Preston into room three and let me worry about that.'

'Actually, sir,' said Pirie, 'I was kinda hoping to sit in on the interview—'

'You've got more important things to do.' The Detective Chief Inspector was on his feet and heading for the door. 'We've got a drugs war on its way and a caravan full of automatic weapons. I will *not* have a bunch of incomers turning my city into downtown Basra.'

'Don't play stupid with me,' Finnie leant on the tabletop and glowered at the prisoner, 'we know you did it.'

Logan got the feeling Steve Preston wasn't playing stupid at all, he was the real deal.

'I'm not saying nothin' without me brief.' The Manchester accent sounded a bit rough at eight o'clock in the morning, but it went with the grey face and bloodshot eyes. Whatever he'd been on the night before was long gone, leaving him to cope with reality all on his own.

Finnie folded his arms and pulled his rubbery lips into a pout. 'Oh, I'm *sorry*, did I confuse your little brain the first *four* times I explained this? You'll get a lawyer when *I* say so, not before.'

'Naw, I been arrested loadsa times: I knows me fookin' rights.'

The Chief Inspector closed his eyes and gritted his teeth. 'For God's sake . . . McRae?'

Logan tried again: 'The Scottish legal system's different, Steve. You'll get to see your brief when we're done here.'

'I knows me rights!'

Finnie: 'Why did you want Kevin Murray to torch the Turf 'n Track?'

'Never 'eard of no Kevin Mornay.'

'Really? Because that's not what Kevin Murray says. He says you and your mates threatened to kill his mum and kids if he didn't do what you said. Got his statement right here. . .' Finnie produced a sheet of paper from a manila folder and slapped it down on the chipped Formica.

Pause.

'Fookin' tosser's lying, ain't he?'

Logan tapped the tabletop. 'You don't remember me, do you, Steve? I was there the night you and your hoodie mates slashed Kevin Murray's face.'

Steve shifted in his seat. 'Nah . . . I wasn't nowhere near nothin'.'

Logan stared at the man's hands. There was a DIY tattoo in the webbing between the thumb and forefinger. It was far too small and on the wrong hand to make him Hoodie

Number One, but what the hell: 'Sure you were. In fact, I think *you* were the one who cut him.' Logan turned to Finnie. 'What are they giving people for assault with a deadly weapon these days?'

Finnie thought about it. 'Eight years. Ten if you get Sheriff McNab, he's a real bastard.'

'I didn't stab no one!'

'Yes you did,' said Logan. 'And you know what? Detective Constable Rennie saw you too. Two police officers as witnesses, that'll be good enough for any jury.'

'It weren't me! It were Baz. . .' And then his eyes went wide, and he clamped his mouth shut. 'I mean, I weren't there. And neither was nobody else.'

Logan made a show of writing: 'IT WAS BAZ' in his notebook in big block capitals.

'What? No, you can't write that: I never said it were Baz.'

'We can rewind the tape and check if you like?'

Finnie pulled another sheet of A4 from the folder. 'Where are you staying, Steve?'

'I never said it were Baz! Tell 'im.'

'According to this you're supposed to report to your parole officer every Wednesday morning. In Manchester.' Finnie checked his watch. 'Ooh, looks like you're *not* going to make it. Do you think he'll be *disappointed* when I tell him you've been picked up for drug dealing and attempted murder in Aberdeen?'

'Attempted murder? Wha? No, it weren't me, you said I only stabbed the bastard—'

'The suspect said, "I only stabbed the bastard. . ."' Logan wrote it down in his notebook.

'Make 'im stop doin' that!'

Finnie sucked a breath through his teeth, like a mechanic about to deliver bad news. 'Not looking good, is it Steve?'

'I didn't do nothin'!'

'Tell you what: why don't we pick up your good mate, Baz, AKA: Barry Hartlay . . . oh don't look so shocked, when I spoke to Manchester Police they gave me a list of your known associates.'

'What? No, I—'

'When we play him that bit of the tape where you grass him up, think he'll do the decent thing? Own up and let you off the hook? Like a good mate?'

Steve was sweating, eyes going from Logan to Finnie and back again. 'I. . . I. . . You can't. . . No. . . He. . .'

Logan watched him stammer for a while, then a thought occurred. He reached across the table and patted Steve on the arm. Steve flinched.

'Did you know that Polish guy's shop had CCTV?' It was a lie, but there was no harm in trying.

Finnie and Steve both said, 'Polish guy?' at the same time.

'Must've been fun, that: smashing the place up. Looked fun anyway. Jars exploding, pickles going everywhere.' Logan whistled. 'That stupid look on the Polish guy's face when the display cabinet hit the deck. . . Sweet.'

The sudden change of subject seemed to confuse Steve for a second, and then an appalled look crawled all over his face. 'There was *cameras* and that?'

'Oh, yeah.' Logan leant forward and dropped his voice to a loud whisper, 'Got a great shot of you smashing stuff.'

'There wasn't supposed to be no cameras. . .'

'Mind you, the shopkeeper told me you were all a bunch of Jessies; said he could take you with one hand tied behind his back. Not going to give you a penny.'

Steve collapsed in his seat, hands covering his face. '"Come to Aberdeen," he sez. "Take over no problem," he sez. . .'

'Apparently next time you and your gay-wad mates show up, he's going to spank the lot of you.'

'Yeah?' Steve came out from behind his hands, scowling.

'We'll see if he's so fookin' brave this afternoon, then! See if he's got the stones to stand there and. . . What you smiling for?' He sat back and frowned at Logan and Finnie. 'What?'

26

Finnie sat in the passenger seat, watching Logan out of the corner of his eye. 'There never was any CCTV in that shop, was there?'

'Nope.' Logan smiled and pulled out to pass a bendy bus that had stopped to pick up passengers. 'Shopkeeper said four hoodies trashed his shop, I thought it was worth a punt. Just like you did with Kevin Murray.'

The DCI nodded. 'You're learning, good.' He let the patronizing compliment hang in the air for a moment. 'And you're sure these hoodies are going to be armed?'

'Knives and machetes.'

'Good. Nothing worse than begging a firearms team then have them sitting about twiddling their thumbs.' He dug something out of his pocket and handed it over when Logan pulled up at the lights. It was a photocopy of an Oedipus note. 'Came in this morning.'

I can not help you any more!!! I have *tried and tried* but you will not listen! I cut out their **filthy eyes**, while you do nothing!! **You are deaf and they are blind!**

***What happens now is* YOUR fault!!!**
I am the **burning** of **GOD** *and salvation will be mine!*

Logan handed it back as the lights went green. 'Eleven exclamation marks: he's getting worse.'

'That's the third note in three days. Before it was one, maybe two a week. Dr Goulding says our boy's escalating.'

There was silence.

And then Finnie cleared his throat, looked out of the window, and said, 'I'm open to suggestions.'

'Ah. . .'

'I don't care how daft it sounds.'

Logan took them up Mid Stocket Road and across Anderson Drive, heading towards Mastrick. 'I spoke to one of the priests at St Peter's this morning.' He filled the DCI in on his chat with Goulding about Oedipus being a religious nut. 'You know what Aberdeen's like. Used to be the most secular city in Scotland, but a lot of these Eastern Europeans are devout. Been a windfall for the Roman Catholic churches, they've actually got bums on pews for a change. Goulding thinks our boy feels squeezed out.'

Finnie stared at him. 'Believe it or not, I *did* actually think of that. Pirie checked every church, mosque, and synagogue in Aberdeen. No joy.'

Damn. Now Logan would have to think of something else to make the DCI put him forward for that promotion. 'Well . . . how about the victims then? We could put a bit of pressure on? See if they'll cooperate?'

Finnie waved a hand, as if wafting away a bad smell. 'I've already got Pirie doing that on a regular basis, they won't budge. They're terrified.' He pointed through the windshield. 'Take a right here.'

* * *

They parked in the shadow of a tower block. Mastrick wasn't exactly Logan's happy place, but it looked a lot nicer in the sunshine than it did in his nightmares. A breeze caught a small drift of empty crisp packets and crumpled pages torn from a lad's mag, sending them into a whirlpool dance of salt and vinegar and half-naked women.

A couple of old men shuffled their way across the road, dragging an unhappy-looking terrier between them, the dog whining and scrabbling against the tarmac.

Logan locked the car, then looked around. 'Why are we here, exactly?'

'Just let me do the talking,' said Finnie, leading the way across a patch of grass. 'And for God's sake, try not to piss anyone off.'

It was little more than a collection of squat concrete buildings, encircled by a rusting chainlink fence. A workshop, a garage, a small two-storey office block with not enough parking space, and a couple of warehouses. A bottle-green Jaguar XJS was up on the ramp inside the garage, a shower of electric-blue sparks marking out some serious welding going on. Old-fashioned accordion music echoed out between the flashes.

And then there was silence.

A pale face watched them from the other side of the car, and then its owner stepped out into the sunshine. He was huge, at least twenty stone, squeezed into grubby blue overalls, wiping his hands on a rag as he waddled towards them. 'Yeah?' The man's face was a topographical map of scar tissue and fat, a patchy beard struggling to conceal the damage. He stank of motor oil and ozone.

Finnie nodded a greeting. 'Reuben. Is Wee Hamish in?'

The man mountain looked them up and down. 'Depends, doesn't it?'

'Like a word.'

'Aye, I'll bet you would. . .' He stared at them for a little longer, then lumbered towards the shabby office block. They went to follow him, but the big man stopped dead, turned and pointed at Logan. 'Where the fuck you think you're going?'

'I'm—'

'No you're not. You're staying right there.'

Finnie patted Logan on the back. 'Don't go anywhere. Fidget doesn't like people wandering around his yard.'

Logan raised an eyebrow and the DCI pointed towards the dark interior of the garage, where the rectangular head of a Rottweiler glared out of the shadows. 'He's called Fidget, because if you don't stand perfectly still he goes for you.'

Logan stood on the forecourt, trying not to make any sudden movements. Bloody hell: Wee Hamish Mowat. . .

Fidget the Rottweiler lumbered out to the garage door and thumped himself down in the sunshine. He was huge. And unlike the McLeods' second-hand Alsatian, Fidget definitely looked as if he could outrun an out-of-shape Detective Sergeant. And then eat him.

It was probably only ten minutes, but it felt like hours before Reuben the man mountain returned, hooking an oil-stained thumb over his shoulder at the offices. 'You: inside.' And then he went back to his welding.

Wee Hamish Mowat's office looked like something straight out of a National Trust catalogue – wood panelling, hunting prints, bookcases, two brown leather chesterfield sofas, and a mahogany desk the size of Switzerland.

Finnie was sitting on one of the sofas, directly across from the office's owner.

Wee Hamish Mowat: grey hair, hooked nose, hands like vulture's feet, and eyes like chips of flint. He looked up at Logan, and a stray beam of sunlight flashed across his rectangular glasses. 'Ah, Detective Sergeant Logan McRae, I've heard so much about you.' The voice was a gravelly Aberdonian with a slight hint of public school. 'Your Chief Inspector was just telling me about his little problem.'

Finnie shifted, making the leather creak. 'Yes, well. . .'

Wee Hamish stood, crossed to an antique sideboard, and pulled out a bottle of whisky and three glasses. 'Macallan, thirty year old. I take it you'll join me?' He pointed at one of the sofas.

Logan sat.

The old man poured a measure of whisky into each glass. '*Slainte mhar*. Or, I suppose we should say *"Na zdrowie"* now, what with all the Polish people we've got over here.'

They returned the toast and sipped in silence.

'So,' Finnie twisted the crystal tumbler in his hands, 'about that caravan. . .?'

'Tell me, Logan, what do you think of the whisky?'

Logan put his glass down on the big wooden coffee table. 'Very nice.'

'Good.' Wee Hamish smiled, showing off a set of perfect white dentures. 'I do like a man who appreciates a good malt. I think we're going to get on perfectly.'

Which wasn't exactly the most comforting thing Logan had ever heard.

The old man took another drink. 'From what I understand, your caravan was full of machine guns and bullets.' The smile faded. 'Some people just don't understand how business works here. They watch all these big American movies, with the gunfights and the explosions, and they think that's what the real world's like.'

Finnie nodded.

'This,' said Wee Hamish, poking his couch with a finger, 'is not some bloody third world country. Guns are for professionals, *not* rank amateurs. Don't you agree, Logan?'

Logan glanced at Finnie, but got no help there. 'I think Aberdeen doesn't need this kind of trouble.'

'Well put, Logan. Well put. You see, your Chief Constable was right – I heard him on the radio the other day – people look at Aberdeen and they see a fat hog, swollen with oil money and ready for slaughter.' He leaned forward in his chair. 'The funny thing about pigs though, is that they'll devour anything. Hair, skin, bones. And if you're not *very* careful, you can end your days as a big pile of pig shit.'

Silence.

Logan cleared his throat. 'Is that what happened to Simon McLeod? He wasn't careful enough?'

Finnie nearly choked on his whisky.

'That was a terrible, terrible thing. Blinded like that. . .' The old man stared across the coffee table. 'According to the papers you're looking for a serial killer who doesn't kill people?'

The DCI glowered at Logan. 'You'll have to excuse Sergeant McRae, he—'

'Nonsense,' Wee Hamish waved a liver-spotted claw, never taking his eyes off Logan, 'I want to hear what Logan has to say. I read that your psycho doesn't like Polish people. Which is a pity; personally I think they're marvellous. I've got one of them retiling my bathroom right now.'

'Why would Oedipus attack Simon McLeod? He's not Polish, he's one of Aberdeen's biggest—'

'Entrepreneurs,' said Finnie. 'Biggest *entrepreneurs*.'

Wee Hamish laughed. 'Oh don't be so sensitive, Chief Inspector. We all know what Simon is.' Then the old man turned his glittering grey eyes back towards Logan. 'Go on.'

'I think this was business related.'

This time the silence went on for an uncomfortably long time, and then Finnie broke it with, 'I want to apologize on behalf of—'

Wee Hamish ignored him. 'So, you think this was someone trying to muscle in on the McLeods' territory?'

'Yes.'

'Maybe someone who saw what happened to those poor Polish people, and decided this was a perfect opportunity to take care of a rival?'

'Wouldn't you?'

There was another uncomfortable silence.

Then Wee Hamish flashed his dentures again. 'You've got balls, Logan, I like that.' He drained his glass and stood. 'Now, if you'll excuse me gentlemen, I have some business to attend to.'

Out in the sunshine Reuben was leaning against the garage wall smoking a roll-up. A pimply youth with green hair appeared at his shoulder, handed him a mug of tea, then they both stared at Logan and Finnie until they were off the premises.

Logan looked back over his shoulder at the small office block with its row of dark windows. 'What did he mean, he'd heard all about me?'

Finnie didn't reply, just marched straight-backed across the grassy patch to the pool car. He waited for Logan to unlock the doors, then climbed into the passenger seat.

'OK. . .' Logan got behind the wheel and started the engine. 'Where to?'

'Exactly what part of "keep your mouth shut and let me do the talking" did you have *difficulty* with, Sergeant?'

'I was—'

'What the *hell* did you think you were doing?' Finnie turned in his seat, face pinched, jowls trembling. 'Accusing Wee Hamish of blinding Simon McLeod? Did you really think that was a *good* idea? Or were you dropped on your head as a child?'

'But he—'

'Let's get something perfectly straight here, *Sergeant*: Hamish Mowat isn't like Simon McLeod, or any of the other two-bit crooks you deal with. Wee Hamish Mowat will chew you up and spit out your *bones*!'

'It was a legitimate question. He—'

'That lovely little story about pigs isn't a *metaphor*, Sergeant. Mowat's got pig farms all over the North East. If he wanted rid of Simon McLeod, Simon McLeod would disappear.' He dragged his seat belt out and rammed it into the buckle. 'You do not *mess* with that man, understand?'

Logan started the car. 'OK, so he can make people disappear, but maybe he didn't want that? Maybe he left Simon McLeod alive as proof of what happens when you get in his way.'

'Don't be ridiculous.'

'Really?' He pulled away from the kerb, heading back towards the centre of town. 'You said it yourself: Simon McLeod's terrified. *Simon McLeod*. Who else is he going to be scared of?'

'One,' said Finnie, holding up a finger, 'if Wee Hamish wanted to teach the McLeods a lesson we'd never find their bodies. Two: the McLeods and the Mowats go back *two generations*. Wee Hamish lets the boys operate in peace because he had a soft spot for their mum.'

A third finger joined the other two. 'Three: YOU'RE AN IDIOT!' He dropped the hand. 'You're lucky he likes you.'

Somehow Logan didn't feel all that lucky.

27

'Well?' Finnie looked up from his newspaper as Logan climbed back into the car.

'Cheese and pickle, or egg mayonnaise?' At half twelve in the afternoon Victoria Road was more like a slice of southern France than a street in Torry. The warm granite glowed in the sunshine, a pleasant breeze off the North Sea keeping it from getting uncomfortably hot.

'Egg.' The Chief Inspector held out his hand and Logan passed him one of the sandwiches, a packet of pickled onion crisps, and a can of Irn-Bru – the metal surface glistening with dew. 'Thanks.' Finnie broke into the sandwich's plastic triangle case, and chewed in silence for a while, staring down the road at the blue frontage of the Krakow General Store. He swallowed, slurped at his can, then said, 'I meant what I said about Wee Hamish.'

Logan peered suspiciously at the sandwich he was left with – all cheese and no bloody pickle. Which just about summed things up as far as he was concerned. 'If he's so dangerous, why'd we go see him?'

'Because . . . because the world isn't black and white, Sergeant. Sometimes you have to work with shades of grey.'

'Is that what Wee Hamish Mowat is?'

Shrug.

Logan tried his sandwich. It was every bit as dry as it looked. 'Ack. . .'

Finnie smacked the open newspaper with the back of his hand, making it crackle. 'We're getting another bloody golf course. Can you believe they gave Malk the Knife planning permission? Bloody idiots. The whole thing'll be one big money-laundering operation. . .' He took a mouthful of Irn-Bru, swilling it through his teeth as if it was fine wine. 'Mind you, surprised anyone wants to come play golf here these days.'

The DCI stuck the front page under Logan's nose. 'Read that.'

Page one of that morning's *Aberdeen Examiner*: 'STREETS NO LONGER SAFE AS POLICE LOSE CONTROL' with a subheading of 'SERIAL KILLER BLINDING VICTIMS • PAEDOPHILE MISSING • DRUG VIOLENCE WORSE THAN EVER • WOMAN RAPED IN PARK'.

Finnie chewed for a while. 'Imagine what it's going to be like when they find out about all those machine guns. . .'

Logan had one more go at his all-cheese-and-no-pickle. It was still dreadful. He jammed it back in the plastic triangle, crumpled it up, and stuck it on the dashboard. 'You got Kevin Murray to make a statement.'

'It's all a matter of leverage, Sergeant. Soon as he saw our little friend from Manchester outside the interview room he was screwed.'

Logan stared straight ahead through the windscreen. 'What about his kids? His mum? What about—'

'Oh, don't be so melodramatic. Your Manchester hoodies turn up to collect their protection money this afternoon, we arrest them. Parole violations, assault with a deadly weapon, threats against minors, resisting arrest – there's no *way* they're getting bail. So tell me, Sergeant: who's going to hurt Kevin

Murray's children? The *revenge* fairies? Tinkerbell with a grudge? Hmm?'

Logan didn't answer that.

'Exactly.' Finnie ruffled his newspaper back to the sports section.

Logan snapped back into consciousness, sitting bolt-upright in the driver's seat. Blinking. Mouth opening and closing on a taste of stale cheese. 'What? What is it? I'm awake. . .'

Finnie let go of Logan's arm and pointed down Victoria Road. 'There.'

Three men in hooded tops were making a beeline for the Krakow General Store. The Chief Inspector clicked on his Airwave handset as they disappeared inside. 'I want everyone ready to go on my mark. And just in case you're a bit confused, we're not playing *Shoot The Civilian* today. OK? Are we clear?' He glanced at Logan. 'We've already bagged our quota for the year.'

There was a small commotion at the front door of the shop and an old lady was ejected onto the street. She stumbled to a halt on the pavement, turned, and hurled a torrent of abuse back through the door.

One of the hoodies appeared, shoved a bottle of whisky into each of her hands and told her to bugger off.

Finnie was back on the handset again. 'All right, get ready. . .'

Shouting.

And then the cash register flew through the shop window. BANG and the glass was a thousand sparkling shards in the sunshine. CRASH and the register embedded itself in the passenger window of a Citroen. Then the air was sliced to ribbons by the blaring car alarm.

One of the hoodies followed the cash register, head first, landing hard on the pavement.

Finnie shouted 'GO! GO! GO!'

On the opposite side of the street, the back doors of an unmarked Transit Van burst open. Four firearms officers staggered out into the afternoon and lumbered across the road, machine pistols at the ready. After baking for three and a half hours in the back of the van they looked knackered. Being dressed all in black probably wasn't helping.

Logan watched Sergeant Caldwell puff and pant her way to the front, line her team up, and give the signal. They lurched into the Krakow General Store.

'You sure four's enough?'

Finnie climbed out into the sunshine. 'Three hoodies with knives versus four firearms-trained officers with sub-machine-guns. I *think* we'll be OK, don't you?'

The shouting from the shop got even louder. Polish, Mancunian, and over the top, Caldwell yelling, 'ON THE FLOOR! I'M NOT GOING TO TELL YOU AGAIN!'

Logan and Finnie ran for the shop.

28

Logan skittered to a halt on the glass-scattered pavement and peered in through the smashed window. The little shop was full of struggling bodies, flying fists, pushing, shoving, and foul language. Mr Wojewódzki was slumped back against the wall, staring down at his stomach and the knife handle sticking out of it. Bright red spreading across his white shirt.

Four firearms officers, two hoodies . . . and two unidentified men.

One was small and wiry, banging a hoodie's head off the counter, blood and chunky KitKats falling on the linoleum. The other man was huge: at least six foot two, broad as he was tall, with a haircut that could only be described as a receding mullet. For a moment Logan thought they might be customers caught up in the fighting, and then he saw the gun. It was a semiautomatic pistol – large, chunky and black – clutched in the big man's hand.

Half of the firearms team were on the ground, struggling with the hoodie who'd slashed Kevin Murray's face, but the two remaining officers had their submachine guns pointing at Mr Mullet's forehead. Sergeant Caldwell yelled over the screeching car alarm, 'DON'T MAKE ME SHOOT YOU!'

The big man sneered. *'Nie wierzę w to. . .'* and then he was glaring at the bleeding shopkeeper, *'Okłamałeś mnie!'*

'PUT THE GUN DOWN!'

'Nie rozśmieszaj mnie.'

'I'M NOT TELLING YOU AGAIN: PUT THE GUN—' She never got any further, because the small, wiry man dropped the hoodie he'd been battering off the countertop, grabbed a bottle of Grass Vodka and smashed it into her face. BANG. The bottle cracked the safety goggles, broke her nose, then shattered against the edges of her helmet. Glass and liquid went everywhere.

Caldwell staggered, slipped and went crashing down onto the shop floor in a slick of blood and vodka.

Her colleague only looked around for a fraction of a second, but that was enough. Mr Mullet lunged, shoved the submachine gun out of the way, and jammed his semiautomatic up under the officer's chin.

'Oh Jesus. . .'

Logan stepped over the hoodie groaning on the pavement, and kicked the door open. The big man swung the gun round.

BOOOM!

Logan dived to the ground and the glazed door exploded in a shower of safety glass behind him.

Nobody moved.

The firearms officer brought his MP5 up again . . . then screamed, blood spurting from a jagged slash in his face. The small, wiry man had stabbed him with the broken end of the vodka bottle. The officer let go of the submachine gun and clutched at his cheek. Bright red spattered all around him.

Mr Mullet yanked open a door at the back of the shop and barged through. His partner leapt the counter and followed, slamming the door behind him.

Finnie shouted at the two officers still struggling with Hoodie Number One on the floor: 'What the *hell* are you doing? Go after them!'

They let go of their prisoner.

Mistake.

Hoodie Number One snapped an elbow into one officer's face and kneed the other in the balls, then ran for it. He leapt through the shattered shop window, landed on the glass-strewn pavement, scrambled over the Citroen with the blaring car alarm, and sprinted out onto the road. Arms and legs pumping like a gold medal athlete. A huge truck slammed on its air-brakes, shuddering and hissing to a halt on the hot tarmac, missing him by less than six inches.

Logan scrambled to his feet and ran for the door behind the counter. Just in time to hear something go, *snickt*. The handle wouldn't budge.

Finnie stormed into the shop. 'Get that bloody thing open!'

'It's locked.'

'Then kick it in!'

BOOM – Logan slammed his foot into the woodwork just beside the lock. Nothing. BOOM – again. BOOM – the whole door rattled on its hinges, but stayed resolutely shut. 'It's not moving. . .' One more go: BOOM. This time there was the groan and creak of splintering wood.

Behind him, Logan could hear Finnie ordering someone to chase the disappearing hoodie.

Last time: BOOM. The door flew open and Logan staggered into a long corridor lined with boxes and crates filled with Polish jars, bottles and tins. A fire exit lay open at the far end.

He took two steps, stopped, then hurried back into the shop.

Finnie stared at him. 'What the hell are you—'

'Gun.' Logan grabbed the stabbed officer's Heckler & Koch

MP5, and ran back through the door, down the corridor and out onto a short flight of stairs. It overlooked a large back garden festooned with washing hanging from lines that criss-crossed back and forth between the eight-foot-high walls. A collection of outbuildings lay down one side, leading to an old washhouse with cobwebbed windows.

No sign of the two men.

He hurried down the stairs and out onto the grass, ducking beneath a batch of assorted ladies' underwear. With all the clothes and sheets, it was impossible to see more than four feet ahead. He ducked down and scanned the grass below the washing, looking for feet and legs. Still nothing.

How was he supposed to. . . Logan froze.

The sound of puffing and groaning came from behind him, getting louder. He span around, snapping the submachine gun up to his shoulder, just in time to see a grim-faced firearms officer limping down the stairs. He had his gun in one hand and his groin in the other, teeth gritted as he picked his way across the grass.

'Are you OK?'

The officer grimaced. 'Right in the bloody balls. . .'

There was a clang, and what sounded like Polish swearing, somewhere down at the far end of the garden. Logan shoved his way through jeans and towels, enveloped in the plastic-floral smell of fabric softener. But by the time he'd reached the bottom of the garden, there was no one there.

'Sodding hell!'

Maybe they'd doubled back, or were hiding in one of the sheds, or—

Next door, someone screamed.

'How did they get. . .' Logan drifted to a halt, staring at the old washhouse. The roof slates were covered in a thin layer of green and grey moss, except for a line of scuff marks that stood out dark grey in the sunlight.

The firearms officer limped up next to him. 'What are we—'

'Give me a boost.' Logan waved him over, then stepped into his cupped hands, using the leg-up to clamber onto the sloping roof. From there he could see into next door's garden.

A woman was hunched up on a sun-lounger, towel clutched over her naked chest. 'Bugger off, you dirty bastards!'

Mr Mullet and his friend were already scrambling over the wall on the far side into the street beyond.

'Damn it.'

'What? What's happening? Help me up!'

Logan didn't. He ran up the roof, and jumped off, landing in a small vegetable patch. He fought his way through the purple sprouting broccoli, then ran across the garden. Behind him, he could hear the firearms officer swearing his way up onto the washhouse roof.

The wall on the far side was only six foot. Logan jumped, got his elbows over and hauled himself up as the firearms officer crashed head-first into a steaming compost heap. 'Aaaagh!'

Logan dropped onto the pavement.

He was on Grampian Road: parked cars, trees covered in emerald leaves, four-storey granite tenements with identical gardens of sun-wilted grass. The looming bulk of Sacred Heart Catholic Church sat in the background, still covered in scaffolding.

The street wasn't busy, just an old man walking his dog, a young woman with a pushchair, and a blond-haired kid on a skateboard.

And there – running across the road – the two men from the shop.

Logan yelled, 'STOP, POLICE! *POLICJA!* UNDERSTAND?'

It didn't work. It *never* worked.

Logan ran after them, bringing his borrowed Heckler & Koch MP5 up to his shoulder. 'HALT, OR I *WILL* SHOOT!'

The small wiry one yanked open the driver's door of a battered Mini Cooper and leapt inside. Mr Mullet spun round, his gun pointing directly at Logan's face.

Logan shot him.

Or tried to.

The MP5 just went 'click'.

'Bloody hell!'

Mr Mullet didn't have the same problem. His pistol worked: the bullet ricocheted off the roof of a Fiat Punto three feet from Logan's head.

The woman with the pushchair grabbed her child and ran for the nearest building. The old man hid behind a rusty four-by-four. But the boy on the skateboard just trundled slowly down the middle of the road, staring, mouth hanging open.

There was a grunt and the firearms officer clattered onto the pavement beside Logan. He stank, eggshells and rotten vegetables smeared all over his back and trousers. Another bullet clanged into the Punto.

The officer returned fire, but Mr Mullet was already clambering into the passenger seat. The Mini roared away from the kerb, leaving a cloud of vaporized rubber behind.

'SHOOT THE TYRES!'

They ran out into the road, Logan fumbling with the breech bolt on his MP5, trying to eject the jammed round, while the officer let off two more shots. Both slammed into the car's boot as it accelerated away.

The Mini was heading straight for the boy on the skateboard.

At the last moment it swerved around him, close enough to make his red tracksuit flap as it passed. He turned to watch it, slack-jawed.

The firearms officer said, 'Bugger this. . .' and thumbed his MP5 onto automatic. BRRRRRRRRRRT. Brass shell casings cascaded onto the street as bullets pinged and clanged into the Mini's boot. Logan lunged, slapping the barrel up.

Silence. Now the only noise was the squealing of tyres as the car fishtailed around the corner onto Glenbevie Road and then it was gone.

The firearms officer turned on him. 'What the hell did you do that for?'

'You've got your gun on automatic, outside, with bloody civilians in the line of fire! What is *wrong* with you?'

'Wrong with me? *You're* the one who let them get away!'

29

The first ambulance roared away from the Krakow General Store, lights flashing as the driver raced to Accident and Emergency. The second ambulance followed thirty seconds later, the wail of the sirens fading into the distance.

Two patrol cars sat on the other side of the road, flickering lights barely visible in the sunny afternoon. A couple of uniforms were making a cordon around the scene, stretching a roll of blue-and-white 'POLICE' tape along a perimeter of orange traffic cones, shutting off this side of the road.

What a disaster. . .

Logan turned away from the shattered shop window.

The place was a mess of broken glass, bloodstains, and overturned display stands – boxes of Eastern European corn-flakes swelling up in a puddle of dark red.

Finnie slapped his hand over the mouthpiece of his phone and scowled at Logan. 'Well?'

'Shopkeeper's touch and go: lost a lot of blood, but if they can get him into surgery . . . maybe. Both hoodies have concussion and one's—'

'Do I *look* like I care about the hoodies? What about the bloody firearms team?'

'Oh . . . right. Sergeant Caldwell's nose is broken, but other than that she's OK. Banks isn't so good. Paramedic says he's going to need a hell of a lot of stitches, probably a skin graft. He's lucky the broken bottle didn't go in half an inch lower or it would've punctured the carotid.'

Finnie swore and kicked a pack of toilet roll the length of the shop. 'It's a bloody cock-up! Go on then,' he pointed at Logan, 'go on, *say* it.'

'Say what?'

'"Told you so." I should've got a bigger firearms team. Should've had uniform backup. Should've set up a bloody cordon to stop the bastards getting away.' A packet of biscuits followed the toilet paper, crunching against the far wall. 'But *no*, I had to play it low key.' He looked around for something else to kick.

'How were we to know there'd be guns? It was only supposed to be three hoodies from Manchester, we couldn't—'

'Oh, really? *Couldn't* we? You said the shopkeeper was already paying for protection: so what *exactly* did you think he was going to do when someone came in and smashed up the place: bake them a cake? What's the point of paying for protection if you don't use it?'

Finnie sent a box of herbal toothpaste flying. Then went back to his phone call. 'Hello? Hello? Of course I'm still here, what did you think: I was *abducted* by aliens?'

Logan left him haranguing whoever was on the other end of the phone, and returned to the shattered window.

A black-clad figure was wheezing its way up Victoria Road, helmet clutched in one hand, face bright red and dripping with sweat. The firearms officer Finnie had sent after Hoodie Number One.

The officer staggered to a halt outside the Krakow General Store and collapsed against the wall. 'Ah . . . Jesus. . .' Puff.

Pant. He dragged out a handkerchief and scraped it across his glistening forehead.

Logan looked around, but there was no sign of Hoodie Number One. '*Please* tell me you didn't let him get away.'

'I didn't . . . I didn't let anyone . . . anything. . .'

'How could you let him get away?'

'He . . . he was . . . he was wearing trainers. . .'

'Oh you're. . .' Logan closed his eyes and swore. 'Trainers? That's it? He was wearing *trainers*?'

The firearms officer slapped his bullet-proof vest, jiggled his Heckler & Koch MP5 submachine gun. 'You got any . . . any idea . . . how much this . . . crap . . . weighs?' Wheeze, cough. He waved his helmet in Logan's face. 'And it's all black! I'm . . . sodding melting here. . .'

'Oh . . . bloody hell.' Logan grabbed a bottle of Polish mineral water from the upturned chiller cabinet and handed it to the sweaty officer. 'Here.'

The man unscrewed the top and drank deep.

'Better?'

'The little sod disappeared on Abbey Place – tried to follow him, but there was no sign. Must be miles away by now.'

Logan glanced back at Finnie; the DCI was still on the phone, moaning about how long it was going to take the Identification Bureau to get its grubby Transit Van up here. Then he snapped his mobile shut, and Logan gave him the bad news.

Finnie kicked a packet of washing powder. 'Why am I surrounded by morons? Did I tick the wrong bloody box for room service? I *wanted* scrambled eggs on toast, but they delivered a family-sized bag of *idiots*!'

The firearms officer threw his empty plastic bottle on the floor. 'It wasn't my fault! He was—'

'Why the hell didn't you just shoot him?'

'I—'

'Do you think we give you lot guns for a *laugh*? And you,' Finnie jabbed a finger in Logan's direction, 'why did I hear automatic fire from your team?'

Logan nodded at the officer who'd accompanied him on the chase. 'Ask Rambo here.'

'Yeah?' The constable stuck out his chest. 'At least I managed to get a shot off. Unlike *some* people.'

'My gun was jammed!'

'Your head was jammed. Jammed right up your arse!'

Finnie threw his hands in the air. 'ENOUGH!'

Silence.

'And what *exactly* do we have to show for this afternoon's little fiasco? Two officers in hospital; one shopkeeper with a knife in his belly; two hoodies I can't question because they've got concussion; and you. . .' Finnie's whole face twitched. 'You useless bunch of *pricks* let everyone else get away!'

No one would look him in the eye.

The DCI pointed at the shop door. 'Get out of my sight.' But when Logan made a move Finnie grabbed him. 'I'm not finished with you yet.'

The two firearms officers sloped out of the shop, across the road, and back to their unmarked Transit Van. A seagull had decorated the windscreen. So Finnie wasn't the only one shitting on them from a great height.

As the van pulled away, the Chief Inspector sank back against the counter and folded his arms. 'I expected better of you, McRae.'

'And what *exactly* was I supposed to do?'

'Shoot the bad guys! Why is that concept so difficult to understand?'

'There was a kid in the line of fire. Can you imagine what the press would do to us if he'd got hit by accident?'

Finnie opened and closed his mouth a couple of times.

'Fair point.' He scuffed the toe of his shoe through a small drift of washing powder. 'Going to be bad enough as it is. . .' A look of hope flickered across his face. 'Don't suppose you're still friends with that journalist scumbag?'

Logan shook his head. 'They're on holiday: three weeks in the Maldives. I'm watering the plants.'

The hopeful look vanished. 'Then we're buggered.'

30

Back at the station things didn't get any better. Half an hour after returning from the crime scene, Logan was summoned by Professional Standards. He sat outside Superintendent Napier's office on a squeaky orange plastic seat, chewing at the inside of his cheek. Wondering how on earth he could put a positive spin on events.

At least no one got shot this time. Maybe he could—

His phone went into a fit of electronic apoplexy and he dragged it out. Frowned at the number. Then answered it. 'McRae?'

'Hello? Yes, right: you said I should call if anything came up?'

Logan frowned. 'I did?'

'Father John Burnett? Used to be at Sacred Heart, now helping out at Saint Peter's in the Castlegate? I've been worrying about your eternal soul.'

Oh God.

'That's very kind of you, Father, but I really don't—'

'I think you should come to confession.'

'But I'm not a Catholic, I—'

'Now would be a really *good time, Sergeant. Trust me. . .'*

* * *

Logan loitered in the day chapel, examining a stained-glass interpretation of Aberdeen's patron saints – most of whom now had a shopping centre named after them – while he waited for the handful of people to filter out from Thursday evening Mass. His mobile had gone off twice already, Inspector Napier's depressingly familiar number appearing on the screen. Probably wanting to know why Logan wasn't sitting outside the Professional Standards office, waiting to be shouted at.

Logan switched the thing off and dropped it in his pocket.

One wall of the day chapel was panelled in dark wood to about waist height, with lancet windows of clear glass above, and from here he could see straight into the main body of the church. An altar sat at the far end, in front of an ornately carved structure of gold-encrusted mahogany, spotlit against the plain white walls.

The three banks of pews might sit four hundred but right now they were mostly empty. A grey-haired man sat in the centre row, head bowed in prayer, while Father Burnett and a little old lady sat off to one side. She was dressed in a thick winter jacket and woolly hat, even though it had to be at least twenty degrees outside, her hands working their way around a string of prayer beads.

Finally the priest rose and made a religious-looking hand gesture. He was wearing a white robe, with what looked like a big inverted CND symbol on the front in red. Very fancy. He helped the little old lady to her feet. She patted his arm, then crabbed her way along the pews, bent nearly double under the weight of a Punch-and-Judy hump.

Logan stepped through the door and into the body of the church.

He passed the little old lady as she reached the aisle and

started to shuffle towards the exit. She had the sour smell that came with clothes left in the washing machine for too long.

Father Burnett stuck out his hand and Logan wasn't sure if he was supposed to shake it or kiss it. He went for the former. 'Thought you said they were packed to the rafters?'

The priest shrugged. 'Come back tomorrow. Today's Mass is always in English, so we don't get many Poles. Just the regulars, like Gladys.' He pointed at the old lady lumbering slowly down the apse. 'Poor old dear. . .' He sniffed.

'So . . . why the sudden interest in my soul?'

Father Burnett pulled out a pair of wire-rimmed glasses, polished them on the hem of his vestments, then popped them on. 'I want you to meet someone.' He led Logan across to the centre bank of pews, then stood there until the man with the grey hair looked up. 'Sorry to disturb your devotions, Marek, but this is Detective Sergeant Logan McRae.'

The man stood, a crooked-teeth smile just visible through his thick grey moustache. 'Please to meet you, Sergeant.'

Logan looked at the priest, then back at the old man. 'Er, likewise. I mean, *dzień dobry*.'

'I was asking Marek here if anyone had complained of being attacked, or abused recently.'

Marek nodded. '*Tak*: yes, there is man, tall with red hair and. . .' He frowned at Father Burnett. 'What is "*piegie*"?'

'Freckles.'

'Yes, is red hair and freckles. He wait outside after Mass sometimes, follow people home. I know one man who chase him away. Punched him on nose. He has not been back since this.'

Logan got him to give a full description, copying it down

into his notebook. 'OK, well, I'll need you to come down to the station and we'll do an e-fit, so—'

'And there is other man, who is sing in pub on machine?' The old man checked with the priest again. 'What is word?'

'Karaoke.'

'Oh . . . is same in Polish. Anyway, Karaoke man like to cause fight. Many, many people. Very drunk.'

Logan made another note. 'So he's—'

'Then is woman who work in shop for coffee. We know she spit in our drinks. We complain but no one does anything.'

'Really? Are you sure she's actually—'

'Then is taxi driver who will not take Polish people. Says we are filthy. We drink too much and make sick in his car.' Marek pulled a sheet of paper from his inside pocket. 'There are others. I make list.'

'Ah, right. . .' Logan took it. 'Thanks.'

Marek shrugged. 'If I can help, is good.'

The priest gave the old man's shoulder a squeeze. 'Thank you Marek, you've been a great help.' And then the two of them shared an exchange in Polish, ending with what sounded like a dirty joke.

The priest stood and watched the old man leave, still chuckling. Logan scanned the list of locals who didn't like Polish people. There was a depressingly large number of them.

'This is going to take forever.'

'Not exactly welcoming is it?' Father Burnett wandered over to a small door in the apse of the church. It opened on a little room with a threadbare burgundy carpet, a safe, an old kitchen table, and a rickety wardrobe. The priest pulled his vestments over his head and hung them up. 'You asked if anyone had stopped coming to Mass. Well, I couldn't think of anyone off the top of my head. It wasn't until I spoke to Marek that I remembered.'

He closed the wardrobe door. 'Once upon a time, about twenty years ago, there was a man called Daniel Gilchrist. Daniel worked in the fish. He wasn't a particularly nice man: he drank too much, and was occasionally a bit free with his affections and his fists, but he came to church every Sunday with his wife and son.'

'This isn't going to be one of those stories where you say it reminds you a bit of Jesus, is it?'

'Daniel got cancer and had to stop working on the boats. By the time he died there was nothing left but bitterness, and tumours. I administered the last rites.'

Logan leant against the wall. 'Then I think we can safely eliminate him from our enquiries.'

'His son kept up the family tradition. Every Sunday he'd be there at Sacred Heart with his mother.' Father Burnett picked up a big spiky gold and silver thing – like a sunburst topped with a cross – from the table and wrapped it in a silk cloth. 'Of course, I went off to Poland for a few years, but when I got back, there he was: still at his mother's side, every Sunday. Then one day he just stopped coming.' The priest opened the safe and slid the bundle inside, then locked it. 'I think his mother fell ill, or something. Haven't seen her since.'

'That's nice.' Logan took another run through Marek's list. Probably best to start with the complaints of actual violence: get a team to identify the individuals and haul them in for questioning. Poke into their backgrounds.

'Daniel's son has red hair and freckles.'

Who knew there would be so many racist shitheads in Aberdeen? 'Can't really arrest him for that.'

'He's the one who was following people home after Mass.'

And now Father Burnett had Logan's undivided attention. 'When did he stop coming to church?'

'Six months ago. Not long before we closed Sacred Heart for refurbishment.'

Right about the time the Oedipus letters started.

31

Logan listened to Finnie's mobile bleeping over to voicemail. He left a message as he marched across the Castlegate, making for FHQ. He tried the DCI's office phone instead. No luck there either. According to the clock, perched high on the Town House tower, it was nearly half past six. By now the dayshift had been over for almost ninety minutes, and given the afternoon's fiasco at the Krakow General Store, Finnie had probably given up and gone home.

Or to the nearest pub. He'd been first in with Superintendent Napier and the other trolls from Professional Standards. God knew Logan would have needed a stiff drink after that.

Maybe he should phone Pirie?

But that DI's position was coming up and it might not be a good idea to share the credit with someone after the same promotion. Assuming it wasn't all just a waste of time. So he gave DI Steel a call. Let it ring three times. Changed his mind and hung up.

Finnie wanted initiative. Logan could do initiative.

He hurried back to Force Headquarters.

Big Gary was on the front desk, chewing on a blue biro

as he perused the duty roster. 'Sodding sod-monkeys of Sod. . .' He scribbled something in the book, then looked up to see Logan. 'Oh no: tell me you're just back because you forgot to sign out!'

'I need a couple of uniform, got anyone spare?'

The huge sergeant rolled his eyes. 'You got any idea what you're doing to my overtime calculations? I'm supposed to be—'

'Rennie'll do if he's about.'

'No. You can't have anyone. We're throwing a surprise party for some Yardies later, I need everyone making paper streamers and blowing up balloons.'

'Come on, Gary. Just one. Don't care who it is, as long as they can walk, talk, and chew gum at the same time.'

'All three at once?' His eyebrows shot up. 'Jesus, you're not asking for much, are you?'

'An hour. Two, tops.' Logan put on his best lost puppy face. 'Please?'

The big man sighed, his huge shoulders rising and falling, making his white shirt creak at the buttons. 'All right, all right. You can have Guthrie. Just try to bring him back in one piece this time, OK?'

'Cheers.' Logan gave the reception area a shifty once over. PC Karim's favourite tramp, Dirty Bob, was slumped in one of the corner seats fast asleep, a line of dribble disappearing into a thick mat of bushy black beard. Other than that they were alone. 'You heard anything about this DI's position coming up?'

Big Gary scribbled something down in the roster. 'Think you're in with a chance, do you?'

'Might be.'

'With *your* reputation?'

'Oh ha, ha. Come on, what've you heard?'

The sergeant leant across the desk, a roll of stomach

annexing one corner of the day book. 'Pirie's odds on favourite, if you fancy a flutter? Or I can give you two to one on Beattie?'

Logan wasn't about to throw his money away. DS Beattie had more chance of being elected Miss World than making Detective Inspector. 'What about me?'

'Eighteen to one.'

Logan pushed away from the reception desk. 'You're all a bunch of bastards, you know that?'

'We do our best.'

Guthrie poked his head over the balustrade and peered down at a bicycle chained up at the bottom of the stairwell. 'How far you think it is?' he asked. His voice still had a slightly bunged-up edge to it, but at least they'd taken the staple out of his nose. 'Fifty feet? Sixty?'

He howched, then spat. Watching the drop dwindle in size.

Logan told him to stop spitting on other people's bicycles.

'Was just checking.'

'Well, just don't.' Logan made sure they had the right address. A top-floor flat in a little block on Balnagask Road, part of a group of seven identical buildings overlooking off-green playing fields, East Tullos Industrial Estate, and the bracken-covered hill behind it.

They'd sneaked into the block using the services button, convincing a pregnant woman with a sticky child that they were there to check the fire extinguishers.

Guthrie took one more peek over the handrail. 'You sure we shouldn't have a warrant? Armed backup? That kind of thing?'

'We're just going to ask a few questions.' Logan pressed the bell. Nothing seemed to happen. 'Besides, all we're doing is following up a lead.' And there was no way they'd have given him a firearms team after this afternoon's disastrous showing at the Krakow General Store.

Someone downstairs was listening to *EastEnders*: cockney accents drifting up the stairwell. The window-ledges were covered in drifts of junk mail advertising Stanna Stairlifts, over-fifties' life insurance, and things to help you get in and out of the bath.

Logan tried the bell again.

Still nothing.

Guthrie said, 'Maybe he's not in? We could—'

'Shhhhh!' Logan held up a finger. He stuck his ear to the door and after a short pause, the constable did the same. There was music playing inside, something with too much bass and not enough melody. The two of them stood like that for about a minute, and then a loud voice behind Logan made him jump.

'Can I help you?'

He scrambled round to see a woman in her mid-fifties, hair dyed a fiery orange, greying at the roots and thinning at the crown. She was weighed down with shopping bags.

'We . . . tried the bell,' Logan pointed at it.

'The bell doesn't work.' It was almost a shout. She looked them up and down, paying particular attention to PC Guthrie in his black uniform. 'Are you Jehovah's Witnesses, then?'

'Er . . . no. We're police officers.'

'We've not had Jehovah's Witnesses for ages. I think our Daniel scares them off. Of course, he's dead now, but he wouldn't let a little thing like that stop him.' She rummaged in her handbag and produced a big bunch of keys, working her way through them until she found one that fitted in the front door lock. 'Here we go.'

The door opened on a small hallway. A rack full of fleeces and coats, an umbrella stand with three golf clubs in it.

A picture of the Virgin Mary. One door led off to a bathroom, drowning in pink, the other through to a small kitchen/living room.

The music was louder now. *Bmm-tchhh, bmmm-tchhhhh, bmmmm-tchhh. . .*

Logan watched her heft a collection of carrier bags up onto the working surfaces. 'Mrs Gilchrist, we'd like a word with your son, if that's OK?' Pause. 'Mrs Gilchrist?'

She was busy stacking tins of sweetcorn into a cupboard.

Logan tapped her on the shoulder. 'Mrs Gilchrist?'

She jumped. Turned. Stared at him for a moment. 'Do I know you? How did you get into my house?'

'You let us in, just a minute ago? Remember? You thought we were Jehovah's Witnesses?'

She smiled. 'We've not had Jehovah's Witnesses for ages. I think our Daniel scares them off. Of course, he's dead now, but he wouldn't let a little thing like that stop him.' She nodded towards a framed portrait on the windowsill, of a stern-faced man with eyes like cigarette burns. 'Sometimes he comes to the shops with me.'

Logan's gaze drifted past the portrait to the view beyond. From here you could see the boxy houses on Burnbank Place. He scanned the rows until he found the one with a skip outside it, where Doc Fraser had done a living post mortem on one of the Oedipus victims. 'We need to speak to your son, Mrs Gilchrist.'

She looked blank for a moment. 'Sorry, I'm a bit deaf. "Deaf and daft," my Daniel used to say. He's dead now.' She pulled a clunky beige hearing aid from a kitchen drawer and waggled it at them. 'Would you like a cup of tea? Jehovah's Witnesses are allowed tea, aren't they?'

'We're not. . .' Logan stopped. 'Yes, we'd love one, thanks.'

'That's nice.' She smiled. 'We've not had Jehovah's Witnesses for ages. I think our Daniel scares them off.'

'Can we speak to your son, Mrs Gilchrist?'

'Of course he's dead now. Got the cancer, didn't he? Terrible shame. . . He was always such a sweet man.'

'Your son, Mrs Gilchrist?'

'Hmm? Ricky?' She seemed to stare at them from very far away. 'Oh, he'll be in his room.' She pointed at a door with a little skull-and-crossbones sticker on it. 'Would you like some tea?'

Logan tried the handle – it wasn't locked. The door opened on a dingy little bedroom. The curtains were closed, but a huge television set cast a flickering pink glow over the debris-strewn room: unwashed plates; piles of dirty washing; a small stack of newspapers; some lad-mags; a laptop, monitor and printer. A CD player on a bookshelf thumping out what could almost pass for music.

The occupant, Ricky Gilchrist, was slumped on a beanbag in front of the telly, earphones on, trousers round his ankles, hammering away one-handed at his erection.

There was a light switch beside the door. Logan flicked it on and brilliant white filled the room, followed a heartbeat later by screaming as Ricky exploded out of his beanbag and tried to cover the enormous television screen with his half naked body. His skin was the colour of yoghurt, sprinkled with dark red freckles, ribs clearly visible. He fumbled for his trousers, shouting, 'Jesus, Mum, you're not *allowed* in here!'

Logan pulled out his warrant card. 'Jehovah's Witnesses: we understand you might be having improper thoughts.'

Ricky span around, cock bobbing in the breeze, framed in a bramble patch of orange pubes. 'You . . . what . . . NO!' He covered himself up, still standing in front of the television. Then pulled off his headphones. 'You can't come in here, you've got no right!'

'Detective Sergeant Logan McRae, Grampian Police.' Logan

tried not to watch as Ricky did up his flies. 'I won't shake hands, if it's all the same to you.'

A blush turned Ricky's pale skin hot pink. 'It's not illegal, OK? It's personal. . . Privacy of your own home. . . I'll sue.'

'Yeah, let's all go to court and you can tell the jury how we barged in on you playing with yourself. That'll do your reputation the world of good.' He leant against the door-frame. 'I hear you've been harassing members of the Polish community, Ricky. Following them home from Mass. Making a nuisance of yourself.'

The young man pulled a T-shirt on over his scrawny chest. 'They're liars. They're all bloody liars. Look.' He pointed at his face, where the last hint of a black eye was slowly fading. 'They hit me. I was assaulted. I should press charges!'

But Logan wasn't listening any more: when Ricky bent over to pick up the T-shirt, Logan had got a clear view of the TV screen. It was Krystka Gorzałkowska, the woman Guthrie had accidentally shot. She was on her knees, biting her lip, trying not to cry out, tears running down her face as the two men behind her kept on going. Krystka was naked, but the men wore cheap plastic Halloween masks – a bulldog and an Alsatian.

Logan grabbed the headphone cable and yanked it out of the socket.

'Hey, you can't just—'

A man's voice boomed out of the television's speakers: *'You like that, don't you bitch? Eh?'* A slap. *'That's right, take it you dirty whore!'*

Krystka let out a sob, but that only seemed to excite them even more. *'Yeah, you fucking love it! Say it, bitch! SAY IT!'*

'Where did you get this?'

Ricky fumbled for the remote control and the screen went black. 'Just a bit of fun, OK? It's private. You can't just—'

Logan shoved him hard, and Ricky fell back into the

beanbag. 'She's being raped! Think that's "just a bit of fun"? Do you?'

Ricky looked away, his voice barely audible over the music. 'Fucking Polish bitch deserves it, doesn't she?'

Logan closed his eyes and tried really hard not to cross the room and smack the living hell out of him. Instead he turned his back, and stared at the laptop in the corner. There was a collage of newspaper articles pinned to the wall behind it, all about the Oedipus case. Newsprint pictures from the *Aberdeen Examiner* of the victims, their eyes scribbled out in angry red biro. 'You don't like Polish people, do you, Ricky?'

No reply, just the thump-thump-thump of another dreadful song. Logan switched the CD off, then walked over to the television. A DVD player sat on top of it, covered in a thick layer of dusty grey fluff. Logan pressed eject and a shiny home-recorded disc slid out. The kind you could buy blank in any supermarket. A laserprinted label read, 'KRYSTKA GET'S F*CK~D DIRTY 3-WAY!!!*!'

'Where did you get this?'

'I didn't do anything.'

Logan pulled on a pair of latex gloves, then slid the DVD into an evidence pouch. 'We know, Ricky.'

There was a long pause. And then the pale man said, 'They're animals. They roam the streets, marking their territory. Worse than dogs. Someone had to do something.'

Logan nodded. 'I want you to come down the station with me, Ricky.'

'Someone had to make the streets safe.' He levered himself out of the beanbag. 'Someone had to make them pay.'

'Are you going to come quietly?'

'Do I need a lawyer? I don't have a lawyer.'

'You're not under arrest, you're coming down to the station voluntarily.'

'Oh . . .' He seemed to think about it for a minute. 'I did it. All of it.' He stuck his hands out, wrists together, waiting for the cuffs. 'I cut their eyes out. It's me. I'm Oedipus. I did it because *you* wouldn't.'

32

By the time Logan had processed Ricky Gilchrist – photos, fingerprints, and DNA swab – the news was all over the station. A handful of uniform and CID loitered in the corridor, watching as Logan led him into interview room two.

An hour later there was a knock on the door, then a custody assistant stuck her head in and said someone needed to have a word with DS McRae.

Logan got PC Guthrie to suspend the interview. Gilchrist didn't even look up, just kept on going with his manifesto for a Polish-free Aberdeen.

Out in the corridor the custody assistant nodded down the hall towards the observation suite. 'He's in there.'

It was DCI Finnie, hunched over the tiny monitor connected up to the cameras in room two. Whoever had called it the 'Observation Suite' had a twisted sense of humour. It was a cramped little place, with bare breezeblock walls, a kitchen-worktop desk, two rickety plastic chairs, and a TV screen for each interview room.

Normally it smelt of armpits and stale socks, but tonight it reeked of second-hand alcohol. All of it coming from

Detective Chief Inspector Finnie. He looked up at Logan, then patted the plastic chair next to him.

Logan sat. 'Sir, I tried calling you, but—'

Finnie held up a hand. 'I know, I know. Had my phone switched off while I was in with Professional Standards.' The words rolled out on a cloud of whisky. 'Bastard rubber-heelers had me in there for three hours. But you did it!' He grinned and slapped Logan on the back. 'You did it. You got him.'

'I really did try—'

'Nonsense. Credit where it's due. You did good. You went out there and you got him! I was on the case for *months* and never even got close. But you, you turn up and POW!' He banged his hand on the working surface, making the picture on the monitor jiggle. Ricky Gilchrist was still at it, babbling away about how Aberdeen had been ruined. 'See – *this* is why I brought you on board.'

Finnie jabbed the grainy image with a thumb, as if he were squashing a bug. 'He cop for the lot?'

'Everything. All the victims, and all the notes. Showed us the original files on his computer. Goulding was right, he wanted us to catch him, and now we have he's Captain Cooperation.'

'Good work. No, really, I mean it: *excellent* work. I'd sit in on the interview, but I've been drinking.' He leant in close, and Logan tried hard not to recoil. 'Just between you and me,' he whispered, 'the guy who replaced DI Insch is going off on the stress. Can't cope with the pace. We're going to promote someone.' He slapped Logan on the back again. 'There's no way they can overlook you this time. Not after this.'

The DCI wrapped an arm around Logan's shoulders and gave him a shoogle. 'You and me, we're going to go through that CID Department and drag it up by its Y-fronts!'

Which was a lovely image.

* * *

By the time Logan staggered back to his flat it was nearly midnight. He locked the front door, kicked off his shoes on the way to the toilet, did his teeth then dragged himself through to the bedroom. He didn't bother switching on the light: the room was a pigsty anyway. A mess of boxes and things from the lounge, all waiting for him to finish decorating so they could go back where they belonged.

He stripped, chucking his clothes on the chair in the corner, then crawled into bed and went, 'WHAT THE HELL?'

'Mmmph?'

He scrambled for the bedside light, and *click*: Samantha's face appeared in the bed beside him. She hadn't taken her makeup off, and the white face powder was all smudged into the black eyeliner and dark purple lipstick.

'What are you doing here?'

She blinked, sat up, and the covers fell away, exposing a black-and-white striped corset. The duvet was covered in rose petals. 'Where am. . .? What time is it?'

'How did you get in?'

'Wanted to surprise you. There was champagne, but I drunk it.' She yawned, exposing her fillings. 'Urgh . . . ooh, need to pee.'

'The door was locked. I'm *sure* I locked it.'

'Give us a minute.' She hauled herself out of bed, and tottered off to the bathroom on what looked like very high-heeled kinky boots.

Logan slumped back, hands over his face, trying not to listen as she filled, then flushed the toilet. She was back ten minutes later with two tumblers full of dark brown liquid and chinking ice cubes. Makeup perfect once more, like a dead Barbie doll, tattoos standing out against her pale white skin.

'Here.' She handed him a glass.

Logan took a sip: Jack Daniels and Coke.

'Best I could do at short notice.' She put one high-heeled foot up on the bed, next to him. 'It's your lucky night, Sergeant McRae: I finished fingerprinting all those sodding guns today, and now I'm in the mood to *celebrate*.'

'But how did you get in?'

'Picked the lock. One of my many talents.' She took the drink from his hands and pushed him back on the pillow. 'Want to see another one?' She popped an ice cube in her mouth, then kissed her way down his neck and chest. Running the cold tip of her tongue over each of the little ribbons of scar tissue that crisscrossed his stomach. 'They taste of iron filings.'

Logan frowned. 'Sam, I've been on duty since seven, I'm knackered. Can we not . . . ooh.'

She'd moved further south. And suddenly Logan wasn't so tired anymore.

33

It was a strange start to the day – at 07:00 Logan was dragged into Professional Standards for what amounted to a bollocking over yesterday's live fire incident at the Krakow General Store, and at 07:30 he was in the Chief Constable's office getting a pat on the back.

'Excellent work.' Chief Constable Brian Anderson, AKA: Baldy Brian, stood with his back to the room, staring out through a picture window at his domain. Early-morning sunlight sparkled back from granite walls and slate roofs as Scotland's third-largest city geared itself up for another day. 'Isn't it excellent, Finnie?'

The DCI passed Logan a copy of that morning's *Aberdeen Examiner*: 'POLICE CATCH OEDIPUS – POLISH COMMUNITY SAFE AT LAST'.

Finnie sniffed. 'Could have done without that "at last" bit, but it's a big improvement on the kicking we've been getting.'

The Chief Constable bounced on the balls of his feet. 'Indeed. And it's not just the local press who've picked it up. We made front page of the *Scotsman, Times, Observer*, and a lot of the tabloids too. The *Guardian* spelt my name wrong, but still. . . Can't knock good publicity.' He turned to face the room, favouring Logan with a smile. 'And I understand you captured him without a warrant or backup?'

'Yes. . .' Not sure if this was a trap or not. 'We were following up a complaint of harassment from members of the Polish community. Gilchrist's mother let us into the property, and materials in his bedroom led me to believe he might be involved in the recent spate of Oedipus blindings. . . Sir.'

'Hmm.' The Chief Constable put his head on one side and examined Logan for a minute. 'I suggest you work on that a bit more before this comes to court, Sergeant.'

Logan blushed. 'I. . . Yes, sir.'

'In the meantime, you say he's made a full confession?'

Finnie held up a manila folder. 'We're going to go over everything with the Procurator Fiscal this morning. Our forensic psychologist's coming in at half two to do a workup. Gilchrist's going nowhere.'

'Good. Very good.' The Chief Constable went back to staring at the city. 'Don't let me keep you, gentlemen.'

DI Steel stuck her feet up on her desk and blew a wet raspberry. 'If you've come here looking for someone to kiss your backside, Hero-Boy, you're in for a long wait.' She picked up an empty plastic cup and waggled it at him. 'Unless you're here to make a deposit? In that case. . .' She puckered up and made kissy-kissy noises.

Logan ignored her.

She stuck the cup back on her desk. 'Anyway, thought you'd be playing with your new boyfriend Finnie this morning.'

'Nope. I questioned Gilchrist last night, Finnie's doing this morning, and we're going in mob-handed with Dr Goulding this afternoon. Keep him off balance.'

Logan sank down in one of the visitor's chairs. 'I found

something yesterday you might be interested in.' He tossed a freshly minted DVD onto the inspector's desk. 'Got the lab to make you a copy.'

'Oh aye?' Steel examined it suspiciously, then slipped the silver disc from its clear plastic wallet. 'It's no' you and Lydia the Tattooed Lady humping in the broom closet, is it? Only I've just had breakfast.'

'A: no. And B: shut up.'

'Don't push it.' Steel stuck the DVD into her computer and fiddled about with the mouse for a while. 'How do I get it to play?'

'Shift over.' Logan got it going and they sat and watched the opening sequence. There wasn't much to it – a woman bound hand and foot, with a pillowcase over her head, being thrown onto a tan leather couch. That was as far as the fore-play went.

It had been filmed in someone's living room: cream carpet, red walls, glass and chrome coffee table, a framed print of some not-very-talented artist's impression of Union Street on the wall.

The inspector frowned. 'You brought porn to work?'

'Just watch.' Logan sent the picture into fast forward, hitting pause when one of the dog-mask men pulled the pillowcase off the woman's head. She'd been gagged with silver duct tape. The camera went in for a close-up as Bulldog slapped her around the face with his erection. And then he ripped off the gag.

Logan hit pause. 'It's definitely her. Look. . .' He dropped a glossy photograph on the inspector's desk: a young woman posing in a studio somewhere, wearing nothing but her underwear and a smile. 'Krystka Gorzałkowska.'

Steel squinted at the photo, then at the screen.

Her mouth became a hard, angry line. 'Where the hell did you get this?'

'Ricky Gilchrist. He was watching it when I picked him up.'

'I want his arse in an interview room *now*, so I can kick the crap out of it!'

Logan shook his head. 'Finnie won't let you anywhere near him.'

Steel jabbed the screen with a nicotine finger. 'This isn't porn, this is *rape*.' She sat back again, worrying at her disaster-movie hair. 'Fine,' she said at last, 'Finnie won't let *me* near Gilchrist but he'll no' stop you, will he? No' now you're best mates.'

Quarter to ten and Logan was hanging about outside interview room one, waiting for Finnie to call a break. The DCI was in there now with Ricky Gilchrist, going over the same ground again and again. Trying to pick holes in Gilchrist's story, making sure his confession would stand up in court. Logan had watched half an hour's worth in the observation suite, crammed in with four CID officers – one of whom *really* needed to cut down on the garlic.

If Gilchrist was angling for an insanity plea he was going the right way about it. Once given the opportunity to open up and tell his side of the story he disappeared into a fantasy world where he was some sort of dashing white knight and the Polish community were all bastards.

Logan wouldn't be surprised if he started chewing on the furniture soon.

But in the end the reek of second-hand garlic was too much, and Logan abandoned the viewing suite for the corridor. He pulled out his Airwave handset, punched in DS Pirie's badge number and listened to it ring.

And then: *'McRae? What, you called up to gloat?'*

'No I—'

'We'd have got him sooner or later, you know that, don't you?'

'Krystka Gorzałkowska.'

Pause. *'What about her?'*

'I got them to do a rape kit when she was in hospital.'

'So? That's my case, remember? Finnie took you off it.'

'Don't be a dick: what was the result?'

'Fine. . .' The sound of far-off rummaging came from the earpiece. *'Not that it's any of your business: evidence of vaginal bruising . . . traces of spermicide . . . no DNA. Why?'*

'She say anything about who attacked her?'

'I don't know, I forgot to ask her.' Pause. *'Of course she bloody didn't. If she had, I would've arrested the bastard. She won't talk about anything, she's terrified. Why do you want to know?'*

'Because—' The interview room door was opening. 'Oops, got to go.' Logan hung up as Finnie stepped out into the corridor.

The DCI frowned at him. 'What's up?'

'Nothing, I just—'

'Is this because you're not in on the interview? I thought we *agreed* on this? What, is your ego so *fragile*, Sergeant, you can't *stand* to be out of the spotlight for two minutes? Hmm? You'll get to play this afternoon, *remember*?'

'Actually, sir,' said Logan, trying not to rise to it, 'I wanted to keep you up to date on the Krakow General Store shooting. They've managed to pull a fingerprint off one of the shell casings fired by the gunman. The one with the mullet?'

'Oh. . .' Finnie took a moment to process that. 'Sorry. Get the feeling I'm banging my head against a brick wall with our lunatic friend in there. Right, so—'

Ricky Gilchrist's voice sounded inside the interview room. 'I'm not kidding, I'm really desperate!'

Finnie raised his eyes to the ceiling for a moment, then shouted over his shoulder. 'Just tie a knot in it for two minutes!' He turned back to Logan. 'Where was I? Ah, OK: what did the database say?'

'No match.'

'Then we—'

Gilchrist shouted, 'I'm bursting!'

'I told you to tie a bloody knot in it!'

'But I *can't*!' It was like the wail of the damned.

'OK, OK: I'll get someone to take you to the toilet.'

Logan glanced up and down the corridor. 'I'll do it if you like? You know, enforce the Good Cop empathy thing? Might help when we go back in with Goulding this afternoon if Gilchrist thinks he's got a friend?'

'Good idea. Just make sure he's back here in. . .' Finnie checked his watch, 'fifteen minutes. That'll give me time to make a couple of calls.'

Logan leant back against the cell wall, reading the advert for Crimestoppers painted on the ceiling above the bed, while Ricky Gilchrist peed his little heart out.

'Ah, Jesus. . .' It sounded as if he'd swallowed a reservoir.

'You know,' said Logan, when the Niagara Falls impersonation came to a dribbling halt, 'you've never said why she was there.'

'Oh God, that's better. . .' *Zip.*

'The woman, in the office building: Krystka Gorzałkowska.'

There was a clunking sound. 'It's still broken! It wouldn't flush last night – I told them. They *said* they'd fix it.'

'The toilets aren't supposed to flush. That way prisoners can't get rid of evidence they've swallowed or cheeked.'

'But they said they'd fix it!' Gilchrist lurched out of the toilet alcove, wiping his hands on his jeans. 'Not hygienic, is it?'

'Tell me about Krystka Gorzałkowska.'

Blank look.

'The woman in the DVD? The one you left in the office building when you blinded Lubomir Podwojski?'

Gilchrist sank down onto the blue plastic mattress, knees

up against his chest. 'Never bother with names. They don't deserve names. They're just bloody animals. . .'

For some strange reason, Logan had the sudden urge to grab the little shit by his ginger hair and bash his head off the wall a couple of times. 'Where did you get the DVD, Ricky? Did you film it? Or are you one of the men in the dog masks?'

'They take *everything*. Polish bastard down the street falls over drunk and breaks his leg – ambulance is there in ten minutes. My mum had a fucking *stroke* and where was *her* ambulance? Eh? Half an hour.'

'Did you rape Krystka Gorzałkowska?'

He looked up at Logan, face covered in freckles and utter disgust. 'Are you mad? I'd never *filthy* myself like that. Do you have any idea how many *diseases* they carry? I told you: they're animals!'

'Then where did you get the DVD?'

'Some bloke in a pub.' He looked away.

'What bloke?'

'Don't remember.'

'Which pub?'

'Don't remember.'

Logan stared at him. 'Why was she there when you blinded Lubomir Podwojski?'

Gilchrist smiled, his voice low and unpleasant: 'Everyone's got to be somewhere.'

34

'Come on, just a little sperm, you'll no' miss it, will you?'

Logan turned off the engine. 'Can we just go *one* day without the sperm talk?'

The ClarkRig Training Systems Ltd car park was busy today, he'd had to squeeze the CID Vauxhall in between a Nissan Skyline and a filthy minibus with '*Brudas* ~ Strong Team!!!' finger-painted in the grime. There was only just enough room to open the doors.

'Don't be so wet.' Steel popped another little white pellet of nicotine gum, chewing with her mouth open as they marched over to the entrance.

The old lady on reception told them Zander wasn't in his editing suite today, he was *filming*. Then she ushered them through in to the studio.

It looked a lot like a converted warehouse, because that's what it was. A large soundstage sat in the middle of the space, everything painted in the same shade of bright blue and covered in a grid of little yellow markers. There was a half-sized humpbacked bridge made of chipboard; two rows of boxes for a riverbank; and a pair of plastic Victorian lamp-posts, the kind you got in DIY stores for the garden. A big lighting rig hung above everything, showering it in a golden glow.

The only things onstage *not* painted Chroma Key blue were the three people on top of the bridge. Two women, one man, grinding away, stark naked.

Steel froze. 'Oooh . . . will you look at that. . .'

A camera swooped in on the end of a long, counter-balanced pole, worked by two blokes who wouldn't have looked out of place in a zoo.

Someone pressed play, and music belted out of a portable stereo.

As Logan watched, a small rowing boat slid out from beneath the bridge. There were little men in the boat. Little men dressed in white dungarees, brown turtlenecks, and white gloves. Little men with orange faces, white eyebrows, and green hair.

Logan blinked twice, but they were still there. 'Oh, you have *got* to be kidding.'

And then they started to sing.

'What do you get with a dose of VD?
An itch in your crotch, and it burns when you pee,
I bet you wish that you'd worn a condom,
Now we are singing our song,
Humpa Lumpa. . .'

Steel stood, rooted to the spot, with her mouth hanging open. Making giggling noises.

When the song was finished, someone yelled 'Cut! Well done everyone; let's get set up for the next shot.' Zander Clark hauled himself out from behind a monitor and marched towards the bridge and its naked tableau.

'Doug, I want you to remember your motivation in this scene, OK?'

Doug stopped what he was doing, and turned to face the director. 'How come I'm the only one who doesn't get a song?'

Logan followed Steel onto the set as the director hummed and hawed for a bit. 'Well, you see, Doug . . . you know *personally* I think you're *fabulous* . . . But it's—'

'Excuse me, Mr Clark,' said Logan, stopping just short of where the fabulous Doug was playing with himself, 'but can we have a quick word?'

Zander, threw his hands in the air and made a noise like a dying balloon. 'How am I supposed to create when. . .' He stopped. 'I know that voice.' The director turned with a huge smile on his face. 'Sergeant McRae, Inspector Steel, how nice to *see* you again. Did you enjoy the films?'

'I mean, doesn't have to be a big song or anything,' said Doug, still keeping his lower portions amused, 'I just want—'

'Hoy!' Steel grimaced at Doug's erection. 'Don't point that thing at me. Might go off.'

'Anyway,' Zander clapped his hands, 'I'm sorry to be rude, but we do have a shooting schedule to stick to. So. . .?'

'Ah, right.' Logan dug the DVD copy from his pocket. 'We wanted you to take a look at this.'

'Really?' He turned the disk over in his thick fingers, the overhead lights sparking off the silver surface. 'I could probably run through it tonight, if you like?' And then he frowned, reading the label. 'Ah.'

'We wouldn't ask if it wasn't important.'

Fabulous Doug coughed. 'Is this going to take long?' He nodded in the direction of the fire escape, and mimed smoking a cigarette with his free hand. 'You know?'

The director nodded, not taking his eyes off the disk. 'Just make sure you keep your robe fastened this time – don't let anyone see you playing "keepy-up".' Zander turned to cast and crew. 'We're going to take a short break, people. I want you back here and ready to go in forty, OK?'

The editing suite was in darkness, just the flickering pink light coming from the bank of monitors as Zander Clark played 'KRYSTKA GET'S F*CK~D DIRTY 3-WAY!!!*!'. Finally the screens went black and he clicked on an Anglepoise lamp.

'That was horrible. I mean, not just the production values – which were *dreadful*, by the way – but the whole thing. Who on Earth wants to *watch* something like that?'

Steel: 'Recognize anyone?'

'Apart from Krystka?' He picked at the skin around his thumbnail. 'Both men are amateurs – they *completely* messed up the money-shot. Camera's not even high definition, probably a home camcorder thing. The worst sort of gonzo operation. And it's obviously not legal: even if the rape's simulated, there's no titles or BBFC classification.'

Steel's voice was alarmingly level. 'You think it's simulated? They were just *faking* it?'

Zander put his coffee down and rubbed at his face. 'I wish they were. But Krystka, God bless her, just isn't that good an actress.' He drooped. 'I should never have let her go. . .'

Logan tapped the nearest monitor. 'You've no idea who might have filmed this?'

'No. And believe me if I did, I'd tell you. The last thing we need is sick crap like this giving erotography a bad name. Doesn't Krystka know?'

'She won't talk: too scared.'

'Well . . . can't you analyse it? Don't you have police scientist people for this kind of thing?'

'Aye,' said Steel, 'if we want to wait three months.'

'OK.' The director took a deep breath, scrunched his face into a pout, then started punching buttons on his keyboard.

A separate scene from the DVD popped up onto each of the monitors; Zander set them all playing at the same time.

A barrage of gibberish, grunting and swearing blared from the speakers. He hit mute. 'I can pull off the audio as a separate file for you, cut out the background noise. Maybe you can do something with the voices.'

His eyes flickered across the screens, the pink flesh reflecting in his trendy rectangular glasses.

Steel sniffed and hauled up her trousers. 'Why are—'

'Shhhh . . .' Zander stared at the images of Krystka Gorzałkowska being raped. 'They never show the men's faces – they're always wearing the dog masks. . .'

'We can bloody well see that!'

He hit a key and one of the screens went blank. Then another, and another until only one screen still showed a picture. He froze it, then wound it backwards. Hit pause again, then play.

As the scene started again a man's voice crackled out of the speakers: *'Take it! Take it! Taaaaaaa. . .'* The last word stretched out into the lower register then stopped entirely as Zander slowed the playback. Backwards: *'Aaaaait. Ti. . .'* Pause. *'. . . it! Take. . .'*

'There.'

Steel stared at the screen, face scrunched up in concentration. Krystka was pinned to the couch, tears streaming down her face while Bulldog-mask abused her. 'Where?'

'Like I said, the men always keep their faces covered, but. . .' He shifted the mouse, highlighting the corner of the picture, and zoomed in. Now they were looking at a grainy close-up of the not-very-good painting of Union Street. A man's face was reflected in the glass. 'Cameraman wasn't so careful.'

Steel went on squinting. 'It looks like Mr Potato Head! What the hell are we supposed to do with that?'

'What we do with *that*, is send it to my computer geeks. They take the next twenty frames or so and subtract all the pixels that are part of the painting. Composite what's left, clean it up, and Bob's your rapist.'

'I still can't believe you got a warrant based on that.' Rennie parked the pool car and killed the engine. The house was at the end of a moth-eaten cul-de-sac, its garden overflowing with weeds, grass, and a rotting bicycle frame. The houses on either side were even worse: boarded-up windows; the corpse of a washing machine; a stack of ruptured bin bags, the contents disappearing into the long grass.

DI Steel sat in the passenger seat, puffing her way to the end of an angry cigarette. 'Aye, well Sheriff McNab might be a sanctimonious old git, but even he's no' going to pass up a chance like this.'

They climbed out into the morning sunshine.

Logan scanned the street. The only visible inhabitant was a grey and white cat, watching them warily from the roof of a plastic Wendy-house.

Rennie marched round to the back of the car and fetched the 'big red door key' from the boot. 'Thing weighs a ton. . .'

'Don't whinge.' Steel started up the path to the door, with Rennie grumbling along behind her.

Logan waded through the knee-high grass, round the corner of the house and into the back garden. At least this time there wasn't a fence to climb, or a dirty big dog, just a whirly listing at thirty degrees and a collection of mildewed garden furniture. He got into position, and waited for things to kick off.

Three crashes of battering ram against UPVC. Shouts. A thump.

Logan tried the back door – it wasn't locked.

Straight through the kitchen and into the hallway. A man in a brown T-shirt and boxer shorts was sprinting towards him as the front door exploded off its hinges. The man saw Logan and slithered to a halt, socks getting little purchase on the linoleum.

Rennie: 'STOP, POLICE!'

Logan: 'Give it up, Gary.'

Gary: 'Fuck!' He turned and scrambled up the stairs with Rennie in hot pursuit. Logan followed, getting up to the landing in time to see Rennie launch a flying rugby tackle.

The constable slammed into Gary, and they both went down in a heap of flailing limbs and swearwords. An ironing board hit the carpet: creased clothes went everywhere.

Grapple. Struggle. *Clunk* – Gary bounced the iron off Rennie's head. The constable let go, wobbled a bit, then fell over.

Logan fumbled in his pocket for the canister of pepper-spray as Gary struggled to his feet, the iron still clutched in his fist.

'I didn't do nothing!' He wasn't the ugliest person in Aberdeen, but he was having a decent stab at the title. One thick eyebrow, face like curdled milk, patchy beard.

'You just assaulted a police officer.'

'He was breaking into my house!'

'Come on, Gary, don't make it any worse. Put the iron down.'

Gary dropped it, turned, and ran, slamming the bedroom door behind him. Logan scrambled past Rennie, and kicked the door open. Double bed. Black sheets with crusty white stains. Mirrored tiles on the ceiling. Camera lights on tripods. Gary was on top of a chest of drawers by the window, fighting with the catch.

'It's not going to happen, Gary. Give it up.'

Gary swore, then climbed down. Moping his way across the carpet, head down. 'Bloody thing was locked.'

'Well, if you'd just come quietly in the first—'

Gary's knee slammed right into Logan's crotch.

Oh God. . . He folded in half, clutching his groin as Gary shoved past out onto the landing. 'Unnnnnnnnnnnnnnngh.'

And then Steel's voice bellowed out from the stairwell: 'Oh no you bloody don't!'

35

Logan winced his way through into the hallway. The bathroom door was shut, but there was a lot of swearing and spluttering coming from inside; the sound of the toilet filling, then flushing, then filling, then flushing.

He stood, holding onto the wall, trying to breathe his way through the burning ache in his testicles, just like they'd taught him at the pain clinic. Then knocked on the door.

'Inspector?'

Flush, splutter, swearing, something thumping on the bathroom floor.

'Inspector, are you OK?' He tried the handle and the door swung open.

She was sitting on the edge of the bath, holding Gary by the scruff of the neck, forcing his head into the toilet bowl. His legs flailed about as water rushed by, both arms wrapped around the porcelain. She'd cuffed his hands either side of the U-bend.

The flushing stopped, and she dragged his head back up. 'I'm no' going to ask you again.'

'Aaaagh, Jesus!' Then a bout of coughing.

'Who were they?'

'You can't—'

She shoved his head back into the bowl again, and there was a clunk as Gary's face bounced off the porcelain. 'Aaagh! Stop it!'

Steel cranked the flush again, but it just made gurgling noises; the cistern wasn't full enough yet. 'Who were they?'

'I don't know!' His voice was distorted and echoey inside the bog. 'I don't!'

Logan froze. 'What are you doing?'

She looked up. 'How's the balls?'

'Sore. You can't—'

She slapped Gary on the back of his wet head. 'You better pray they're no' broken! If he can't get my wife pregnant. . .' The cistern was full again.

Flush.

'Aaaaagh!' And then gurgling.

'Stop it!' Logan limped into the small room. 'What the hell do you think you're doing?'

'This is what you do with shite, you flush it down the bog.' She dragged Gary's head back above the rim. 'I said: who – were – they?'

'I can't, they'll kill—' Gurgle, thrash, gurgle.

Logan lurched forwards and grabbed her arm, pulling her off. Gary surfaced again, retching up toilet water.

'Please. . .'

'Let go of me you daft—'

Logan hauled her to her feet. 'That's enough.'

Gary was crying now, tears and snot running down his wet face. 'Make her stop. Please . . . make her stop. . .'

Steel shook herself free and kicked him in the backside. 'Who were they?'

'Allan Rait and Duane Cowie. OK? Allan and Duane. . .' More coughing.

Another kick. 'Who sold you the girl?'

'Aaaaaagh, we didn't buy her! We just . . . rented. . .'

And this time there was no stopping the inspector. She leapt forwards, and plunged Gary's head into the bowl again, flushing, holding on for grim death while Logan tried to drag her off.

'She's a HUMAN BEING!'

Splutter, gurgle.

'Stop it!' And then Logan did something really stupid – he slapped her. Just like they did in the movies. Only instead of shaking her head and saying, 'Thanks, I needed that.' DI Steel slapped him back. Hard enough to split his lip.

'The *fuck* you think you're doing?'

But at least she'd let Gary go. He surfaced like a dolphin, only not so attractive, and with a distinct smell of mouldy dog food.

This time the retching brought up a couple of pints of water, and then what looked like a not-so-happy meal. Gary laid his head on the toilet rim and sobbed like a child.

Steel's face was clenched, Logan's handprint beginning to show pink across her left cheek. 'If you *ever* hit me again—'

'You can't do this, OK? You can't!'

'They raped that girl—'

'This isn't the way we do things!'

'Well maybe it *should* be.' She rubbed a hand across her cheek, then kicked Gary again.

Gary dragged in a shuddering breath, tears and toilet water dripping from his face. 'I'm sorry, I'm so sorry . . .'

Logan pushed past Steel, getting between her and Gary before she did him some permanent damage. 'Who was it? Who rented Krystka Gorzałkowska out like she was a bloody Transit Van?'

'We got . . . we got her from this guy Allan knows. Some Polish bloke. . .'

'Name.'

'I don't know. . .'

'*Name,* Gary. I want a name and address, or I'm out of here; you can go back to your swimming lesson.'

'I don't know! I swear, on my mother's grave! I never met him, Allan did all that stuff.' Gary howched up a mouthful of something foul and spat it into the bowl. 'He said they were like a company that did porn actresses and stuff.'

'What company?' Logan got the sinking feeling he knew where this was going.

'Cost Key Internal somethings . . . She was two hundred pounds for the day. . .'

'Kostchey International Holdings Limited.'

Steel was in the back garden, sitting on an upturned wheelbarrow in the long grass, smoking a sulky cigarette. The sound of Radio One wafted over from three houses down – some TV talent show wannabe murdering an Elvis song.

Logan settled back against the wall. 'That was out of order.'

'Rape's a nasty thing, Sergeant. You should try it some time, see how tolerant you are then.' She flicked a little swirl of ash into the still morning air.

'You can't assault a prisoner in custody. Look what happened to DI Insch.'

'Aye, well, *technically* he's no' in custody yet. He's just had an unfortunate toilet-related mishap.' She took a deep drag on her fag. 'He going to press charges?'

Logan looked away. 'I had a word with him.'

'Oh aye?'

'Still got a pile of those Polaroids from Rory Simpson's flat: little girls running about with their panties on show. Told Gary it would be a shame if we find some of them when we search his house. Might not go down too well when he gets to prison.'

'Ta.'

'You owe me.'

'Aye. . .' The grey cat was back, picking its way along the fence at the bottom of the garden. Steel dug in her trouser pocket and came out with a five pound note. 'Here.' She handed it over. 'For the swear box. Should only be three fifty, but I'm planning on calling Gary a worthless sack of shite a couple of times.'

Logan watched the cat jump down and disappear into the long grass. 'You can't ever do that again, you know that, don't you?'

'Like you said, I owe you one.' Steel ground her cigarette out on the wheelbarrow, then flicked the remains away into the jungle. 'How's Rennie?'

'Got bashed on the head with an iron. Might be brain damaged, but who'd know the difference?'

She hauled herself to her feet, brushing dust and cobwebs from the seat of her trousers. 'Better get on the blower to your mate the fat pornographer. I want to know who these Kostchey International Dickheads are and where I can find them.'

'Already did it. No answer, so I left a message.'

She nodded. 'Right, let's go see what the Little Mermaid has to say for himself.'

Gary was sitting on a ratty brown armchair in the lounge, staring off into the middle distance, hair plastered to his head, T-shirt soaked through all the way down to his waist.

Rennie was perched on the sofa, a bag of frozen sweet-corn clutched to the side of his head. He looked up as Steel creaked down beside him, then handed over his notebook. 'Mobile number.'

Gary sniffed. 'We had to call it when we was finished with the girl.' He raised his cuffed hands and rubbed at his pink eyes. 'They'll kill me if they find out.'

'Oh aye? That'd be *such* a shame.' Steel produced her phone and dialled with her thumb, held the thing to her ear. 'Ringing. . .'

Gary wiped his nose on his arm. 'You got to get me that witness protection, yeah?'

'Oh don't be so wet. They're just—' Steel stopped, then spoke into the phone, 'Hello?' Pause. 'Aye, got your number from a friend. Said you had . . . *women* for hire. You know, for doing films and stuff? . . . His name? . . . Aye, aye, keep your shirt on, it was Duane Cowie. You. . . Hello? Hello?'

She clicked the phone shut, pursed her lips, then said, 'Hung up. Some people got no manners.' The inspector slapped Gary on the back of the head again, sending little droplets of water flying. 'Backside in gear, Toilet Boy. Got a nice warm cell waiting for you.'

He only had ten minutes before Dr Goulding was meant to come in and do a psychological workup on Ricky Gilchrist, but Logan's stomach sounded as if he'd swallowed an angry bear. He sealed the interview tapes and signed them into evidence, then headed up to the canteen, on the off chance there was something nice left.

For once the interview had gone without a hitch: Gary had been a good boy, repeated everything about his co-conspirators and where he'd got the girl from – on the record this time – and kept his mouth shut about his underwater adventure. Going to prison would be bad enough, he didn't want someone carving 'PAEDOPHILE' into his forehead with a homemade knife when he got there.

Logan grabbed an egg mayonnaise sandwich and a packet of salt and vinegar crisps, eating them on his way back down to the interview rooms.

Goulding was early – Logan could hear him chatting with DCI Finnie in the observation suite. Today the psychologist was wearing a sharp, collarless suit and a tie that wouldn't have looked out of place on a carnival Wurlitzer. He smiled at Logan and shook his hand. 'Ah, Sergeant McRae. You got him! Great stuff.'

'Well . . . you know . . . team effort.'

Finnie snorted. 'No it wasn't, you— bugger.' His phone was ringing. He excused himself, and took the call out in the corridor. 'What? Yes . . . What do you mean they won't talk?' He closed the door.

Goulding pointed at one of the observation suite monitors. Ricky Gilchrist was already in room two, sitting alone at the interview table, a burly PC standing against the window behind him. 'Fascinating, isn't he?'

The psychologist pulled up one of the creaky plastic chairs and sank into it. 'He fits the profile perfectly. Dead father, emotionally distant mother – I know it's not her fault, after the stroke and everything, but it's still true. Ricky's a single white male, in his mid twenties, and he used to work as a labourer on a building site until the company fired him and took on Polish migrants instead. . .' Goulding rested the tips of his fingers against the screen, just like he'd done with his whiteboard. 'Fascinating.' There was a thoughtful pause. 'Do you know if he has any history of violence? Fire-raising? Cruelty to animals?'

Logan checked the file. 'Nothing he was caught for.'

'Ah, well, I'm sure it'll all come out in the fullness of time.' Goulding tapped the image of Gilchrist. 'I can't wait to open up that little head and see how it ticks. . . Do you know he won't refer to any of his victims by name? It's just like the notes he sent: he's completely dehumanized them.'

'He told me they don't deserve names. "They're just bloody animals."'

'I know. . .' And then, 'How about you? Sleeping any better?'

'Eh? What's that got—'

'You look tired.'

'Busy day yesterday.'

Goulding turned and stared at him. 'I meant what I said: therapy could really help you.'

'Can we just focus on Ricky Gilchrist? Please?'

'It would be in the strictest confidence. You could tell people you were following up on offender profiles if you like?'

The door opened again and Finnie grumbled into the room. 'Right, McRae, I've got a job for you.'

Thank God for that. 'Good cop, or bad cop?'

The DCI paused. 'Actually, I want you to give DS Pirie a hand. He's getting nowhere with Harry Jordan's tarts.'

'What? But I—'

'Look: you caught Gilchrist and you got him to confess. You're getting full credit for it. What we're doing now is just a tidying-up exercise. And let's face it, Pirie hasn't exactly been setting the world on fire recently, has he?' Finnie patted Logan on the shoulder. 'I need a right-hand-man who can get results.'

Harry Jordan's manky flat-cum-brothel was a tip. Not just dirty, but ruined. As if someone had gone on the rampage with a sledgehammer. The furniture was all smashed: the grey sofas flattened and broken, huge chunks of stuffing spilling out onto the bare chipboard floor. The smell of industrial bleach made Logan's eyes water, even with the windows open.

Detective Sergeant Pirie gave a tattered paperback a half-hearted kick. 'I don't need you here to hold my bloody hand.'

Logan leant against the windowsill, between the dead bluebottles. 'This wasn't my idea, OK? Blame Finnie.'

'You're a sodding jinx, you know that?'

'Thanks, it's great working with you too.'

'Why don't you kiss my—'

The living room door opened and Kylie's sister, Tracey, shuffled into the room, rubbing at the crook of her arm. 'Been through this,' she said, eyes flicking around the room. Licking her lips. Trembling. Her skin slick and shiny. 'Wasn't Creepy battered Harry's head in, OK? Was some black bloke.'

Logan pointed at the wreckage. 'You had the decorators in since I was here last?'

She sniffed and stared at the chipboard floor. 'Some blokes came round from the Environmental Health. Tore up all the carpet coz of . . . you know . . . the blood, like.'

'They break all the furniture too?'

'We had a party.'

'Course you did,' said Pirie, 'a happy house-wrecking. Bring your own crowbar.'

She glanced at him, then back at the floor. 'Does he have to be here?'

'Course I do, you silly c—'

Logan spoke over the top of him. 'Maybe DS Pirie could go make us all a nice cup of tea?'

Pirie sneered. 'Up yours. If there's anyone—'

'*Now*, would be good.'

He looked as if he was about to say something, then huffed, stuck his hands in his pockets. 'Fine.' He turned and stomped from the room.

'He's a right wanker, you know? Total.'

Logan shrugged. 'He's got a point though. Either you're *way* behind on the housework, or someone's trashed the place.'

She wouldn't look at him. 'Wasn't. . . We. . .' Deep breath. 'It wasn't Creepy, OK? I told you, it wasn't him.'

'You sure?' He let the silence grow uncomfortable. 'I meant what I said, Tracey: I can help. Get you away from. . .' he waved his hands, taking in the squalor and destruction, '. . . all this.'

She rubbed at her arm again. 'I can't. . .'

'If you help me put Colin McLeod away, I'll get you *and* Kylie into witness protection. You could start over again somewhere new. Anywhere you like.'

She looked up for the first time. 'Used to go to Lossiemouth when me and Kylie was kids, you know?' Then her eyes drifted back to the chipboard, fingernails worrying at a scab on her wrist till it started to bleed. 'We was happy there. . .'

'Lossiemouth, then. All you have to do is make a statement, and *stick* to it this time. We'll even get you into a rehab programme if you like?'

Tracey sniffed, then wiped her nose on her sleeve. 'Kinda on one now. They cut us off. Won't let anyone sell us gear . . . coz of what we said about Creepy.'

She crouched down and fumbled in the broken sideboard, coming out with a litre bottle of cheap vodka. 'Two blokes came round with Mrs McLeod. She was all, like, "This is what happens when you lie about my family." And then the blokes started smashing everything. You know? Then the old bag asks if we've learned our lesson yet. And Kylie says, "Yeah," you know?'

She cracked the seal on the vodka and took a swig. 'And Mrs McLeod says, "No you haven't. But you will." And the big bloke grabs Kylie and starts smacking her around.' Tracey's voice was getting quieter and quieter. Another swig. 'Like she's not still hurting from when Harry knocked her about, you know, for the wheelchair joke? So I wades in, and they take it out on me instead. . .' She stared at the bottle in her hands. 'Used to work with our stepdad too.'

'And Mrs McLeod was there the whole time?'

'She was the one said they'd be back if we didn't tell the

police it was someone else who battered Harry.' Tracey knocked back another mouthful. 'But it wasn't, you know? Creepy did it, I *saw* him do it.'

Logan slipped his notebook back in his pocket. 'Then all you have to do is come down to the station with me. We'll get it all typed up properly, you can sign it, then I'll get something sorted with Witness Protection. OK?'

The lounge door creaked open and in came DS Pirie with three steaming mugs. 'Milk was off, so you've got some sort of soya crap instead.' He clumped the mugs on the windowsill, sending a slop of weak coffee over the edges and onto the dusty paintwork.

Logan took one. There was lipstick on the rim, and a thin brown line to mark a previous high tide. He put it back down again. 'No offence, but I think I'll wait till we get back to the ranch. How about you, Tracey? You want to get Kylie and we can head off?'

She looked up at Pirie, then back at the floor again. 'I don't want to come back here. You know? After.'

'Pack whatever you need. We're in no rush.'

Pirie perched himself on the edge of the broken sofa, hands in his pockets, face turned to the window. Outside, a couple of small children were running about on the communal drying green, screeching happily. 'So,' said Pirie, 'you got them to talk.'

Logan shrugged. 'Yeah, well. . .'

'Thought you were supposed to be a complete fuck-up?'

'Thanks.'

Pirie cleared his throat, paused. 'I. . .' Another pause. 'Finnie's going to cream his pants when he finds out.'

The sounds of muffled conversation came from the hallway – Kylie and her sister picking through the debris of their flat for anything worth salvaging.

Logan watched as one of the small children outside, looking over his shoulder at the kid chasing him, ran right into a metal clothes pole. *CLANGGGGG* . . . He went flat on his back, then started to wail. 'Why's Finnie so obsessed with the McLeods?'

'What, other than all the unsolved armed robberies, punishment beatings, drugs, loan-sharking, prostitution, tobacco smuggling. . .? You name it they're up to their ears in it.'

'What about Wee Hamish Mowat?'

'Ah . . . Yes.' Pirie ran a hand through his curly orange hair. 'Let's just say that it's *complicated.*'

'You mean Finnie's dirty?'

'What? No. . .' He drifted off into silence for a moment. 'The thing you got to remember about Wee Hamish is that he's a bit like background radiation. You can live with it for generations, then suddenly all your teeth fall out.' He cleared his throat again. 'Look, I'm sorry if I was a dick earlier, OK? I've been. . . This sodding caravan full of guns: I'm getting nowhere. And I just. . .' Pirie sighed, shrugged, stuck his hands in his pockets. 'Well, you know.'

Out on the communal green, the screaming child's mother had arrived, all hugs and kisses. If anything the kid's bawling got even louder.

Pirie prodded the remains of the shattered coffee table with his toe. 'You heard about the DI's position coming up?'

'Gray's going off on the stress.'

'Yes, well,' said Pirie, 'I was odds-on favourite. . . Don't suppose it matters now. Finnie's going to put you forward, isn't he?'

'No idea.'

'Be mad if he didn't.' What was left of the coffee table collapsed. A handful of DVDs and dog-eared dirty magazines slithered onto the carpet. 'Sod it. . .' He bent down and picked up a copy of *Naughty Nuns 2: Hardcore Devotions*. 'Suppose we'll all have to start being nice to you. Just in case.'

Logan smiled. 'Wouldn't hurt.'

Ten minutes later they were out in sunshine again, Pirie helping Tracey and her sister pack their stuff into the CID pool car while Logan listened to DI Steel whinging on the other end of his mobile.

'Hope you're happy,' she was saying, sounding out of breath. *'I had to take that idiot Beattie. . .'* There was some rustling, then she told someone, *'Well, ring the damn thing then!'*

Logan heard the sound of a doorbell in the background. 'Where are you?'

'Where do you think? Got a warrant for Gary the Cameraman's rapist chums. Did you get an address for Kostchey International Whatevers?'

'Not yet.'

There was a pause.

'Right, first thing tomorrow we'll— Hoy! You! Stop right there!' Some rustling, and then the inspector's voice was all over the place. *'Come . . . back . . . here . . . you . . . little . . . shite!'* Puffing, panting, then what sounded like the ocean crashing repeatedly against a stony shore.

She'd probably stuffed her phone in her pocket.

Logan listened for another minute, but the only thing he could hear was the SWOOOSSHH, PWSHHHH of fabric on the mobile's microphone. He hung up. If it was important she'd call back.

36

Quarter past six and Logan was just starting the report on their visit to Harry Jordan's train-wreck brothel. It wasn't the interview that had taken the time – that was the easy bit – it was haggling with the Witness Protection people. Then filling in all their bloody forms. But finally Tracey and her sister had been picked up by an extremely plainclothes officer in a dented Citroen Picasso.

Both stick-thin junkies had given Logan a big hug before they left.

And now, the paperwork beckoned.

Two pages into it, DS Pirie stuck his head round the CID room door and grinned. 'You're going to want to come downstairs and see this.'

The back doors boomed open, and a pair of uniformed officers dragged an old lady out of the back of a police van. Mrs McLeod's housekeeper: hands cuffed behind her back, face red and swollen from a good dose of pepper-spray, kicking and screaming.

'YOU FUCKING PIG BASTARDS, I'LL FUCKING KILL THE WHOLE FUCKING LOT OF YOU!'

Pirie waved her goodbye as she was hauled down the corridor. 'Isn't she sweet? When they kicked the door in, she went for someone with a kitchen knife.'

Next out of the van was Mrs McLeod herself. She was dressed in her black and white silk and cashmere ensemble again, jewellery glittering as she stepped down from the van and into the station's fluorescent lighting.

Finnie came strolling in behind her. 'Ah yes, Agnes, you'll love it here. The rooms are a bit snug, but the views are terrific.' He did a little skip-step, then winked at her, 'Make sure you tip the bell-boy, OK? They might put bogies in your tea otherwise.'

She paused for a second, looked him up and down, then spat. 'My Tony was worth ten of you!'

Finnie wiped the glop of spittle from his leather jacket with a paper handkerchief. 'Thanks, Agnes, but we'll get a DNA sample *after* they've done your fingerprints.' Then to the pair of constables escorting her: 'Show Mrs McLeod to the penthouse suite, gentlemen.'

They went to move her, but she dug her heels in. 'I can walk myself!' She dusted herself down, then let them lead her away.

'Ahhh. . .' DCI Finnie leant back against the wall – eyes closed, head thrown back – as they disappeared down the stairwell to the cells. 'I've wanted to do that for *years*.' Then he turned and slapped his hands together. 'Right, now we—'

There was a commotion outside. Raised voices and the high-pitched yapping bark of a small dog. A police officer saying, 'I'm sorry, ma'am, you can't come in here.'

A woman shouting, 'You have no bloody right!'

Finnie's smile grew even wider. 'Get the doors, will you Pirie?'

The DS did as he was told, throwing them wide open. It

was Hilary Brander, and her scabby terrier. Today the dog was dressed in a blue and green raincoat decorated with little sheep; it ran around on the end of its leash, barking at the uniformed officer blocking the way. 'All enquiries from the public have to be made at the front desk!'

'It's all right, Constable,' said Finnie, 'let the nice lady in.'

She stormed into the station and straight up to the DCI. 'You dirty, conniving, underhand bastard!'

'Ah, *Ms* Brander. How *nice* to see you. If you're looking for your mother-in-law, you've just missed her. But don't worry, she'll only be here till we can get her a court appearance.' He checked his watch. 'Which will be Monday.'

'*Monday*? You can't do that!'

'I'm so sorry, Ms Brander, but the court doesn't operate Saturday or Sunday, so your mother-in-law's just going to have to enjoy our hospitality till then. It's *such* a pity, but what can I do?' He gave a theatrical shrug, not bothering to hide the smile on his rubbery face.

'You should be ashamed of yourselves: arresting an old woman when her son's been blinded!'

'I know, it's a wonder I can sleep at night.' The DCI crossed his arms and leant forwards till he was inches from her face. 'Now, would you like to tell us your whereabouts on Wednesday night?'

'What?' She backed up a step. 'I was at home, with Simon.'

'Really? Shame. . .'

'A *shame*? He's *blind*, you moron.'

'You see, I've got Colin on attempted murder, his mum for perverting the course of justice, and I only need Simon to make the *full* set.'

'You're an arsehole.'

'Why, Ms Brander, such language from a young lady!' Finnie picked himself off the wall. 'Anyway, *lovely* though this is, I really do have to get going. I'm sure *someone* will see you out. McRae, my office: ten minutes.' He turned on his heel and sauntered away, whistling a happy tune.

As soon as Finnie was gone, the terrier stopped barking.

Pirie slapped Logan on the back, 'All yours mate,' and hurried after the DCI.

There was an uncomfortable silence.

'I'm sorry about that,' said Logan. 'Chief Inspector Finnie can be a bit—'

'He's a slimy git.'

The little terrier gave a yap, and Logan bent down to ruffle the tuft of fur between his ears. 'How's Simon doing?'

'How do you think? He's blind!' She snatched the dog up, clutching it to her chest. 'And you useless bunch of bollocks should be out there finding whoever did it, not arresting his mother!' Her voice was getting louder and louder and louder. The terrier started to bark again.

Logan held up his hands. 'Look, I'm sorry, but we—'

'You should be catching the . . . the bastards. . .' She was fighting it, but the tears were there. Making her green eyes sparkle. Deep, shuddering breath. 'You should be out there.'

'Then tell me who's trying to move in on Simon's territory?'

'I told you he's a legitimate—'

'How are we supposed to catch them if you won't co-operate?'

She bared her teeth. 'So it's *my* fault now? Bloody typical! Blame the *victims*!'

'Was it Wee Hamish Mowat?'

Hilary stood, staring at him. 'You're an idiot. No wonder you can't catch the people who attacked my Simon. Call yourselves policemen? You useless bastards couldn't catch a bloody cold!'

'. . .and PC Buchan says, "listen up, you old boot, either you drop the knife or I'll. . ."' Finnie's anecdote drifted to a halt as Logan walked in. The DCI had his feet up on the desk, hands tucked behind his head. 'Ah, McRae, bang on time. Did Ms Brander give you any trouble?'

'Just an ear-bashing.'

'Oh . . . Never mind, can't have everything I suppose. Assaulting a police officer would have rounded off the day nicely.' He waved Logan towards one of the visitor's chairs. 'I was just telling Pirie about the battle for Mrs McLeod's parlour.'

There was a knock on the door.

'Enter.'

It was PC Karim. He held up a plastic bag with the Oddbins logo on it. 'One bottle of champagne, from the chiller cabinet. . .' He stuck it on the chief inspector's desk, then went rummaging in a trouser pocket, coming out with a few pound coins and a smattering of silver. 'And your change.'

Finnie took the bottle from the bag, 'Heidsieck Monopole, vintage. Good choice.'

'Thank you, sir.' Karim stayed where he was, looking hopeful as DS Pirie rummaged three crystal tumblers out of the filing cabinet's bottom drawer and blew the dust out of them.

Finnie ripped the gold foil off the cork. Then stopped and frowned at the constable. 'Is there something else?'

Karim blushed. 'No, sir.' He stomped out; Logan could hear him muttering about what a bunch of tight-fisted bastards CID were.

Finnie popped the cork – Pooom! – and sloshed champagne into the tumblers, froth rushing up the glass and over the lip. Soaking into the ballistics report he was using as a coaster.

He stood. 'Gentlemen, a toast: the Clan McLeod. May they rot in jail.'

They repeated, 'Rot in jail,' then drank.

Pirie smacked his lips. 'Not bad at all.'

Finnie topped them all up then sat back down, feet up on the desk again. 'You know what, I fancy a curry tonight. Anyone? My treat.'

Logan took another mouthful of champagne. Stifled a burp. 'Aren't you going to interview Mrs McLeod?'

'Nope. The old battleaxe can stew in her own juices till tomorrow. She's already been charged, so there's no rush. She's not going anywhere till Monday. A weekend in the cells will do her the *world* of good. Be practice for when she gets sent down.' He grinned. 'Oh, and before I forget: we have *another* reason to celebrate. Baz Hartley, our escaped Manchester hoodie, tried to kill Kevin Murray's mum last night. Broke into the family home and had a go at her with a butterfly knife. Revenge for her Kevin grassing them up.'

'Oh Jesus.' Logan sank into one of the chairs. 'What about the kids?'

'Didn't wake up till the ambulance got there. Seems our mate Baz was off his face at the time: slipped on the way in through the kitchen window and banged his head on the working surface. Mrs Murray finds him staggering around on the linoleum and beats him unconscious with a stainless steel breadbin. Wonderful woman.' Finnie held up his glass, twisting it to catch the fluorescent light. 'Oedipus is no more, the McLeods are behind bars, God is in Her heaven, and all's right with the world. Well . . . except for that caravan load of guns.'

Finnie raised his glass again. 'To Detective Sergeant Logan McRae. Believe it or not, you've actually made my week.'

37

The alarm went off at six fifteen – as usual. Logan slammed his hand down on the off button, rolled over, and burrowed deeper into the duvet. A Saturday off was something to be treasured. He only dragged himself out of bed when the double call of headache and straining bladder ganged up on him. They'd finished off the champagne, then hit the Light of Bengal: king prawn jalfrezi and four pints of Cobra beer. Filthy McNasties: two pints of Stella. The Bells: another two pints, and a whisky chaser. . . After that things started to get a little fuzzy.

Did they go to the Howff next, or the Grill? Probably both from the feel of things: a pair of overweight rhinoceroses were skateboarding around the inside of Logan's skull to very loud rap music, and his stomach wasn't much better.

Two aspirin, a carton of orange juice, two paracetamol and an unsuccessful rummage in the fridge later, Logan winced his way out of the front door, heading up to Archibald Simpson for breakfast.

The pub was relatively quiet, just a few old men in for their Saturday-morning pint. Logan ordered the vegetarian fry-up and a huge mug of tea.

He was wiping up the last remnants of egg yolk with a chunk of veggie sausage when PC Karim crumpled into the seat opposite.

'God, it's murder out there. . .'

He wasn't in uniform, so Logan didn't tell him to sod off. 'Shopping?'

Karim grimaced. 'Wedding present for Her Indoor's sister. "Oh," she says, "why don't you hit the shops when you get off night shift?"' He sighed. 'Tell you, never get married. I thought I was getting a life partner to love and cherish, she thought she was getting a taxi driver, private bank, and personal shopper.' He hauled a plastic bag from John Lewis onto the table. 'Keep an eye on that while I go for a slash, eh?'

Logan thought about taking a peek, but pulled his phone out instead. He switched it on and called Samantha. Listened to it ring for a bit. And then a muzzy voice came on the other end.

'Emmmph?'

'Did I wake you?'

'Wmmmm?' Yawn. *'What time is . . . oh Christ. . .'*

'Sorry. I can call back later if you—'

'It's not you. I'm supposed to be at the sodding lab in twenty-five minutes. Didn't get home till three. Urrrgh, sambuca. . .' Another yawn crackled through the phone. *'What happened to you last night? Tried to call.'*

'Teambuilding with Finnie and Pirie. How about tonight? I've got the day off and—'

'Done. . . Oh God, look at the time!' And she was gone.

Karim came back to the table, carrying two mugs of coffee. 'Here.' He handed one over. 'Look like you need it.'

'Ta.'

The constable sank back into his chair. 'God what a night. Bloody Union Street's like Beirut after the pubs shut.' He shuddered, then dunked his biscuit in his coffee. 'Oh, and by the way, word to the wise: if you see Steel coming, *run*. She's in a bloody horrible mood. That bloke she was after? He turned up last night with his arms, legs, and jaw broken.'

Logan rattled his mug back in the saucer, stood, said thank you for the coffee and legged it for the station.

Sergeant Eric Mitchell was on the front desk, slumped over a copy of that morning's *Aberdeen Examiner* with a ballpoint pen, drawing moustaches on people. But however much ink he used, it was never going to come close to the huge furry creature lurking on his own top lip: a full-blown Joseph Stalin job.

He looked up as Logan puffed and panted to a halt. 'Thought you were supposed to be off this weekend?'

Logan grabbed the edge of the reception desk and tried to get some oxygen back into his lungs. 'I . . . ahh . . . it. . .'

'Jesus. Where did you run from, Inverness?'

'Arch . . . Archies.'

'That's just round the corner! How unfit do you have to be to—'

'Karim told me . . . Rory Simpson . . . turned up . . . last night.'

Blank look.

Logan tried again, 'Beaten up? Broken arms . . . and legs?'

Sergeant Mitchell pulled out the day book and flicked through it. Frowning. 'Nope. . . No one's seen your child-molester friend since he did a runner.'

That bastard Karim had been winding him up.

'What we *do* have,' said Mitchell, running a finger across his facial topiary, 'is a Duane Cowie. Anonymous call from a pub payphone: said they'd seen a man being assaulted on the Kings Links, down by the beach. Alpha Sixteen found him about two hundred yards from the petrol station.'

'Duane Cowie? Who the hell is Duane Cowie?'

'No idea.' Sergeant Mitchell punched away at a keyboard beneath the level of desk. 'Says here Steel had a lookout request on him. Something about a Polish girl getting raped in a porn film?'

'Damn. Knew it was too good to be true.'

'Aye, well I'm sure Duane Cowie shares your disappointment.' He went back to vandalizing the paper. 'And speaking of Steel: she wants a word, if you're about?'

'I'm not. You've not seen me.' Logan turned to leave. Stopped. Then went back to the desk. 'What's the book at now for the new DI's position?'

Sergeant Mitchell smiled. 'You should've put money on when you were eighteen to one. Steel did.' He raised an eyebrow. 'Speaking of which. . .'

The side door banged open and DI Steel marched into reception with a face on her that would curdle linoleum. 'Where the hell have you been?'

Logan sidled towards the exit. 'It's my day off. I just came in to—'

'My office. NOW!'

Steel slumped behind her desk and glowered at Logan. 'This is all your fault.'

'What? How is it my—'

'Don't interrupt. You sodded off yesterday and I had to take DS Beardy Sodding Beattie! Continental drift moves faster than that fat git. Duane Cowie did a runner.'

'Yes, but Eric said he was—'

'Which part of "don't interrupt" are you having problems with?'

Logan shut his mouth.

'If you'd sodding well been there, Duane Cowie wouldn't have got away, someone wouldn't have battered the crap out of him, and I'd have another suspect to sodding question!' She dug a folder out from her in-tray and tossed it across the desk at him. 'Read it.'

Inside was an interview transcript: present DI Steel, DS Beattie, and Allan Rait. The other dog-mask rapist. Logan skimmed through it. 'That's one pound fifty: "sodding" still counts as a swearword.'

'No it sodding doesn't.'

According to Allan Rait's statement, Krystka Gorzałkowska was acting. There was no rape. It was all make-believe. The magic of cinema. Logan stuck the transcript back in the folder. 'What does Krystka say?'

'What the hell do you think? Like interviewing Marcel Marceau.' Steel slumped back in her chair. 'If she made a complaint I could nail them to the wall, but right now we've got fff . . . sod all.'

She scowled for a bit, drumming her fingers against her forehead. Then: 'What about the company who hired her out?'

'Kostchey International Holdings Limited.'

'Aye, you got that address yet?'

'Er. . .' Logan dragged his phone out and checked for messages from Zander Clark. 'No.'

'Oh for God's sake! You're now officially in my bad books.'

'Oh, come on. That's not fair—'

'Boo-hoo. Life's not fair.'

'It's my day off—'

'Want to know how you can get back in my *good* books?' She pulled out the empty plastic cup and stuck it on her desk.

Logan groaned. 'Not again with the sperm!'

'Aye, *again* with the sperm. You've got millions of the wriggly little buggers, you'll no' miss a couple of tablespoons, will you?'

'*Tablespoons*?'

'Oh don't be such a drama queen.' She dug a hand into her shirt and started hauling on her bra strap. 'Susan's being a complete nightmare. Now she wants to cash in all our savings, sell *my* car, and go pay for artificial insemination in the States.'

'Well, maybe that's not a bad—'

'If I don't want Rennie's sperm, why the hell would I want some American tosser's? Gene pool's bad enough as it is.'

There was an uncomfortable silence.

Logan stood. 'Well, I'd better get going, you know: day off and—'

'No' so fast. What else we got on Kostchey International Whosit?'

Shrug. 'Nothing.'

'What about that mobile number we got from Gary the Toilet Diver?'

'Pay-as-you-go – no registered details.'

She hauled at her bra for a bit. 'What did the Polish police say?'

'Eh?'

'You were supposed to chase them up! You forgot, didn't you?'

'Well . . . McPherson's the liaison officer, and he's still off on the sick. . .'

Steel spoke very slowly and very clearly. 'And it never occurred to you to phone them yourself?'

'Er . . . well, I—'

'For God's sake, you're supposed to be a Detective Sergeant!'

'But if Krystka Gorzałkowska won't make a complaint, how does it—'

'Don't be an idiot: half the girls they import are probably

from Christ-knows-where-istan. Illegal immigrants. People trafficking. And the mucky film industry's no' exactly booming in Aberdeenshire, is it? So what happens to the poor cows who can't be porn stars?' She tapped her desk with a finger. 'Do the words "forced into prostitution" mean anything to you?'

Logan opened his mouth, but the inspector got there first: 'And before you say anything, you'll phone them because I sodding well told you to. Me: organ grinder, you: monkey, remember?'

Silence.

'Now get the hell out of my office.'

Detective Inspector McPherson's room was a mess of file boxes, sandwich wrappers, and random bits of paper. Coffee mugs lurked on various surfaces, full of brown-green scum, evolving their own life forms in the heat of the radiator: turned up to full. The whole room smelled musty and stale.

Logan cleared a copy of Monday's *Aberdeen Examiner* off the chair and settled – carefully – behind the desk, looking at McPherson's piles of paperwork and plague of Post-it notes. The contact details for the Polish Liaison Officer had to be in here somewhere.

Not that Logan really wanted to touch anything.

There was a half-eaten Mars Bar in the top drawer and a stack of ancient receipts. Next drawer: notebook, paper-clips, pens, hundreds of random business cards. He dragged open the bottom drawer. It was meant to be for files, but McPherson seemed to be using it as a paperwork glory hole.

On top of the pile was the same memo Logan had seen on Steel's desk: the one asking for nominations for a new Detective Inspector. Blah, blah, blah, regret to inform you that DI Gray has tendered his resignation; blah, blah, blah;

opportunity to reward performance; blah, blah, blah; suggestions by next Wednesday.

McPherson had scribbled, 'BEATTIE?' in the margin in red biro.

Idiot.

Logan stuck the memo back in the drawer. Detective Sergeant Beattie couldn't arrest his own backside with three patrol cars and a search warrant.

The Polish contact details were nowhere to be found, so Logan fired up McPherson's computer. Hacking into the inspector's email wasn't that difficult – the idiot had left his password on a Post-it stuck to the monitor. DI Gray wasn't the only one who needed replacing.

McPherson's computer files were every bit as disorganized as his real ones, but eventually Logan found one marked 'Staff Sergeant Cyrek Łukaszewski ~ Warsaw FHQ'. Telephone number and email address.

He was tempted to fire off a quick email and escape, but that would just give Steel another excuse to whinge. So he picked up the phone, made sure there was nothing sticky on the mouth or earpiece, then dialled Poland.

Strange foreign bleeps, that went on and on and on and—a bored voice: *'Posterunek Policji, Kryminalne Biuro Śledcze, słucham.'*

Logan did his best. 'Hello? I mean: *dzień dobry, czy pan mówi po angielsku?*'

'Yes, I speak English.'

Thank God. 'I need to speak to a Staff Sergeant Cyrek. . .' He had a stab at the surname, 'Wookas-view-ski?'

'Łukaszewski?'

'Yes, that's right: Łukaszewski.' Hurrah.

'No: is Saturday. Try again Monday.' Not Hurrah.

'Oh. . . Can I leave a message? I need details on a "Kostchey International Holdings Ltd."'

The officer on the other end laughed. *'You are joking, yes?'*

'No. Why would I be—'

'In Poland, Kostchey is lord of the underworld. Kostchey the Deathless.'

'You don't have anyone called Kostchey over there?'

More laughter. *'Criminals and gang-people all want to be Kostchey the Deathless. Think it make them sound tough. Is not real name.'*

Another dead end. Logan put his hand over the mouth-piece and swore. Steel wasn't going to be pleased.

'Hello?'

'Give me a minute. . .' There was a memo on the cluttered desk from Finnie, telling McPherson to get his finger out and chase up the list of Oedipus victims with the Polish police. McPherson had scrawled 'Do This First Thing Monday!!!' at the top of the sheet. And then 'Monday' had been crossed out and replaced with 'Tuesday'. By which time the silly sod would have been flat on his back in the hospital, sleeping off a concussion. Which probably meant it still hadn't been done.

'Hello? You are still there?'

'Yeah, sorry. Look, we've had a bunch of blindings recently—'

'Blin-dings?'

'Blindings: eyes cut out and burnt?'

Logan could almost hear him shrugging.

'All the victims are Polish, we need to know if there was any connection between them. Can you get someone to do a background check for me?' Then he went through the names, making the man on the other end repeat them back to him.

'OK, I tell Łukaszewski *when he come in on Monday.'* And then the officer hung up.

So much for that. Logan shut down McPherson's computer,

switched off the lights, and closed the door on the inspector's pigsty. Now he'd have to go tell Steel the bad news.

Thankfully she wasn't in her office, so he scribbled a note and left it on her desk: 'POLISH POLICE THINK "KOSTCHEY" IS A JOKE NAME. THEY'LL PHONE BACK MONDAY.'

And escape.

38

Sunday morning dawned . . . and was ignored. It was half past ten before Logan and Samantha surfaced, rumpled and still pleasantly tired from the night before.

He stuck the kettle on while she bumbled about in the shower.

Breakfast: croissants, cream cheese, smoked salmon from Marks & Spencer; freshly ground coffee from a little shop on Little Belmont Street; and a dusty jar of black cherry jam from the back of the cupboard. He laid it all out on the coffee table in the lounge, then whipped the dust sheet off of the sofa and draped it over the stepladder in the corner.

Samantha emerged, wearing knee-length stripy socks and a black T-shirt featuring a dead teddy bear. Rubbing her bright-scarlet hair with a towel. 'I'm impressed. Thought you'd be more of a fry-up kind of guy.'

Logan poured the coffee. 'My body is a temple.'

'Aye, right.' She settled on the couch, legs crossed underneath her.

It wasn't a bad way to spend a morning: eating breakfast, drinking coffee, and reading the Sunday papers. Watching a square of sunlight slowly crawl from left to right across the bare floorboards and empty paint pots. A little canoodling.

And then the phone went.

Logan stayed where he was – lips locked on Samantha's, one hand up the front of her T-shirt. Eventually the ringing stopped and the answering machine picked up. Then the phone started ringing again.

He swore. 'It's probably—'

She pulled him back to her. 'Leave it.'

The answering machine went bleep. The ringing stopped. And then started again. She sighed. 'Go on then.'

'Bloody hell.' Logan grabbed the phone. 'What?'

'How come you never answer your phone the first time?' It was Big Gary.

'What are you, allergic to the answering machine?'

'I got someone from the Polish police on the line for you—'

'I'm not on duty.'

'And I'm not shagging Keira Knightley, but you don't hear me whinging about it, do you?'

'It's my day off! I'm—'

'Here you go. . .'

A new voice came on the line: a woman, sounding as if she were speaking into a tin can on the end of a length of soggy string. *'Hello? Hello?'*

Bloody Gary.

Logan did his best not to sound as hacked off as he felt. 'Detective Sergeant McRae. Can I help you?'

'You called Warsaw Police Headquarters yesterday?' The accent was lightly flavoured with Eastern European, but her English was perfect, if a little stilted.

'Yes. Is this Staff Sergeant Łukaszewski?'

'Łukaszewski is fifty-six years old. And a man.'

Definitely not Łukaszewski then.

'My name is Wiktorja Jaroszewicz,' she sounded it out for him, *'Yahr-oh-SHAY-veetch. And before you ask: no, no relation.'*

Relation to who, Logan had no idea. If in doubt, change the subject. 'Did you find anything out about Kostchey International Holdings?'

'You asked about blindings – men with their eyes gouged out and the sockets burned? We have victims here too.'

And Logan started paying a lot more attention. 'Really?'

'Do you want to come and speak to them?'

Detective Chief Superintendent Bain sat behind his desk, listening as Logan went over everything Senior Constable Wiktorja Jaroszewicz had said on the phone. Finnie had one of the visitor's chairs, DS Pirie the other, all dragged in on their day off, dressed in casual clothes instead of the standard cheap suits.

'Let me get this straight,' said DCS Bain, Sunday afternoon sunshine glinting off his shiny head, 'you're saying it's the same MO: eyes gouged out and burnt?'

Logan checked his notes. 'The last one was in 2004. According to Jaroszewicz, the attacks started around 1974, but it could be earlier. She says when the Communists were in power the police were more interested in rooting out political subversives than actually solving crimes. And a lot of the records disappeared when Poland got its independence.'

'Covering their tracks in case of repercussions,' said Finnie.

'I see. . .' DCS Bain steepled his fingers, tapped them against his lips, then turned to Finnie. 'Tell me, Chief Inspector, why didn't anyone bother contacting the Polish police until now?'

'McPherson was supposed to do it *weeks* ago. Pirie's been chasing him up two, three times a day.'

Pirie nodded. 'Kept coming up with excuses, he—'

'Besides, with Ricky Gilchrist in custody it's immaterial.

There's no way he could have been blinding people in 1974 – he wasn't even *born* in 1974. No, this is something else.'

'Maybe it's a family thing?' Pirie looked around the room for support. 'His father worked in the fish, who knows where he sailed to?'

'*Or,*' said Logan, 'he's been using the Polish attacks as a template.'

'What does our pet psychologist say?'

Finnie scowled. 'Can't get hold of him, sir. Apparently playing *cricket* is more important.'

'I see. . .' The head of CID was silent for a while. 'Well, we have a confession, and you say Gilchrist's cooperating?'

'Fully. Doesn't even want a lawyer. He's proud of his *accomplishments*.'

'Still, I want someone to go out there and interview these victims. See if we can either make a link with Gilchrist, or rule one out. The last thing we need is some slimy defence lawyer muddying the waters when it comes to court.'

Finnie hauled himself out of the seat. 'I'll be on the first flight to Warsaw tomorrow morning and—'

'I need you here looking into that caravan full of guns. With Oedipus out of the way it's our number-one priority. Whatever's going on, I want it stopped before we've got running gun battles up and down Union Street.'

'But—'

'You're needed *here* Chief Inspector. Send someone you can trust.'

Pirie sat forward. 'I'll go. I can—'

'No,' said Finnie, 'you've got those drug dealers in Bucksburn to find, *remember*?' He folded his arms across his chest and nodded in Logan's direction. 'McRae caught Gilchrist, *and* he came up with the Polish lead. He should go.'

* * *

'Warsaw?' Samantha stood in the doorway, watching him pack. 'Jammy sod. Furthest they ever sent me was Thurso, and that wasn't exactly a bag of laughs.'

'It's only for a couple of days.'

He went through every drawer in his bedside cabinet: what the hell had happened to all his clean socks?

Samantha settled onto the edge of the bed. 'Some farmer walked into his local Post Office with a shotgun and blew this old guy's head off. Then he did the same thing to the cashier. *Then* he stuck the barrel in his own mouth. Blood and brains all over the ceiling.'

Logan tried the wardrobe. 'And Poland's in the EU, so it's not like I'm even getting duty free out of it.'

'Two old ladies, a single mother and her kid were standing right there. Saw the whole thing. Got covered in most of it. . .'

'You haven't seen a pile of socks anywhere, have you?'

'Apparently the only thing he said was right before he topped himself. Said, "Told you it wasn't funny." And then bang.'

How could three dozen socks just disappear?

'Took us days to scrape up all the bits.'

Logan found them lurking under the bed, hiding from the dust and paint. Four pairs went in the little suitcase, followed by just enough clothes to see him there and back. ''Scuse me. . .' He squeezed past Samantha, made for the bathroom, and started packing a toilet bag.

'Come on then,' she said, watching him rummage for the spare toothpaste, 'it's half six already. What we doing for tea?'

'Carry out?'

'We could go clubbing? Paint the town a bit.'

The toilet bag went in the little suitcase. 'Can't really do a late night; I've got a briefing at seven.'

'Oh.'

'Sorry.' He zipped the case shut and hefted it off the bed. Then started the hunt for his passport.

Samantha picked at the edge of the makeshift dustsheet draped over the wardrobe. 'They're talking about shutting the lab again. Shift everything down to that new place they're building in Dundee.'

Logan stopped mid-rummage. 'What idiot thought that'd be a good idea? What are we supposed to do with no lab?'

'They'll have to keep some IB techs up here for the crime scenes and stuff, but we'll just be glorified monkeys. Pick it up, pack it up, and post it off to Dundee.'

'What about you?'

Shrug. 'Who knows? They're not saying anything about redundancies yet.'

Logan gave up on the search and wrapped her up in a kiss.

Later. The sound of drunken singing drifted up from the street below, coming in through the open bedroom window. Logan lay on his back in the bed, the duvet rumpled around his knees, Samantha on her side next to him. Head resting on his chest as she ran a finger through the scars on his stomach. Tracing the pattern.

Logan frowned up at the ceiling as she bent forwards to kiss one. 'Sam?'

'Mmm?' Another kiss.

'Why do you . . . This thing . . . with my scars. It's kind of creepy.'

She froze. 'What?'

'Is it some sort of Goth thing?'

She sat upright. No more kissing. 'I can't believe you just said that.'

He looked up at her, silhouetted in the light from the

window, her red hair tinged with gold, as if her head were on fire. 'Well . . . is it?'

'I'm a freak, is that what you're saying?'

'I didn't say that.'

'But you're thinking it.'

Logan pulled the duvet up, covering himself to the nipples. 'Every time we're naked you play with them. I'm beginning to worry about it, OK?'

'You are *such* a shit, McRae.' She wiped a hand across her face and clambered out of bed. 'I can't believe you.'

He snapped on the bedside light. She was struggling a leg into her pants. 'I've got to go.'

'Sam, don't be like that, I—'

'Where's my bloody bra?'

'Oh for God's sake. I'm sorry, OK?'

'I can't believe I actually thought you were different.' She grabbed her T-shirt from the bedroom floor and dragged it on over her head. Then she scooped up her leather trousers and boots, turned and stormed out, slamming the door behind her.

Logan slumped back on the bed, put his hands over his face and went, 'AAAAAAAAAAAARGH!' He couldn't find someone *nice* and *normal* to go out with, could he? No, *he* had to pick the ones who'd make him miserable.

The bedroom door flew open and she was back.

'You want to know? Do you?' Samantha dumped her leather trousers on the floor and marched over to the bed. She grabbed his hand and slapped it on the jagged tribal spider tattoo that wound its way from the inside of her left thigh all the way up onto her belly. 'There, feel it. Go on! Right there.'

'What? I'm not feeling—'

'Not there, *here*, you idiot.'

A collection of little ridges, four to six inches long. Curves, straight lines, zigzags. Scar tissue, hidden beneath the tattoo's black ink – the ones Logan thought were stretch marks. Then she slapped his hand away and got back into her trousers. 'That's why.'

This time when she slammed the door, she didn't come back.

39

Most of the Monday morning briefing was spent going over the caravan-full-of-guns inquiry: codenamed Operation Tailback. Then came the usual updates and warnings about gang violence, and a bit of gloating from Finnie about Agnes McLeod being in the cells all weekend. They finished with the day's assignments and the announcement that Logan was off on a jolly to Poland for three or four days.

DI Steel grabbed Logan as he tried to slip out. 'What the hell do you think you're. . .' She caught the head of CID watching her, stopped, smiled, nodded a greeting, then bustled Logan out into the corridor. 'Poland? You forgetting we've got bloody work to do?'

'Look, Bain said—'

'What about those Kostchey idiots: did you get an address yet?'

'Yup.'

There was a pause and Steel stared at him. 'Well? Are you going to tell me, or am I supposed to sodding guess?'

Logan gave her the address Zander Clark had emailed through – a business unit on Greenwell Road, East Tullos Industrial Estate.

'Right.' She hauled up her trousers. 'Get a pool car organized, we'll stake the place out and—'

'I can't. My flight's at five to eleven; got to be at the airport an hour before that.'

'Fine. You go to Poland, see if I care.' Steel poked him with a nicotine finger. 'But if I have to take Detective Sergeant Beardy Sodding Beattie, I'm holding you responsible, understand?'

Rennie winced his way into the CID office; face, neck, and ears bright shiny pink. Even the backs of his hands were sunburnt. That, and the blond crown of spiky hair, made him look like an unsqueezed spot. He perched himself, gingerly, on the edge of Logan's desk and said, 'Ow. . .'

'Nice tan.'

'It's not funny.'

'Should have put on some suntan lotion then, shouldn't you?'

Rennie loosened his collar, wafting his scarlet face with a burglary report. 'Fancy an ice-cream or something? I'm boiling.'

Logan sent Dr Goulding's latest report to the printer in the corner and shut down his computer. 'Can't: have to go home and get my suitcase; Finnie's got a patrol car taking me to the airport in twenty minutes.'

'Ah well. . . Bring us back some vodka, eh?'

'Speaking of Finnie,' Logan grabbed the printout, 'he about?'

Logan could tell Rennie was thinking: he could smell the burning dust.

'Nope,' the constable said at last, 'got a phone call and went scurrying out of here. Back door I think?'

Logan said his goodbyes, signed out, then sauntered outside, making for the keypad controlled door that led onto Lodge Walk.

The door was ajar. Logan pushed it open, going from bright sunshine into the blue shadow of the alley.

DCI Finnie was just turning back towards the station, stuffing a brown envelope into his inside jacket pocket. He looked up and saw Logan standing there, then frowned. 'What are—'

'Going to get my suitcase.'

'Oh, right.' Finnie said something about interdepartmental cooperation with the Polish police, but Logan wasn't listening. He was looking over the Chief Inspector's shoulder at a spotty youth marching away down the gloomy alleyway and out onto Union Street. The sunlight caught in his bright green hair, making it shine like electric grass. And then he was gone.

A hand thumped down on Logan's shoulder breaking the spell. 'Good luck, I'm counting on you.'

'Oh, right . . . thank you, sir.'

'Soon as you're back I want you on Operation Tailback. It'll probably be a couple of days before we can make the announcement – about the promotion I mean – but I want you heading up a team ASAP. OK?'

And then Finnie's phone rang. The DCI dragged it out and headed back towards the station: 'What? . . . No, of *course* I don't mind waiting *three days* for a warrant. He's only wanted for *armed robbery* after all, not like it's anything *important*. . .'

Logan stayed where he was, staring down the alleyway to the patch of glowing street at the far end. Green hair. Spots. And a brown envelope.

No doubt about it: background radiation could be a dangerous thing.

40

At least he'd managed to get a window seat. Logan was halfway across the North Sea, with a strange cheese and pesto sandwich and a tiny bottle of white wine. The wheezy old woman sitting next to him had lasted a whole fifteen minutes before falling asleep, twitching as she dreamed, like a cat.

The report he'd printed out before leaving the office didn't make very scintillating reading – Goulding went on and on about 'behavioural indicators' and 'stress-point escalators', none of which made any sense to Logan.

> Gilchrist continues to refuse to discuss his victims, or even acknowledge their existence. By removing their eyes he has removed the very essence of their humanity; many cultures believe the eyes to be the gateway to the soul, and Gilchrist has removed that gateway, rendering them spiritually inert (an important distinction for someone with Gilchrist's strong, though twisted, religious convictions {*see Appendix B, section 3.2*}), as such they have no meaning to him.
>
> It would not surprise me if Gilchrist later admits to consuming the eyes. Possibly as part of a ritual based on his

somewhat individual views on the sacrament, designed to absorb his victim's immortal soul.

However, this remains conjecture at this point.

Blah, blah, blah . . . Logan skimmed forward a couple of pages. The whole thing was a great steaming pile of conjecture as far as he could see.

Certainly Ricky Gilchrist represents a very real danger to the public, and while there are no current indications that he may be suicidal, I recommend that he be kept under close observation.

Which seemed to be a long-winded way of saying what they'd known all along: Ricky Gilchrist was a nut-job.

Logan put the report down and stared out at the glittering blue surface of the North Sea.

Should have brought a book with him.

The woman sitting next to him had stopped twitching and started snoring, the noise barely perceptible over the plane's engines.

Logan polished off his wee individual bottle of white wine, then asked for another one, and settled down for some industrial-strength brooding. First about Samantha. And then about Detective Chief Inspector Andrew 'Brown-Envelope' Finnie.

And then he went back to brooding about Samantha again.

Playing with his scars, then acting as if *he* was the one with the problem. Logan shifted in his seat. OK, so he had a problem. . . But that didn't mean she had to yell at him and storm off.

Away on a trip to Poland, two high-profile arrests under his belt, a promotion to DI coming up – God knew he'd been waiting long enough – and then *this* had to happen. Tainting it all.

He placed a hand on his stomach, pressing until he could feel the old familiar tug of knitted tissue, the stitches, the months in hospital.

Bloody Angus Robertson: even after all these years he was still screwing up Logan's life.

Za Naszą I Waszą Wolność

[For Our Freedom And Yours]

41

Logan stifled a yawn and joined the shuffling queue for passport control. The place was even more soulless than the one back at Aberdeen airport. Plus all the security guards were wearing drab-olive military uniforms, complete with side arms. Even after doing his firearms training, there was something about seeing policemen with guns that gave Logan the willies.

He picked up his suitcase and slouched into the arrivals lounge – a big empty room with white walls and a glass ceiling. A couple of men held up sheets of paper with indecipherable names scribbled on them. A handful of small children squealed around a businessman, their mother hanging back. Scowling and heavily pregnant.

There was no sign of anyone who looked like a 'Staff Sergeant Łukaszewski', or a 'Senior Constable Wiktorja Jaroszewicz'.

Typical.

Logan dumped his luggage at his feet, and stood there looking gormless for a minute. Until a balding man in a shabby grey pullover sidled up and said, 'You tourist? You want taxi, yes?'

Alarm bells.

Logan pulled out his warrant card. *'Policja.'*

The man backed away, stammering, *'Przepraszam, pomyliłem się. . .'* and then froze as a hand slapped down on his shoulder.

The woman standing behind him couldn't have been an inch over five foot five, mid-thirties, blonde hair scraped back in a severe ponytail. 'Damn right you made a mistake!' At least she was speaking English.

Mr Shabby Pullover closed his eyes and winced. *'Cholera jasna. . .'*

She spun him around. 'How many times have I told you?'

'Przepraszam: sorry, I am sorry. . .'

'You are lucky I am busy, Radoslaw.' She let go. 'Go on, get out of here you dirty *zboczeniec.*'

A smile scrambled onto his face. *'Dziękuję, dziękuję bardzo!'*

And then he all but ran for it, her parting shot ringing around the arrivals hall as he scampered away: 'Next time I catch you, you will not be thanking me, you will be clutching your balls and crying like a little baby: stay away from the airport!'

There was silence as her threat echoed away, everyone staring at Logan and the woman. 'Come on.' She grabbed Logan's bag and strode for the exit. 'I am parked outside.'

They stepped through the sliding doors and emerged under some sort of flyover, surrounded by grey concrete on all four sides. Rain poured down a set of stairs. The distant rumble of thunder. Welcome to Warsaw.

Her car was a right-hand-drive Opel hatchback in grubby silver. She threw Logan's luggage in the boot, and jumped in behind the wheel. It wasn't until Logan walked around to the passenger side that he saw the damage – it was one long collection of dents and scrapes. The door squealed as he hauled it open, and groaned when he pulled it shut.

The woman shook her head. 'You have to slam it hard, or it will pop open every time we go over a pothole.'

Logan did as he was told.

'Piece of shit, yeah?' She stuck the car in gear, and floored it.

'Jesus. . .' Logan grabbed onto the handle above the door as she roared around the corner and nearly into the back of a bus.

She didn't seem to notice, just shifted down and swerved round the outside, bumping up onto the kerb on the way past. And then they were out from under the flyover, swapping grey concrete for an even greyer sky.

Rain hammered down, making the tarmac shimmer, reflecting back the car headlights, even though it was only ten to five on a Monday afternoon.

She took one hand off the steering wheel and offered it to Logan. 'Senior Constable Wiktorja Jaroszewicz. You say it: Yahr-oh-SHAY-veetch.'

'I know, you told me when—' Logan tried not to close his eyes as she threw them around the roundabout and onto a tree-lined dual carriageway, but she was still shaking his hand while she did it. 'Detective Sergeant Logan McRae.' Forcing his voice down the two octaves it had suddenly jumped.

'Look at this idiot. . .' She leant on the car's horn and raced up the back end of a mouldy Volvo estate. 'Move it grandfather!' BRRRREEEEEEEP! 'I tell you, rush-hour brings them all out.'

And then she accelerated past, nipping between an articulated lorry and a telecoms van. 'You were lucky I turned up,' she said, swerving back into their original lane, 'Radoslaw would have taken you for everything you had.'

'I wasn't going to—'

'He turns up at the airport, pretends to be this helpful old taxi driver, and if you go with him you end up on the wrong side of the river.'

'Not a very good taxi driver then?'

'Not unless you like being robbed at gunpoint, no. We think he gets two or three tourists a month, but we can't prove anything.'

Lightning flickered across the clay-coloured sky, silhouetting the trees and ugly concrete buildings on either side of the road. Then came the deep, bass rumble of thunder.

Senior Constable Jaroszewicz hunched closer to the steering wheel. 'Bloody rain. What happened to summer?'

She launched into a stream of weather-related invective, but Logan was too scared to listen to it, holding on for dear life as she leapt from one lane to the other.

A horn blared at them, Jaroszewicz ignored it. 'I checked the records again. We have twenty-three victims since 1974; most of them happened after we kicked the Communists out. I brought everything I found with me, you can read it on the train.'

'Train? I thought we were going to—' He closed his eyes as the rear end of a truck suddenly appeared in front of them. 'Oh God.'

The tyres squealed on the wet road. Jaroszewicz leant on the horn: BRRRRREEEEEEEEEP! 'Asshole! Are you trying to kill everyone?'

And then she was roaring past on the inside, sticking one finger up at the old lady behind the wheel. 'There are no living victims left in Warsaw, so we are going to Krakow.'

'Can we slow down please?'

'No.'

Logan tried not to think about what his body was going to look like when the Polish fire brigade finally cut it out of the wreckage. 'What happened to the other victims?'

'Dead. Some had accidents, some got ill, some died of old

age, and some killed themselves.' Shrug. 'It must be a hard thing to live with.'

The bland communistic apartment blocks opened up, revealing central Warsaw. It was a vista of skyscrapers: huge chunks of glass and steel reaching up into the downpour. A big Marriott hotel sat in the background, the top seven floors covered in white lights that flashed messages out across the gloomy, rain-drenched city. The other skyscrapers were slightly less vulgar, but everything paled into insignificance next to the huge Palace of Culture: an evil wedding cake in rain-blackened sandstone, dominating the skyline.

Jaroszewicz must have seen him staring, because she said, 'A gift from Uncle Stalin. Are you hungry?'

'Kind of. Are we—'

'We will eat on the train.'

The Palace of Culture sat in the middle of a vast square, surrounded by buildings that looked as if they'd been thrown up by some city planner who'd had one too many vodkas. And the closer they got to Uncle Stalin's gift, the slower the traffic got, until they were crawling along. Rain drumming on the roof, windscreen wipers going full pelt, watching the people stomping past on the pavement.

Everyone looked suicidal.

Aberdeen could be miserable in the rain, but it was *nothing* compared to Warsaw.

Jaroszewicz jerked the steering wheel and squealed the car across a set of lights and down a little alleyway, threading round behind an ancient-looking hotel. Parking next to the bins.

'Now,' she said, reaching through into the back of the car and pulling out a large shoulder bag, 'train station.'

They got Logan's luggage out of the boot and tramped back to the main square in the pouring rain, across four lanes of traffic, and down into the station.

It didn't look too bad from the outside, but inside it was Bedlam. A collection of low-ceilinged concrete corridors, lined with booths selling everything from science fiction novels, to doughnuts, to hardcore pornography. The smell of kebab meat and hot falafel, the smoky tang of grilling sausages and frying onions. Voices. Shouting. People bumping into one another. Yellow and red lights blazing out of every shop front.

Up till now, it hadn't been too bad – pretty much like any modern European city – but suddenly Poland was a very foreign country.

Jaroszewicz marched up to a booth with a handwritten sign saying *'Nie Informacja'* Sellotaped to the glass. No information. He couldn't understand a word of the ensuing argument as Jaroszewicz and the man behind the counter shouted at each other, but eventually she stomped away from the booth with a pair of tickets and seat reservations.

'Bloody place.' She wandered through the throngs of people and joined a small crowd staring at a poster covered in a bewildering array of stations and times. Two minutes later she said, *'Peron* five.' And then headed off for a dirty grey escalator down to a dirty grey platform.

Logan hurried after her. 'What do you know about the victims?'

She shrugged, settling back against an information board. 'Before 1989 it looks political. We do not have much detail, but all the victims were accused of undermining the Communist regime: union leaders, clergy, activists, people like that. After 1989 there is a gap, then it starts up again: mostly small-time crooks.'

The platform started filling up, a mixture of businessmen and students.

Jaroszewicz dumped her bag at her feet. 'What about yours?'

Logan went through the Oedipus victims one by one, finishing up with the fact that none of them would talk to the police. 'They're all still terrified, even though we've got the guy in custody.'

She shrugged. 'I am not surprised.'

An announcement crackled out of the platform speakers – and everyone started shuffling towards the edge of the platform. Then a battered green diesel engine rumbled out of the dark tunnel, dragging behind it ten lilac-and-white carriages, the bright orange 'ICC PKP INTERCITY' logo painted on the side.

A whistle blast and the doors opened. Jaroszewicz pulled out their tickets and squinted at them. Then dragged Logan down the platform and onto carriage number nine.

Inside, it was like something out of a transport museum: a corridor stretched down one side of the carriage, lined with sliding glass doors that opened onto little individual eight-seat compartments.

She checked the tickets again, then hauled a door open and stepped inside. It was already crowded. Six students sprawled on the seats, laughing and sharing a loaf of bread – ripping off handfuls and popping them in their mouths.

Jaroszewicz swore, hauled her bag up onto the overhead rack and told a man with long brown hair to get out of her seat. Then told his girlfriend to get out of Logan's. They just shrugged, then moved.

Logan apologized his way between everyone's knees to the window seat, and manhandled his suitcase up onto the rack.

Another announcement. Then a clunk. And slowly the train pulled away from the platform, through another dark tunnel, and out into the rain-soaked evening.

Senior Constable Jaroszewicz made small talk for a while, mostly about movies she'd seen, and then lapsed into silence, staring out of the window as the graffiti-covered sidings drifted past.

A girl sitting across from Logan, slumped down in her seat, exposing pale thighs as her skirt rode up. Tattoos poked out of the top of her V-neck jumper.

Samantha. How was he supposed to know she had scars high up on the inside of her thighs? What was he, a mind reader? He shifted in his seat. And how the hell did you get scars there anyway?

The student looked up and saw him staring at her tattooed chest. Their eyes met and Logan looked away, embarrassed. Great, now she thought he was a pervert.

'*Bilet.*'

Logan looked up. An official-looking man in a dark blue uniform was standing in front of him.

'Erm. . .'

Jaroszewicz dug about in her handbag, 'He wants to see your ticket.'

'Oh right. . .'

The conductor made his way around their little compartment, stamping everyone's ticket, before lurching back out into the corridor, pulling the sliding glass door shut behind him. As soon as he was gone, Jaroszewicz stood and rattled off something in quick-fire Polish to the students.

They complained, but she didn't seem to care. She pulled out a police ID and flashed it at them, then gave them another earful.

The students got to their feet and shuffled out of the compartment, full of bad grace, angry backward glances, and mutterings of, '*Kurwa, komucha. . .*'

Jaroszewicz waited till the door was closed before dragging her bag out of the rack and collapsing back into her seat, grinning. 'They say I am a Communist bitch.' She pulled a swollen, green folder from her bag and handed it over. 'This is everything I could find.'

Logan removed the elastic band holding the file together,

and opened it up. A bundle of photographs sat at the front – each one showing someone's mutilated face in graphic close up. Most were taken pre-hospital as well, the sight making Logan's stomach lurch in time with the train on the tracks. The damage was identical to the Aberdeen victims: Ricky Gilchrist had copied the MO perfectly.

He flipped past, finding dozens of reports, statements, interview transcripts. . . Somewhere in this lot would be the connection between Gilchrist and whoever mutilated these poor sods.

And Logan couldn't read a word of it.

42

Outside the carriage window there was nothing but fields and trees. Every now and then they'd pass a village – little more than a handful of houses with wooden outbuildings slumped in defeat. Chickens strutting back and forth in the mud.

The rain had stopped about an hour out of Warsaw, but the landscape still lay beneath a lid of heavy grey clouds.

'And this was the last one.' Jaroszewicz poked the file in Logan's hand. 'He was a baker in Sromowce Niżne. Arrested two times for drug dealing. They found him in the garage: he hanged himself six months after he was blinded.'

There was a photocopy of the note he'd left, and a police photo of the body dangling from a roof beam.

Logan stuck them back in the file. 'Twenty-three victims since 1974. So if it's the same man doing them he's got to be, what . . . mid fifties, early sixties by now?'

'*If* it is the same man.' Jaroszewicz accepted the folder and put it back in her bag. 'Before 1989 all our victims are dissidents, and after 1989 they are all criminals.' She snapped her bag shut and hefted it into the overhead rack. 'I think the men who are doing this are copying what happened under the Communists. It is a warning to everyone who will not do what they are told. In Poland it is not a serial killer, it is mob enforcement.'

By quarter past eight they were in the dining car, getting scowled at by the evicted students. Jaroszewicz sat with her back to them at one if the five long tables that stuck out from one side of the carriage, leaving an aisle at the end just big enough for the waitress to walk down, carrying plates of food from the little kitchen by the door. The smell of frying chicken filled the air.

A couple of businessmen sat at the other end of their table, poking away at laptops and drinking bottles of lager. Everyone had to perch on little bar stools that had been bolted to the floor, as the train swayed and rattled its way across Poland.

'It will be too late to do anything when we get to Krakow,' Jaroszewicz was saying, 'so we will start first thing tomorrow morning. Hit the local police for information.'

'Information?'

'Addresses for the Krakow victims.' She took another mouthful of unpronounceable beer. 'The only records I could get in Warsaw are out of date. They. . .' She stopped talking as a smiling woman in an apron appeared at the table with their food – flattened slabs of chicken fried in breadcrumbs, mashed potatoes covered in dill, and pickled gherkins. Served on paper plates with plastic cutlery.

A long way away from British Rail sandwiches.

Outside the sun was setting, a heavy orb of red fire just visible between the clouds and the fields, gilding a three-storey house made entirely of breeze blocks, all on its own in the middle of nowhere.

Logan scooped up another forkful of mash. 'If the records are out of date, how do you know the victims are still alive?'

'I do not.' She took one look at the expression on Logan's face and laughed. 'Relax, they cannot all be dead. I spoke to the *Komisariat Policji* yesterday, there is at least one they have heard about recently. Now eat your chicken.'

The first sign of Krakow was the local football team's name, scrawled in red spray-paint on a dilapidated building at the side of the railway tracks, just visible in the fading glow of a setting sun. The distant sparkle of houses gave way to huge blocks of concrete apartments, with the chimneys of a massive steelworks in the background – crowned with blinking red and white lights to ward off aircraft.

Then mile after mile of densely packed houses and tower blocks, sulking beneath thick grey clouds.

The students braved a return to the carriage, grabbing their luggage and grumbling as the train pulled into the station. Not quite defiant enough to make eye contact with Senior Constable Jaroszewicz.

Logan followed her out onto the platform. A cold wind whipped a discarded newspaper apart and sent it dancing across the expanse of grey concrete. Warsaw had been depressing, and right now Krakow didn't look much better.

The taxi dropped them outside a hotel in the old city, on a street packed with people, bars and kebab shops. The high buildings and narrow streets cut out the worst of the wind, and it was almost balmy. Tourists wandered through the fading twilight wearing T-shirts and shorts, taking photographs.

Logan couldn't blame them, it was actually pretty impressive, just the way old Eastern European cities were supposed to be. Cobbled streets, ornately carved frontages . . . like something out of a *Hammer House of Horror* film. Well, except for all the neon and flash photography.

Jaroszewicz pushed through the wrought-iron gates into the hotel, and after a pause, Logan followed her. 'So, what's the plan for tonight then?' Hoping it would involve beer.

She puffed out her cheeks and made a deflating noise. 'I am going to have a bath and go to bed.' She checked her watch. 'You can meet me for breakfast at eight o'clock.'

Upstairs in his room, Logan pulled the net curtains wide and stared out at the street below. He'd already unpacked everything and laid it away, played with the room's safe, checked out the contents of the mini-bar, thought about stealing the little plastic bottles of shampoo and conditioner, and read all the tour leaflets.

And then he remembered to switch his phone back on. Three messages, all from DI Steel, telling him to phone her back, urgently.

He checked his watch: half nine. That would make it half past eight back home. He dialled Steel's number and rested his forehead against the window, watching a pair of drunken girlies staggering out of what looked like an off-licence.

Then Steel's voice barked out of the earpiece: *'What took you so sodding long?'*

'Had my phone turned off. Airline safety rules.'

'Blah, blah, blah. I went to that address you got from your fat pornographer, and you know what I found?'

Outside, one of the girls slipped and clattered bum-first onto the cobbles. Her friend started laughing. 'No idea.'

Steel blew him a big, wet raspberry. *'That's what. No' a damn thing. The whole place was empty.'*

'You sure you went to the right—'

'Finish that sentence and you're getting a shoe-leather suppository. Of course we went to the right place: manky wee Portakabin on Greenwell road, backing onto the railway line. Anonymous and sodding empty. A rest home for spiders and dead wasps!'

'Oh . . . Sorry.'

'Aye, well "sorry" doesn't help Krystka Gorzałkowska, does it?'

Logan closed his eyes and counted to ten.

'You still there?'

'Did you want me to phone you back *urgently* just so you could shout at me?'

'Don't get lippy.' Pause. *'Susan wants you to come over for dinner when you get back.'*

And he knew what that meant. 'Ganging up on me?'

'Nope. Just a nice family dinner, couple bottles of wine, and if you still don't want to get Susan up the stick you can tell her yourself.' Then she hung up.

Logan snapped his phone shut. Swore. Then doinked his head gently off the window.

Sod it. He hadn't travelled one thousand, two hundred and sixty-seven miles just to sit in a hotel room. It was time to see what the local pubs were made of.

The alarm on his mobile phone sounded as if someone was trying to ram a xylophone up a chicken. Half past seven. Logan cracked one eye open and prepared for the hangover to hit. He'd stayed in the nearest bar till nearly midnight, drinking the local beer and experimenting with different kinds of flavoured vodka until the place shut. So he should have been feeling dreadful this morning. Only he wasn't.

Shower, shave, and down to breakfast. Still waiting for the other shoe to drop on his head from a great height.

Senior Constable Jaroszewicz was already sitting at a table for two, eating a huge mound of muesli. She pointed at him with her spoon. 'Your hair is wet.'

He helped himself to the buffet – ignoring the cold meat in favour of cheese, gherkins and bread, then sat down and perused the menu. Looking for a vegetarian fry-up. There wasn't one, so he settled for the scrambled eggs with mushrooms.

'I was thinking,' he said, while Jaroszewicz went back to her muesli, 'how well known are these blindings?'

She chewed for a while. 'No idea.'

'Well, how would someone from Aberdeen find out about them?'

'The Internet?'

'I tried that before I left yesterday and couldn't find anything.' A waitress turned up with his scrambled eggs. 'Oh, thank you. I mean: *Dziękuję.*' The young woman smiled at him and wandered off. Then Logan saw what he'd actually been served.

Jaroszewicz watched him pulling faces. 'What?'

'This isn't scrambled eggs. . . Looks like someone's sneezed on the plate.' Instead of a fluffy mound of yellow, it was a ribbony mix of white and yoke, oozing out across the plate, speckled with brown lumps. Not exactly appetizing.

'We will go to the police station straight after breakfast.'

He risked a bite. It actually wasn't that bad. 'What about jurisdiction?'

'Juris. . .?'

'Are you allowed to interview people here? Or do we need a local officer to hold our hands?'

'Pffffff. Warsaw and Krakow do not get on very well. We call them "villagers". They call us "freaking yuppies". They sulk because they used to be the capital of Poland, and now we are.' She shovelled in another spoonful and chewed. 'We are unlikely to get any help from the local police. I will be amazed if they even give us addresses for the victims.'

Somehow that didn't exactly fill Logan with confidence.

The street outside the hotel was a lot less crowded than it had been last night; the kebab shops dark and lifeless, the tourists still asleep, or enjoying a leisurely breakfast of something almost entirely unlike scrambled eggs.

Jaroszewicz took a right at the hotel's front gate, heading down towards the main square, under the shadow of the looming red-brick spire of St Mary's Basilica. Up above, the sky was a crystal blue, the sun already warming the cobblestones. Little cafés were setting up for the day, unfolding awnings and umbrellas to shade tables clustered around the outside of the square. The smell of charcoal fires and barbecued sausages filled the air, wafting out from a half dozen food stands, part of the permanent market that sprawled alongside the ornate rectangular bulk of the Cloth Hall.

She led Logan around to the other side of the square, marching towards a small, nondescript shop front on the ground floor of a yellow-painted building. The windows on the upper floors were surrounded by elaborately carved architraves, but the police station looked more like a minicab office, only blander. If it weren't for the little red sign mounted above the dark frontage with 'KOMISARIAT POLICJI I wKRAKOWIE' on it, there would be no indication it was there at all.

Jaroszewicz stopped about a dozen feet from the entrance. 'You had better wait out here. Go get yourself a cup of coffee or something.' And then she marched inside.

Logan wandered over to a nearby café, settled into the shade of a green Heineken umbrella and ordered a cup of coffee.

He checked his watch: twenty past nine. Twenty past eight in Aberdeen. He thought about calling Finnie to see if they'd got anything useful out of Gilchrist yesterday, but that would probably sound a bit needy. Much better to call when he had something to show for his trip to Krakow. So he sent Rennie a text instead, then sat and debated sending one to Samantha too. But what would he say? 'SRY I SED U WR A FR3K – MSSNG U – LGN.' Not exactly Shakespeare, was it?

His phone squawked: Rennie replying.

'NO PROGRS – STL IS A TTL BIATCH :-(FNY IS A DIK :-(BT IS

A WNKR :-(HWS POLAND?' Which made even less sense than normal. Maybe getting an iron bounced off his head had rattled something loose in that great big empty space between Rennie's ears?

Logan fired off a quick response about vodka and dancing girls. Then drank his coffee, watching a pair of armed policemen get off their bicycles to buy cigarettes from a small, round kiosk.

He was thinking about ordering another coffee, and maybe a sticky bun, when Jaroszewicz finally reappeared.

She hoiked a thumb over her shoulder. 'They played nice and gave me three addresses to try.'

Logan stood. 'What about transport?'

'Are you on expenses?'

'Yes.'

'Then we will take a taxi, and you can pay.'

By half past eleven the morning had gone from pleasantly sunny to stiflingly hot and sticky. Logan slumped against the roof of the taxi, sweating, as Jaroszewicz emerged back onto the street, slamming an old wooden door behind her.

The buildings in this part of town looked just like the ones around the hotel, only shabbier. Their paintwork faded and peeling, as if the inhabitants had given up a long time ago. Some were so dirty it was impossible to guess what colour they'd started off. It should have been quaint and olde-worlde, but it was just drab and oppressive. No wonder they'd shot *Schindler's List* here.

'Any joy?'

Jaroszewicz scowled back at the building she'd just stomped out of. 'The apartment has been empty for six years, according to the man next door. He says Mr Gibowski moved to America to be with his daughter after his wife died. He could not cope on his own with no eyes.'

'Three for three.'

She did a slow pirouette, staring at the shabby street. 'That is it. I have no more idea what to do.' By the time she came round to face Logan again, her eyes were shining. Bottom lip trembling. 'All this time. . .'

And Logan didn't know what to say. So he tried, 'Are you sure the police gave you all the info they had? I mean, if Gibowski's been gone six years?'

Sniff. She ran a palm across her eyes. 'I told you they hated us "freaking yuppies".'

The taxi driver stuck his head out of the car window and said something too quickly for Logan to catch any of it, but Jaroszewicz rattled back a brittle reply, then climbed into the back, saying, 'Are you hungry?'

Lunch was in a labyrinthine restaurant called Chłopskie Jadło, five minutes walk from the main square, with some sort of witch carved out of dark wood standing guard outside. The place was nearly deserted, just a woman and a small child stuffing themselves with dumplings. Jaroszewicz picked a table in another room, far away from the roaring fire.

She slumped into her chair and sighed at the menu. 'So that is it, we are finished. You had a wasted trip. I am sorry.'

'You seem to be taking this very . . . personally.'

She shrugged, eyes scanning the menu. 'You should try the *pierogi* – potato dumplings. Very good.'

'Come on, you were nearly in tears back there.'

'I. . .' Pause. 'This is a big case for me. If I. . . My sergeant says that if I do not get this one right, my career is over.' She turned the menu over in her hands. 'Do you want a drink? I want a drink. Let us get something to drink.'

There was a pause, then Logan stuck out a hand. 'Let me see those files again.'

'Why?'

'Because I'm not going home without a connection between Ricky Gilchrist and what happened here. And I don't care how tenuous it is – there has to be something. He didn't just come up with the exact same MO as your Polish mobsters by accident.'

She dug the file out of her cavernous handbag. Then went back to the menu.

Logan spread the individual case files out on the table. It was a cut-down version of the huge stack he'd seen on the train from Warsaw, with all the non-Krakow victims removed. Five victims: all men.

He arranged them in date order, '1973, 1981, 1993, 1997, and 2004. Five victims. Gibowski is in America, Wisniewski's dead, and no one's seen Bielatowicz since 2003. Which leaves us Gorzkiewicz in eighty-one, and Löwenthal in ninety-seven.'

The waiter turned up, but Logan hadn't even looked at the menu, so he let Jaroszewicz order for them both, and went back to the two remaining files, trying to remember the details. Löwenthal was allegedly involved in people-trafficking from Russia to the UK, and the odd spot of gun-running. Ex-Soviet weaponry being sold off on the cheap by soldiers who hadn't been paid for months, then passed on at a huge mark-up to gangs all over Europe.

Gorzkiewicz was a different kettle of borscht entirely. He'd been a lance corporal in the Polish army, under the Communists, invalided out after some sort of accident. A law-abiding citizen whose only transgression was being active in the Solidarity movement in the early eighties.

Logan pulled Löwenthal's file to the front. 'Right, this is the guy we have to concentrate on.'

She sniffed. 'Why him? Why not Gorzkiewicz, surely he would be more—'

'No he wouldn't. Gorzkiewicz was blinded in 1981: while

the Communists were still in power. Anything we got out of him would be nearly thirty years out of date. And if this *is* mob enforcers copying what happened back then, it wouldn't help us anyway. But Löwenthal was done in 2004. What *he* knows might still be worth something.'

'But we have no idea where he—'

'We hit the land registry, census records, telephone books. We talk to informers, known associates.'

She sat back and frowned. 'Oh . . . I had not . . . Yes. Of course.'

The waiter returned with two large glasses of beer and a wooden board covered in bread, a tub of what looked like lard, and a huge knife. Jaroszewicz thanked him, then handed Logan one of the beers, their fingers touching on the cold glass. A droplet of condensation ran down the side and dripped onto the tabletop.

'Er . . . thanks.' Logan took a mouthful, pretending not to notice that Senior Constable Jaroszewicz was blushing. 'I'll call my DCI after lunch: get him to speak to whoever's in charge in Krakow. If they won't play with the Warsaw police, maybe they'll cooperate with Aberdeen?'

She helped herself to bread and lard. 'Just make sure you tell him not to mention me. If they think a freaking yuppie is using Aberdeen to put pressure on them, they will deny everything.'

43

The room was too hot to concentrate, sunlight streaming through three huge, dirty windows into the airless space. Stifling and soporific. A big lunch of beetroot soup and potato dumplings hadn't exactly helped. Krakow's municipal records hall was undergoing some sort of refit, the huge stacks of files and documents relocated to a grimy four-storey building, sandwiched in the middle of a row of other grimy four-storey buildings that overlooked two construction sites and a tram stop.

The City Council obviously didn't believe in air-conditioning: a single electric fan sat in the middle of the room, oscillating back and forth – hummmmmmmm *click*, hummmmmmmm *click*, hummmmmmmm *click* – doing little more than stirring up a cloud of dust in the oppressive summer heat. The only other sound was the low murmur of American tourists, tracing their ancestors through stacks of old town records.

Logan's head snapped back to the upright position. Blink. Shudder. Yawn.

Jaroszewicz didn't look up – she was pouring over a stack of newspapers from 2004, looking for coverage of the

Löwenthal blinding. If they were lucky it would at least give them an area of the city to start looking. Cross reference it with the listings for Löwenthal in the Krakow phone book and they might actually be on to something.

Logan stretched out in his chair, making the ancient wood creak. 'Are you sure I can't do anything?'

'Why,' she turned to the next page of yellowing newsprint, 'have you learned to read Polish since the last time you asked? Or the four times before that?'

Logan sighed. 'I'm not doing anything here.'

He could see her gritting her teeth. 'Then go do something else. *Please*. And let – me – work – in – peace!'

He found a little internet café, just off the main square, paid his twenty zloty, and checked his email. There were the usual memos; directives; calls for witnesses; a couple of missing persons; a leaving do for DI Gray in Archie's next Friday; something from the Witness Protection people saying Kylie and her sister Tracey were doing remarkably well on the rehab programme; something from Big Gary saying if Logan didn't get his expenses in by the end of the week there'd be trouble; and a huge email from Staff Sergeant Łukaszewski with attached background reports for all the Aberdeen victims. Logan spent five minutes wading through the data, then forwarded it to Finnie. Let him do some work for a change.

Last up was one from Rennie, complaining about being dumped with DI Steel's 'Sperminator' inquiry and finishing off with an invite to join half of CID to watch the football on Saturday, followed by dodgems, curry, and lots of beer.

No messages from DI Steel or Finnie. And nothing from DCS Bain either. . . Mind you, nominations for DI Gray's replacement didn't have to be in until tomorrow, so Bain probably wouldn't make the announcement until next week.

Logan hit the 'NEW EMAIL' button and wrote a message to Samantha. Deleted it. Started again. Deleted that one too. Replied to Rennie's invitation instead.

Two minutes later he had a response:

```
Were you been? No footy for us, been another
blingding! Just got out the breifign ~ another
polish bloke!!! ACC going mental: All leave
canselled. Oops, got to go, Finny's on the warpath.
Can only see Pirie's feet now, he's so far up the
DIC's arse!!!! LOL
   ;-)
```

Logan read the email three times. Trying to convince himself that Rennie was just having a joke. There wasn't really a new Oedipus victim. There *couldn't* be another Oedipus victim: Ricky Gilchrist was in custody, he'd confessed, the threatening notes were on his sodding computer.

Logan pulled out his mobile and called Finnie. 'Is it true? Someone else's been blinded?'

'No, I made it up for a laugh. Of course *it's true. Where are you?'*

'Krakow.' He told the DCI about the lack of living victims in Warsaw, and Senior Constable Jaroszewicz's opinion of the local police. 'They're not really cooperating.'

'And what, exactly, *do you expect me to do about it? Do you not think I've got enough to worry about, without* you *adding to it? Is that it? Not enough excitement in my life with the wrong man in bloody custody?'*

'Wrong man?'

'Ricky Gilchrist, who did you think I meant, Ronald Mc-Sodding-Donald?'

'Well . . . it. . .' Logan slapped his hand on the table.

Eureka. 'This new victim, it could be the people who attacked Simon McLeod.'

'God, that's brilliant, *Sergeant! I hadn't thought of* that. *Gosh, what a* good *idea, maybe it was the* same person. *Only victim number seven is a Polish roughneck with BP. And he was found on a disused building site in Torry. We even got the gloating phone call. It's definitely Oedipus.'*

'Damn.'

'That's an understatement. The press haven't got hold of it yet, but when they do. . .' Finnie went quiet for a moment. *'What a cock-up.'*

'We're not letting Gilchrist go, are we?'

'Do I look *like an idiot? Goulding's already started paperwork to have him sectioned. He's either going to prison or a secure psychiatric facility for the rest of his unnatural, twisted, little life.'* Logan could hear the background noise change. The babble of voices giving way to an echoey silence. Probably Finnie leaving the incident room for the corridor outside. Now the DCI's voice sounded almost desperate. *'I need you to find something out there, OK? I don't care what, but you find me* something *I can use to catch this bastard.'*

'We're trying to chase up alternative sources of info: see if we can track down our two possible survivors. But like I said, local plod aren't cooperating. Wouldn't hurt if you could put in a good word. . .?'

'Anything else?'

'Might be best if you leave Senior Constable Jaroszewicz's name out of it. Apparently Krakow and Warsaw can't stand each other.'

'I'll call them now. Just make sure you find *me something, understand?'*

And then the DCI hung up.

According to the computer, Logan still had another five minutes before his money ran out, so he called up a fresh email and forced himself to write something to Samantha. Apologetic, but not crawly. At least this time he managed to send it.

Then he grabbed his jacket and wandered out into the afternoon.

Just after five and the streets were beginning to liven up: locals tramping past on their way home from work; yet more tourists with their cameras; little old ladies standing on the street corners selling smoked cheeses in bizarre, slightly phallic shapes. He was wandering back towards the hotel, pausing to read the menu outside every restaurant he passed, when his phone went off – Jaroszewicz.

'I found somebody! I cannot believe it!'

Logan listened to her babbling on about how difficult it was and how many newspapers she'd had to read, and how many phone calls she'd had to make.

'So,' he said, when she finally paused for breath, 'who is it?'

'Löwenthal's brother. And do you want the good news? He is meeting us tonight. Nine o'clock!'

Quarter to ten and there was still no sign of him. Logan and Jaroszewicz waited in a little basement bar on Floriańska – just up from the hotel – a brick catacomb with red tablecloths and white napkins. Candles. Red-stained pine booths, the wood going pale at the edges where the varnish had worn off. A big oil painting of a bald man in militaristic clothes with a green cockade hat, moustache and vast mutton-chop sideburns.

The air was thick with cigarette smoke.

Jaroszewicz was slumped over a half-empty pint of Guinness, poking a lonely peanut across the tabletop. 'He said he would be here.'

Logan finished his beer and pointed at her glass. 'You want another one while we wait? Half, or something?'

She shrugged and he went back to the bar, watching goldfish swimming around a tiny beer-sponsored aquarium while the barman poured him another pint of Tyskie and a half of draft Guinness.

Voices behind him.

Logan turned to see Jaroszewicz on her feet, talking to a man with the kind of moustache a walrus would be proud of.

Jaroszewicz introduced him. 'This is Henryk Löwenthal.'

They shook hands, and Logan said, 'Good evening.'

The man looked puzzled, and Jaroszewicz shrugged. 'He does not speak English.'

'Oh . . . OK,' Logan tried again, '*Dobry wieczór.*'

'Ah!' Smile, nod. '*Dobry wieczór.*'

They sat at the table, under the watchful gaze of the military man in the painting. Löwenthal cleared his throat, took a deep breath, then rattled out a long speech that Logan couldn't understand a word of.

Jaroszewicz: 'He says we have to remember that no one in his family had any idea what his brother was doing. None of them have ever been in trouble with the police before. They are good people and are very ashamed.'

'Ask him where his brother is now.'

She stared at him. 'What did you think I was going to do?'

'OK, OK. Sorry.'

She fired off the question, and got another speech in reply.

'He says he does not know.'

'Oh for God's. . .' Sigh. 'Ask him if he's got a telephone number, or an email address.'

Stony silence. 'Now why did I not think of that?'

'I didn't mean—'

But she was already talking over the top of him. Löwenthal's brother said something back and then they both laughed.

'What? What did he say?'

'He said that all you British are the same – you never bother to learn anyone else's language. You think you can still rule the world by shouting slowly at the natives.'

'What did he say about the number?'

More Polish.

'He says they cut off all ties with his brother years ago. He was drunk all the time, violent, on drugs, he stole things.'

The evening got worse from there. Jaroszewicz and Löwenthal's brother talking for longer and longer in Polish, leaving Logan to sit on the outside drinking lager and waiting for a translation. Pressing her to ask more questions.

In the end she turned to him, eyes flat as knife blades and said, 'Sergeant McRae: I am perfectly capable of questioning a witness without you pointing out the obvious every two minutes. Now sit there, shut up, and concentrate on looking pretty. OK?' She gave him a nasty smile, then turned her back on him, sharing another joke with Löwenthal in Polish.

So much for international cooperation.

44

Seven thirty, Wednesday morning. Logan lay on his back and stared up at the hotel-room ceiling. What a *great* idea this trip was. He killed the alarm on his phone and slumped back into his pillows. She was a nightmare. The evening had gradually deteriorated to the point where Logan might as well have been on his own in a strange pub in a foreign country. Only a lot less pleasant, because he was pretty sure Senior Constable High-And-Mighty Jaroszewicz and Löwenthal's brother were laughing at him. And they weren't even doing it behind his back – they were doing it to his face.

'I am a professional,' he told the bedside lamp, 'I promise I will not sulk.'

Like hell he wouldn't.

He dragged himself through the shower and down to breakfast, disappointed to see that Jaroszewicz was already there, tucking into another bowl of muesli. For a brief moment he thought about giving her the cold shoulder and grabbing another table, but he'd made a promise to his bedside furniture.

The scrambled eggs were going to be every bit as alternative as yesterday's, but he ordered them anyway.

Jaroszewicz watched him eat in silence for a minute. 'I was thinking, I was unfair to you yesterday.'

'Really.'

'It is not your fault you do not speak the language.' She shrugged. 'But you cannot read the documents, and you cannot question witnesses. So. . .' She reached into her cavernous handbag and dug out a pile of tour brochures. 'Go do something. See Krakow. Löwenthal's brother gave me some addresses to try, I will call you if I get anything.'

Logan was feeling too petty to argue with her. The bedside light could go screw itself.

The sun was a chip of gold, shining between slivers of white cloud. Logan sat on a park bench and grumbled and swore: Who the hell did she think she was, telling him to go see the sights, as if he was a child who needed to sod off so the grown-ups could talk? Detective Sergeants should be seen and not heard.

He ripped another chunk from the bread he'd bought from a brown-faced old woman on a street corner, and hurled it at a bunch of stupid-looking pigeons. Doing his best to hit one of them and failing miserably. Bloody Jaroszewicz.

A group of nuns tottered past, dressed in the traditional black and white penguin outfits you never saw in Scotland any more. No, in Aberdeen it was all grey twinsets and sensible shoes.

What was the collective noun for nuns? Flange? Flock?

Logan watched as they stopped to harangue a young man for dropping his McDonald's wrapper on the path. The guy held out for a whole thirty seconds, before grabbing up the wrapper and hurrying away to the nearest bin.

A Terror of nuns.

Logan had another go at braining a pigeon with a chunk of crust.

The park would have been a nice place to sit and watch the world go by, if he'd been in a better mood. A two-mile-long avenue of dusty green that encircled the Old Town, lined with huge trees, their leaves dappling the sunlight, making it almost cool on Logan's bench as he tried to concuss birds.

The next lump of bread bounced off a pigeon's head and Logan awarded himself twenty points. This was such a waste of time. He was a police officer, surely there was *something* he could—

His mobile phone rang. Probably Jaroszewicz checking to see if he was away sightseeing like a good little boy. But it wasn't her, it was Finnie: *'Where were you? I've been trying for an hour.'*

'Twiddling my bloody thumbs. Jaroszewicz won't let me—'

'I've spoken to the Krakow police and they don't have anything on Gorz-kie-wicz?' Sounding it out. *'Too long ago – as far as they know he's pushing up Polish daisies somewhere. But they know all about Löwenthal.'*

Logan jammed his phone between his shoulder and his ear, pinning it there while he dug out his notebook and pen. 'Go ahead.'

'They fished him out of the river eight months ago. Turns out he crossed someone over a shipment of rocket-propelled grenades heading for France. Beat him to death with his own white stick.'

'Oh.' So Logan had put up with all that humiliation last night for nothing. 'Then we're out of victims. Everyone's either dead or gone.'

'Well that's just perfect. We spent a fortune sending you out there and what do we have to show for it? Nothing. Finish up and get yourself on the next flight home. We'll try and pretend this whole disaster never happened.'

'There isn't anything to finish, I—'

But Finnie had already hung up.

Logan snapped his phone shut, scowled at it for a bit, then stuck it back in his pocket. Wonderful. This was going to look *so* good when they were deciding who got the new DI's job. I know: let's give it to Logan who's just wasted a couple of thousand pounds with a pointless trip to Poland.

Gibowski was in America. Wiśniewski was dead. Bielatowicz – missing for years. Löwenthal – dead. And Gorzkiewicz was anyone's guess.

Sodding hell.

Logan tore the last of the bread up and hurled it at the birds, feeling petty and vicious. And then guilty. He stood, apologized to the pigeons, and mooched back towards the Old Town. At least he wouldn't have to put up with Senior Constable Jaroszewicz for much longer. A quick goodbye, pack his bags and off on the next train back to Warsaw. She could stay here and sod about if she liked: he was going home.

Back in the main square, wood smoke drifted out in scented wafts from food stall braziers. He stopped to buy a little paper plate of grilled, smoked cheese served with a dollop of cherry jam.

Logan finished the lot before crumpling up his plate and dropping it in a bin – not wanting a row from any passing nuns – then froze. There was a pamphlet lying amongst the litter, advertising some sort of concert. It was all gibberish to him, but one thing did stand out loud and clear – the band had written their name in the same red, blobby, run-together block capitals Solidarity used. They even had a little flag-like scrawl over the 'N' in their name, just like the union.

Gorzkiewicz – his file said he'd been active in Solidarity while Poland was under Communist rule.

Logan looked out across the town square, then down at the poster again. A smile spread across his face. Maybe he could salvage something from this disaster after all.

45

It took longer than he'd thought, but eventually Logan managed to track down the local Solidarity headquarters, just off the main square in Krakow. And best of all, the woman behind the reception desk spoke English.

She gave Logan a seat and a cup of coffee, then told him the person he needed to talk to would be down in about fifteen minutes. And he was.

Gerek Płotkowski certainly looked the part – squarely built, greying hair, massive soup-strainer moustache, handshake like a steelworker. In thickly accented English he invited Logan to follow him to a nearby café for a drink. 'Is all *herbata* and coffee in office. When it is hot like this a man needs something cold. No?'

Yes.

They got a table on the edge of the square, not far from someone who'd painted himself gold and was standing motionless on an upturned bucket, pretending to be a statue. Płotkowski ordered two beers from a waiter, then sat and scowled at the statue-impersonator. 'We fight Communist oppression for years, for what? So *idiota* like that can exist.' He took a big mouthful of beer, leaving a high-tidemark of foam on his moustache. 'What do you want to know?'

'They told me you were in Solidarity from the very start. I'm trying to find a man who was a member back in the early eighties.'

'Ah. . .' the big man got a misty look in his grey eyes. 'They were good times. Hard, but we stood shoulder to shoulder. Like this. . .' He held his two fists up, side by side. 'We mean something.'

'The man I'm looking for is called Gorzkiewicz. Rafal Gorzkiewicz. Did you know him?'

The misty look disappeared, replaced by something much harder. 'Why?'

'I'm a police officer.' Logan pulled out his warrant card and slid it across the table. 'Gorzkiewicz was attacked in 1981 – somebody blinded him.'

'I do not know this man you are talking about.' He wrapped his pint in one huge fist and threw half of it down his throat. 'I must get back to work.'

Logan grabbed the man's sleeve . . . took one look at the scowl it got him, and let go again. 'Please, it's important. Where I come from, people are being attacked just like he was: someone cuts their eyes out and burns the sockets. Shopkeepers, businessmen, fathers.'

Płotkowski turned his face back to the living statue. 'They should not be allowed on the square. It cheapen everything we fight for.'

Logan let the silence stretch.

'We. . .' Płotkowski coughed, took another drink, 'Not everyone agreed with getting rid of Communists through political protest. Some thought armed struggle was only way. A revolution. *Solidarnosć*, written in blood on cobbled streets of Kraków.' The big man shook his head. 'Gorzkiewicz – he was explosives expert in army. The Communists sent him to Afghanistan in seventy-eight. . . He come back two years later with a hole in his thigh size of fist. Bitter. "Political is too slow," he say. "Blood is only thing these Russian bastards understand."'

Płotkowski finished his beer and called for another – getting one for Logan as well, even though *he* was nowhere near finished his first pint – and two shots of vodka too.

The big man didn't say anything more until the drinks arrived, handing Logan a shot glass of clear spirit, so cold it steamed in the warm afternoon. *'Na zdrowie!'*

He knocked his vodka back in one and Logan followed suit.

'Gorzkiewicz want *Solidarność* leadership to call for armed resistance, but they would not. Too much violence and Russia will use excuse to march in, like they do in Afghanistan. Soviet soldiers with Soviet tanks and guns. . . We want our freedom the right way.' He was silent for a minute, looking not at Logan, but at a time nearly thirty years ago. 'He want to blow up anything that support Communist regime. And he have enough friends to make him dangerous.' The big man seemed to shrink a bit. 'On twenty-sixth of November 1980 there was explosion at the SB headquarters.'

Logan must have looked confused, because Płotkowski said, 'SB is stand for *Służba Bezpieczeństwa*. They were Security Service of Ministry of Internal Affairs: Communist secret police who try to make dead anyone that stand up to regime.' He leant over and spat at his feet. 'When SB headquarters explode authorities say it gas leak, they do not want people to know it is really bomb. So they start rounding up members of *Solidarność*. . . Beatings. Disappearings.' His huge shoulders rose and fell. 'Police Station in Kazimierz blow up two weeks later and Communists declare *stan wojenny*: martial law. Close the borders, curfew, censor our mail, tap our phones, arrest our teachers, shut down newspapers. Then the riots start.'

He stared into the depths of his glass. 'People shot in the streets. . . It was too soon, we did not *want* this. But Gorzkiewicz say, "This is progress! Now we will have freedom." He want to blow up more police stations. . . We have no choice.'

The old man finished his second beer in silence.

Logan pulled out his notebook and pen, and put them on the table. 'Do you know where Gorzkiewicz is now?'

Płotkowski scribbled an address down, then got up and left without another word.

Logan pushed his way back into the records office. Jaroszewicz was sitting at the same desk as before, the electric fan still making its soporific hummmmmmm *click*, hummmmmmm *click*, hummmmmmm *click*. . .

He pulled out a chair on the other side of the desk and settled into it. 'Find anything?'

She scowled up at him. 'Nothing. I went to all the places Löwenthal's brother mentioned and no one knows where he is.'

'That's because Löwenthal's dead. They dragged his beaten body out of the river eight months ago.'

Jaroszewicz slammed the document she was reading down on the desk, and swore. 'Then it is true,' she said, 'this was all a stupid waste of time!'

Logan took his notebook from his pocket, opened it at the relevant page, and placed it on the table in front of her.

She picked it up, frowning as she read. 'What is this?'

'That's where Rafal Gorzkiewicz lives.'

And Jaroszewicz started swearing again.

'Why are you looking at me like that?' Jaroszewicz shuffled forward two paces in the queue.

Logan looked up at the towering bulk of St Mary's Basilica.

The huge red-brick cathedral sat at a jaunty angle on the edge of the old town square, surrounded by tourists, bathed in the smell of charcoal-grilled meat. 'You want to pray before we go see Gorzkiewicz?'

She shuffled forwards again. 'You think you are so perfect.'

'It's not exactly standard police procedure where I come from.'

'Well, you are not where you come from. You are where *I* come from, and this is how *we* do things.'

'Thought you said you were from Warsaw.'

'I moved there when I was a little girl. I was born just outside Krakow.' They were nearly at the entrance now, a pair of stout wooden doors in an ornate hexagonal porch. 'Are you a Catholic?'

'Nope.'

'Then you cannot use this door. It is for worshippers only. You will have to wait outside.'

Logan took another look at the sun-drenched square. 'You going to be long? Only it's baking out here.'

'Then go and have a beer, or a coffee, or *something*.' And then she stepped into the darkened porch, leaving Logan on his own outside. Except for the queue of the faithful and another one of those bloody living statues.

Logan wandered down the side of the cathedral, following a small clot of American tourists to a sign that said visitors were permitted to use the side entrance. *If* they bought a ticket. Why not?

Inside it couldn't have been more different from St Peter's back in Aberdeen. Instead of austere white walls, this place was done up in cheery shades of blue and gold, plastered with statues, friezes and paintings of saints. Hundreds of them.

The nave was cut in half by a waist-high set of wooden barriers, keeping the faithful at the back safe from the heathens at the front. Logan scanned the faces of the men and women deep in prayer on the dark wooden pews, but there was no sign of Jaroszewicz. Probably still in the queue, or lighting a candle or something.

He found an empty seat and sank into it, looking up at the incredible display of shiny stuff around him. The walls were covered in biblical scenes, all painted directly onto the stonework. The pulpit was festooned with spines and dripped with gold. A huge crucifix hung between the nave and the presbytery, where there was even more gold and gaily coloured paint. Like a gaudy fairground ride, only with pictures of martyrs and Madonnas instead of ripped-off Disney characters.

He'd never seen anything like it.

Logan peered back over his shoulder. . . There she was, just kneeling down on one side of confessional stand number fourteen – it said so on a little beige sign taped to the wooden screen. In a way the setting was appropriate, because God was probably the only person who knew what had got into her. Logan certainly didn't. Ever since he'd shown her Gorzkiewicz's address she'd been twitchy.

Which probably wasn't a good sign. But it was too late to worry about that now.

Jaroszewicz was mumbling, head down, hands clasped in prayer . . . and then Logan realized she was actually fiddling with her mobile phone: texting while she confessed. That was modern Catholicism for you.

Five minutes later his bum was starting to go numb, so he stood, sneaked his own mobile out of his pocket – if it was good enough for true believers, it was good enough for him – and took a couple of photos while the man in charge of stopping people doing just that was looking the other way. Then Logan wandered back outside into the sunshine. It wasn't long before Jaroszewicz joined him.

'Right,' she said, sticking her hands deep into her pockets, 'we have to pick up two things, then we can go.'

Stop number one was the off-licence opposite the hotel, for a litre bottle of good vodka; stop number two was the hotel itself. She told him to wait for her in the lobby, and disappeared into the lift. When she came back her face was set like a painted martyr.

The taxi beetled down the dual carriageway, heading East with the sun at its back. Half past six and the traffic was starting to get a little better, even if the road was getting worse – the taxi rolled about on the rutted tarmac like a ship at sea. The driver turned to grin at Logan. Early twenties, long dreadlocks, thin face, and a pierced nose. 'You can always tell when driver is drunk in Poland: he drive in straight line, not swerve to avoid pothole. Ha!' The car bounced through a pothole.

Sitting in the back seat next to him, Jaroszewicz had gone a worrying shade of grey.

'Are you OK?'

She glanced at him and then back out of the window again. 'It is probably nothing. Nothing to worry about. Nothing at all.'

'When people tell me not to worry, *that's* when I start worrying.'

'It is just not the best part of Krakow. . .'

The taxi driver laughed again. 'Is not part of Kraków at all. Is Nowa Huta!' He grinned at Logan again. 'Where you from? America? Like on *Friends*? Like Joey and Chandler?'

'No, Scotland, like Sean Connery. . .'

'Ah! James Bond. Very good. Shaken not stirred.' And as if to emphasize the point the car lurched through a series of tarmac ruts. 'Nowa Huta is mean: "New Steelworks". Uncle Joe give them as gift to people of Kraków. Make them suffer for being broken bourgeois.' He leant on his horn and hurled abuse as a little black Trabant puttered by on the inside lane. 'You want go to milk bar? I know nice place.'

Jaroszewicz waved a hand at him. 'Just take us to the address.'

He shrugged, and the car lurched again.

She went back to staring out of the window, clutching her massive handbag to her chest.

Logan was beginning to get a very bad feeling about this.

46

The taxi pulled a juddering U-turn on the wide, tree-lined street and roared away in a cloud of oily smoke, leaving Logan and Jaroszewicz standing outside a block of flats. Five storeys of grimy grey, with white-painted window frames. The word '*Hutnik*' was daubed in red paint next to an archway that led all the way through the building and into some sort of square on the other side.

'This it?'

Jaroszewicz checked the bit of paper he'd given her, then walked through the archway. On the other side it opened up into a little park of paving slabs and trees, a rickety children's play area that looked about ready to collapse in the corner. The green space was surrounded on all sides by walls of identically bland apartments.

One half of the square looked much cleaner than the other and when Logan asked why, Jaroszewicz just shrugged, mumbled something about it depending on which way the wind from the Steelworks was blowing, then marched across to a plain blue door.

She glanced over her shoulder at the empty windows surrounding them. 'Stalin built it like this so people would spy on their neighbours. Every house overlooks at least a dozen more.' She dug into her handbag, brought out something wrapped in a paisley-pattern handkerchief, and handed it over. 'Here.'

Heavy. And worryingly familiar.

Logan peeled back one edge of the cloth and slapped it back again.

'Why do I need a gun?'

'Just keep it. . .' She pointed at his pocket. 'In case.'

'What's going on, Jaroszewicz?'

'Please, call me Wiktorja.'

'Either you tell me what's going on, or I'm turning round and walking out of here.'

She pulled another bundle from her bag, slipping it into her coat pocket. 'This man, Gorzkiewicz, he is dangerous.'

'He's blind.'

'He knows dangerous people. And dangerous people are looking for him.' She blushed. 'I . . . ahem . . . I do not want you to get hurt.'

She scanned the list of names on the intercom, running her finger lightly across the handwritten labels. 'He is not here: no Gorzkiewicz.'

'Well, if dangerous people are looking for him, he's not going to put his real name on the buzzer, is he?'

Her finger froze over one. '*Zegarmistrz* . . . Ah.' And then she pressed the button.

Silence. Then a crackle. Then silence again.

Logan put a hand on the door and pushed. It swung open.

It took a moment for his eyes to adjust to the dark. There was a short corridor with a block of letter boxes on one pistachio-green wall, three doors leading off to separate apartments, and a set of concrete stairs with wrought-iron balustrades and a scarred wooden handrail.

Jaroszewicz – Wiktorja – pointed up, then started to climb.

Each landing had a small square window set into the thick wall at knee height, but they didn't do much more than emphasize how gloomy it was in here. The apartment doors were all different, some elaborately so, trying to impose a little individuality on this communist workers' paradise of grey bland buildings.

At least the stairwell didn't stink of piss.

Logan froze. 'Wait a minute, how do you know dangerous people are after him?'

She kept on going. 'It was in the file.'

'Then why didn't you say anything about it?'

'I did not think it mattered – we thought he was too long ago, remember? We were concentrating on Löwenthal. Now come on. . .'

They stopped again on the fifth floor, outside the only door that didn't want to be different. It was a plain, bland slab, painted black. 'This is it.'

Wiktorja reached into her pocket, the one with the gun. Then she knocked.

A voice muffled out from the inside. '*Otwarte.*'

She tried the door handle and it creaked, then the door swung open, groaning like a sound effect from a horror movie.

The corridor on the other side was dark and cluttered – piles of old newspapers, a broken sewing machine, shoe boxes, bricks, an ancient radio with the valves poking out. The walls were covered in 70s-style red velveteen wallpaper, the swirly pattern disappearing into the darkness, and the only illumination came from a twisting ribbon of little white fairy lights.

The same voice as before came from a room further down the hall, saying something about *pierogi*?

Wiktorja placed a finger on her lips and crept into the gloom, picking her way around the obstacles. Swearing quietly, Logan followed her, closing the front door behind them – shutting out what little natural daylight had oozed in from the stairwell. And now there was nothing but the fairy lights.

It was impossible to walk in a straight line, the piles of junk made the confined space into a twisting maze. Claustrophobic.

Wiktorja held up a hand and stopped, peering through an open door into the room beyond. She stepped inside, motioning for Logan to follow her.

It was the living room that time forgot, and just as dark as the hallway. More piles of junk, more Christmas lights. And as Logan's eyes slowly grew accustomed to the gloom he could see the stripy wallpaper, the swirly-patterned rug, the fake-teak sideboard, the old Bakelite phone, the framed pictures of Jesus, Pope John Paul II, and the Virgin Mary. The boarded-up windows. A broken alarm-clock-radio sitting on top of a stack of boxes. The man sitting in the armchair pointing a gun at them.

He had grey hair, liver spots, dark glasses, big rounded shoulders and hands like dinner plates. A bear in a cardigan. A three-quarters empty bottle of vodka sat on the table by his side. He was right in the middle of his maze of junk. A minotaur with a semi-automatic pistol.

He waggled the gun at them. *'Co zrobiliście Zytka?'*

Wiktorja answered him in English, 'We have not done anything to Zytka.' She eased her hand slowly out of her pocket – bringing her own gun with it. 'We are not—'

'Stop right there.' His accent was a strange mix of Polish and American. As if he'd learned to speak the language from watching Hollywood movies. 'You stop, or I will shoot you.'

She froze. 'I'm not doing anything.'

He raised his arm and aimed straight for her chest. 'Put it on the floor.'

She looked back at Logan, then did as she was told, laying the gun down with a clunk on the threadbare carpet.

'Good, now you sit. Over there, in the seat.' The gun waggled again, this time in the direction of a rickety dining-room chair, hard up against the wall. He kept the gun on her until she was sitting, ignoring Logan. 'You tell that *cholernik* Ehrlichmann I am not an idiot. He touches one hair on Zytka's head and I'll blow him and his whole *pierdolony* family back to the Stone Age. Do you understand?'

'I . . . I don't know who Ehrlichmann is.'

Logan stepped into the room. 'She's telling the truth.' And the gun snapped round. Oh God. . . He was looking right down the barrel. He put his hands up. 'We're not here to hurt anyone.'

'Where is Zytka?'

Logan glanced at Wiktorja, and edged a little closer. 'We don't know. We've not seen anyone since we got here.'

The man grunted. 'Then what do you want?'

Wiktorja: 'We're police officers.'

He swung the gun round again. '*Pierdolona suka!*'

Logan lunged.

47

He smashed through a stack of hardback books, sending them flying into the shadows. The string of little white lights caught around his waist, hauling things from the walls of the junkyard maze – a glass lamp hit the floor and shattered – Logan kept on going.

The gun came back round, the old man was *fast*, but Logan was already too close.

He ducked under Gorzkiewicz's arm, grabbed the vodka from the table and swung it like a tennis racket: using the man's head as the ball.

Only Logan's foot went down on one of the scattered books and it shifted beneath him mid-swing. The bottle missed its target, just catching the edge of Gorzkiewicz's sunglasses as Logan crashed into another pile of junk, sprawling out flat on his back. Something sharp digging into his spine.

The old man swore, '*Kurwa!*' and Logan was looking down the barrel of the gun again. Gorzkiewicz was trembling, clutching the armchair, sunglasses skewed off to one side, exposing a twisted knot of scar tissue where there should have been an eye. 'You made a *big* mistake, *piździelec*! I'll blow your fucking—' He stopped dead.

Senior Constable Wiktorja Jaroszewicz had a slab-like chunk of Soviet-built semiautomatic jammed in his cheek hard enough to force his face into a lopsided smile. 'No,' she said, twisting the barrel, 'you are going to drop the gun and hope I do not paint this shitty little apartment with your brains.'

The kitchen was another blast from the past: old-fashioned units, painted a sickly shade of avocado, lurked in the darkness; yellow linoleum floor worn almost through to the underlay; a rectangular, mahogany clock with the hands stuck at twenty to two; kitchen gadgets that looked as if they'd fallen off the back of a dinosaur. There was just enough room for three people to sit around a tiny table, bathed in the faint glow of yet more fairy lights, and the gurgling hummmm of an antique refrigerator.

Gorzkiewicz opened a bottle of vodka and poured three stiff measures, keeping a finger on the lip of each shot glass – filling them right up to the brim and never spilling a drop.

He raised his glass. 'May we live to bury our enemies.'

Logan and Wiktorja joined the toast – her throwing the drink back in one, Logan taking an experimental sip . . . then deciding it was probably better not to taste the stuff on the way down. He coughed and spluttered as the alcohol hit: raw and bitter.

She pounded him on the back. Then asked Gorzkiewicz why all the windows were boarded over. 'I mean,' she said, filling their glasses again, 'I know you are blind, but do you not like to feel the sun on your face?'

'A sniper's rifle only works if he can see his target.' The old man downed his vodka, then removed his sunglasses. Both eyes were gone, and all that was left were deep furrowed scars, following the contours of the sockets. 'In my line of work, it is not good if people can see you, when you can't see them.'

'Uh-huh. . .' Logan looked around the cramped kitchen, 'Your line of work?' Whatever it was it couldn't be paying too well.

Gorzkiewicz smiled, his teeth too perfect to be true: dentures. 'They call me *Zegarmistrz*: the Watchmaker.'

Logan looked over his shoulder at the boarded-up windows. 'So why does a watchmaker need to worry about snipers?'

'It is a very competitive marketplace.'

Logan stared at him. Those scarred sockets were the most disturbing things he'd seen in a long time . . . which was saying something. The longer he looked at them, the more convinced he became that they were staring straight back. He suppressed a shudder. 'Who's Ehrlichmann? He make watches too?'

'Ehrlichmann is a German . . . businessman. He is not important.' Gorzkiewicz glanced up at the dead clock. 'What time is it?'

Logan checked his watch. 'Seven forty-three.'

Frown. 'Zytka should be here by now.'

'We want to talk to you about the man who. . .' Logan tried to think of a tactful way to put it, and couldn't. 'The man who blinded you.'

Gorzkiewicz felt for the vodka bottle again, filling their glasses. 'There is a story that long ago the wealthiest families in Kraków would build clock towers to show how grand and important they were. But every time a family unveiled one, someone else would commission an even more beautiful clock.' He knocked back his vodka. 'And so one day the head of the greatest house in all of Kraków called for the best watchmaker in the world and asked him to make a timepiece so wonderful that no clock would ever outshine it.

And the watchmaker did. He made a clock so beautiful that the angels stopped singing, just to hear it chime.'

He slipped his sunglasses back on, hiding the scars. 'But the head of the house was a jealous man: he knew that the next clock the watchmaker made would be even more beautiful. Then *his* would no longer be the finest in the land. So he called the old man to him, and burned his eyes out with a poker from the fire; that way the family's clock would always be the best.'

Wiktorja shook her head. 'That never happened.'

'It is a good story all the same.' He turned to Logan. '*That* is why they call me the Watchmaker.'

'Only you didn't make clocks, did you?'

He smiled again. 'Sometimes the things I make go tick, tick . . . BOOM!' Gorzkiewicz slammed his hand on the table, making everyone jump. He laughed. 'Or so people say.'

'Who was it? Who blinded you?'

There was a long pause. Then Gorzkiewicz reached up beneath his sunglasses, rubbing the place where his eyes used to be.

'The SB – secret police bastards – come to my house in the middle of the night, they throw me in the back of a truck and I never see my wife or daughter again. Someone said they ran away. Someone said they were sent to Warsaw, sold to some Politburo *skurwysyn*. And someone said they were just taken out to the steelworks and shot. That my wife and child fuelled the furnaces to make more Soviet steel. . .'

He poured himself another drink. 'The SB beat me for days. Lied to me: said my comrades had informed on me because I was a liability to Solidarity – too dangerous.' He laughed, cold and hard. 'All *lies*! The SB wanted me to confess to the bombings in Kraków, tell them who else was involved. But I wouldn't tell them *anything*.'

Gorzkiewicz shivered. 'Then *he* came. He. . .' There was silence for a moment as the old man fidgeted. 'He came with his knives and pliers. And I talked. I screamed like a woman and I told him everything he wanted to know.' This time the vodka slopped over the edge of the glass, soaking into the red-and-white checked tablecloth. 'Then he cut out my eyes and burned me.'

Wiktorja swore, reached out, and put her hand over the old man's.

He didn't seem to notice. 'The SB rounded up my friends two hours later. They were never seen again. And when the bastard was done with me he drove me back to Nowa Huta and threw me out onto the street for everyone to see. With a sign around my neck saying, "Communist Spy".' Another refill disappeared. 'I could hear the crowd: shouting, swearing. . . They tied me to a tree and beat me until everything was blood and darkness. Broke both my legs. My jaw. My arm. Left me tied there for two days, without food or water, until my brother came and cut me down.'

Logan winced. 'Dear God. . .'

'It was 1981 in the People's Republic of Poland. There was no God, there was only Lenin.' He finished the bottle. 'If it was me, I would have killed me. . . But maybe that would have been too kind.'

Wiktorja said, 'Then why do you stay here? Why not get out, somewhere else, far away from the people who did this?'

'Because Nowa Huta is my home. I fought for these streets, I killed for them, I was *blinded* for them. They are my streets. That is why I stay.'

'Who was he? The man?'

Gorzkiewicz stood, then hobbled to the rattling fridge. The open door cast a sudden bloom of cold white light, then it clunked shut and they were back in the gloom again. The old man returned carrying a fresh bottle of vodka and a jar of pickles. 'He was Old Boney. King of the Underworld. Kostchey the Deathless.'

48

Wiktorja threw back her head and laughed. 'The *Devil* gouged out your eyes?'

Gorzkiewicz shrugged and poured three fresh shots. 'That's what he called himself in those days: Kostchey the Deathless. But his real name was Vadim Mikhailovitch Kravchenko. He was an army Major when I was in Afghanistan, forced to fight for those Russian bastards. I never met Kravchenko, but I heard of him. Every time they wanted a prisoner questioned. . . The screaming would last for days.'

The old man downed his vodka. 'He ended up in the SB, running the hunt for dissidents and anti-Communist sympathizers. And people like me – people he blinded – we were his warning. We were what happened if you disobeyed the regime.'

'Where is he now?'

'If I knew, he would be dead. I heard a rumour he was working for some gangsters in Warsaw, but that was many years ago.' Gorzkiewicz helped himself to a tiny yellow pickled squash. 'The shopkeepers in your Aberdeen, they are blinded yes? Eyes gouged out, sockets burned?'

'What does Kravchenko look like?'

There was a long, slow pause, then the old man took off his sunglasses, giving Logan another look at the mess where his eyes should have been. 'I haven't seen him since 1981, remember?'

Stupid question. 'Sorry.'

'But. . .' He scraped his chair back from the table and hobbled from the room, navigating the twisted maze of junk with surprising ease. He was back ten minutes later with a tatty brown folder. He held it out, and Wiktorja took it. 'This,' he said, 'is everything I know about the man. I did a Russian *entrepreneur* a favour involving a business rival and sixteen pounds of Semtex. He arranged for the Politburo to misplace Kravchenko's file. Started asking questions for me.'

Wiktorja flicked through the contents in the semi-darkness, then whistled, pulled out a photo, and showed it to Logan. 'Do you recognize him?'

It was a black-and-white shot, head and shoulders, of a man in military uniform, staring at the camera. Hard eyes. Squint nose. Short black hair. A small scar on the tip of his chin.

'Never seen him before.'

A buzzing noise sounded from somewhere out in the hall, and Gorzkiewicz's head snapped up, as if scenting the air. 'Wait here.' And he was gone again.

'So,' said Logan, holding out his hand to Wiktorja for the folder, 'how the hell does a blind man make bombs?'

'Very carefully.'

'You're all mad.'

There wasn't a huge amount in the Kravchenko dossier. Twenty or thirty sheets of A4 – all in Russian and Polish – a handful of fading photographs, and a lock of hair. Logan pulled it out, twisting the brittle strands in the dim light. Long and blonde – the same colour as Wiktorja's – wrapped up with a red silk ribbon.

'It is belong to his daughter.' A young girl appeared at the kitchen door. She was thirteen, maybe fourteen years old – wearing far too much makeup – carrying a strange stacked pot thing. Her eyes were huge, the pupils so dilated in the dark that there was almost no colour visible. 'Are you make mess in Uncle Rafal front room? Now I must to spend much time making tidy.'

Logan dropped the hair back in the folder, feeling guilty for even touching it. 'Are you Zytka?'

The young girl hefted the pot onto the working surface and unclipped the lid. There was a *poom* of steam, and the smell of warm food filled the little room. 'I am look after him.'

The sound of a toilet flushing came from somewhere in the flat.

Zytka opened a cupboard and came out with two plates. 'You must to go now. He is old and tired.'

'And hungry.' Gorzkiewicz – fastening his belt. '*Jakie masz pierogi?*'

'*Ruskie.*'

Whatever that meant it must have been good, because the old man smiled.

Logan held up the folder. 'Can we borrow this?' Then he realized Gorzkiewicz couldn't actually see him doing it. 'I mean, the file on Kravchenko?'

'No. But Zytka will make a copy for you tomorrow. Write down your address for her.'

Logan dug one of the Grampian Police business cards out of his wallet and scrawled down the name of the hotel they were staying in.

They left the old man sitting at his table tucking into a plate heaped with pale white dumplings.

The young girl showed them to the door, weaving her way through the gloomy corridor's maze of books and newspapers just as easily as the old man had. Logan and Senior Constable Jaroszewicz stumbled along behind her, trying not to fall over anything.

At the door, Zytka stopped and fixed them with a stare, dark eyes glittering like a feral animal in the fairy lights. 'You must to find this Kravchenko and you must to kill him.'

'Excuse me?' Wiktorja loomed over the little girl. 'We are *police officers,* we do not go around—'

'Uncle Rafal is hero of Poland. Kravchenko – he deserve to be dead for what he do. And if you not kill him, Kravchenko kill you. Now you go away and you leave Uncle Rafal alone.' She slammed the door on them.

They stood in the corridor outside, listening to the rattle and clank of chains and deadbolts being fastened. 'Well,' said Logan, 'she was . . . nice.'

Wiktorja turned and started down the stairs. 'At least we found a victim that was still alive.'

'Yeah, a blind bomb-maker who does favours with Semtex, and wants us to kill a sadistic ex-secret policeman for him.' It was even gloomier in the stairwell than before, music oozing out from behind closed doors. 'And did you see the state of that apartment? He's off his head.'

They pushed through the door at the bottom and out into the muggy evening. The sky was the colour of fire, high clouds laced with burning gold against the red. In the square between the buildings, the yellow lights of occupied apartments shone in the blue-grey shadows.

Wiktorja stopped halfway down the concrete slab path, then dug about in her huge handbag, coming out with the litre of vodka they'd bought on the way out here. 'I forgot to give it to him.'

'Well, too late now. Unless you want to go back up there and—'

The bottle exploded in her hands. One heartbeat it was

there, the next it was all over the ground – shards of glass and puddles of liquid – leaving Wiktorja holding onto the shattered neck. They both stood, staring as the vodka seeped away between the warm paving slabs.

'Do they usually—'

This time he heard it: a muffled crump. And Logan looked over his shoulder to see a fresh hole in the stairwell door. Bullet-sized.

'I think someone's—'

Wiktorja screamed. She stared at her right arm as bright red soaked through the sleeve of her jacket. Logan grabbed her and dived behind a tiny, Lego-block-shaped car.

'Are you OK?'

She gritted her teeth, tears rolling down her cheeks, blood dripping from one trembling hand. The other was wrapped tightly around her bicep, trying to staunch the bleeding. '*Cholera jasna. . .*'

Logan poked his head over the bonnet of the car and scanned the shadows. No sign of anyone. Why couldn't they hear any gunshots?

A little chunk of concrete path exploded, followed by the sound of a ricochet.

Wiktorja flinched back against the car, then stopped. A look of horror crawled across her face. 'We have to move!'

'What? Where? This is the only cover for—'

'This is a Trabant! Made of fibreglass: the bullets will go straight through it!'

And right on cue a fist-sized hole appeared in the car's bodywork next to Logan's head. 'Shit!'

'Shoot back!'

'At what? I can't see anything.'

THUMP – another hole.

'JUST SHOOT!'

'Jesus. . .' He scrabbled through his jacket pockets, looking for a pair of latex gloves, pulling out evidence bags, a notebook, little yellow forensics stickers . . . the collected debris of a dozen crime scenes back home. There was a pair of gloves buried at the bottom, sealed away in their own sterile plastic pack. He stuffed everything else back in his pockets, peeled the pack open, then snapped the gloves on.

'What the hell are you doing?'

'You think I'm leaving my fingerprints all over a strange bloody gun?' He unwrapped the thing from its square of paisley-patterned fabric. It was some sort of heavy-duty semi-automatic pistol and it weighed a ton. Nothing like the nice light Glock 9mm they'd taught him to shoot with during firearms training. Logan ejected the clip, checked it was full, then slapped it back in. He hauled the slide back and let go – it clacked forward into place. Ready.

'Well?' Wiktorja was starting to go pale, her lips taking on a delicate shade of blue. No way she'd lost that much blood already, so it was probably shock. 'What are you waiting for?'

'I can't just shoot into the dark at random! I might hit someone.'

'That is the point!'

THUMP – another hole in the Trabant.

He rolled the paisley handkerchief into a thin rope and tied it above the hole in her arm. 'Try not to pass out on me, OK?'

She grabbed him by the lapel, leaving a bloody handprint. Then kissed him. 'For luck.' Pause. 'You know, like in Star Wars?'

He was right: they were all mad.

Logan snapped up, tried to pick a spot in the shadows where he wasn't going to accidentally shoot someone through their living-room window, and squeezed the trigger. Nothing happened. Of course: it wasn't a Glock, was it? He flicked off the safety catch as the car's windscreen blew cubes of glass everywhere. This time when he squeezed, the gun roared, kicked like a mule, and pinged a brass cartridge case out to bounce along the fibreglass bonnet.

BOOOM!

'Bloody thing's a cannon!'

Two more shots came in reply. One shattered the wing mirror and the other thunked into the nearest tree. And this time Logan actually heard a '*futttt*' in the darkness. Silencers. He fired a couple back, trying to aim for the noise.

BOOOM! BOOOM!

Ears ringing, he ducked back down again as they retaliated. The Trabant was beginning to look like a badly engineered piece of Swiss cheese.

Voices in the darkness – shouting instructions.

'What are they saying?'

Wiktorja closed her eyes. 'They . . . they're going to rush us from both sides.'

'How many of them?'

She shrugged, then hissed in pain. 'Three. Maybe four.'

'Sodding, bastarding hell.' He popped his head back over the bonnet, scanning the darkness. There were people standing at their apartment windows now, looking out. One by one the lights went off. No one was coming to help. 'We've got to make a run for it – back into the apartment block, OK? Can you do that?'

Wiktorja bit her bottom lip and nodded.

'Right, on three. One, two. . .' Logan jumped to his feet, ready to give covering fire. A man was charging towards them: mid-thirties, big moustache, dark curly hair, leather jacket. Gun. Logan shot him.

The man didn't fly backwards like they did in the movies, he just folded up, his momentum carrying him forwards into the other side of the Trabant. The whole car rocked as he slammed against the bodywork.

'Oh God.'

The man started to scream.

Wiktorja grabbed Logan by the sleeve and tried to drag him back towards the building. 'Run!'

'I shot him. . .'

The car's rear window exploded in a shower of glass.

'You have to move!'

Logan backed up a couple of steps. 'I . . . I've never shot anyone before. . .'

She tugged at his sleeve again as chunks of brickwork flew from the wall behind them. 'They are getting closer.'

Logan started forwards. 'We need to get him an ambulance!'

'SHUT UP AND RUN!'

49

They burst through into the building's stairwell. The sound of screaming trailed away as Logan dragged Wiktorja up the stairs. Now the only noise was the blood pounding in his ears, their feet hammering on the concrete steps, and the angry shouting outside. Oh God, the man he'd shot was dead. He'd killed someone. Or maybe the man had just passed out? Please dear God, let him have passed out.

One more storey to go and they were back at Gorzkiewicz's front door. Logan hammered on the plain wooden surface. There was music playing inside: something cheery and upbeat. Down below he could hear feet clattering up the stairs after them.

'GORZKIEWICZ, OPEN THE BLOODY DOOR!'

Nothing.

Footsteps getting closer.

Logan backed up to the banister, and slammed his foot into the wood, next to the lock. The frame burst as the deadbolt tore loose, but the chain still held firm. He kicked again and the chain ripped free in a shower of splinters.

He shoved Wiktorja into the darkened apartment, then

turned and fired two shots at random down the stairwell. BOOOM! BOOOM!

Outside the gun had been loud, in here it was deafening, the roar bouncing back at them from the solid walls.

Swearing came from the floors below.

Logan charged in after Wiktorja, shutting the door behind him, looking for something to jam against it . . . only he couldn't see a thing. The fairy lights had been switched off, and with the windows all boarded up the place was in utter darkness.

The cheery music boomed out of speakers somewhere deep inside the flat – Katrina & The Waves singing *Walking On Sunshine*. Not exactly appropriate.

Where the hell were Gorzkiewicz and his bloodthirsty niece?

Junk – there was junk everywhere, they could use that to barricade the door. Logan grabbed whatever was closest to hand and dragged it against the wood. Then had a moment of epiphany. This was stupid – they didn't have enough time to make a barricade out of newspapers and assorted crap. The men would barge straight through and kill them. And Logan didn't want to die in a crappy flat full of rubbish and 1970s wallpaper.

'Gorzkiewicz?' Wiktorja was moving, he could hear her stumbling through the maze of junk. Logan charged after her, tripped over something in the darkness and went sprawling. The gun bounced from his hand and skittered away.

'FUCK!'

He scrabbled forwards on his hands and knees, trying to find the bloody thing.

Wiktorja muttered something in Polish and Logan froze.

'What?'

He could hear the footsteps patter to a halt on the landing outside. The gunmen had caught up with them.

Wiktorja's voice was high-pitched and trembling. 'There is something in here. . .'

Someone out in the hall started shouting. The only word Logan recognized was 'Ehrlichmann', but the intention was clear enough: come out or we'll kill you. Or more likely, come out *and* we'll kill you.

No thanks.

He scrambled through a stack of what felt like magazines and fell into the living room.

It wasn't completely dark in here – a faint red glow came from something in the middle of the room. An alarm-clock-radio, the one he'd thought was broken. The one sitting on a big pile of boxes within easy reach of Gorzkiewicz's chair. The one counting down from sixty. That was where the music was coming from.

00:00:58

'Oh fff. . .'

00:00:57

Wiktorja was standing in front of it, just visible in the red glow, staring with her mouth hanging open.

00:00:56

Bomb. Bomb. BOMB!

Logan grabbed Wiktorja's collar and yanked her backwards. They hit the wall and he fumbled for her handbag.

00:00:54

'What are you doing?'

00:00:53

'Gun! Give me your gun!'

'In my coat pocket . . . the other one!'

Another heavy chunk of Soviet engineering. At least this time Logan remembered to flick off the safety catch.

00:00:49

He hauled Wiktorja out of the living room and into a pile of something that clattered to the ground. The hallway was still pitch black. The men outside hadn't got past the shouting threats stage, probably working up the courage to charge into a confined space after an armed man.

Logan had a go at dissuading them, putting two rounds through the front door, the shots so loud it was like being smacked around the head. A dim light blossomed beside him. Logan stared at it. 'Why didn't you tell me you had a torch?'

'We have to get out of here!'

'Where did Gorzkiewicz go? He didn't pass us on the stairs . . .' Logan grabbed the torch.

'Hey!'

He swept it along the hallway. There was a room next to the lounge, the door lying ajar. Logan gave it a shove and it opened onto a tiny bedroom – single bed on one side, coffin-like wardrobe on the other.

'What are we going to do?'

Logan stared at the wardrobe – it was squint, one corner sticking out into the middle of the tiny room. 'In here!'

He stuck the torch between his teeth, the gun in his pocket, and hauled at the wardrobe. It rumbled across the threadbare carpet, exposing a hole in the plasterwork, right through to the brick. And a heavy steel door, covered in weld-marks and rivets.

Logan grabbed the handle and yanked, but the whole thing was solid. Gorzkiewicz had made sure no one would be following him. 'Fuck! Why did we have to break into a bloody bomb-maker's house?' The torch was already beginning to dim as the batteries died.

Out in the hallway he could hear the shouting and swearing getting louder, and then a *thunk*. A bullet punched through the door, leaving a perfect circle of light behind.

A shop mannequin propped up against the wall rocked as half of its chest disappeared in a shower of brittle plastic.

Logan staggered into the kitchen, stumbling through stacks of God-knew-what in the semi-darkness as Katrina & The Waves kept on singing their happy song.

He tried to shake some life back into the dying torch. 'How long?'

Wiktorja: 'Until what?'

'What do you think?'

'Oh. . .'

He fumbled through the gloom, feeling for the boarded-up kitchen window.

And then there was light: bright and white.

Logan waited for the blast to hit, but it was just the huge, ancient refrigerator. Wiktorja had opened the door.

At least now he could see what he was doing . . . And that it was bloody hopeless. The window was covered with a thick sheet of plywood, nailed into the surround. He'd need a claw hammer and half an hour to shift it.

They were going to die.

Wiktorja pointed at the fridge. 'In here! We could climb inside and—'

'It's a bloody fridge, not an air-raid shelter! The blast'll rip it to shreds.'

THINK!

'Bathtub!' He grabbed her hand, yanking her back out into the hallway, just in time to see the front door slam open. Three figures were silhouetted against the faint orange glow of the sunset filtering in through the tiny stairwell windows.

Logan dived through the bathroom door, snapping off a single shot as he fell. The muzzle flash was bright enough to sting his eyes, and screw up what little night vision he had. One of the figures clutched at their leg and went down swearing. And then the other two returned fire, the *'futttt'* of their silencers barely audible over Logan's tinnitus.

The first shots went high, thunking into the bathroom's back wall, just above the stained porcelain cistern. If Logan had been standing up they would have been just above his bellybutton.

The bathroom wasn't huge, just the toilet, a wooden chair, a pile of towels on the floor, and a collection of grey Y-fronts dripping over a large, old-fashioned enamel bathtub.

'Get in the bath!'

He fired off two more shots in swift succession, the gun kicking, lighting up the bathroom with strobe flashes. Each BOOOM followed by the cling-clink-clink of a shell casing skittering across the linoleum, in perfect time to the music. The harsh smell of cordite.

The silhouettes ducked and Logan struggled to his feet, then slammed his foot into the open bathroom door, forcing it back against its hinges. One more kick and the top one gave way.

A bullet ricocheted off the wall beside his head as Logan grabbed the door's edge and ripped the whole thing free.

'futttt'

He staggered under the weight as something thumped into the wood.

'Logan!'

He clambered into the bath, trying to drag the door on top of them, like a lid. It was a tight squeeze, elbows and knees sticking in uncomfortable places. The two of them a jumble of limbs. The door awkward and heavy.

He could see the men framed in the doorway of the flat, lunging forward into Gorzkiewicz's maze of junk. Logan swore and pulled the door into place.

'What's Polish for "bomb"?'

'What?'

'WHAT'S POLISH FOR "BOMB"?'
Flames.
Blinding light.
Shockwave.
Noise.

Six Days Later

50

A grey pall hung over Aberdeen, threatening rain but never quite getting around to it. A pair of plastic bags played chase across the road outside the primary school, swirling up for a moment, before disappearing over the railings and into the empty playground.

'Uh-huh.'

Logan rested his forehead on the steering wheel, mobile phone clamped to his ear as Samantha said, *'And I thought we could go out for a drink, Friday. Celebrate you being allowed back to work?'*

'Uh-huh.'

'Rennie wants to go. And Steel. Maybe Big Gary and Eric?'

'Uh-huh.'

Pause.

'Uh-huh.'

'Are you OK?'

'What? Oh, sorry, yeah.' He pulled himself upright and rubbed a hand across his gritty eyes. 'You know what it's like. All this varnishing . . . the fumes.'

'You're not still at it are you?'

He looked across the road at the bland granite lump of

Sunnybank Primary School. 'Just giving the lounge floor another coat right now.'

'The doctor said you should take it easy for a bit.'

Silence.

'Logan?'

'Sorry.'

'Is that journalist moron still camped out on your doorstep?'

A light breeze ruffled the leaves overhead, making little ovals of sunshine dance across the car's dirty bonnet. 'What? Oh . . . no. Guess he's got more important things to do than stalk some idiot who got himself blown up.'

Another pause. *'Logan, are you sure you're all right?'*

'Sorry, I just. . . Look, that's the doorbell, I gotta go, OK?'

They said their goodbyes and he hung up. Slipped the phone back in his pocket. Scowled at himself in the rear-view mirror. 'You're a lying bastard.' And an ugly one too: his face was a mass of scratches and white butterfly stitches. Dark purple bags under his eyes to match the bruises on his forehead and chin. Six days worth of stubble. He couldn't shave without taking the top off half a dozen scabs.

Logan reached for the glove compartment and pulled out the packet of cigarettes he'd bought from the corner shop. There was something wrong with the lighter – it wouldn't hold still, the flame trembling past the end of the cigarette until he used both hands. He dragged the smoke deep into his scarred lungs.

Coughed. Spluttered.

Then wound down the window.

At least it was a bit cooler for a change. Yesterday the ratty little car he'd picked up for two hundred pounds at Thainstone Mart was like an oven. His very first car and it was a piece-of-shit three-door Fiat in diarrhoea brown that smelled of old lady, stale cigarettes, and mould. But it'd been cheap, and it would do.

He sat there, smoke curling out of the window, trying not to shiver. Wasn't even that cold. Stupid.

Logan didn't trust the dashboard clock – half the electrics were shot – so he checked his watch instead. Nearly half ten.

Bloody doctor. What did he know? Not fit to return to work. Logan wasn't the one they should be sending home, it was that moron Beattie. Detective Inspector Beardy Beattie. How the hell could they promote Beattie? What idiot thought *that* was a good idea?

The cigarette tasted like burning flesh, so Logan ground it out in the car's ashtray, along with the corpses of its half-smoked friends.

He covered his mouth as a jaw-splitting yawn tore free. Then shoogled about in the lumpy seat, trying to get comfortable. Two whole days sitting outside a closed school. Must be mad. . .

Everything goes bright.

The noise hits a fraction of a second later, and then the heat: blistering the paintwork on the door, flames billowing into the room. Screaming—

Logan sat bolt upright, banged his knee on the steering wheel, then slumped back into his seat. 'Fuck!'

He sat there, clutching his leg, heart thumping, feeling sick. Struggling to breathe.

There was a packet of caffeine tablets in the carrier bag at his feet – he washed four down with a tin of Red Bull. Shuddered. Swore. Lit another trembling cigarette.

Jesus. . .

Every.

Single.

Time.

Someone slumped past on the other side of the road, head down, shopping bags in hand. Bowed by the weight of the world and every bastard in it. Logan toasted him with the tin of Red Bull. 'Screw them all.'

The scruffy old man stooped to tie his shoelace. Then stood and stared across the road at the empty school.

He was wearing a brown corduroy jacket with frayed cuffs, a pair of faded jeans with turn-ups. Scrappy beard. Grey hair sticking out at all angles. Glasses.

'Ah. . .' Logan smiled. 'About time you showed up.'

He waited for the old man to shamble across the road, then stepped out of the car; not bothering to lock it – what self-respecting thief would be seen dead stealing something like that?

The old man stopped at the playground fence, looking wistfully through the railings at the dark, silent building beyond. And then he turned and started to walk away again.

Logan shouted, 'Want to see some puppies, Rory?'

The old man dropped his carrier bags and ran for it.

He didn't get far. Logan grabbed him by the scruff of the neck and rammed him into the nearest tree, hard enough to make the man's glasses fly off into the gutter.

'Aaaagh . . . get off me! I'm not—'

'The schools closed last week, you idiot: summer holidays. No kiddies for you.' Logan pulled him back and slammed him into the tree again, bouncing the little sod's forehead off the bark.

'Aaaaagh. Jesus. . .'

When Logan let go, Rory Simpson slumped to the pavement, holding his head as if it were about to split in two. Up close he stank of BO, greasy hair, and unwashed clothes.

'You look like shit.'

He scowled up at Logan. 'You can talk . . . attacking innocent people like that. . .'

'Innocent?'

'I think I'm bleeding. Am I bleeding? I need to go to the hospital.' He pulled his hands from his forehead and checked them for signs of blood. Nothing. 'Probably got a concussion. I— Hey!'

Logan hauled him to his feet. 'The glasses your idea of a disguise, Rory? What, you think you're Clark Kent? That shite might work on the good people of Metropolis, but you're in Aberdeen now.'

The little man went back to massaging his forehead. 'That's police brutality, you know.'

'It's called resisting arrest.' He tightened his grip on Rory's collar and dragged him towards the car.

'Wait! Wait – my shopping! My glasses. . .' Hands flapping towards his fallen possessions.

Logan didn't let go, but he *did* let him pick up his stuff. Then marched him back to the ratty little Fiat. 'Get in.'

Rory stopped, peered in through the window, curled his top lip. 'Doesn't look very clean.'

Logan yanked the door open, hauled the driver's seat forward, and shoved him between the shoulder blades. Rory sprawled across the back seat, face down.

'Wrists together, behind your back.'

'But—'

'Don't fuck with me, Rory, coz I've had a shitty week and I'm just dying for someone to take it out on. Understand? Now put your bloody hands behind your bloody back!'

He did as he was told, and Logan slapped the handcuffs on.

'Ow! Do you have to be so rough?'

Logan slammed the driver's seat back into place, then climbed in behind the wheel as Rory struggled upright again. 'Where are we going?'

'Skipping bail, failing to appear, and resisting arrest. Where do you think?'

'No.' He shuffled forwards, eyes wide in the rear-view mirror. 'You can't take me back to the station! They're waiting for me!'

Which was stating the bloody obvious.

'Of course they are: with jelly and ice cream, because you're so fucking popular.' Logan started the engine – it sounded like a washing machine full of ball-bearings – then fought with the groaning gearbox. 'Now sit still and shut up.'

Rory managed to do as he was told for a whole two minutes. Then he was leaning forwards again, his head poking between the front seats, bottom lip trembling. 'Please! I'm begging you. You can't take me back there. Please.'

Logan pulled up at the junction, waiting for the lights to change. 'Not going to happen, Rory.'

'Please. . . It was. . . A policeman tried to kill me.'

'Bollocks.'

'That's why I ran: I swear on my sainted mother's grave. A policeman and that Russian you were after: they tried to kill me!'

The wind had picked up. Logan sat in the driver's seat, watching the North Sea churn against the beach, smoking another cigarette he didn't really want. A seagull lurched past on the pavement outside, giving him the evil eye on its way somewhere important.

There was a knock on the passenger window and DI Steel peered in. 'Where'd you get this piece of junk? A skip?'

Logan got out of the car. 'You took your time.'

'Don't you bloody start – I get enough of that from DCI Frog-Face.' She pointed at the cigarette still smouldering in his hand. 'Thought you'd given up the demon cancer sticks?'

Logan shrugged and took another drag. 'You going to give me a hard time?'

'No' if you lend us one.'

He did and she lit up, then blew a long stream of smoke across the roof of the car. 'You know this stuff'll kill you, yeah?'

'It can join the queue.' Logan walked round to the Fiat's boot. 'Got a present for you.'

She followed him, stepping forward as Logan unlocked the lid and swung it open. She looked inside. Looked at Logan. 'Why is there. . .?' Looked back inside again. Rory Simpson lay on his side in the boot, tucked in beneath the parcel shelf, next to the threadbare spare tyre. Hands still cuffed behind his back. He blinked up, eyes squinted against the light.

Steel poked him. 'Rory, you daft sod: normal people ride up front in the seats. The boot's for dead bodies.' She puckered up for a moment. Then said to Logan, 'Mind you, we could always drive him out to the middle of nowhere: do the world a favour? I've got a shovel in my car.'

Rory blinked, grumbled something about pins and needles, then tried to sit up. Steel pushed him back down again and slammed the hatchback shut.

'Laz, why have you got a kiddy-fiddling scumbag handcuffed in the boot of your crappy car?'

The inspector slumped back into the passenger seat, brushed the rust and dust from her hands, and said, 'This better be good.'

Rory Simpson's voice whined out behind them, 'I'm getting cramp in here.'

Logan turned, staring through the gap where they'd put one of the back seats down so they could see into the boot. 'Shut up and tell the inspector what you told me.'

The old man wriggled, probably trying to get comfortable. 'Can you at least take these things off?'

Steel popped a pellet of nicotine gum in her mouth, talking and smoking and chewing all at the same time. 'Clock's ticking Rory.'

'Fine. . .' Big sigh. 'They were waiting for me when I got home. You know, from court. The building's front door was kicked in. "Oh-ho," I thinks, "bloody kids up to no good again." And then I go upstairs and someone's broken into my flat.' He shuddered. 'If I hadn't gone past the shop on the way. . .'

'Should've called the police.'

That got her a dirty look. 'I could hear two men talking in the lounge, and I'm about to leg it – just in case it's . . . you know, concerned parents or something – when I realize they're talking about how to get rid of my body. My body! Like I'm already dead. . . One of them sounds Russian, but the other's a policeman.'

'Who?'

Rory went silent, staring down at the grubby surface of the back seat.

'Rory, who was it?'

'I didn't see him.'

'You're such a liar.' Steel stretched her gum with the tip of her tongue, then popped it. 'If you didn't see him, how do you know he was a police officer?'

'Because the other man said so, OK? *That's* how I know. He said, "You call yourself a policeman and you can't even catch one little. . ." He called me the "P" word. And the other one said he'd get patrol cars looking for me. So I snuck back out and ran for it.'

Rory started fidgeting again. 'Are you sure you can't take these handcuffs off?'

Steel said, 'Positive.'

'But my nose is *itchy*.'

'So I'm supposed to believe some anonymous Russian and a bent copper are trying to kill you?'

'He's *not* anonymous: I *saw* him. When I got back outside I looked up, at the flat. The Russian was standing at the window, talking to someone on the phone. It was him – the man from the house when that gangster got blinded. Grey hair, eyes like a rapist.'

There was a thunk on the bonnet and Logan looked around. A fat seagull was glaring at them through the windscreen. Logan honked the horn, but the bird didn't even blink. 'You lied when we put together that e-fit, didn't you.'

'Didn't want to get involved. And now look. . .' He sagged, until his head was resting on the spare tyre. 'If you take me back to the station, they'll kill me.'

Steel chewed in silence for a minute. Then turned back to face the front. 'Sounds like a load of old bollocks to me.'

Logan cleared his throat. 'Actually . . . I think he's telling the truth.'

'You soft git.' She pulled the gum from her mouth, rolled down her window, and pinged it at the seagull, then did the same thing with her cigarette butt. Missed both times. 'Fine, we'll give him the benefit of the doubt.' Steel turned back to scowl at Rory. 'Looks like it's your lucky day. But if you're lying to me, you'll be digging your *own* shallow grave, understand?'

51

The rear podium car park was nearly empty, just the Chief Constable's flash new Audi, DI Steel's MX-5, and a couple of patrol cars. Logan pulled into one of the free parking spots and turned off the engine. As it coughed and spluttered to a halt, a muffled whisper came through from the back. 'Where are we?'

'Force Headquarters.'

'What?' The whisper turned into a panicky yelp. 'No! You said! You promised!'

'Shhhhhhh! We're just stopping here till Steel has a word with the head of CID.'

'WHAT?'

'You *want* someone to hear you?'

And he was whispering again: 'She shouldn't be talking to anyone. What if he's the policeman I heard?'

Logan turned and stuck two fingers up at the man in the boot. They'd put the back seat up again, so Rory couldn't actually see, but it was the thought that counted. 'Detective Chief Superintendent Bain was *not* in your flat, plotting to kill you with a Russian gangster, OK? He's. . .' Logan drifted to a halt, watching as Steel stuck her head out of the back doors and made come-hither motions. 'We're on.' He unbuckled his seatbelt. 'Stay where you are and keep quiet.'

'But—'

'No. And stop moving about: someone'll see.'

Logan climbed out of the car, locked it, then followed DI Steel inside.

Drunken singing echoed up from the cell block, punctuated by someone shouting, 'SHUT UP YOU NOISY BASTARD!'

'Right,' said Steel, marching down the corridor, 'took a bit of convincing, but Bain's going to let us keep Rory at a secure location: your place.'

'What? No! Why can't he stay at a safe house?'

'Because the less people know we've got him, the better. He's staying at yours.'

'No chance.' Logan followed her through a set of double doors. 'It's a one-bedroom flat, where's he supposed to go? You've got a bloody huge place, why can't he stay there?'

'Oh aye, Susan'll love that, won't she? "Honey, I'm home! I know you're desperate for a kid, but I've brought a paedophile to stay for a bit instead." She'd have his balls off with a pair of pliers, two minutes flat.'

'Then don't tell her.'

'I'm no'—'

'He's not staying at mine!'

Steel threw her hands in the air. 'Fine! Act like a baby, see if I care!' She stomped to a halt. Turned. And poked Logan. 'But if he ends up with his knackers ripped off it's *your* fault.' She marched off again. 'Go get the bloody laptop.'

Logan headed up one flight of stairs and through the keypad-controlled door to reception. Big Gary was sitting behind the counter, nibbling on a Ryvita and looking miserable.

Logan leant on the desk. 'Better watch that, you'll waste away. . .' He stopped. Sniffed. Winced. The reception area stank. 'What the. . .'

Big Gary pointed at the row of seats against the window, where PC Karim's best friend Dirty Bob was slumped, picking things out of his beard and eating them.

'God almighty. . .'

'Tell me about it. He's been here since half ten.'

'Then chuck him out!'

The fat sergeant sighed. 'Can't: his mate Richard died last night. He's got to wait here till the great Detective Inspector Beattie deigns to interview him.' Big Gary shook his head, setting off a ripple of blue-stubbled chins. 'Can you believe it? DI Beardy Beattie: all the people they could've promoted, and they picked *him*.'

Big Gary took another bite of Ryvita and crunched. 'Anyway, what you doing in? Thought you were off on the sick till tomorrow.'

'Need to pick up something for Steel.'

'You look like crap, by the way.'

'At least I'm not eating stale cardboard.'

The huge sergeant took a slurp of tea and grimaced. 'Who invented camomile?' He put the mug down. 'What you after?'

'I need a laptop with e-fit software on it.'

'Aye, hud oan.' He disappeared from the desk, then there was some grunting, and he returned with a battered laptop bag. He thumped it down in front of Logan, then forced it through the gap between the glass screen and the desk. 'One laptop.' It was followed by a clipboard. 'Sign there. And no taking the piss! The amount of bastards who've signed stuff out as "Mickey Mouse" or "Adolf Hitler". . .'

'Who rattled your cage?'

'Not my bloody job, is it? Sooner they get that refit done the better.' He snatched the clipboard back and peered at Logan's signature – checking. 'Right, it's all yours. And before you go. . .' He produced a stack of Post-it notes. 'Your messages.'

'Off on the sick, remember? I'll pick them up tomorrow, and—'

'No you sodding won't: I've had enough of the bloody things cluttering up my desk.'

Logan picked up the pile of sticky yellow notes. 'You were a lot more fun before you gave up the chocolate.'

Logan sat on the bonnet of his crappy car, a cigarette sticking out of the side of his mouth as he read his messages and waited for Steel. One by one he stuck the Post-it notes on the rusty brown paintwork beside him, making a little chequerboard pattern. Two from Father Burnett, reminding Logan that he was always welcome at St Peter's if he ever wanted to talk about anything. Three from Hilary Brander, demanding he call back. One from *DI* Beardie Sodding Beattie saying how much he was looking forward to them working together, now he'd been promoted – tosser. Three from Rennie moaning about the aforementioned tosser treating him like his personal slave. One from Tracey and her sister Kylie, about how great Lossiemouth was, and like, thanks, you know?

And four from Doctor Dave Goulding.

Logan read those ones last, cigarette clamped between his teeth, smoke curling up around his eyes. They were all pretty much the same: trying to set up a meeting about a fictitious case. 'REMEMBER THOSE RAPES WE WERE TALKING ABOUT? I REALLY THINK I CAN HELP.' All of them ended the same way: with the words, 'I CAN HELP' and the psychologist's phone number. Subtle.

Logan pulled out his mobile and dialled.

A perky Liverpudlian voice said, *'Hello, Dave Goulding?'*

'What's wrong with you?'

There was silence. Then, *'Who is this?'*

'Are you after a restraining order? Is that it?'

'Look, I don't know who you are, but I'm sure I can help. Why don't you—'

'No, you can't. OK? You can't bloody help!'

Pause. *'You have to tell me who you are, I can't—'*

'Leave – me – the fuck – alone.' Then Logan hung up.

He took the cigarette out of his mouth, his fingers shaking so much that ash went everywhere. Maybe now—

His mobile was ringing. Logan checked the number on the screen and swore: it was Dr Goulding calling back.

He let it ring.

Took another trembling drag on his cigarette.

Then answered. Why not? He was in the mood for a fight.

The psychologist's voice had lost none of its infuriating cheeriness, *'Logan, Dave Goulding.'* He said it as if it was all one word: LoganDaveGoulding.

'If you've—'

'Just wanted to have a quick word about Ricky Gilchrist.'

'You. . .' Logan trailed off. Not what he'd been expecting. 'Ricky Gilchrist?'

'Yeah: thought I'd keep you up to date, as we've not talked since you went off to Poland.' Diplomatically ignoring the fact that they'd just spoken thirty seconds ago. *'I've been working with Gilchrist since his arrest – made some very real progress. Fascinating character.'*

Logan pulled the Post-it notes out of their pattern, stacking them back into a block as the psychologist droned on.

'This morning he remembered a story his dad used to tell about how Ricky's great grandmother abandoned three kids and ran off with a Polish airman during World War Two. Isn't it strange how something all those years ago can echo through people? Generations of bitterness, all distilled into Ricky Gilchrist. Can you imagine being spoon-fed that your whole life?'

'And that's why he did it?'

'Well, there's going to be more to it than that, but it's a great start, don't you think?'

'You helped Gilchrist, so you can help me. That supposed to be the idea?' Logan mashed his eyes with the palm of his free hand. 'You keep leaving messages.'

'Of course, we've had another Oedipus victim since he was arrested, so it's all got a bit complicated. Gilchrist now claims he's got thirteen disciples, and they're the ones carrying on His Holy Work.'

Logan took one last drag, then ground the stub out on the bonnet. 'I want you to leave me alone. I don't need any help.'

'It's possible he's been working with an accomplice, but I doubt it: Gilchrist's not the type. He's a fantasist, I think he's just been taking the credit.'

'Did you hear me?'

Pause. *'It's called Post-Traumatic Stress Disorder. Let me guess: you've got problems sleeping? Nightmares? A heightened feeling of anxiety? You're irritable, have difficulty concentrating, feel numb? It's perfectly natural. And I know you don't want to hear it right now, but you don't have to feel this way. Talking about it* will *help.'*

'There's nothing to talk about. I'm fine.'

'You don't have to decide right now. Just think about it. I'm free tomorrow – well, I'll be working on the revised Oedipus profile, but I'd appreciate your help?'

Logan hung up on him again.

52

Logan parked on the street outside DI Steel's house, and sat there, waiting for the inspector to turn up in her little sports car. Sunshine danced across the road and pavement, filtering through the leaves of ancient beech trees.

A voice from the Fiat's boot: 'OK, my turn. I spy with my little eye, something beginning with S.T.'

'Spare Tyre. *Again*.'

There was a gurgling roar and Steel pulled up on the street in front of him. She had the roof down on her car, her hair whipped up into an asymmetric shambles. She hopped out, dug a tatty carrier bag out of the passenger-side footwell, then marched over to the garage and hauled open the heavy red door.

Logan reversed his manky Fiat up the drive and into the gloomy interior.

It was a glory hole of cardboard boxes, random tools and half-empty tins of paint encrusted with emulsion tears.

Steel hauled the garage door down, flicked on the overhead light, then marched round and opened the Fiat's boot. A little flurry of rusty snowflakes fell on the curled-up figure of Rory Simpson, hands still cuffed behind his back.

'Hokey Cokey time, Rory.' She held up a tatty carrier bag. 'Stick your left leg out.'

'Give me a minute . . . Ow . . . Ooh . . . Eee. . .'

'We haven't got all sodding day!' Steel grabbed Rory's right ankle and pulled.

'AAAAAGH!'

'What now?'

'Pins and needles.'

'Oh, don't be such a Jessie.' She yanked down Rory's sock, then dug an electronic tag out from the plastic bag, wrapped it around his ankle, and Logan fastened it with the special pliers, making sure it was on nice and tight. Steel gave the thing a good tug, just in case.

'Ow! Not so rough.' Rory rolled to the lip of the boot and struggled there until Logan grabbed a double handful of brown corduroy jacket and hauled him out. He limped a couple of paces, then stopped. 'Still don't see why this is necessary.'

'Then you're dafter than you look.' Steel slammed the hatchback shut and more rust escaped. 'Only way that tag's coming off is if your foot goes with it. You go more than twenty yards from this house and a wee man with a big computer will tell me *exactly* where you are. And after I've beaten the living crap out of you, I'll drag you down to the station by your one remaining bollock.'

'But. . .' Rory looked down at his crotch, then back up at Steel. 'I've got two testicles.'

'No' when I've finished with you.'

'Oh.'

Steel shoved him towards the plain wooden door in the side wall. 'And if you do *anything* to upset my wife, if you so much as think about wee kiddies, or fucking *sneeze* out of place, I'll do for you. Understand?'

* * *

The dishwasher gurgled in one corner of the kitchen, cleaning up after a microwaved lunch of leftover macaroni cheese and oven chips. Then they had a pot of tea on the breakfast bar, with a plate of chocolate digestives. All very civilized.

They drank in silence, Rory dipping his chocolate biscuits in his tea before methodically licking all the topping off with a yellowy slug-like tongue.

Steel wrinkled her nose, then turned to Logan. 'So come on, Sherlock, how did you find him?'

'You said he was a creature of habit, so he was bound to turn up at that primary school sooner or later. All I had to do was wait.'

'Really?' Rory sagged. 'Didn't think I was so predictable.'

Steel took the plate of digestives away from him. 'You smell like a hoor's armpit too.'

'Been living rough – sleeping in people's sheds, public toilets . . . that kind of thing. Can't say it's a lifestyle I'd recommend.' He raised an arm and sniffed his own armpit. 'Is it really that bad?'

'Worse. There's a guest bathroom upstairs; take a shower before we all suffocate.'

'But I don't have any clean—'

'Don't worry.' She gave him an evil smile. 'I'll find you something to wear.'

Rory looked at himself in the mirror. Frowned. Then pulled at the lemon-yellow sweatshirt DI Steel had given him. 'Are you sure you don't have anything else?'

Logan smiled. 'I think it suits you.'

'But. . .' He pulled at the sweatshirt again. A big pink triangle sat in the middle of the chest, with the words, 'OUT, LOUD, GAY AND PROUD!' reversed out of it. A pair of pastel-pink jogging bottoms finished off the ensemble, one leg ruffled up over the electronic tag attached to his ankle. 'But I'm not gay. What if people think I'm gay?'

Steel smacked him over the back of the head. 'You're a sodding paedophile! World would be a happier place if you'd been born gay. And what's with the face?'

Rory was bright red, double chins wobbling in time with his bottom lip. 'I don't like the "P" word, it's . . . it's horrible.'

'If you don't like it, you shouldn't interfere with little girls, should you?' She took a handful of yellow sweatshirt and frogmarched him to the door. 'Come on, *Gaylord*. Time to sing for your supper.'

'God,' said Steel, lying on the couch, grey-socked feet dangling over the arm, 'why's it taking so *long*?'

They'd decamped to the living room, Logan and Rory working at the coffee table while the inspector slumped about like a badly designed cat. 'They built the sodding pyramids quicker than this!'

Rory licked his lips. 'Well, maybe if I had a little smackerel of something wet it would help? Like a brandy. . .?'

'When you're finished.' She lifted her head and scowled at him. 'Now get back to work, or you'll get a swift snifter of my boot up your backside.'

Logan went through every combination of nose, eyebrows, ears, mouth and chin the e-fit software had, until they finally came up with two faces. One was angular, with a broad forehead, the hair receding at the front and shoulder-length at the back. The other had hard eyes, a nose that listed to the left, and short grey hair.

'You're sure?' said Logan, mouse hovering over the 'SAVE' button.

'Hmm. . . Well . . . maybe. . . No. This one had a scar or something, on his chin. About. . .' he leant forward and tapped the screen, 'there.'

Logan selected a scar from the menu and moved it into place. 'Like that?'

'Perfect.' Rory hopped down from his chair, and struck an *I'm-A-Little-Teapot* pose in his lemon and pink ensemble. 'And now, His Royal Gay-For-A-Dayness demands a brandy!'

Steel peeled herself off the couch. 'We'll see if you deserve one first.' She loomed over Logan's shoulder and squinted at the e-fits. 'Recognize them?'

He closed the laptop with a small click. 'I think we're *all* going to need a drink.'

'You took your sodding time!' Steel scowled at Detective Constable Rennie as he hobbled into the kitchen, bent under the weight of a massive, lumpy holdall.

He dumped it on the floor. 'Any chance of a cuppa? I'm parched.'

'Do I look like a sodding char lady?' She hoiked a thumb at the kettle. 'You know where it is.'

Logan nudged the holdall with his foot. It rattled. 'What's this?'

'Videos and DVDs. And for your information, I got here as soon as I could.' Rennie filled the kettle from the tap. 'You only called half an hour ago. Takes that long to find a sodding parking space.'

The inspector peered at the bag. 'Videos, eh? Better no' be porn. . . Is it porn? If it's porn you can leave it here.'

'It's not porn, it's CCTV footage and you're welcome to it.' He stuck a teabag in a clean mug. 'Anyone else want one?'

Steel stood. 'Who knows you're here?'

'No one: Secret Squirrel all the way. They think I'm off questioning security guards about the Sperminator case. Mind you, Beattie isn't happy about it. Bastard thinks I've got nothing better to do than run about after his beardy arse all day. Rennie, do this; Rennie, do that; like I'm his bloody sidekick!'

'Boo hoo.' She grabbed her car keys from a pegboard by the fridge, then shouted, 'RORY!'

A muffled voice came from somewhere upstairs: 'I'm in the toilet.'

'A NICE CONSTABLE'S HERE TO LOOK AFTER YOU. DON'T SOD HIM ABOUT!'

The sound of flushing. 'OK.'

'AND PUT THE BLOODY SEAT DOWN THIS TIME!'

Clunk.

Rennie went for another rummage in the cupboards. 'If you're going back to the ranch, Finnie's looking for you.' He emerged with a packet of Jaffa Cakes. 'Tell you, ever since that bloody drugs bust on Friday he's been insufferable.'

'OK, first off,' said Logan, 'since when did you start using words like, "Insufferable"?'

'Emma says I need to improve my vocabulary if—'

'And second: what drug bust?'

'Big consignment of heroin from Leeds. Couple of old farts in a motor home packed with the stuff. Been dropping off consignments for dealers every couple-hundred miles. Finnie caught them making a delivery to our friendly neighbourhood Triads.'

Logan frowned. 'He did?'

'Aye, Metropolitan Police and SOCA are going mental: been trying to crack that supply chain for three years. Finnie's so full of himself it's not real!'

Steel grabbed Logan and dragged him towards the door. 'All right, that's enough of the Frog-Face Appreciation Society. We've got work to do.'

* * *

'And you're sure about this, are you?' Detective Chief Superintendent Bain sat back against the windowsill in his office, arms crossed.

Logan nodded and laid the e-fits side by side on the DCS's desk. 'Positive.' He poked the picture with the receding mullet. 'That's the man who shot at us in Torry.'

'And the other one?'

'I can't be a hundred per cent, but I think it's the man we were warned about in Poland. Just before the. . . Well. . .' He coughed. Tried not to fidget. One leg starting to tremble. 'The . . . em . . . The only photo I saw was about forty years old. But. . .' Shrug. 'Maybe. The eyes are right.'

'Name?'

'Vadim Mikhailovitch Kravchenko. Worked for the Secret Police in Krakow and Nowa Huta under the Communists: torturing dissidents. Word is he's freelancing for Warsaw gangsters now.'

'Hmm. . .' Bain ran a thoughtful hand over his shiny head. 'Inspector?'

'Makes sense. Been hearing rumours of Eastern Europeans trying to muscle their way in for ages. Simon McLeod won't play nice, so they carve his eyes out and burn the holes. Same crap they've been pulling back home since the seventies. It's no' revenge, it's a warning to everyone else.'

'Right.' The DCS picked up his phone and started to dial. 'Let's get Finnie in here and—'

Logan stabbed his finger down on the cut-off button. 'Actually, sir, it might be better to keep this low-key.'

Bain stared at him. 'Sergeant McRae, I understand you've been through a lot recently, but DCI Finnie needs to be here.'

'You can't—'

'One: he's in charge of the Oedipus investigation. And Two: until DI McPherson gets back from sick leave, Finnie's looking into that caravan full of guns.'

'That's got nothing to do with—'

'They finished processing all the prints from our weapons cache. The fingerprint recovered from that empty shell casing at the Krakow General Store matches latents on weapons *and* the caravan. If you've got an ID, he needs to know.' Bain looked down at the phone, then up at Logan again. 'Now move your finger.'

'We. . .' Logan licked his lips. 'I think Finnie's dirty.'

'Don't be ridiculous—'

'I saw him taking a brown envelope from one of Wee Hamish's goons. I-C-One male: green hair, spots, late teens, early twenties.'

Steel whistled. 'Johnny Urquhart? Thought he was still in borstal?'

Bain put the phone down. 'Are you *seriously* accusing Detective Chief Inspector Finnie of taking bribes from Hamish Mowat?'

Silence.

'I know what I saw.'

'Finnie's got the highest rate of drug busts in the force, he's like a sniffer dog. Last week: three-quarters of a million in heroin from that motor home case. If he's on the take, why does he arrest so many people?'

'I don't know . . . maybe he's overcompensating?'

'Aye,' said Steel, 'and how comes he drives that crappy Mondeo? It's an estate, for God's sake.'

DCS Bain shook his head. 'I don't see it.'

'Well . . . what about Rory Simpson? He said he heard a police officer talking to Kravchenko when they wrecked his flat, and—'

'Sergeant McRae, I will *not* let Polish gangsters run amok in my city, just because a wanted paedophile is feeling a little paranoid. Now I gave you considerable leeway in allowing you to keep Rory Simpson at DI Steel's house, but enough is enough. If we don't nip this in the bud, we're looking at all-out gang warfare. With machine guns!'

'But—'

'I said no, Sergeant.'

'This is stupid!' Logan's voice was getting louder and louder. 'You have to—'

'No I don't!' Bain was on his feet, leaning on the desk. 'I'm beginning to wonder if you're really ready to come back to work.'

Logan opened his mouth, but Steel slapped a hand down on his arm before he could speak.

'Tell you what, Laz,' she said, 'why don't you go get us all a nice cup of tea.'

'I don't want a—'

'Cup of coffee then. Rowie with jam. Photo of Gloria Hunniford with her boobs hanging out. I don't care, just sod off for ten minutes.'

'Fine.' Logan stood and stomped out. Slamming the door behind him.

He kept up the strop all they way out to the rear podium car park, then sparked up a cigarette in the last remaining square of early evening sunlight. Five to five and people were heading back to the station. Beat officers wandering up the steps from street level, patrol cars and CID Vauxhalls competing for Aberdeen's daily 'Who Can Park The Worst' award.

Logan smoked his cigarette right down to the stub, grunting and nodding hellos at the people he knew. Ignoring those he didn't. Brooding the whole time about DI Steel and DCS Bain. Probably up there working out how to get him permanently signed off on the sick.

Indefinite leave, a sorry-to-see-you-go handshake, and a partial pension.

He ground what was left of his cigarette into the tarmac with the toe of his shoe.

Maybe it'd be for the best anyway. Sodding police force. Wasn't as if it was a dream career was it? Getting shouted at, spat at, threatened . . . and that was just the senior officers, the bloody public were even worse.

Screw the lot of them.

He checked his watch. It'd been eleven minutes since he'd been banished. Time to go back upstairs and face the music.

53

He didn't bother to knock, just pushed straight into Bain's office. The head of CID was sitting behind his desk, scowling, mouth clenched like an angry chicken's bum.

But Steel smiled as Logan entered. 'Ah, about time.' She stood. 'We'll be off then. Don't worry, Bill, you've made the right decision.'

And as they left, Logan could have sworn he could hear the man grinding his teeth from the other side of the room.

Steel led the way down to her own office, waiting until the door was closed before deflating like a week-old party balloon. 'Dear God. . .'

'What happened?'

'You got any more fags on you?' She waved her hands at him. 'Come on, faster, faster.'

Logan handed one over and she lit it, drawing in a deep lungful before cracking open her window. 'You and me,' she said over the sounds of distant traffic, 'are now running a separate investigation into these Polish gangsters. Finnie knows nothing about it, and no one else gets to either.'

Logan settled onto the edge of her desk. 'How the hell did you manage that?'

She shuddered. 'You don't want to know. But you sodding well owe me one, understand? Maybe two.'

'What did you say to him?'

She took another drag and grimaced. 'Next time you go back on the fags, try a man's brand, eh? These are like smoking my granny's pubes.' She picked a thread of tobacco from her lip. 'You're lucky I didn't let Bain fire you: handing out crap cigarettes like these. . .'

It didn't stop her smoking them though.

'What next?'

'Normally I'd get your e-fits done up as big posters, plaster them all over the place, in the papers . . . maybe on the telly. This time?' She smoked and frowned. 'Never done a low-key manhunt before.'

They spent the next twenty minutes trying to work out how to run the investigation with no resources, no staff, and no backup, and no one finding out about it. 'It's just no' possible,' said Steel, feet up on her desk as Logan scribbled things on the whiteboard. 'We need at least one uniform. Who's going to make the tea?'

'We could probably get Rennie? He already knows about Rory anyway.'

'*And,*' said Steel, 'it'll really annoy Detective Inspector Beardy Beattie if we take his plaything off him, so it's win-win!'

Logan scowled and wrote a very rude word on the whiteboard.

She sighed. 'It's no' like I didn't try, OK? Apart from anything else, I'd've won a fortune if they'd promoted you.'

'Beattie. They promoted *Beattie*. He couldn't investigate his own arse with toilet paper!'

'I argued with Bain till I was blue – aye, and so did that frog-faced tit Finnie – but. . .' She shrugged.

'Who caught Gilchrist? Who found Rory Simpson? Who

ID'd the guys that blinded Simon McLeod? What about those gonzo porn makers? Who caught them?' Logan slashed the whiteboard with the tip of the pen, underlining the filthy word over and over again. 'What's Beattie *ever* done? Eh? What's he—'

'Enough, OK? I get it: Beattie's a complete nipple. *I agree*. But you. . .' She looked away. 'All that shite last year with the Flesher, and the seven-month bad patch, and the whole . . . *attitude* thing.'

'But Beattie—'

'You're a good officer, Laz, you really are, but you've got a high fuck-up to brilliance ratio. And Bain. . .' She stopped. Frowned. Made a face that looked as if she'd just soiled herself. 'Oh God, what time is it?'

Logan rammed the cap back on the whiteboard marker. 'Don't change the subject.'

Steel went scrabbling for her watch. 'Aaaagh!'

She grabbed her jacket and sprinted for the door, screeched to a halt on the threshold, then grabbed Logan by the sleeve. 'We've got to get back to my place!'

'What? But—'

'Rory Simpson: what's Susan going to say when she gets home and there's a bloody paedophile in the living room?'

'It's not my fault they're digging up half of Aberdeen!' Logan followed Steel up the path to her house.

'Should've stuck on the siren like I told you!'

High overhead, a plane left a snail-trail of white across the blue sky. From the nearby houses came the sound of lawnmowers and the smell of freshly cut grass. And from DI Steel came a long stream of muttered obscenities as she rummaged through her pockets for a key.

'If he's lying on the bathroom floor with his nuts ripped off, you're taking the blame, understand?'

She unlocked the front door and hurried inside, 'Susan? Susan, I can explain!'

Through the hall, past the living and dining rooms, past the staircase, past the downstairs bathroom, into the kitchen. . .

Rory Simpson was sitting at the breakfast bar, sharing a pot of tea with DI Steel's wife. She was still in her work suit, Rory was still in his yellow and pink ensemble, and still camping it up from the look of things.

He threw his arms wide and said, 'Inspector, *darling,* so nice to see you again!'

Susan smiled. 'Explain what?'

'I. . . We. . .'

'It's all right,' Rory winked at her, 'I told Susan all about it.'

'You did?'

Susan tutted, then filled three mugs from the teapot. 'I don't know why you've got to be so secretive sometimes. It's not like I'm going to tell anyone we've got a key witness in a big London gangland case staying with us, is it?'

'It . . . London?'

'Personally I think Rory's very brave: informing on the people who gunned down his boyfriend must take a lot of courage.'

Rory simpered for a bit. 'Oh, well, I wouldn't say courage, *per se,* I just want to make sure my Barry didn't die in vain. We've got to stand up to these people Susan, or what's going to happen to society?'

Steel plastered on a smile. 'Rory, can I have a word, please. In the hall. *Now.*'

The old man hopped down from his stool. 'Certainly. And when I come back, Susan, you just have to give me the recipe for that *fabulous* carrot cake!'

The inspector dragged him out of the room, leaving Logan behind.

'So. . .' Susan handed him a mug of tea. 'How have you

been? We've not seen you since before . . . well, Poland.' She placed a hand on his arm. 'Are you OK?'

Logan pointed at his face, the patchwork of scabs and butterfly stitches, the bruises, the heavy purple bags under his eyes, the stubble. 'Looks worse than it is.'

'You'll stay for dinner?'

'Thanks, but I can't.'

'Nonsense: you're staying, and that's final. You look like you haven't eaten in a week. I'm doing fish pie.' She frowned. 'You still eat fish, don't you?'

'I really—'

The door flew open and Rory struck a pose. 'Did you miss me? . . . Hey!'

Steel shoved past. 'Alright if Laz stays for his tea? Maybe crash here tonight?'

'What? No, I can't, I—'

Susan nodded. 'It's already settled.'

'But I can't—'

'*Aye* you *can*.' Steel's smile wasn't pretty. And as soon as Susan's back was turned, she grabbed Logan and pulled him over to the patio doors, her voice lowered to an angry whisper: 'You're no' buggering off and leaving me with Rory Sodding Simpson all night! Any more of his gay stereotype act, and he's spending the night in the morgue.'

'Rory's just trying to be funny, you know what he's—'

'I *will* kill him.' She stepped back and slapped Logan on the shoulder, raising her voice for, 'We'll make up the other spare room, you can sleep there.'

'But I've got plans.' Which was true – he was going to go home and sit in the dark drinking vodka until he passed out. Same as he'd done every night since getting back from Poland.

'I don't care: you're sodding well staying!'

* * *

Rory shuffled off to bed almost immediately after dinner, and as soon as the kitchen door swung shut, Steel was on her feet. 'OK. . .' She coughed, licked her lips, fidgeted. Shared a look with Susan. 'How about some vodka?'

They abandoned the dishes and headed out to the patio to drink shots of neat vodka. The bottle was fresh from the freezer, covered in a thin film of frost, steaming in the evening air as Steel and Logan sank three shots to Susan's one.

A citronella candle fizzed and crackled as midges and flies committed suicide in the hot wax.

The inspector filled their glasses up again, proposed a toast, 'To good friends!' then threw it back.

'Actually,' said Susan, fiddling with her hair, 'we. . .' She ground to a halt.

Steel filled Logan's glass. 'They won't let us adopt.'

Logan froze, vodka halfway to his lips. 'Do we have to—'

'We can't get IVF on the NHS,' she said, 'and we can't afford to go private.'

Susan sniffed. 'Well, we could sell the house.'

'We're no' selling the house!'

'I'm just saying—'

'Been in my family for three generations.'

'Well, there won't be any more generations if we can't get pregnant!'

There was an awkward silence.

Steel downed her vodka and poured more for everyone. 'I ever tell you about the Sperminator, Susan? Goes about smearing his spunk on handrails in shopping centres. All you'd have to do is take your knickers off and slide down every banister in Aberdeen – probably get pregnant somewhere between Markies and John Lewis's.' She laughed, trailing off into silence as Susan's face went pink, tears glinting in her eyes.

'I have to tidy up.' She snatched up the plates, clattering them together, not saying a word, then marched back into the house and slammed the patio doors.

Logan helped himself to more vodka, then pulled out his cigarettes, the lighter sparking in the fading light.

Steel slumped back in her chair. Closed her eyes. And swore. 'Great, isn't it? That's what I have to live with.'

He didn't say anything, just poured them both another glass. Threw it back. Already working on a nice numb haze.

'You know. . .' Steel took a sudden interest in the shed over Logan's shoulder. 'We could . . . ahem . . . threesome. I mean, it's what all you men fantasize about isn't it?'

Logan spluttered, vodka exploding from his nostrils, making his eyes water. 'I. . . With. . .'

Steel threw a coaster at him. 'Oh thanks. That's very sodding flattering, that is!'

'It's just—'

'It was Susan's idea, OK?' She stood, chair legs grating on the tiles. 'Me? I WOULDN'T TOUCH YOU WITH A FUCKING CATTLE-PROD!' And then Logan was all alone.

54

Fire – blaring through the walls and the floor, curling across the ceiling in violent yellow sheets. Heat. Pain. A sound like the world tearing apart—

A crash of breaking glass.

Logan jerked awake. Heart pounding. Eyes wide in the darkness. Everything was soggy. Oh fuck . . . he'd wet himself.

No, it was just sweat. He folded his arms across his face and muffled a scream. Then slumped back in his chair and stared up at the dark orange sky, waiting for his heartbeat to go from thrash-metal to slow waltz.

Every – bloody – night.

He tried to stand, but his legs weren't working properly. Finally, he managed to haul himself upright, leaning heavily on the table to stay that way, something scrunching beneath his shoes. It was the vodka bottle, spread in glittering shards all over the patio tiles. Good thing it'd been empty.

He blinked. Swallowed. Peered at his watch until it came into focus. 03:45. Probably still a bit drunk. But not feeling too bad. Thirsty. A bit achy after falling asleep in a wrought-iron garden chair, but other than that he was . . . he was. . .

That's when the nausea kicked in.

Logan staggered across the garden, in through the patio doors, the kitchen going by in a blur as he lurched out the other side and into the hall.

He was going to be sick, going to be sick, going to be sick, going to be. . .

A thin sliver of light seeped out under the downstairs bathroom door, but Logan didn't care. He wrenched the door open.

And stopped dead.

Rory was in there, bent nearly double over the bathroom sink. Trousers around his ankles. Pounding away. And then he froze: one hand wrapped around his erection, the other clutching a thick catalogue. Children's clothes. Little girls running around, grinning for the camera. 'It's . . . it's not what you think. . .'

Logan stepped inside and closed the bathroom door.

55

'. . . further protests expected this morning as part of the ongoing budget crisis at Aberdeen City Council. Here's our business correspondent Craig Connel. . .'

'Do you want another cup of tea?' Susan sat on the opposite side of the breakfast bar, and handed Logan a floral plate with a slice of hot buttered toast on it. She watched him nibbling on a corner. 'Are you feeling OK?'

Logan shrugged. Paused. 'Think I've got a cold coming on.'

At least Susan didn't pick him up on the lie.

The man on the radio babbled on about *'strike action'*, and *'disruption to public services'*.

Logan crunched toast and wallowed in his hangover. DI Steel had been long gone by the time he'd crawled out of the spare bed and into the shower. Right now, the clock on the microwave said 07:30 – half an hour after he was supposed to report for duty – but Rennie still hadn't turned up to watch Rory. And it wasn't as if Logan could leave a wanted paedophile to his own devices.

'I. . .' Susan put her mug down. 'I'm sorry about last night. It's just. . . We. . . Well, we're sort of going through a bit of a bad patch.'

He shook his head. 'It's OK.'

'I don't know what else to do. She won't sell the house. Stupid isn't it? House like this: should have children running through it.' Susan wiped a hand across her eyes, smudging the mascara. 'It's so unfair.'

Logan took her hand as the radio news came to an end. 'She really loves you.'

'I know, it's just. . . We want this *so* badly.' She stared at him, her eyes pink and needy. It was the same look he'd seen a thousand times before, usually from emaciated junkies, sitting on the opposite side of the interview table, desperate for their next fix.

He let go of her hand.

The DJ said something about a concert at the Music Hall that evening, and then he stuck a record on: *Walking on Sunshine*, by Katrina and the Waves.

Dizzy. Mouth full of bees. Heart pounding. Nausea.

Logan staggered back from the breakfast bar, the stool clattering down against the floor. 'Don't feel so good. . .' He turned and sprinted for the downstairs bathroom, locking himself in, wrapping his arms around the porcelain until tea and toast exploded from his throat. Vomiting and shivering until there was nothing left but bile.

God, how much did he drink last night?

He lay on the bathroom floor, waiting for the tremors to pass.

Must've been something wrong with that vodka.

He closed his eyes, resting his cheek on the cool tiles. Definitely the vodka. . .

The whole room shakes, chunks of concrete smashing against the bath, making it ring like a bell. The smell of burning rubbish and blistering paint. Singed hair. The deafening roar that went on and on and on and—

He jumped, bashing his forehead on the underside of the toilet bowl. Then rolled over onto his back, clutching his throbbing head and swearing.

There was a voice in the hall. 'Logan? Logan are you all right?'

He lay there, tears squeezing out from the corners of his eyes. 'I'm fine.'

Susan paused. 'I've got to go to work . . . will you be OK?'

He gritted his teeth. 'Never better.'

'. . . OK, if you're sure.'

Logan knocked on the bedroom door. Waited. Then tried again. 'Rory?'

It'd taken nearly quarter of an hour for the trembling and tears to subside. Fifteen minutes of lying on the bathroom floor feeling like an idiot.

'Rory? You awake?'

The response was muffled. 'Leave me alone.'

Logan opened the door and stepped into a cocoon of pink fluffiness. Everything was pink: walls, ceiling, bedding, wardrobe, curtains, desk, comfy chair. Even the carpet was pink. It was kind of creepy: like being inside someone, but not in a good way. The only thing not pink was a faded poster of the Bay City Rollers, cheesy pop-star grins with big, seventies hair and tartan trim.

Rory Simpson was a lump beneath the duvet, not a single portion of his anatomy sticking out into the land of pink.

Logan sat on the end of the bed. 'Brought you a cup of tea.'

More silence.

'Look, I'm sorry. . . I shouldn't have done that.'

'You hit me.'

'I know, I'm sorry it was—'

'You're just like all the rest of them.'

'You were wanking over a catalogue of little girls!'

Rory's head poked out from under the duvet. His left eye was swollen almost shut, skin the colour of ripe aubergine. Another bruise sat on the right side of his face, giving his head a lopsided look, as if it hadn't been put on properly. 'I can't help it, OK? I'm sorry, but I can't.' He sniffed, and turned his head into the pillow. 'This is what I am.'

'You want breakfast?'

'Think you cracked one of my teeth.'

'Rory, I said I'm sorry.'

'Go away.' The older man buried his head beneath the pink duvet again. Retreating into his shell. 'Please . . . just leave me alone.'

It was half past eight before Rennie turned up – dropped off at DI Steel's front door by a petite brunette in an open-topped Jaguar. The driver gave the constable a long, slow kiss, then he hopped out and round to the boot, emerging with the same holdall he'd been dragging behind him yesterday. He waved and the car pulled away, the driver blowing him another kiss as she disappeared.

Rennie stood there with a soppy smile on his face for a moment, then hefted the lumpy holdall over his shoulder. Turned, and spotted Logan leaning against the front door, smoking a cigarette and drinking tea.

'Morning.'

Logan sucked the last gasp from his cigarette, then pinged it away into the street. 'That your mum then?'

Rennie stuck two fingers up at him. 'You look like crap, by the way.'

'You're late.'

'Yeah, well, blame Steel.' He clumped up the garden path.

'She's in a right grump this morning. What did you do to her?'

'Nothing.'

'Well, she's making little effigies of you out of Blu-Tack and whacking them in the balls with a stapler.'

Logan swigged back the last mouthful of tea, handed the empty mug to Rennie, and made for the garage. 'Keep an eye on Rory this morning, OK? He's feeling a bit delicate.'

He hauled the door up and slipped inside.

Rennie followed.

The crappy Fiat looked as if it had aged overnight; it was covered in a thin film of dust, fresh cobwebs stretching from the wing-mirrors to the windows.

'This yours?' Rennie wandered around Logan's car, kicking the tyres. 'Nice colour: looks like a motorized turd.'

'It was cheap. And shut up.' Logan climbed in behind the wheel. The key skittered around the ignition before finally going in. The engine started the long squealing grind into life. Then died.

Rennie leant on the roof and peered in through the driver's window. 'Want a push?'

'Go away.'

'Just being nice.' He stood back as the Fiat's engine finally resurrected itself with a loud backfire and a cloud of black smoke. 'Jesus, this thing doesn't need a push, it needs a decent burial.' He waved a hand in front of his face, coughing. 'And before I forget: someone's waiting for you at the station. Woman called Branding?'

'Branding?'

'Branding, Branson? Something like that. Blonde, pretty, about this tall, nice boobs. Got a little dog in a stupid-looking coat?'

Wonderful. As if today wasn't going to be bad enough.

* * *

She was pacing up and down in reception, picking the varnish off her scarlet nails. The terrier scurried along in her wake, wagging its tail, and sniffing the passers-by. Today the dog was wearing pastel blue with lime-green diamonds, as if it was heading off for a round of golf later.

All the interview rooms were in use, so Logan steered her through the front doors and out into the sunshine.

She peered up and down the street. 'Can we not go somewhere private?'

'Still haven't told me what you're doing here.'

'A whole *hour* I've been waiting!' She stooped and picked up her Westie, clutching it to her chest. 'What if someone sees me talking to you?'

'Hilary: what – do – you – want?'

'It's. . .' She looked at her dog, a passing car, the strange little shop across the road with its windows jammed full of shoes and boots and jackets and hats. Everywhere but at Logan. 'You have to let Colin go.'

'No I don't.' He hopped down from the wall and started walking back towards the station. 'Bye, Hilary.'

'Wait!' She grabbed his arm. 'It wasn't him; he wasn't even there. He was . . . He was with me.'

'It's an offence to give a false alibi, you know that don't you? Attempting to pervert the course of justice: look what happened to your mum-in-law.'

'It's not a false anything, we were *together*, OK?' A blush raced all the way up from her cleavage to her forehead. 'Simon was still in hospital and we. . . It was. . .' Silence.

'Your husband's in hospital with his eyes gouged out and you're at home shagging his brother?'

She let go of Logan's sleeve, turned away. 'It wasn't like that.'

'How long's it been going on?'

'You can't tell anyone. He'll kill me if he finds out. And I don't mean figuratively: I mean he'll *kill* me.'

Logan gave her a small round of applause, and she stared at him.

'Got to hand it to you, Hilary: that was a great performance. "He'll *kill* me!" Classic. You should try for tears next time though, give it a bit of realism.'

'It's *true*!'

'No it's not. You're lying to get Colin out of prison. You McLeods are all the bloody same. If he *was* with you all night, playing hide the sausage, why did he have a hammer in his garage with Harry Jordan's blood on it?'

'Because . . . That was from before, when. . .' She went back to staring at the shop across the road. 'When he did Harry's knees.'

'So you're saying Colin crippled him, but didn't go back for seconds?'

Hilary laughed, short and bitter. 'If he had, Harry wouldn't be in a coma, he'd be in a coffin.'

Logan ran a hand across his stubbly chin. 'I still can't believe you're having an affair with Creepy Colin McLeod.'

'Six years, off and on. It was . . . Simon's not the easiest man to live with. People always think gangsters are all violence and virile, but he's. . .' Her eyes sparkled, rimmed in red. 'Thank God for Viagra, eh?'

'Well—'

'He wakes up screaming in the middle of the night now. Ever since. . .'

Logan put a hand on her shoulder. 'Come on, we'll go inside. You can make a statement and—'

'No! No statements!' She clutched her scabby dog even tighter and the thing barked at Logan. 'I told you: he'll kill me!'

'What's the point of giving Colin an alibi if you won't do it properly?'

'Can't you just . . . you know: investigate, or something? If it wasn't Colin it must've been someone else. That's who you should be doing for attempted murder. Not him!'

56

The CID office was empty except for Logan and a single bluebottle. It buzzed and battered against the window, then disappeared up behind the Venetian blind, the plastic amplifying the noise. According to the duty whiteboard by the door, everyone else was off on a job: burglaries, muggings, fire raising, drug dealing, assaults, prostitution. The whole colourful pageant of big city life.

Logan made himself a cup of tea and slumped behind his desk. The paperwork had backed up while he'd been off on the sick, piles of forms, reports, spreadsheets and statistics all needing urgent attention so some government idiot could pretend they were tough on crime. . .

But really Logan was just hiding from DI Steel.

And besides, how much of an idiot did Hilary Brander think he was? Having an affair with Creepy Colin McLeod? Who was she kidding? Everyone knew the man had a hard-on for junky prostitutes. She wasn't even a good liar.

Logan took a mouthful of tea, looked at his pile of paperwork, sniffed, then made a start.

Half an hour later he unearthed a padded envelope addressed to 'DETECTIVE SERGEANT LOGAN MCRAE,

GRAMPIAN POLICE, FORCE HEADQUARTERS, QUEEN'S STREET, ABERDEEN, SCOTLAND' in a child's painstaking block capitals.

He fought his way through the straightjacket of Sellotape and poured the contents onto his desk: photocopied bits of paper in Polish and Russian. Rafal Gorzkiewicz's file on the man who blinded him: Vadim Mikhailovitch Kravchenko.

There was even a copy of the army photograph they'd seen at the flat. Rory's e-fit had been spot on. Kravchenko hadn't changed much. Obviously he was older and had a few more wrinkles, but other than that he was exactly the same, right down to the scar on his chin.

'Still alive then?'

'Hmm?' Logan swivelled his chair.

DS Pirie was standing in the doorway, running a hand through his curly red hair. 'Not seen Rennie have you?'

Logan picked a couple of burglary reports from the pile and dumped them on top of the Kravchenko file, burying it from view. 'No. Well, not since this morning. Think he's off questioning security guards for DI Steel again. Or something.'

'Ah. . . Finnie's not going to like that. He's already pissed off she's got *you* assigned full time. Says it's pandering to the sick-note culture: we should all be thrown in at the deep end, not mollycoddled.'

'That's nice.'

'If this was the First World War, he'd probably have you taken outside and shot.' Pirie settled back against the door frame. 'Seriously though: you OK?'

'Why does everyone keep asking that?'

'Only you look like a pile of shite with a hangover.'

Logan stiffened. 'I've got a cold!'

The DS snorted. 'Yeah, good luck with that. Might work better if you eat a pack of Lockets though, menthol might cover the smell of stale booze.' He pulled himself upright. 'We all know Beattie's going to screw up sooner or later. And when he does, they'll bust his beardy arse back to sergeant, and that DI's post will be up for grabs again. Twenty quid says I get it.'

'Make it thirty.'

Pirie nodded. 'Be a pleasure taking your money, McRae.' Then he was off, dragging out his mobile phone and shouting at someone on the other end.

Logan listened until Pirie's voice faded away down the corridor.

Silence.

He unearthed the Kravchenko file again. It was all still gobbledygook, but right at the bottom was a sheet of pale-violet notepaper, covered in the same childish handwriting as the address on the envelope.

'DEAR MR SERGEANT,

UNCLE RAFAL IS SORRY YOU ARE BLOWNUP. HE SAYS THIS WAS ~~AXIDENT~~ ACCIDENT MEANT FOR BAD MENS WITH GUN WHO TRY KILL UNCLE RAFAL. HE HAPPY YOU STILL ALIVE. I HAPPY YOU STILL ALIVE ALSO. THIS IS COPY OF FILE ON *KURWA MAĆ* KRAVCHENKO. IF YOU FIND HIM, PLEASE TO KILL HIM AND SEND ME PHOTOGRAPH. THANK YOU.

LOVE, ZYTKA X

P.S. UNCLE RAFAL SAYS THERE IS BOAT GO TO WHERE YOU LIVE WITH MANY GUN FOR KRAVCHENKO. IT CALLED "BUCKIE BALLAD" AND IT GO ABERDEEN 15 JULY.

P.P.S. PLEASE TO REMEMBER PHOTOGRAPH.'

Logan sat back in his seat and whistled. A boatload of weapons on their way to Aberdeen. . . Probably replacements for the ones they'd found in that caravan in Stoneywood. Finnie wasn't going to like that, and neither was his paymaster: Wee Hamish Mowat. An all-out drug war was getting closer, and a lot of innocent people were going to get caught in the crossfire.

But the *worst* part of all was that Logan would have to go speak to DI Steel.

The inspector was in her office, glowering at her computer screen as Logan entered – bearing two cups of coffee and a peace offering from the canteen. 'Got you a bacon buttie.'

She looked at the tinfoil-wrapped parcel and sniffed. 'You were a complete shite last night.'

He settled into a visitors' chair. 'If you're not hungry, I can give it to someone else.'

She snatched it up. 'Didn't say that, did I?'

He watched her tear into the thing, tomato sauce making a bid for freedom at the side of her mouth, then unwrapped his own mid-morning cholesterol treat. A booby-trap buttie: two fried eggs in a buttered roll, ready to explode yolk all over the place

They ate in silence for a minute, then Logan pulled out his notebook, flipping through it with floury fingers to the correct page. '*Buckie Ballad*. It's a fishing boat registered out of Peterhead, belongs to one Gerry McKee. It's been out at sea since last Tuesday, due back early Friday morning.'

Steel washed down a chunk of buttie with a mouthful of coffee. 'Big deal. This is Aberdeen: fishing boats come and go the whole time.'

'Not with a hold full of ex-Soviet weaponry they don't.'

She stopped, halfway into a bite. 'Seriously?'

'Seriously.' He dropped a clear evidence pouch onto her desk: Zytka's note. 'I spoke to the Harbour Master this morning – the *Buckie Ballad* always comes into port when there's nobody about. I got him to go through the surveillance footage of its last visit and he's got blokes unloading fish boxes in the dead of night, straight into the back of an unmarked Transit Van.'

Steel picked up the note and peered at it. 'A boat full of guns? Bloody, God-damned, bastarding. . .' She frowned, polished off her buttie, then sucked at her teeth for a minute. 'Number plate on the van?'

'Image is too grainy.'

'You're dripping egg yolk on my desk.' She swivelled back and forth on her chair, while Logan mopped the wrinkly yellow drops up with his thumb. 'Right, who else knows about this?'

'Just you and me. And that's two quid you owe the swear box.'

'Oh . . . bloody hell!' She was scowling again. 'I was swearing all day yesterday, how come you didn't whinge then?'

'Wasn't on duty. And it's two fifty, now: I'll let you off with the "hell".'

They spent the next twenty minutes working out Operation Creel on the whiteboard, then Steel got Logan to type up everything and get rid of the evidence while she went to the toilet. He was wiping the board clean by the time she got back. Everything else was done: requisition forms, risk assessment, contingency plan, and warrant application. She shuffled through the lot, then wandered off to look for the head of CID.

Logan didn't tell her there was nearly a foot of toilet paper sticking out of the back of her trousers.

There was no point just sitting there waiting for her, so he wandered outside for a cigarette. A clump of uniforms had gathered on the rear podium, laughing and drinking tea, so Logan went out the front instead, wandering down Queen Street, listening to the rumble of traffic, and the screech of seagulls.

He pulled out his cigarettes, but his fingers were so twitchy the damn things went everywhere. Half a packet, all over the pavement at his feet. No way he was smoking those now.

Stupid bloody habit anyway. Wasn't even as if he enjoyed it.

He carefully winkled the last remaining cigarette from the packet and stuck it in his mouth. Then reached into his jacket pocket for his lighter. He scritched the wheel, but nothing happened. Tried again. Gave the lighter a shake. This time sparks burst from the lighter's tip, tiny explosions, bright and painful, then there was flame.

Logan shivered.

Closed his eyes.

Listened to the thump and swirl of the blood in his veins.

Wrinkled his nose at a sudden, pissy smell.

'Are you no' needin' them then?'

Logan peered out at a dishevelled man: swollen nose, red eyes, bushy black beard; monk-tonsure bald patch; blue parka jacket with half the fur trim missing; trousers that had seen better days and some sort of curry, going by the stains; filthy grey trainers. Robert Danavell, AKA: Dirty Bob.

'What do you want, Bob?'

Karim's favourite tramp gave Logan a gap-toothed smile. 'Yer fags.' He pointed at the fallen cigarettes with a grimy finger. 'You no' needin' them oany mair?'

'Knock yourself out.'

'Ah, cheers min, yer a fine loon.' Dirty Bob creaked his way down to his knees. 'No' like that fat bugger yesterday. Tellin' me I'm stinkin' up his reception. Me! Wie ma best pal lyin' deid in the morgue. . .'

Logan watched him picking through the gutter. It wasn't much of a life, but at least Dirty Bob knew what mattered to him: drink, fags and the occasional half-eaten fish supper, or discarded kebab – whatever he could forage from the bins.

No life-or-death decisions. No moral or ethical dilemmas. No screaming heebie jeebies, just because some stupid song comes on the radio.

It probably said something about your life when you started envying people like Dirty Bob.

Bob was sitting on the pavement now, one of the windfall cigarettes clamped between his lips, patting round his pockets until he found a book of matches. Lighting up with a sad little smile on his face. He looked up at Logan. 'Kin yeh spare oany money fer an aul mannie tae have a wee drink tae his best mate's memory?'

'Aul mannie? You're forty-two Bob, not seventy.'

Dirty Bob shrugged. 'Aye, but forty-two's a lot older in tramp years. Lookit poor Richard.' He sniffed and wiped a sleeve across his nose, leaving a clean-ish streak. 'Deid afore his time. . .'

Half past ten. Some of the pubs down on Regent Quay would have been open for hours, catering for the nightshift crowd and early morning drinkers. Tempting. Logan produced his wallet and dug out a fiver. Then changed his mind and made it a twenty instead. 'Here.'

Dirty Bob eyed it suspiciously. Then grinned and grabbed the note. 'Aye, that'll dae Richard proud.' He grunted his way upright, threw Logan a salute, then turned and hobbled away in his filthy trainers.

Twenty quid wouldn't make a dent in a seasoned alcoholic like Dirty Bob, not in a pub anyway. But it would probably buy a whole load of white spirit.

Logan ran a hand across his chin, feeling the stubble scritch. Maybe Bob had the right idea, burying his troubles in a bottle. Fuck the outside world. Make everything go away. . .

If nothing else it might get rid of his hangover.

Logan wandered out onto Union Street, across the road, and down Marischal Street towards the docks. The Regents Arms was a dingy little place, the windows covered with a thick layer of black paint, shrouding the drinkers in dim, artificial light. After the brightness of a sunny morning it was like stepping into a tomb. A collection of apostrophes hung behind the bar – postcards, photographs, plastic ones stolen from shop signs, all there to make up for the missing one in the pub's name.

The place was almost empty. Two old men sat in the corner by the cigarette machine, nursing their pints. A haggard woman in a very short black skirt was hunched up on a bar stool, wrapped around an empty glass, a cigarette smouldering away in her hand. Skin pale as milk, blue veins visible in the depths of her cleavage. She looked up as Logan took a seat at the other end of the bar and smiled at him. At least she'd remembered to put her teeth in.

'Hey, sweetheart, you look lonely.'

'Not today, Carol.'

She squinted, then dug about in her handbag for a pair of scratched glasses. 'Aw fuck.' She raised her voice. 'It's the pigs!' The two old men didn't seem to care, so she waved her cigarette at Logan, and a flurry of ash fell across the bar. 'What, you going to arrest me for smoking a fag? Eh? Not got anything better to do?'

He shrugged. 'Carol, I couldn't give a fuck if you want to shoot-up right here. Be my guest.'

A pot-bellied barman poked his head out from the back room. 'What's all the. . .' He looked at Logan, shifted from foot to foot, then turned on the ageing prostitute. 'You can't smoke in here, it's against the law.'

She looked daggers at Logan, then dropped the cigarette into her empty glass, swirling the thing around until it fizzled out in the residue of dying ice cubes. 'Happy now? Bloody fascists.'

Logan pointed at the taps. 'Pint of Stella, large Grouse.'

The barman stared at him for a moment. 'Yes, Officer.' He poured the pint of lager, then stuck two measures of blended whisky in a tumbler. Paused, then added a third. He put the lot down in front of Logan. 'On the house.'

Logan put his hand out and touched the pint glass, cold beneath his fingertips, beads of condensation running down to soak into a curling beer mat. God he was thirsty. . . The last time he'd been in here, as soon as they realized he was a policeman, someone had offered to take his head off with a pool cue. And now, all of a sudden, they were handing out free drinks.

'I appreciate the offer,' he pulled out his wallet and put two fivers on the bar, 'but I'd rather pay.' Logan picked up the whisky. It wasn't even eleven yet, on his first morning back at work, and he was about to get hammered.

The glass trembled as he brought it up to his lips.

A police officer, drinking whisky in the morning. Way to go. Way to be a fucking stereotype. Detective Sergeant Cliché.

The shaking was getting worse. He steadied the glass with his other hand.

Closed his eyes.

Tried not to think about fire, and tearing concrete, and blistering paint.

Logan slammed the glass down and bolted for the toilets, barging through the door and into the eye-stinging reek of stale urine. He grabbed the edge of the sink and vomited, spattering the cigarette-burnt porcelain until he was empty. Then stood there, shivering.

He spat, cranked open the cold tap, and washed his mouth out, leaving the water running until all the chunks were gone.

Logan pulled out his phone, found the number he wanted from the memory, and made the call.

* * *

Goulding's mousey assistant ushered Logan into the psychologist's lair, told him the doctor would be there in a minute, and asked if he'd like a cup of tea.

Milk, three sugars.

It was shudderingly sweet when it arrived, but at least it took away the taste of bile. Besides, it was what you were supposed to drink when you'd had a shock. Hot, sweet tea: that good old-fashioned British spirit of the blitz. Bollocks.

He looked around the office.

This was a stupid idea. Just the latest in a long list of stupid ideas.

Shouldn't even be here.

Logan stuck his empty mug on the glass and chrome coffee table, and stood. Sod this. He didn't *need* any help. He'd—

The door opened and Dr Goulding bounced into the room. A Liverpudlian Tigger in an ugly tie. 'Sergeant McRae, Logan, great you could come. Just working on the new profile, could really use your help.' He stuck out his hand. 'How you been?'

Logan coughed. 'I . . . can't stay too long, you know, operational stuff. Just came to . . . see how you were getting on.'

'Right, yes, take a pew.' The psychologist marched over to his scribble-covered whiteboard and launched into a presentation on his new Oedipus theories, now that Ricky Gilchrist was out of the picture. Goulding was so enthusiastic, Logan didn't have the heart to tell him it was all wrong. Oedipus was Vadim Mikhailovitch Kravchenko, and had been all along. OK, so Logan had no idea *why* a thug in the pay of Warsaw gangsters would want to torture and mutilate Polish shopkeepers, but it couldn't be anyone else – it would be too much of a coincidence if it was.

Goulding got to the end of his presentation, paused as if he was expecting applause, then settled into the couch's matching black leather armchair. 'I spoke to the Procurator

Fiscal this morning: we're releasing Gilchrist on licence, Friday. I've asked for a supervision order, make sure he attends outpatient counselling, but. . .' Shrug. 'Of course, that's not really why you came here, is it?'

'What? Of course it—'

'There's nothing wrong with asking for help, Logan. *Especially* after everything you've been through.'

'I don't need help. I'm fine.'

The psychologist sat back, made a little wigwam out of his fingers, tilted his head to one side, then said, 'You don't trust me. That's OK, I understand, a lot of people are scared of therapy—'

'I'm not scared, and I don't need—'

'—they're not comfortable opening up to someone they don't know. It's not easy to take that first step, so why don't we meet half way?' Goulding inched his chair closer to Logan. 'You'll admit that you're having trouble sleeping?'

No point denying it: he looked like crap and he knew it. 'So?'

'I'm going to prescribe you a mild sedative to help you sleep. It's OK, nothing to worry about, just Zopliclone. Take one pill, two hours before you go to bed, and steer clear of booze. They won't knock you out, but they will help you get some rest. You'll feel a lot better.'

'I don't want sleeping pills.'

'And I'll give you some breathing exercises to help with any anxiety, or mood swings.' Goulding reached over to his desk and picked up a BlackBerry, tapping at the screen. 'We should set up a regular appointment. . . How's Thursday mornings for you?'

'Are you deaf? I said no!'

Goulding popped the top back on his pen. 'Logan, we both know that if you weren't ready for this, you wouldn't have come here.' The psychologist gave a big, theatrical shrug. 'Of course, if you're *happy* the way you are? Feeling the way you do?'

Lunch was a microwaved mushroom risotto that tasted like rice pudding with sliced slugs in it. A factory-produced ready-meal manufactured by someone with a serious grudge against the world. Logan pushed sticky grains of rice around the plastic carton, not even bothering to tip the congealed sludge out onto a plate. It would just mean more washing up anyway.

The flat was a tip, a mess of paint pots and brushes, dust sheets and bits of unidentifiable DIY crap. He'd cleared a spot in the kitchen, just enough room for his microwaved yuck and the pills he'd got from the chemist's on the way home.

Logan stared at the packet of sleeping tablets. Read the list of possible side effects: confusion, hallucinations, memory loss, breathing problems. Might not be so bad. Take the whole lot at once and wash them down with the bottle of vodka he'd picked up from the supermarket. . .

He got up and dropped his lunch in the bin.

Then got the vodka out of the freezer.

57

'Where the hell have you been? And before you say anything, "hell" doesn't count, remember?' DI Steel had appeared at Logan's side like the shopkeeper from Mr Ben. One minute: nothing. The next: there she was in the CID office, standing right next to him. As if by magic. She wrinkled her nose. 'Why do you smell like an auld wifie's drawers?'

Logan crunched his way through another menthol sweet. 'I've got a cold.' He blew his nose for added effect. 'IB were looking for you. They say your Sperminator boy's got full-blown AIDS, so probably best if Susan keeps her panties on. You know . . . for sliding down banisters.'

Steel poked him in the shoulder, leaning in to engulf him in a haze of Chanel N° 5. 'You been drinking?'

He shrugged. 'Got a lot of paperwork to do.'

'You have, haven't you? You're pished as a—'

BOOM, the door flew open and Finnie marched in, flanked by DS Pirie on one side and PC Karim on the other. Finnie paused dramatically, then flung a hand in Steel's direction. 'Ah, Inspector, how *kind* of you to join us.'

She hauled her trousers up and scowled. 'I've been busy.'

'Oh, have you? Tell you what, do you think you could

possibly spare fifteen minutes from your *hectic* social schedule to attend the strategy meeting I invited you to?'

'Are you—'

'The meeting about trying to avert a drugs war? Or is that not important enough for someone of your *calibre* to bother with?'

Her chin came up, dragging her droopy neck with it. 'Five minutes.'

Finnie gave a small bow. 'I know we'll all be *thrilled* to see you.' And then he turned to Logan. 'I'm glad to see you're back, Sergeant. Hopefully it won't be too long before you're fit for *proper* duties.' Then he turned and marched off, calling over his shoulder, 'Five minutes, Inspector.'

DI Steel said something that cost her three pounds fifty.

Twenty minutes later, she was in her office, grinding her teeth and smoking one of Logan's cigarettes. 'Pompous, sarcastic . . . flipping . . . *sod*.'

Logan stood at the window, watching the sunshine glinting off cars and buses out on Broad Street. The lunchtime vodka buzz was beginning to fade, leaving him tired and headachy. Thirsty too.

'You know,' said Steel, flicking ash onto the stained carpet, 'I hope to God you're right, and that rubber-faced-fffff. . . That he's bent. I *really* do. Be a sodding pleasure to help him fall down some stairs.'

'You want something from the canteen? Tea, coffee?'

'And you: coming to work pished, what the hell were you thinking?'

'You ever dealt with Wee Hamish Mowat?'

She sniffed, then hauled her feet up onto her desk. 'We've been after the wrinkly old git for as long as I can remember.'

'So how come there's nothing in the files?'

'Because we've no' caught him for anything. *Ever*. And

we're no' allowed to keep rumour and innuendo on file, coz of the bloody Data Protection Act.' She held up a hand and counted the points off on nicotine-stained fingers. 'We know he's behind half the crap goes down in Aberdeen, but we can't prove it. No one'll stand up against him in court, and anyone daft enough to try is never seen again. He's got that pig farm out by Rhynie – we've no' found a single body. We've got sod-all on him.'

'Oh. . .'

'Everyone thinks Aberdeen was crime-free before the oil money hit, just a peaceful wee city of shiny streets and happy people. Rubbish: Wee Hamish's grandad was into protection and loan-sharking when Queen Victoria was on the throne. They called him "Big Hamish". His son, "Hamish Junior", expanded into smuggling and prostitution.'

She stuck the cigarette in the corner of her mouth and had a scratch at her armpit. 'Anyway, when his dad dies, Wee Hamish inherits two generations worth of criminal empire. Then the oil comes and suddenly everyone's flush with cash. Wee Hamish goes global. And we can't bloody touch him.'

'Surely after all this time someone would've caught him for *something*.'

'Nah: Bain's been after Wee Hamish Mowat for as long as I can remember. The guy who ran CID before him was at it for fifteen years. And the guy before him, and the guy before him too. There's this bottle of thirty-year-old Knockdhu sitting up in the Chief Constable's office for whoever gets Mowat. Closest anyone's come was Basher Brooks in 1975: Post Office job. Only witness vanished and the Fiscal dropped the case. No evidence.'

Logan knew what that meant: 'Pig farm.'

'Aye, pig farm.' She blew a long stream of smoke across the desk. 'Now bugger off home before anyone notices you're three sheets to the sodding wind!'

Logan shrugged and hauled himself upright. He stifled a yawn, then scrubbed his hands across his face. 'You want me to come round tonight?'

'After yesterday's performance? No I sodding don't.'

No skin off Logan's nose. He grabbed his jacket and made for the door. There was half a bottle of vodka waiting for him back at the flat.

Steel shouted after him: 'Oy! If you *do* get anything on Wee Hamish, I want in on it. Might even split the whisky with you.'

58

Someone said, 'Wake up!'

Logan broke free from the bed, arms and legs thrashing the duvet aside, then *thump*, he was lying in a heap on the floor. His own bedroom. His own flat. Not a pile of rubble in Poland.

'Jesus, you're drenched. . .' Samantha sank down on the floor next to him and ran a hand down his chest, sending beads of sweat trickling away through the assault course of scars.

He dragged in a shuddering breath. 'Fuck. . .'

'You were screaming.'

'Oh God. . .'

She let her finger drift further down, tracing the little knots of scar tissue. Echoes of the knife.

Logan grabbed her hand. 'Don't, OK? Please, just . . . don't.'

Samantha's voice was small in the darkness. 'I'm not a freak.'

Here we go.

Logan groaned. 'Can we not do this now?'

'I thought you'd understand . . . when I . . . when I let you feel my scars.' There was a long pause, and he felt her stand then settle on the edge of the mattress. 'I started when I was twelve – cutting myself. Never anywhere anyone would see, but . . . Don't know why; just seemed to make sense at the time.'

Logan looked at her, bathed in the faint green glow of the clock radio. A little after three in the morning.

Samantha sniffed, tying her fingers in knots. 'Wasn't like my parents were beating me or anything, it just . . . I don't know. They left these shiny marks on my skin. Do you know what I mean?'

She pulled at the flesh of her inner thigh, examining the black ink of the tribal spider. 'Soon as I was old enough I started getting them tattooed over.'

'Sam—'

'And then I saw yours and I thought . . . I thought it made us . . . connected or something.' She shrugged and rolled over until she was lying on the bed. 'Stupid, isn't it?'

He crawled in next to her. 'Might as well face it: you *are* a freak. And so am I. There's no such thing as normal people, it's a myth us freaks put out to torture ourselves. Just something else we can't live up to.'

She smacked him on the arm. 'I am not a freak.' But he could hear the smile in her voice.

Twenty minutes later, Logan stood in the dark kitchen, in front of the open fridge door. They'd made love then lay there in silence until Samantha drifted back to sleep. Then Logan had slipped out of bed. He gulped down half a carton of orange juice, not bothering with a glass, washing down three paracetamols. He turned and stared at the kitchen table. The sleeping pills were still there, pristine and untouched, caught in the fridge's pale light.

OK, so he woke up screaming every night – just like Simon

McLeod – but at least he could still get it up. No Viagra needed.

Logan took another swig of orange, slooshing it around his mouth. Pity there wasn't any vodka left.

Poor old Simon McLeod. What would he say if he found out his wife was telling people he was impotent? Go bloody mental. . .

The smile faded from Logan's face.

Sandilands, 1998: Andy Howard – a small-time drug dealer with a big mouth – called Simon McLeod a 'big poof' and ended up eating through a tube for six months. There was no way in hell Simon would let Hilary tell people that his dick didn't work any more so she was shagging his brother instead. Not even to get Colin out of jail.

So either Hilary had come up with this scheme on her own, or she was telling the truth about her and Creepy.

Bugger.

Froghall was silent. Weak, jaundiced streetlight bounced back from dark windows, and glittered on the paintwork of parked cars. Twenty past four: far too early in the morning to be sodding about at an abandoned crime scene, but that's exactly what Logan was doing.

He ducked under a line of blue-and-white 'POLICE' tape and unlocked the door to Flat C. A damp, musty smell greeted him as he stepped over the threshold into Harry Jordan's place.

Logan clicked on the light . . . and nothing happened. Someone must have turned the electricity off.

He pulled out his torch and ran it across the grubby carpet. The place looked exactly the way Kylie and her sister had left it: piles of ruined furniture and broken things. Logan shuddered. In the dark it was far too much like the Watchmaker's flat in Nowa Huta for comfort.

He stopped in the lounge, turning a slow three hundred and sixty degrees.

The girls – Tracey and her two friends – they'd *seen* Creepy batter the living hell out of Harry Jordan with a claw hammer. Hilary Brander was playing him for an idiot. And he was shell-shocked enough to fall for it.

He wandered from room to room, letting his torch drift through the bedrooms with their damp-stained woodchip wallpaper, the bathroom with its mildew and cracked tiles, the kitchen with its sink full of dirty dishes and bin full of something rancid and rotting.

How could anyone live like this? Even before the place had been trashed it was a hovel.

He found himself back in the smallest of the three bedrooms, the one where Kylie had been holed up with her bruised and swollen face. Mrs McLeod's pet thugs had flipped the bed up on its side, then slashed the mattress, the grey stuffing sticking out. A small chest of drawers lay on its back. They'd tried to tip the wardrobe over as well, but the room wasn't big enough and now it was wedged at forty-five degrees between the two walls, one door broken off its hinges, letting an avalanche of cheap shoes spill across the equally cheap carpet.

Logan poked a toe through the debris. There was nothing here. He was wasting his time. Should be home in bed with his slightly deranged girlfriend, not rummaging through some junky prostitute's bedroom.

But he was here anyway: might as well *try* and do a half decent job.

He snapped on a pair of latex gloves and started with the chest of drawers, hauling it back the right way up and then going through the drawers one by one, the torch stuffed in his mouth so he could see what he was doing.

Top drawer: vibrators, condoms, lubricants, hardcore porn

magazines. Everything your discerning punter could want. All yours for fifty quid a go; twenty for a blowjob.

Jesus, you'd have to be desperate.

Middle drawer: cheap tarty underwear. Peek-a-boo bras and crotchless panties, frilly nylon things, a basque, fishnet stockings.

Bottom drawer: a stack of letters and a pile of woolly socks. Most of the letters had never been opened, but Logan read the couple that were, then put them back where he'd got them. Our dearest Kylie, you know your dad and I miss you and your sister, why won't you come home?

The wardrobe was next. He dragged it upright and it bounced off the wall, denting the woodchip wallpaper. All the clothes lay in a heap at the bottom – cheap jeans, shirts, a couple of rugby tops, pink fluffy bath robe.

The impact had knocked the chipboard moulding round the bottom loose. Logan gave it a little kick, but instead of going back on, the whole front piece fell off.

He bent and tried to force it into place again, but it wouldn't fit. What did it matter anyway? Everything here was destined for the tip when the council got around to clearing the place out.

He was about to stand up when he saw it: two parallel indents in the carpet, right in the corner of the room, where the little chest of drawers would have sat.

Logan ran the torch along the skirting board.

Everywhere else the carpet was tucked down flush with the wall, but in the corner it was all curled up. Pinned underneath that chest of drawers for who knew how many years, it should have been flat.

He took hold of the edge and pulled – about eighteen inches of cheap, corrugated carpet peeled back without so much as a ripping sound. And then it stopped, where the gripper strip started.

No underlay – the carpet had been laid straight onto the chipboard.

Someone had cut an uneven, shoebox-sized rectangle out of the chipboard, then put it back again. Probably nothing. Just a jury-rigged access point for the electrics, hacked out by a sparky too lazy to do the job properly. But it looked far too well-used for that, the join covered in grimy fingerprints.

Stash for drugs?

Logan poked a biro down into the crack and used it to lever the lid off. He was right, it *was* a hiding place. Bundles of photographs, held together with fraying elastic bands. Family snapshots of a much younger Kylie and Tracey on holiday, or at someone's birthday, or just playing Mexican banditos in the back garden. Kylie looked happy, a million years away from the stick-thin drug addict who couldn't get out of bed because her pimp had beaten her.

There was a small tin in the hole, complete with a syringe and spare needles. A bong in the shape of Yoda's head. A little porcelain ballerina. A set of tarot cards.

Logan took everything out, and lined it all up on the carpet. Not much to show for a life.

Then he stuck the torch back in the hole and swung it round for one last look.

Something glinted in the darkness.

He stuck his hand down into the gap between the chipboard and the dusty concrete.

Couldn't quite reach . . .

He lay on his side, getting as much of his arm down the hole as possible, then walked his fingers along the gritty surface. Nothing . . . nothing . . . nothing – and then a faint rustle. Carrier bag? He teased it closer with his fingertips, took a good handful of plastic and pulled the whole thing out.

It was an anonymous blue-and-white-striped plastic bag, the kind you got from a corner shop. Heavy. He lowered it to the floor and peered inside.

It was a claw hammer, crusted with dark-brown, partially wrapped in a bloodstained copy of the *Aberdeen Examiner*.

59

'I don't care, OK? Get out of your sodding bed and put her on the phone!' Logan sat on the arm of the broken couch, the pre-dawn light just beginning to trickle in through the lounge window as he waited for the Witness Protection Officer to do what she was told.

'Quarter to five . . . Jesus.' A yawn. There was some muttered swearing, then a rustling noise then – *'Some bastard from Aberdeen . . . What? . . . I don't know, do I?'* More rustling. And finally knocking. *'Kylie? You awake? Kylie?'*

Pause.

Then the officer was back: *'I think she's asleep.'*

'Of course she's asleep, it's the middle of the night. Wake – her – up!'

'OK, OK, Jesus. . .' The knocking turned into thumping. And a minute later Kylie was on the other end of the phone.

'Whhhhu?' Some wet chewing noises. *'Whssleepin'. . .'*

'Kylie, it's DS McRae. Remember me?'

'Mmmnhmmmm? You're the guy saved us. Tracey says we owe you, you know? For the doctor, and gettin' us outta that shite-hole and into rehab.' A huge yawn came down the line from

Lossiemouth. *'No one was ever nice to us before. Always thought police was bastards, but you're like, a hero and that. . .'*

'I know about the hammer.'

Silence.

'I . . . eh?'

'Under the floor: in your little hidey hole, there's a claw hammer in a plastic bag with blood all over it.'

'What? No. But. . .'

'It wasn't Creepy, was it? It was you. You battered Harry Jordan and tried to frame Colin McLeod.'

'No! It can't. . . Me and Colin, we're . . . you know? He said he'd take me to Australia, start over . . . maybe even get married. Have babies. . .'

Another voice in the background, asking who it was, and then Kylie's sister Tracey was on the phone. *'You found a hammer, yeah? Must've been that old bag Mrs McLeod. Planted it, like. Make it look like it wasn't Creepy smashed the bastard's head in.'*

Logan hefted the carrier bag in his gloved hand. It was a long shot, but what the hell: 'Then why has it got your fingerprints all over it?'

Pause. *'It has?'*

'What do you think?'

This time the silence dragged on for so long Logan had to check his phone to see if he'd lost the signal. 'Well?'

'Kylie, love, get us a can of Coke, or something, eh?' Pause. A door closing. *'It wasn't her, it was me. I did it. She doesn't even know.'*

Score one for the educated guess.

'Why?'

'Why do you think? Harry was going to hurt her again. Sooner or later, and maybe next time she's not so lucky, you know?' Her voice was starting to wobble. *'Maybe next time he kills her, or she ends up a vegetable. I had to, OK?'*

She sniffed. *'Told him we was leaving, but he wouldn't let us. He's got this big knife and he's off his face on smack. Going on about how no one fucks with Harry Jordan, how we belong to him, got to learn respect, he's going to cut off our faces. . . I was scared, OK?'* Her voice dropped to a whisper, *'I kicked over Harry's wheelchair and he goes sprawling on the carpet. Hits his head on the sideboard.'*

Logan looked down at the broken sideboard with its missing leg. 'You're saying it was an accident? How stupid do you think I am?'

'He . . . he hit the sideboard – and there's blood pouring from this gash in his forehead, you know? And it's all down his face and he's trying to drag himself along the carpet, shouting and screaming how he's going to kill the pair of us . . . I got a hammer from Harry's toolbox, and I made him shut the fuck up. You know? Once and for all. No more threats, no more fists, no more of his shite.'

Logan closed his eyes and swore quietly. 'And you thought you could blame Colin McLeod.'

He could almost hear her shrugging all the way from Lossiemouth. *'Was a hammer, wasn't it? Creepy likes hammers . . .'* She sniffed again, but her voice was a lot calmer than before. *'I'm glad I did it, OK? Harry Jordan was an evil bastard. And Creepy's just as bad. Way I see it, I did the world a favour. Harry's in a coma and Creepy's in prison, and they can't hurt my sister no more.'*

Bloody hell. Logan sat on the ruined couch, holding the carrier bag with the claw hammer still in it. The one piece of evidence that would damn them all.

Tracey was right – the world would be a much better place without Colin McLeod and Harry Jordan. And all Logan had to do was lose the hammer. Pretend he'd never found it.

Hammer? What hammer?

Kylie and Tracey get to start their new life in Lossiemouth, off the drugs and off the game. No one would miss Harry

Jordan, and Creepy Colin McLeod deserved to rot in jail for the rest of his natural life.

All Logan had to do was drive out to the middle of nowhere and ditch the hammer. Or chuck it in the River Dee. Or just drop the damn thing in a wheely bin.

No one would ever know.

DI Steel's cough rattled out of the phone's earpiece, followed by some light blasphemy. Logan let her get it out of her system. Dawn had finally arrived, the sun slowly crawling its way up the sky, casting a rectangle of watery gold through the lounge window. Making the smoke from Logan's third cigarette shine like ivory.

'It's half five!' Steel groaned. *'Someone better be dying. . .'*

'I need to ask you something.'

'If it's no' about you filling a wee plastic cup with spunk, I'm no' interested.'

'I've got an ethical problem.'

Pause. *'And you phoned* me*? Jesus, things must be bad. Hold on. . .'* He could hear her bumbling about, then she was back. *'Well, come on then?'*

'Suppose there's someone who's going to get sent down for attempted murder, but you've got proof he didn't do it. He did heaps of *other* stuff, but always gets away with it: drugs, beatings, extortion, maybe a couple of deaths. . . But if you tell anyone what you know, the bastard walks and someone else has to take the blame. Someone who maybe doesn't deserve it.'

'You got me out of bed for this?'

'But it—'

'Who we talking about?'

'No one. It's . . . hypothetical.'

'Hypothetical my sharny arse. You don't wake me up at five thirty in the morning for hypo-bloody-thetical. Who is it?'

Logan took a long draw on his cigarette, the smoke burning deep in his scarred lungs. 'Colin McLeod.'

'Creepy Colin? But he's. . .' She swore. *'Are you telling me someone* else *bashed Harry Jordan's brains in? Oh, that's just bloody brilliant. First chance we've got to put him away and the son-of-a-bitch didn't do it? . . . What's Chief Inspector Frog-Face say?'*

'Haven't told him.' Logan dropped his cigarette to the grubby carpet and ground it out with his foot.

'He'll go bonkers.'

Logan walked over to the window, rubbing a clear patch in the dusty glass. Looked like another beautiful day to be a police officer, with outbreaks of infighting, sulking and recriminations. 'What if we don't say anything?'

There was a pause. *'We? When the hell did it become "we"? You're no' dragging me into this.'*

'But—'

'Just hypothetical you said.'

'But—'

'Look, Laz, I love you like a slightly retarded little brother, but you know what you've got to do. Wouldn't have called me otherwise. I am your conscience, your Jiminy Cricket, your Fairy Sodding Godmother. Soon as you told me, it's no' a secret any more: truth's out. You've got to tell Finnie.'

'Oh . . . bollocks.'

'Aye, and if you're lucky you'll still have yours by the time he's finished with you.'

60

There was a slightly bleary edge to Force Headquarters at seven in the morning: constables, sergeants and inspectors slouching around like half-shut knives, bent under the weight of a night in the Illicit Still, celebrating DCI Finnie's recent drug bust.

Logan asked around and finally tracked the DCI down in the canteen, tucking into a fry-up.

'Mmmph.' Finnie looked up, mouth full, a bean juice cold sore on his top lip. He chewed and swallowed. 'What happened to you last night?'

'I . . . ahem. . .' Logan sat, and tried not to watch as the Detective Chief Inspector got stuck into a glistening disk of black pudding, little flecks of oatmeal and fat peppering the cooked blood.

Finnie stuffed down a forkful, talking while he ate. 'Got a table booked at Toni's tonight: you, me and Pirie. Celebrate you getting back on the job after your accident.'

Accident. . .

Logan tried a smile. It wasn't easy with his stomach churning. 'I had a visit from Hilary Brander yesterday.'

'Oh aye?'

Logan told him about the affair, the other claw hammer, and the call to Kylie's sister Tracey.

Finnie stopped eating, his voice a strangled whisper: 'Why the bloody hell didn't you call me? You knew how important this was!'

'I. . .' Logan scanned the rows of breakfasting police officers, but no one seemed to be looking in their direction. 'I thought Brander was just taking the piss. How was I supposed to know it would pan out?'

'So now you're *exempt* from the chain of command, is that it? You're too damn *special* to tell me when there's a major screw-up on *my* investigation?'

'What was I supposed to do, stick the hammer back where I found it? Pretend it never happened, just because we can't get Colin McLeod for anything else?'

Finnie screwed his rubbery lips into a scowl, and his eyes into narrow, evil slits. Then he stabbed his last chunk of sausage and jammed it in his mouth. Chewing and glowering. And then he sagged.

'You're right,' he said at last. 'I fucking *hate* it, but you're right. Just because Creepy's a nasty little bastard, it doesn't mean we can fit him up for something he didn't do.' Sigh. 'Bloody hell, it was going to be such a good day as well.'

Finnie threw back the last of his tea, then stared into the empty mug. 'Better get onto that witness protection lot: I want those prossies back here ASAP.' He scraped back his chair and stood. 'Suppose I'd better go tell the Procurator Fiscal. Bloody hell. . .'

And then he was gone, leaving Logan and a half-eaten breakfast behind.

Logan pulled out his mobile and put in a call to the Witness Protection Officer he'd spoken to earlier. Finnie's plate was awash with animal fat and little flecks of gristle, smears of blood-red tomato sauce. . . Logan pushed the plate away, but he could still smell it.

It took a while, but eventually the Witness Protection Officer answered the phone. Loan told her to go get Kylie and her sister packed up – Finnie wanted them back in Aberdeen. *Now.*

There was some grumbling, an almost inaudible, *'Make up your bloody mind. . .'* and then Logan could hear the officer marching out into a different room, the phone pressed against her chest.

The muffled noise of a conversation in the hallway. *'They're all the same at bloody Queen Street. . .'*

Some knocking.

The Witness Protection Officer's raised voice: *'Kylie? Tracey? Hello?'* A moment of silence, then a door opening. *'Oh fuck . . . Bill: get an ambulance! . . . JUST GET A FUCKING AMBULANCE!'*

And then the phone went silent.

'Are you deaf or something?'

Logan looked up from the report he was supposed to be writing; Big Gary was standing in the doorway, nursing a mug of tea and a packet of custard creams.

The CID office was deserted, just Logan and a dying pot plant.

'Hospital called.' The huge sergeant sniffed then hauled at the belt straining around his middle. 'Pumped their stomachs, but it's touch and go. Drain cleaner. I mean, you'd have to be desperate, wouldn't you?'

Logan didn't want to think about it. 'Any news on Colin McLeod yet?'

'Last I heard the PF and the Sheriff were in with Finnie and the ACC. Mucho shouto, mucho swearo. Apparently your name's coming up a lot.'

'Very funny.'

'I thought so.' Big Gary grinned, adding an extra couple of chins to his collection. 'Anyway: you got a call on line two. Some Polish bint, been on hold for five minutes. I tried calling, but you never bloody answer.'

Logan swore, then dug his desk phone out from beneath a pile of search reports. Sure enough, the little red light was winking. He reached for the handset.

'Before I go,' said Gary, 'we still on for that meal tonight? Coz if we are, stick a paper bag over your head, eh? All those bruises and scabs'll put me right off my grub.'

For a big lad, he moved fast, getting safely out of the door before Logan hurled a stapler at his departing backside. It bounced off the wall and fell to the carpet.

Logan stabbed the button on his phone. 'DS McRae, how can I help—'

'Logan? This is Senior Constable Jaroszewicz? From Poland?'

'Wiktorja?' Just the sound of her voice was enough to make Logan break out in a cold sweat. 'What—'

'Can we talk?'

'Hold on, let me close the office door—'

'No, not on the phone, I need to talk to you in person. It is important.'

'What?' His bowels clenched. Oh God, he didn't want to go back to Poland. He really, *really* didn't want to go back to Poland. 'But I can't—'

'I am at Aberdeen Airport. I can get a taxi to your police headquarters?'

'No!' Even though he knew he was alone, Logan glanced around the empty CID offices, then lowered his voice. 'Don't come to the station. I'll give you an address. . .'

The taxi pulled up outside DI Steel's house. The back door opened and a familiar figure struggled out into the hot July sunshine. Wiktorja. Her face was speckled with yellow-green bruises, a patch of white gauze taped to her forehead above a collection of brown-scabbed scrapes. She struggled one-handed with a bright yellow 'DUTY FREE' carrier bag – her right arm useless in a sling – until Logan lumbered up the path and paid the driver.

He hefted her battered brown leather suitcase out of the boot, and they stood there, not saying anything as the taxi pulled away from the kerb. Logan coughed. She looked at her feet. DI Steel's fluffy grey cat slouched past on the garden fence.

'How's the arm?'

Wiktorja grimaced. 'My stupid doctor says I am not fit to return to duty, and my stupid sergeant agrees with him.' She smiled, but her eyes were dead, her voice full of artificial cheer. 'So I decided to take a holiday. I have always wanted to see Aberdeen. . .'

'For a police officer, you're a bloody lousy liar.'

This time her smile looked more genuine. 'Do you think so?'

They rummaged a clear spot in Steel's freezer for the bottle of vodka Wiktorja had brought from Poland, then sat in the back garden, in the sunshine, Wiktorja shivering slightly, Logan trying to light up. The cigarette wouldn't hold still, dancing back and forth away from the flame.

Wiktorja took a sip of instant coffee. 'I did not know you smoked.'

'I don't. Gave up years ago when someone made a pincushion out of my innards with a six-inch knife.' He tried to steady the cigarette. 'Come on you little sod. . .' And then it caught. He dragged in a lungful. Coughed. Spluttered. Winced.

'You should think about giving up again. You are not very good at it.'

'Think it'll be cold enough yet?'

'No. Twenty minutes.' She picked up the photo of Kravchenko again and frowned at it. 'And you are sure he is here?'

'Yup.' Logan slid the e-fit across the little cast-iron table. 'See?' He spread out the rest of Gorzkiewicz's file on Major Vadim Mikhailovitch Kravchenko.

Wiktorja bent over the photocopies, lips moving soundlessly as she read.

Logan spotted another photograph, stuck between two photocopies. It was in colour, the tones muted and faded; a dour-looking man, a pretty woman, and a little girl. He was canted over to one side, as if there was something wrong with his leg. Gorzkiewicz – after his discharge from the Polish army, and before Kravchenko blinded him. With his wife and daughter. Dead in the furnaces of Nowa Huta's steel works, or sold on to some Politburo stooge in Warsaw.

The little girl's hair really was *exactly* the same colour as Wiktorja's. And the mother looked a bit like her too. And Wiktorja said she was born just outside Krakow . . . Nowa Huta was just outside Krakow . . .

Maybe that's why she'd been so keen to track down Gorzkiewicz?

'You know,' said Logan, trying to think of the best way to put it, 'your hair's the same colour as Gorzkiewicz's daughter.'

Wiktorja didn't even look up from the report she was reading. 'Maybe she uses the same hair dye.'

'Oh.' He let the photo fall back to the tabletop, feeling like an idiot. So much for that theory.

The back door opened, and Rennie sauntered out into the garden, hands in his pockets. He stopped and stared at Wiktorja, his eyebrows going up and down like randy caterpillars. 'Going to introduce me to your friend then?'

Logan balanced his cigarette on the edge of a saucer. 'No.' He excused himself and marched over to the house, shoving Rennie back inside.

'Hey? What'd I do?'

'We're not here, understand? You haven't seen us.'

Rennie looked blank for a moment. Then understanding crawled across his face, leaving a leer in its wake. 'Gotcha.' Wink. 'Playing away from home, eh? Don't want Sam to find out.' He nudged Logan. 'You dog, you.'

Logan stared at him. 'You're an idiot. Where's Rory?'

The constable hooked a thumb over his shoulder. 'Living room, watching a Sponge Bob Square Pants marathon. Are you taking over, paedo-sitting? Coz I got places to go, things to do, people to arrest.' He grinned. 'You know I've been watching all those CCTV videos? Well you see—'

Logan didn't care. 'You've got till three. If you're not back by then, I'm telling Steel you've been trying on Susan's underwear. She'll kick the crap—'

'I don't wear women's underwear!' The constable coughed. 'Well, you know, not . . . with the . . . Emma says. . .' He clamped his mouth shut.

'Just get your arse back here by three.'

Logan made sure the front door was locked, then went to check on Rory Simpson. Sure enough the old man was sitting in the living room, watching kids' cartoons. When asked if he wanted anything for lunch, Rory just shrugged. His black eye hadn't improved any, and neither had his sulk.

'My tooth hurts.'

'Then microwave some soup.'

'I don't *want* soup.'

Logan sighed. 'You going to pout all day?'

'I'm not pouting.' He went back to staring at the television. 'And you hit me.'

'I said I'm sorry.'

Rory shuffled his backside, worming his way deeper into the couch. 'DI Steel never hit me.'

'Fine,' said Logan, closing the door again, 'sod you then.'

He stopped off in the kitchen to collect a pair of shot glasses, and the bottle of Wyborowa from the freezer, taking everything back out into the garden. The vodka was thick and slippery as he poured out two measures.

He handed one to Wiktorja. 'Well?'

She raised her glass, said, '*Na zdrowie*!' and tossed it back. Closed her eyes. Then smiled. 'That's better.'

Logan downed his own vodka, then topped them up again.

She picked up a sheet of paper from the pile on the patio table. 'This,' she said, 'is an army report about six aid workers suspected of being Mujahideen spies. Kravchenko cut off their ears and fed them to a stray dog.' Wiktorja picked up another. 'In this one he tortures an old man for information on local Muslims.' She pointed at a third. 'They suspected one of his troops was selling military supplies on the black market. Kravchenko gouged out the man's eyes and poured petrol into the sockets. The staff sergeant lived just long enough to be dragged outside and shot.'

'Jesus.'

It was warm in the garden, the cold vodka bottle steaming in the sunlight. They drank, and Logan filled their glasses again. 'What about the modern stuff?'

'Nothing is conclusive. Some say he is working for the Russian mafia. Some say he is working for a Polish gang.' She puffed out her cheeks. 'It is very hot. Are you hot?' She tried to get out of her jacket, but the sling made it nearly impossible. Logan helped her, revealing a T-shirt, stretched tight across her chest. 'But,' she said, 'it does not matter who Kravchenko works for, the end result is the same. He is interested in two things: fear and power. If he is in Aberdeen it is because his masters want to move in and take over.'

Logan stuck the note about the *Buckie Ballad* and its hold full of guns on the table. 'It comes in tomorrow night.'

'Then you have a war on your hands.'

Time for more vodka.

61

DI Steel was home first: half past five, and by then DC Rennie had returned, scrounged a cup of tea, and gone again. The inspector slumped through the back door into the garden, then froze, staring at Wiktorja. 'Who the hell's this?'

Logan did the introductions and offered Steel a shot of vodka.

'Aye, go on then.' She settled into one of the garden chairs as Logan went inside to raid the freezer again. By the time he got back, Steel was deep in conversation with Wiktorja, heads together over the scattered contents of the Kravchenko file.

As soon as Logan reappeared they both shot upright.

'Am I interrupting anything?'

Steel: 'No.'

Wiktorja: 'We were just talking.'

Pause. 'OK. . .' He stuck a clean glass in front of the inspector and filled it to the brim. The bottle was well on its way to being empty.

Steel picked up her drink, sniffed at it, threw it back, then clunked her glass back on the table. 'Same again.'

Logan did the honours.

'Tell you,' she said, 'won't *believe* the sodding day I've had. Finnie's been a right pain in the backside: they've got to let Creepy Colin out on bail and suddenly it's *my* fault?' She downed her second shot. 'Frog-faced git needs taken out and given a stiff sodding kicking. Any more in that bottle?'

Another refill. 'Right,' said Logan, gathering up the file, 'we'd better get going, I'll phone you tomorrow morning and—'

Steel slapped a hand down over his, pinning his fingers over a photograph of one of Kravchenko's victims. 'No' so fast. Susan and me are off out tonight, some woman's-support-group-knit-your-own-tampons thing. *You're* watching Rory.'

Logan groaned. 'Can't you get Rennie to—'

'Oh don't be such a sodding girl. All this top secret rubbish is your fault in the first place, least you can do is take your turn. We'll be back about ten. Till then,' she pointed at the kitchen window, where a pale face with a black eye peered out at them, 'Git-Features is all yours.'

'I'm no' comfy.' DI Steel wriggled in place, hauling at the armpit of a blue silk shirt.

'Would it have killed you to brush your hair?' Susan dipped into her handbag and came out with a comb. 'Here.'

Logan watched them both through a slightly fuzzy haze of vodka. They'd abandoned the garden in favour of the kitchen when Logan's forehead started to go red. Now the skin was stretched tight as an over-inflated balloon, greasy from a liberal smearing of after-sun. It stung a bit, but he was anaesthetized enough not to care. Especially after Steel had broken out the ten-year-old Highland Park.

Wiktorja had taken to whisky almost as quickly as Logan had taken to Polish vodka. She was still out there, at the garden table, her mobile phone clamped to one ear telling her sergeant back in Poland about the Kravchenko file, and the boatload of guns.

'Honestly,' said Susan, fussing around her wife, 'you're a disaster area. And eat a mint or something: you smell like a brewery. . .'

Rory sat at the breakfast bar, still wearing his 'OUT, LOUD, GAY AND PROUD!' sweatshirt, munching away on a packet of Mini Cheddars, popping each disk into his mouth and sucking them to mush before having another. 'Well, *I* think *you* look *fabulous*, Susan.' His tongue was covered in a thin film of cheesy sludge. 'First impressions are *so* important, that's what . . . that's what my Barry used to say.' He wiped away an imaginary tear.

'Oh Rory, I'm so sorry. . .'

Steel hauled at her trousers. 'Can I no' just wear jeans?'

'No.' Susan stepped back and examined her handiwork. 'Suppose you'll have to do.'

'But I *hate* these trousers, they bunch right up the crack of my—'

'You look *nice* in them.'

Rory hopped down off his stool, helping himself to a couple of chocolate biscuits. 'You should listen to Susan, those trousers do *wonderful* things for your bum. Trust me: as a gay man, I know these things.'

She scowled at him. 'I'll do wonderful things for your bum with the toe of my sodding boot!'

Susan blushed. 'Roberta! You be nice to our guest!'

'Ah,' Rory took Susan's hand, 'if only everyone was as understanding as you.' He spun her into a fast waltz around the kitchen floor. She was giggling as he started singing *Thank Heavens for Little Girls* in a high, wobbling tenor.

Little bastard.

Nasty, little, child-molesting *bastard*.

Logan swallowed the last half-inch of whisky in his glass, stood up and blocked their way.

'I say, old chap,' Rory winked at him, 'this isn't a gentleman's excuse me, you find your own—'

Logan slapped him across the face. Hard.

Everything stopped dead. Rory clutched a hand to his cheek, stumbled back against the working surface and stared up at Logan with tears in his eyes. 'What was that for?'

'Stop it.' Someone was grabbing at Logan's sleeve, but he shook them off.

'But I didn't do—'

'Stop it! Stop with the bloody comedy paedophile act! It's not fucking funny!' He was shaking, whisky and outrage surging through his veins, both hands curled into fists, just waiting for Rory to say something. Anything.

'Paedophile?' Susan stared at Logan, and then at Rory. Then she turned on Steel. 'He's a *paedophile*? You brought a *paedophile* into this house?'

'I . . . we . . . I didn't want to worry—'

'How dare you? How fucking *dare* you?'

Steel reached for her. 'Susan, I can explain: it was—'

'DON'T TOUCH ME!' Susan backed off, glowering at them. 'How could you bring that *filthy pervert* into my house? How could you lie to me?' She took a deep breath, then spat in Rory's face. 'You should've been drowned at birth!'

The little man bit his bottom lip and blinked. Blinked again. A fat tear welled over the edge of his red-rimmed eye and trickled down the side of his nose. Then he struggled to his feet and walked out of the kitchen. Didn't even slam the door behind him.

The evening was balmy, an ocean-blue sky dotted with islands of high white cloud. The sound of a sprinkler came from a nearby garden, the *'Fsssssssss, ftt, ftt, ftt, fsssssssssss. . .'* overlaid with the sound of laughing children. Fat pigeons, cooing in a thick green hedge. All managing to make Logan feel even more depressed than he already was.

Wiktorja emerged from the back door, pulled out the chair opposite and sat down in the shade of a big holly bush.

Logan didn't look up. 'How's Rory?'

'You should not have hit him.'

Fair point.

'He just. . .' Logan closed his eyes. Deep breath. 'He's OK most of the time, but. . .'

'I do not think your inspector is very pleased with you.'

Which was an understatement. Susan had stormed off to her mother's, with Steel hurrying after her, trying to explain that it wasn't her idea and she hadn't wanted to do it and it was all Finnie's fault and if Susan would just slow down they could talk about it and it was only supposed to be for a couple of days and she was really, *really* sorry. . .

Logan took another sip of whisky, trying not to think about the look of betrayal on Rory's face. 'It was an accident.'

'He says it is not the first time you have hit him.'

'I didn't . . . I didn't mean to. It just sort of happened.'

Wiktorja looked at him, but Logan couldn't meet her eyes.

'I know Rory Simpson looks like this nice little old man, but he's not. We've caught him four times interfering with little girls, none of them older than six. God knows how many times he's got away with it. I just. . .' He pulled out his cigarettes, but the pack was empty. He scrunched it up. Threw it away. Ran a hand across his face. 'I don't know.'

They sat in silence for a while, listening to the sounds of a balmy Thursday evening. Then Wiktorja said, 'I was suspended, because of what happened in Nowa Huta. Eight months undercover work, wasted just like that.' She snapped her fingers. 'Eight months convincing Ehrlichmann I was a drug dealer from Warsaw, looking to move up. Eight months pumping his thugs for information on the Watchmaker: Gorzkiewicz.'

Logan stared at her. 'You *what?*'

'I have not been entirely honest with you, but—'

'Damn right you haven't!'

She finished her whisky. 'What was I supposed to do? It was bad enough you knew I was a police officer.'

'How could you be undercover?'

'Did you really think we had to go to the cathedral in Krakow to pray? I had to contact my handler, tell him we had an address for Gorzkiewicz.'

Logan scowled. 'And the next thing you know we're getting our arses shot off.'

'I am sorry. I should never have taken you with me to Nowa Huta. It was irresponsible.'

Logan reached for his whisky, the liquid sloshing in the trembling glass. 'Did they find his body? The man I shot?'

'I should have called for backup. . .'

'Did they check the hospitals? Doctors? Maybe he's not dead.'

'Do you know how many departments are after Gorzkiewicz? All of them. I had him at the end of my gun and I let him go.'

'Wiktorja!'

She looked up. 'What?'

'Did they find the man I shot?'

'There was a lot of blood near the Trabant, but. . .' She shrugged. 'Hospitals must report anyone admitted with gunshot wounds, so Ehrlichmann has his own doctors. He does not want the *policja* involved.'

'You're sure it was Ehrlichmann?'

'I am sure.'

'And your handler?'

'Disappeared.'

Logan sagged in his chair and took a mouthful of whisky, not really tasting anything but cordite and concrete dust. 'Every night. I dream about that bloody apartment and that bloody explosion every bloody night.'

She reached across the table and took his hand. 'I know.'

The clock on the cooker was broken or something: wouldn't stay in focus for more than a couple of seconds. Logan squinted one eye shut and tried again. Seven o'clock and they'd just about killed the bottle of Highland Park. He lurched back out into the garden with a couple of packets of things. You know: crunchy things. Salt and vinegar, stuff like that.

He bumped into the table and let the packets fall from his hands. 'Help yourself.'

Wiktorja did, fumbling with a yellow bag, and then there were prawn cocktail Skips all over the place. 'Oops.' She levered herself up and wobbled back and forth a bit.

Probably a bit drunk. She'd had quite a lot to drink.

Logan took one step forward, and leant on the garden wall, only the damn thing wasn't where it was supposed to be, and he sort of staggered a little.

Wiktorja laughed at him. 'You are *pijany*.'

'No I'm not.'

'Yes you are. You are *pijany*. Drunk.'

'I'm not *pijany*, you're *pijany*.'

Wiktorja held up her good arm, posing like the Statue of Liberty. 'OK, I am *pijany*.' She picked up one of the little shell-like disks and stuck it on the end of her tongue. Then stepped in close. 'We are both *pijany*.'

Logan grinned. 'I'm not *pijany*, I'm an idiot.'

'No, you are not an idiot.' Her face softened. And then she was kissing him; prawn cocktail tongues on a sun-soaked Thursday evening.

Upstairs in one of the spare bedrooms they struggled out of their clothes, Logan helping Wiktorja with the buttons and zippers she couldn't get at because of her arm being in a sling. They collapsed onto the bed, wrapped around each other. Kissing, groping, fondling. She'd been telling the truth – not a real blonde after all. . .

And then it all went wrong.

Logan let go and rolled over onto his back. 'I can't do this.'

She lurched up until she was looming over him, breasts brushing the scars on his torso. 'You do not like me any more?'

'I do. I just. . . I can't do this.' He let out a little grunt as she grabbed him somewhere private.

'This bit says you can.'

Dead puppies. Warts. DI Steel in a thong. The last image had the desired effect, and Wiktorja said, 'Oh. . . Not any more.'

'I like you, I really do, but we're *pijany*. And I'm seeing someone.'

'You are? *Cholera*.' She sat back on her haunches. 'Is she prettier than me?' Then she punched him in the thigh. 'How can you be seeing someone?'

'It's complicated and—'

The long, sonorous *biiiiiing-bonnnng* of the doorbell saved him. Logan scrambled out of bed and into his trousers, in too much of a hurry to bother about socks or pants. 'I'd better get that.'

'Wait, but we have not—'

He shut the bedroom door behind him, pulling on his shirt as he thumped down the stairs, barefoot.

Biiiiiing-bonnnng. . .

'Coming.' He was all buttoned up and tucking his shirt into his trousers as he reached the front door.

Biiiiiing-bonnnng. . .

'I said I'm coming! God's sake. . .' Logan could see the distorted shape of whoever it was through the rippled glass on one side of the door. He unlatched the chain – having to concentrate to make his drunken fingers work – then undid the deadbolt.

The door opened.

A mountain of muscle stood on the top step: six foot tall and almost as wide, arms like tree trunks, angular features, receding mullet. Kravchenko's right-hand man.

Logan got as far as, 'Oh f—' before the fist slammed into his stomach. He crumpled, all the breath rushing out of him in one painful wheeze, and then his legs gave way and he crashed onto the black-and-white tiles.

Mr Mullet stepped inside, grabbed Logan by the ankles and dragged him further back into the hall. Then went back and closed the door.

Logan tried to roll over, tried to get up, but he could barely move.

Shout. Warn Wiktorja. DO SOMETHING!

Mr Mullet flicked the deadbolt into place.

Logan dragged in a rattling breath. Oh GOD that hurt.

The huge Polish man squatted down over Logan's chest. Grabbed a handful of hair, drew back a massive fist. '*Dobranoc policyjna suko.*'

Darkness.

62

Sharp stabbing pain. Logan groaned, coughed, opened his eyes. Then really wished he hadn't.

He was in some sort of warehouse. Golden sunlight streamed through a series of small windows twenty feet above his head, a row of partially dismantled metal shelves casting shadows across the dirty concrete floor.

He was lying on his side, arms behind his back, shoulders aching along with everything else. Handcuffs, or cable-ties around his wrists, the same around his ankles.

Fuck. Not good. Not good at all.

His stomach ached, and his head felt as if something was trying to claw its way free. A rabid hangover fighting with a punch in the face. His mouth tasted of blood, and one of his teeth was loose.

Sodding hell.

Logan coughed again, the movement sending another wave of fire through his scarred stomach. He hissed in pain. . .

'Ah, you are awake. This is good.' Foreign accent, heavily laced with Eastern Europe. 'Turn him around, Grigor.'

Mr Mullet appeared, grabbed Logan by the collar, hauled

him around through ninety degrees, then dropped him back to the floor again. And there he was: Vadim Mikhailovitch Kravchenko, looking almost exactly as he had in Rory Simpson's e-fit.

Only this time he was smiling. 'So glad you can join us, Detective Sergeant. I begin to worry Grigor hit you too hard. He is still have grudge from when you pepper-spray him.' He looked up for a second. 'Grigor, please to fetch our other guests.'

Another grunt and Grigor marched into view, then out through a side door. There was a sudden flash of blue sky and green weeds before the door swung shut again.

'Now,' said Kravchenko, squatting down in front of Logan, 'Detective Sergeant, you are man of honour, yes?'

Logan coughed again, then spat out a mouthful of blood – aiming for the old bastard, but getting nowhere near.

The Russian smiled. 'A man of fire as well. I like that.' He unbuttoned the cuffs of his shirt, rolling the fabric up to his elbows. 'You know who I am, yes?'

'You won't get away with it.'

Laughter. 'Do people really say this? Like in bad movie, is big cliché.' He pulled something from his pocket. It was a Swiss Army knife. 'I have business proposition for you.' He put the knife on the dusty concrete between them. 'I want Aberdeen. I want her drugs and her prostitutes. You want long, happy life. Is fair swap, yes?'

'I'm a police officer. If you kill me—'

'No, no, is not worry. I not kill you.' He produced a small tin of lighter fluid and placed it next to the knife.

Oh dear Jesus.

The side door banged open and Rory Simpson staggered in, hands tied together, his nose at a jaunty angle to his bloody face. Grigor was next, with a half-dressed, struggling woman thrown over his shoulder. Wiktorja – wearing a pair of jeans and a bra, bound hand and foot. She was screaming something behind a gag of duct tape.

Kravchenko pointed. 'Thank you, Grigor: over there.'

The big man put a hand on the small of Rory's back and shoved, sending him tumbling to the floor. Then Wiktorja was unceremoniously dumped next to him.

Logan thrashed against the concrete. 'Let them go!'

'I am think not.' Kravchenko picked up the knife. 'You will work for me. You will be my . . . how is called: eyes and ears? Yes?'

'Thought you already had a bent copper in your pocket.'

Kravchenko frowned. 'What is "bent copper"?'

'A policeman. You've already got some bastard working for you, why do you need me?'

'Ah, I see . . . sorry, my English is not so good sometimes.' He unfolded a curved blade from the knife. 'A businessman never have too much staff. So: you will work for me, yes?'

Logan closed his eyes. Screwing them tight, as if that would make them stab-proof. 'Yes. Yes, I'll work for you. Just let everyone go.'

'Good. This is good.'

Logan felt a hand on his shoulder and flinched.

'Now, just in case you are lying . . . Grigor, bring the fat one.'

Rory screamed.

Logan opened his eyes. Grigor was dragging Rory across the floor, the little man kicking and struggling all the way, tears streaming down his face. 'DON'T LET THEM HURT ME! PLEASE! PLEASE DON'T LET THEM HURT ME!'

Logan looked up at Kravchenko. 'You've made your point. I'm not lying – I'll do whatever you want. Let him go.'

Kravchenko shook his head. 'First we must take care of Mr Simpson. Grigor?'

'YOU PROMISED! YOU SAID YOU'D. . . ulk—'

The burly man wrapped one arm around Rory's throat, pulling his head up, the other arm clamped over the top to keep it in place. Now when Rory screamed all that came out was a muffled squeak.

Kravchenko pinched Rory's bottom eyelid between his finger and thumb, pulling it down. 'How can you be eye-witness with no eyes?'

Logan: 'You don't have to do this! I said I'd work for you!'

The curved blade shone in the cavernous warehouse. And then it went in, between the lid and the eyeball. A twist of the wrist and blood poured down Rory's face, soaking into Grigor's sleeve. Another muffled scream. And then a bloody eye sailed through the air, bouncing in the dust at Logan's feet.

'Oh Jesus. . .'

More screaming.

He was going to be sick.

The second eye joined it a minute later, rolling to a halt, its surface speckled with bits of grit and spots of blood.

Blue. They were both blue. Lying there, *staring* at Logan.

The screaming stopped. Rory slumped, and Grigor let him slide to the floor.

Kravchenko picked up the lighter fluid. 'You must to be very careful with the burning. Too much and they die. To little. . .' Shrug. 'There is no point burning them at all, yes?'

He flipped up the little red cap and Grigor nudged Rory over onto his back. The little man's eyes were just two ragged slits, surrounded by glistening red. Logan couldn't look.

The smell of burning meat.

The sound of crackling skin.

63

The car door opened and Logan fell. With both hands still tied behind his back, he couldn't do anything but slam into the hard ground, then lie there, groaning in claustrophobic darkness. No idea where he was.

'*Clunk*' Then the crunch of feet on dry earth, getting closer – someone walking around the vehicle towards him. Rough hands on his shoulders, dragging him backwards until he was completely out of the car. And then the darkness lifted as Kravchenko pulled the bag off Logan's head. The change from pitch black to bright sunshine was sudden and painful.

They were in a lay-by surrounded by trees. A grass verge full of yellow dandelions and tangled brambles. An abandoned armchair, the fabric stained and fraying. A ripped open bin-bag with its contents strewn across the undergrowth.

Kravchenko smiled down at him. 'Please to remember, Detective Sergeant, you do what you are told. And everything is happy.'

'Let her go.'

'I am sorry, Senior Constable Jaroszewicz is stay with me until I trust you.' Kravchenko put his foot against Logan's shoulder and pushed him over onto his back. 'You have been ask questions about Krystka Gorzałkowska, yes? Very pretty girl, is good, but she not like to make film with men, want go to *policja*, but Grigor is play with her. Very rough.' The smile vanished. He hooked a thumb at his driver. 'If I can not trust you, Senior Constable Jarosewicz is blinded. Only I let Grigor play with her first. And when he is finished with her, I let him play with you.'

Leaning back against the black BMW, Grigor grinned.

'And please to remember I have, as you say, the "copper who bends", and if you try fuck me, I will know.' Kravchenko pulled a mobile phone from his pocket and placed it on the ground by Logan's head. 'If I need you, I call, yes?'

Logan squinted up at the clear blue sky, trying to gauge how much time had passed since they'd left the warehouse. Half an hour? Forty minutes? 'You have to get Rory to a hospital.'

'Why do you care? He is children rapist, yes?' The old man opened his arms wide. 'But you are alive, you have still both eyes. This is happy day for you.'

Logan struggled on the ground for a moment, tugging against his bonds.

'You want perhaps I should untie you, yes?' Kravchenko's smile was back. 'But you are resourceful man. You can manage I am thinking.' And then he climbed back into the car. 'I will to be in touch. Grigor?'

The car door slammed, and the engine roared, wheels spinning on the dry earth, sending grit and pebbles flying as the BMW shot out onto the road. Logan waited for it to disappear from view, then rolled over and threw up.

He limped and hobbled along the side of the road in his bare feet. He'd tried walking on the verge, but the grass was full of sharp stones and broken bottles. And Logan *really* didn't need another serious laceration.

He sucked at the heel of his left hand. Probably going to need a tetanus shot. That's what happened when you had to saw through a set of cable-ties with the rusty lid from a tin of baked beans.

Lucky he didn't lose a finger.

He dug out the mobile phone Kravchenko had given him, and fiddled with the buttons again, like he'd done a dozen times since getting himself free. Still no luck. Somehow they'd managed to lock the handset so it would only accept incoming calls. Kravchenko could call in, but Logan couldn't call out.

He kept on walking.

It was a quiet road, somewhere north of the city, judging by the helicopters that occasionally droned by, far overhead, going to and from the offshore oil platforms.

And then there was a new noise: a car's engine, getting closer. About time too. He limped into the middle of the road and started waving his arms.

A red hatchback roared around the corner, doing at least sixty. No intention of stopping. Logan jumped back onto the verge as it flew past, the driver leaning on the horn. '*Brrrrrrrrreeeeeeeeeeep!*'

Logan gave it the two-finger farewell. 'Bastard!'

Five minutes later a tractor rumbled up the road, huge heavy tyres churning up the tarmac on one side of the road, the farmer too busy blethering away on his mobile phone to notice Logan standing there waving at him. He looked up at the last moment and his eyes went wide.

The tractor lurched to a halt in a squeal of air-brakes and foul language.

Logan marched up to the cab, hands up in the universal sign for stop. 'I need you to—'

'You bloody idiot!' The farmer yanked his door open and shouted down at Logan, 'Trying to get yourself killed?'

'Police – give me your phone.'

'*What*? Do you lot have nothing better to do than harass innocent motorists?'

Logan stuck out his hand. 'Phone. Now.'

'I was only listening to my messages!'

'I don't care if you're having phone sex with the Duke of sodding Edinburgh, give me your bloody mobile!'

The farmer scowled. 'Bunch of bastards. If it was up to me—'

'You want let off with a warning, or locked up?'

He shut his mouth. Shifted in his seat. 'Sorry, Officer.' He tossed the phone out of the cab and Logan grabbed it before it hit the dirt, then dialled DI Steel's number from memory.

She picked up on the second ring. *'Who's this?'*

'I need you to—'

'YOU!'

Logan flinched, holding the phone away from his ear as the inspector shouted and swore.

'What did you do to my bloody house? I leave you in charge for five bloody minutes and it looks like a bloody bomb went off! That TV cost thousands, you—'

'They've got Wiktorja. Kravchenko and his sidekick . . . they gouged Rory's eyes out.'

There was a pause.

'Inspector?'

More swearing. *'You* sure *they did Rory? We've no' had a phone call or anything, so maybe he's just—'*

'I was there: I watched them do it.'

'You WHAT?'

'It's not like I had any choice, is it? I was tied up. The point is they've got Wiktorja.'

'Where are you?'

'Are you listening to me?'

'Just answer the bloody question.'

'Oh for God's sake. . .' Logan did a slow turn, but he still couldn't recognize anything. 'Hold on.' He walked back to the tractor and shouted up at the driver, 'Where's the nearest town?'

The man pointed out of the cab. 'Whitecairns is about two miles that way.' Then he harrumphed. 'This phone call . . . not long distance is it? I've only got five quid credit left and—'

Logan turned his back on him and limped down the road a bit. 'They dumped me north of the city. You need to get the tracking thing on Rory Simpson's ankle bracelet turned on. Wiktorja might still be with him.'

'Sodding hell, Bain's going to do his nut when he finds out. . . Why did I let you talk me into this?'

'It's not my fault! They broke in and—'

'I don't care: get your arse back here, ASAP.'

Logan said he'd see what he could do.

The farmer gave him a lift as far as the industrial estate on Denmore Road, Bridge of Don. Then Logan flagged down a taxi. He'd given Steel the number of the anonymous mobile phone Kravchenko had left, and now Logan held it clutched in his hand, unsure if he wanted the thing to ring or not.

Outside the taxi windows the sky had faded to a pale blue-grey, the sunset already gone from a fiery pink to a faint yellow haze on the horizon, soon lost behind the dark hulks of buildings and tower blocks. They were most of the way down King Street before the sinister mobile started making irritating bleeping noises.

He checked the display – DI Steel.

'. . . look like a sodding mind reader? Get your finger out and—'

'Hello?'

'—hold on a minute. Laz? Where are you?'

'Almost at the station: two minutes tops.'

'Change of plan. We got a location for Rory's – I don't care. Do I look like I sodding care? Just do it! – Hello?'

'Hello?'

'Playing fields, other side of the river from Duthie Park. And when you get here you can tell me how the sodding hell I'm supposed to organize a search party without telling anyone!'

The grass was cool beneath Logan's bare feet as he picked his way down the slope from Abbotswell Road, trying not to step in anything nasty in the growing gloom. A high, chain-link fence ran down the right-hand edge of the park, the skeletal frame of a building behind it just visible against the darkening sky.

A couple of people were walking dogs on the other side of the park. They didn't seem to notice the small clump of flashlights working their way through the scrub and bushes at the water's edge.

Logan hobbled on.

DI Steel was standing with her hands in her pockets twenty feet from the river bank, cigarette dangling from the corner of her downturned mouth, staring out at the water. 'They wrecked my house.'

A car horn blared from the road above.

Logan glanced back. 'Can someone lend me a twenty? I've got to pay the taxi and—'

'How could you let them blind him?'

'I didn't let—'

'He was a sodding prisoner in *your* sodding care!'

'They broke in! I didn't have a—'

She poked Logan in the chest. 'If he's dead I'm no' taking the blame, understand?'

Logan looked up at the sky, then back down at the inspector. 'What was I supposed to do? I was tied up, dumped miles out of town.' He held up his palm, showing off the jagged dark red line where the can lid had sliced into the skin. 'I nearly cut my bloody hand off getting free!'

'You should have. . .' Silence.

'What? What should I have done? Please: tell me, because I can't think of a fucking thing!' He was shouting now. 'WHAT SHOULD I HAVE FUCKING DONE?'

She sighed, took the cigarette from her mouth, and pointed with the glowing tip at the little circle of torches, still at it down by the river. 'I've got four people looking for him. *Four*. That was all I could get without Bain or Finnie finding out we lost Rory. Because soon as they do, you and me are well and truly screwed.'

'I didn't have any choice.'

The taxi horn sounded again and this time Logan shouted back, 'AND YOU CAN FUCK OFF AS WELL!'

He slumped to the ground, sitting with his knees against his chest. Trembling.

'You OK?'

'They've got Wiktorja.'

'I know.' Steel put a hand on his shoulder. 'We'll find her. Bain's setting up a big press conference, the whole three-ring circus. And don't look at me like that, I had to tell him, OK? We'll keep Rory a secret for as long as we can, but – oh sodding hell. . .' The Airwave handset in her pocket was ringing. She dragged it out and went, 'Uh-huh, is he. . .? . . . Aye.'

Down by the water, someone was waving their torch back and forth, trying to attract their attention.

They'd found Rory Simpson.

64

What he really wanted to do was to climb inside a bottle of ice-cold vodka and stay there. Instead he was sitting on his own in his ratty brown Fiat; parked on Commercial Quay in the shadows with the lights off, listening to the buzz and chatter of a typical Aberdeen nightshift.

'Aye, this is Alpha One Niner, we've been roon the Trinity Centre and there's naybiddy here. Must've been a hoax. . .' – 'Just picked up three teenagers drunk and disorderly on Holburn Street. . .' – 'Roger that Control, on our way tae Seafield Road noo. . .' – '. . . can I get a PNC check on a blue Renault Clio, registration number Sierra Wilko Zero Seven. . .'

You had to hand it to the head of CID, the only people who knew about Operation Creel were the officers involved – all handpicked by Bain. Complete radio silence as they waited for the Buckie Ballad to chug into port.

ETA 01:50.

Aberdeen Harbour was huge: two man-made inlets of greasy water and a chunk of the River Dee, all lined with warehouses and massive tanks of chemicals and fuel. Commercial Quay was right in the middle and this section of it, down by the fish market, was almost empty – just a handful of parked cars and a vast pile of lumber bound for Finland.

The small grey Royal Navy training craft was the only thing tied up here tonight, the nearest ship a vast offshore supply vessel on the opposite side of Albert Basin.

Nice and quiet. Nice and dark. Nice and secluded.

Logan drummed his fingers on the steering wheel, caught the edge of his bandaged hand and winced. Four stitches, a tetanus shot, and a small packet of low-grade painkillers. Little more than paracetamol, as if that was going to do any good.

Quarter to one – an hour and a bit to go.

He wiped his good hand across his eyes.

What the hell was he going to do? When Kravchenko found out his boatload of weapons had been seized, he'd blind Wiktorja. If she wasn't already dead. Raped, strangled, and dumped in a lay-by. All because Logan screwed everything up.

'Control from Alpha Three Niner, we've got a fatal RTA on South Anderson Drive. . .' – '. . . can you attend a domestic in Hazlehead?' – '. . . peeing in a shop doorway. . .' – '. . . fight outside that new nightclub on Windmill Brae. . .'

The passenger door opened and DI Steel groaned her way into the seat. 'Bain's going mental.'

Logan kept his eyes on the windscreen. 'How's Rory?'

'Fucked. And don't tell me that's fifty pence I owe the swear tin, because I don't care. There's nothing they can do, just keep him sedated and doped to the eyeballs . . . Well . . . you know what I mean. Poor sod crawled sixty feet, through a hole in the fence and out onto the river bank. Lucky he passed out before he fell in and drowned.' Sigh. 'Course, maybe that was the idea?' She wriggled in her seat. 'Got any fags on you?'

There were only three left in the packet; he gave Steel one and she lit up, blowing a cloud of smoke out of the open door and into the night. Logan joined her.

'Apparently,' she said, 'we're going to be the subject of a "rigorous Professional Standards investigation". And you know what that means.'

She puffed away in silence for a minute. 'What's the time?'

Logan told her and she groaned.

'Tell you, this better no' be a wash-out tonight. We don't come up with a boatload of guns, we're screwed.'

'I'm going to stretch my legs, you want anything?'

'Tea, bacon buttie, and a sodding miracle.'

He found a little bakers on Market Street that was still open, flogging artery-clogging delights to the harbour night shift. Logan bought two cheese and onion pasties for himself and a buttie for Steel, then headed back across the road to the harbour, clutching a warm carrier bag and a pair of polystyrene cups. He was almost back to the car when something in his pocket started ringing.

Probably Steel wanting to know where her tea was. He stuck the carrier bag on the ground and dragged the phone out. 'I'm coming, OK? Give us a bloody chance.'

'Detective Sergeant, you are not still tied up, I am thinking.' Not Steel: Kravchenko.

Logan nearly dropped the polystyrene cups.

'You are still there, yes?'

'Yes.'

'Is good. Detective Sergeant, I have the delivery of something come to Aberdeen, and I want to make sure is safe. Policja *can be so . . . suspicious. Is right word? "Suspicious"?'*

'I want to talk to Wiktorja.'

'She is safe. Grigor is not touch her yet.'

'I – want – to – talk – to – her.'

There was a pause, then a discussion in rapid Polish, and then a woman's voice came on the line. *'Logan?'*

Thank God. 'Are you all right?'

'Logan, proszę*: please, I am scared. I am so scared.'*

'It's OK, it's going to be OK. I'm going to take care of everything. . .' How the hell was he going to do that? 'They're not going to hurt you, it's—'

'No?' Kravchenko was back again, he sounded disappointed. *'If you think this, what is incentive for you? Grigor: break something.'*

A muffled scream came from the other end of the phone.

'There. Now you have incentive, yes?'

Logan stared at the phone, he could hear Wiktorja moaning in the background. 'What did you do?'

'Is my delivery to be safe, Detective Sergeant?'

'WHAT DID YOU DO?'

'Senior Constable Jaroszewicz has two arms. Do you like to hear the other one?'

Logan closed his eyes and listened to her crying.

What was he supposed to do: let them get away with flooding Aberdeen with automatic weapons? Then it wouldn't just be Wiktorja getting hurt, it'd be God knew how many people. Indiscriminate drug war. Machine guns in Mastrick. Handguns on Holburn Street. Bullets in Bon Accord Square.

'Grigor, perhaps you break the other—'

'No! It's not safe. They know about the boat: the *Buckie Ballad*. There's a team waiting for it.'

There was some Polish swearing, and then the sound of a muffled conversation.

'Hello?'

Logan checked his watch – 01:03 – they were probably trying to contact the fishing boat, get it to turn around and sod off back out to the middle of the North Sea until they could find somewhere safe to land the guns.

'Are you still there?'

Silence.

'Hello?'

The Airwave handset in Logan's pocket crackled then a disembodied voice said, *'Harbour Authority say they've got the* Buckie Ballad *on the radio. . .'* There was a pause, and then: *'Aye, they're cancelling their berth. Not going to be back till Wednesday at the earliest'*

Steel: *'That's no' sodding funny!'*

'Skipper says he got a tip about some haddock sixty miles off Peterhead: he's had a crap trip, so they're going to give it a go.'

'Get the bastard back here!'

'How are we meant to do that?'

Kravchenko was back. *'Well done, Detective Sergeant. You are good man. But Grigor, he is disappointed, yes?'*

Logan watched DI Steel clamber out of the Fiat and hammer a fist down on the thing's rusty roof. *'I don't know, do I? Call the sodding coastguard: do something!'*

He turned down the volume on the Airwave handset, so he wouldn't have to listen to her rant. 'I've proved you can trust me. Now let Wiktorja go.'

'You only cooperate because Grigor hurt her, I am thinking. So I keep hold of Senior Constable Jaroszewicz for moment.'

'I did what you wanted!' And now Logan was responsible for a boatload of automatic weapons getting away. They'd bring it in somewhere else, up or down the coast and when people started dying it would be all his fault. He was going to be sick again. . .

'Next time we see if you can cooperate without her have bones broken, yes? Perhaps then *there is trust.'*

'But—'

'I will speak later.' And there was nothing more for Logan to say: Kravchenko had hung up.

Logan closed his eyes, swore, and stuck the mobile back in his pocket. He stood for a moment, taking deep breaths, hands on his knees, trying to settle his roiling stomach. Finally it passed and he straightened up. It was time to go back to the car and suffer the consequences.

'Well I don't sodding know, do I?' DI Steel slumped back in one of DCS Bain's visitor's chairs and scrubbed at her face, pulling the wrinkles about in a strange, moving topographical map. 'Someone must've leaked the info, told the Polish gitbag we were waiting on him.'

Behind the desk, Bain looked as if he'd been dragged into work at two in the morning to shout at people. Baggy, tired, and angry. 'I hand-picked the operational team *myself*.'

'Aye, well you screwed up on one of them then, didn't you?'

Standing at the back of the room, Logan tried not to look as guilty as he felt.

'You. . .' Bain pointed across the desk at Steel. 'You're in enough trouble as it is, Inspector: you promised me you could look after Rory Simpson—'

'Oh don't give me that, Bill, we've been over this.'

'—and he turns up with both eyes gouged out! I had to stand up at that press conference and tell the world a Polish police officer's been *kidnapped,* and the key witness in the Oedipus case has been *blinded* when he was supposed to be under *your* protection! Do you have any idea what kind of lawsuits we're looking at? The Media are having a field day!'

Logan stepped forward. 'It wasn't her fault – it was mine. I was the one in charge when they broke into the inspector's house. DI Steel—'

'Aye, and they wrecked the sodding place and all!'

'DI Steel isn't responsible for what happened to Rory Simpson, I am.'

Bain scowled at him. 'Shut up. And sit down.'

Logan did as he was told.

'Right now you're both looking at suspension.'

Steel bristled. 'That's no' bloody fair!'

'If you'd actually managed to get something out of this *Buckie Ballad* nonsense it might have been different, but you didn't. There's only so much I can cover for, and you passed that point the minute Rory Simpson was attacked and blinded.'

The inspector looked as if she was about to say something else, but Bain slammed his hand on the desk, cutting her off. 'You will *both* report to Professional Standards at oh-seven-hundred hours. You will cooperate *fully* with their investigation. And then you *will* hand over all your open cases to Detective Chief Inspector Finnie.'

'What?' Logan sat forward in his seat. 'You can't do that, he's—'

'DCI Finnie has been investigated and *cleared* of any wrong-doing, Sergeant, which is more than we can say for you. I kept him out of the loop on this operation, on *your* word, and look what a disaster *that* turned out to be.'

'But he—'

'Enough! No more. Go home. And have a serious think about whether or not you're actually suited to police work.'

65

Logan slumped back onto the clammy sheets, slapped both hands over his eyes and swore. He lay there until the shaking stopped, then hauled himself out into the kitchen. The vodka bottle was empty, and so was the litre of Bells his brother had given him for Christmas. All he had left was an inch of OVD rum. He swigged it straight from the bottle.

It wasn't even enough for a warm fuzzy feeling. So he made a cup of tea, then sat at the kitchen table, trying to figure out when it was that his life had gone down the crapper.

According to the microwave it was five in the morning. Two hours to go till his bollocking from Professional Standards, and already the sun was up: golden highlights slowly spreading across the old granite buildings outside his kitchen window, pushing the deep blue shadows back into their corners. What was the point of getting fired on a lovely day?

It should have been pouring with rain.

'Where you been? Going to be late for the morning briefing.' Detective Constable Rennie bounced up and down on his heels, grinning like the happy little idiot he was.

Logan had one last go at getting the tip of his vibrating cigarette to meet up with the flame from his lighter.

Success. He pulled in a deep lungful, then coughed it all back out again.

'Anyway,' said Rennie, 'come on: briefing.'

Logan settled back against the wall. Ten to seven and the rear podium car park was still in shadow. High up above, the sky was blue, but down here it was miserable and grey, like his mood. 'Why the hell are you so cheerful?'

'Ah . . . all will be revealed at the morning briefing!'

'I'm not going.'

'Eh?' The constable deflated a bit. 'But it's the morning briefing.'

'Don't care.' Logan took a long draw on his cigarette. At least this time he didn't bring up a lung. 'I'm off to see the Wizard, the wonderful Wizard of Professional Fucking Standards.'

'But I've got a thing. . .'

'Congratulations.'

'No, I really have – I caught the Sperminator. The bloke smearing his spunk on the handrails? Arrested him last night. Had to go through seven gazillion hours of CCTV footage, but I finally got him climbing into a car in the Bon Accord Centre car park. Ran the number plate and: Bob's shagging your mother's sister.' He paused, hands out, obviously waiting for applause.

'I'm actually impressed.' Logan flicked the first flurry of ash from the end of his cigarette. 'Not like you to use your initiative.'

'Yeah, well, now Beattie's made DI, it means there's a Detective Sergeant's job going begging, doesn't it? Emma thinks I can—'

'Emma says, Emma thinks. You're like a broken record.' He stuck his fag back in his mouth and made a pair of naked sock-puppets with his hands. 'Blah, blah, blah, blah.'

Rennie pouted. 'You're getting as bad as Steel, do you know that?'

Logan blew a stream of smoke at the sky. 'Your arse.'

Silence.

'So . . . you coming to the briefing then?'

'Are you deaf?' He ground his cigarette out against the wall and turned towards the back door. Then stopped. 'And don't worry about that DS's job, there's going to be another one free by lunchtime.'

'You look like shite.' DI Steel collapsed into the uncomfortable chair next to Logan's, outside Superintendent Napier's lair. 07:00 precisely.

Logan raised an eyebrow. 'You can talk.' She was wearing a dark grey trouser suit that wouldn't have looked out of place on Worzel Gummidge. Neither would her hair. Scarecrow chic, if you were feeling generous. The bags under her eyes belonged on an airport carousel.

She punched him in the leg. 'Didn't get any sodding sleep, did I? Susan won't come home, says I'm an "insensitive cow". Says, first I won't give her a baby, and now I'm turning the house into a B&B for perverts.' The inspector pulled out a packet of nicotine gum and popped a couple out of their foil packaging. Stuck them in her mouth and chewed as if they were live wasps. Then offered the pack to Logan.

He shrugged, took two, and discovered why she made that face. 'Urgh! What's this stuff made of?'

'My house is a bombsite, I can't get my wife pregnant, and my career's fucked.'

Logan slumped back in his seat. 'I'm sorry, OK? I am. None of this was. . . I'm just sorry.'

'So what's the problem?' She stared straight ahead. 'You don't think I'd make a good parent for your sprog? That it?'

'No . . . I. . .' He scrubbed his face with his hands, wincing as he touched the fresh bruise where Kravchenko's henchman, Grigor, had punched him. 'I don't know.'

'Yeah, well, what does it matter to you, eh? No' like your relationship's going down the toilet, is it? No' like your life's screwed up beyond all sodding recognition!'

Logan looked at her. Then burst out laughing.

'What the hell is so funny?'

But now he'd started he couldn't stop.

Steel scowled at him. 'What the hell's wrong with you? I'm asking for your help! They won't let us adopt, we can't get IVF on the NHS, and we can't afford to go private. She's going to leave me, I bloody know it.'

There were tears running down Logan's cheeks.

'You are such a *cock*!' Steel hit him again. 'It's no' some sort of joke, OK? This is my life we're talking about!'

He had to fight to squeeze the words out, bent almost double in the chair: 'I've been blown up; shot at; I can't sleep; I have nightmares, even when I'm awake; all I want to do is drink until I can't . . . *fucking* . . . feel anything; I've started smoking again; I got Rory blinded, and Wiktorja's going to be next; I think I killed someone in Poland; I ruin everything I touch; and I'm about to get fired.' He looked up at her. 'And you think *my* life's not fucked up?'

Logan stood in front of the machine on the third floor, trying to decide if he felt like a coffee, a tea, or a chicken noodle soup. Not that it mattered, they all tasted the same. He punched the buttons and reconstituted brown slurry gurgled into a thin plastic cup.

He picked it up by the rim, trying not to burn his fingers, then wandered upstairs to the CID office. Rennie was there, boring PC Karim with his 'how I caught the Sperminator' story.

'. . . and I'm piecing together, like, a *million* hours of CCTV footage, trying to track the guy back from the shopping centre and all the way down Union Street. . .'

Logan's desk was a disaster area of forms and files. Again. Half of them weren't even his. He stuck his cup of plastic coffee on top of a memo from DI Beattie, and gathered up an armful of witness statements. Then dumped them on the next desk over.

He sat in his creaky swivel chair and stared at the dead computer. Thinking about booting it up and writing his letter of resignation.

```
Dear Bastards,
  I quit.
  Screw you all.
Detective Sergeant Logan McRae
```

Karim kept glancing at his watch and shuffling towards the exit, but Rennie wouldn't stop droning on, and on, and on. 'Worked in a shoe shop. . .' Blah, blah. 'Confessed right away. . .' Blah, blah. 'Wife waited till he was handcuffed, then kneed him in the balls. . .'

'Yeah, great,' said Karim, when he could finally get a word in. 'Got to go: post mortem in ten minutes.'

'Ooh,' Rennie grabbed his notebook. 'Someone dead?'

'Dirty Bob. They found him yesterday evening in the St Nicholas graveyard, round the back near the shopping centre?' Karim sighed. 'He was pretty broken up about his mate Richard dying. . . Doc Fraser says sometimes they're like married couples: first one goes, then the other. I suppose it's kind of sweet. Poor sod probably drank himself to death – stank of white spirit.'

Logan's stomach curdled. 'White spirit?'

'His tipple of choice.'

And Logan had given him twenty pounds to go buy booze

with. Great, something else for him to feel guilty about. He didn't listen as Karim said his goodbyes and left the office.

Rennie waited for the door to close before rummaging through his desk drawers, then scooted his chair across the CID office floor, until he was sitting next to Logan. 'Got something for you.' He handed over a carrier bag.

There was something heavy in it, a rectangular box – about a foot long and three inches on either side – wrapped in brown paper. Instantly recognizable to every Scotsman over the age of twelve.

The constable nodded. 'Came for you yesterday – didn't want to leave it lying on your desk, you know what a thieving bunch of bastards they are in here.'

Logan tore the paper off, levered open the cardboard box's top flap, and pulled out the bottle of whisky inside. Thirty-year-old Knockdhu. There was a hand-written note Sellotaped to the bottle:

'Dear DS McRae,

Thank you so much for sorting out that wee misunderstanding with Colin McLeod and Harry Jordan. We all appreciate it.

Best wishes,

H.M.'

'H.M.' Hamish Mowat. Brilliant. That was *just* what Logan needed. A gift from Aberdeen's top crime lord, thanking him for getting Creepy Colin off with attempted murder. Professional Standards were going to love that.

Rennie took one look at the bottle and said, 'Cool! Not your birthday is it?'

Logan slid the bottle back into its box, then locked it in his bottom desk drawer. It could stay there until he figured out what he was going to do with it. 'Don't you have work to be getting on with? People to impress, arses to kiss?'

'Jesus, you're a happy little pixie since you got back from Poland, you know that?' He stuck his feet flat on the floor and pushed, squeaking his chair back to his own desk. 'Anyway, thought you were in with the rubber-heelers this morning.'

'Steel went first: privilege of rank. I get to wait for my bollocking.'

'Oh. . .'

'Now sod off and leave me alone.'

Logan poked away at paperwork for a while, but couldn't work up any enthusiasm. What was the point? They were probably going to suspend him anyway. So he gave up and borrowed an *Aberdeen Examiner* from the media office, flipping through to the Jobs pages at the back.

Everyone wanted years of experience. No one wanted a failed ex-Detective Sergeant with a crappy track-record and talent for disaster.

He checked his watch. Steel had been in with Superintendent Napier for nearly three hours.

Logan let his head sink forward until it was resting on a pile of uncompleted burglary reports. Sod this. He wasn't just going to sit here and wait for Napier to summon him.

He went to the IB lab instead, hoping to grab a couple of minutes with Samantha, but she was off at a crime scene in Blackburn.

What now? Back to the CID office to sulk some more? Scrounge a cup of tea and some cake from the CCTV room? Or just walk out and never come back. Or he could do what he should have done last night: march into DCS Bain's office and tell him who really tipped off Kravchenko about the *Buckie Ballad*. Slam the Polish bastard's mobile on Bain's desk and tell him where he could stick it. . .

Logan dug the phone out of his pocket and stared at it. How could he be so *stupid*? He turned the thing on – Kravchenko called last night, his number would be in the call history. They could run a GSM trace, turn Kravchenko's handset into a homing beacon.

He worked his way through the phone's menus until he got to the right bit. 'Sodding hell. . .'

It was listed as 'UNKNOWN'. Now he'd have to get a warrant to force the phone company to ignore the Data Protection Act and give him the details of who called. It would take days – maybe weeks – and there was no way Kravchenko's 'copper who bends' wouldn't find out about it.

Back to plan A. He stomped up the stairs to Bain's office, but the head of CID wasn't there, he was having a shouting match with Finnie in the middle of the corridor.

Logan took one look at them and froze.

Finnie: 'I should have been informed—'

Bain: 'It was on a *strict* need to know basis, and you—'

Finnie: 'I am a senior officer in this—'

Bain: 'Then try acting like one! I do not expect this kind of behaviour from—'

Finnie: 'Oh no, I *bet* you don't. God forbid *anyone* should stand up to the Almighty Head Of CID!'

Someone tapped Logan on the shoulder and he flinched. It was DS Pirie, curly ginger hair glowing in a shaft of sunlight. 'I'd stay out of his way this morning, if I was you. Soon as he heard about Operation Creel he went ballistic.'

Bain: 'You're on thin ice Chief Inspector!'

Finnie: 'Oh don't give me that, you *know* I'm right. This whole disaster was mismanaged from the start.'

There was no way Logan was wading into the middle of that. 'I'll come back later.'

'Ah, it'll blow over. It usually does. Just keep a low profile.

And it just so happens I've got something that might get us both back in his good books.' Pirie paused. 'Interested?'

Tempting. 'I'm supposed to wait for a summons from Professional Standards.'

The DS slapped Logan on the back. 'Yeah, I heard. But think how much easier it would go if you had a success under your belt? I got a phone call from a Chiz I use, says he's got a lead on the guys behind that boatload of guns.'

'Did you get an address?'

'I was going to tell the guvnor, but he's mid-rant . . . If you want to tag along instead?'

Damn right he did.

All the pool cars were out, so they took Logan's knackered Fiat. Sometime during the night the seagulls had paid a visit, and now the bonnet and roof were polka-dotted with acrid splatters of white and grey.

Pirie held onto the seatbelt strap as Logan ground his way through the gears. 'Tell me you didn't give someone money for this piece of shite.'

'Very funny.' Logan gave the gearstick one last yank and took them around the roundabout onto Wellington Road, the dirty bulk of Craiginches Prison crawling past on their left as he did his best to accelerate up the hill. 'About Finnie—'

'I told you: it'll blow over. You just gotta give it time.'

'No. I mean him and Wee Hamish Mowat.'

Pirie's left eyebrow shot up so fast it looked as if it was about to break free of his head. 'Oh aye?'

'I saw Finnie take a brown envelope from one of Wee Hamish's boys.'

'Ah. . .' Pirie ran a hand through his wire-wool hair, watching as a scooter overtook them. 'I can get out and push if you like?'

'I'm serious.'

'Finnie gets brown envelopes from Wee Hamish all the time.'

'What?' Logan stared at him. 'You *knew* about it?'

Shrug. 'Course I did. Power behind the throne, remember?'

'But. . . Why. . .?'

'Why didn't I report it? Because they don't have money in them, they've got information. Look at it from Wee Hamish's point of view: someone tries muscling in on his turf, what's he going to do? Yeah, he can fight back, or whatever, but that costs him time, money, manpower, and there's always the risk something will get connected to him. Never been arrested in his life, think he wants to start now?'

Logan slumped, said, 'Fuck', then banged his head off the steering wheel.

Pirie's voice jumped up an octave. 'Think you'd like to keep your eyes on the road? *Please*?'

'He's using us.'

'Where did you learn to bloody drive?'

'He doesn't need bent coppers, he gets us to do his dirty work for free.'

'It's a two-way thing, OK? Wee Hamish sends Finnie a wee brown envelope with all the details. We make the arrest – bad guys are off the streets, and no one gets fed to the pigs. It's win, win. . .' Pirie frowned. 'Wait a minute, it was you, wasn't it? You set Professional Standards on him: told them about the brown envelopes.'

'I thought he was on the take.'

'Do you have any idea how much pain and extra work you caused him? They crawled all over every inch of his record, picked him apart for two whole days. Made his life a living *hell*.'

Logan sighed. 'I'm sorry, OK?'

Pirie threw his head back and laughed. 'Sorry my arse – it's been great. I owe you a drink!'

66

Peterseat Drive was a loop of dirty tarmac on the northernmost edge of Altens. Most of the buildings were new or not even finished yet: warehouses and storage depots. Stacks of offshore containers were locked away behind chain-link fences. Piles of drilling pipe. Huge chunks of metal, painted bright primary colours.

Logan pulled the rattling Fiat up to the kerb and killed the engine, before it died of its own accord.

'Right.' Pirie unfastened his seatbelt and popped the passenger door open. 'Got to have a quick word with my Chiz: find out what he knows.'

Logan clambered out of the car, but Pirie held up a hand. 'You know the rules – total anonymity for all Covert Human Intelligence Sources; my guy sees you, he'll run a mile. Hell, I shouldn't even be *talking* to this guy without Bain's say so.'

'But—'

'I'll only be two minutes, OK? Just chill till then.' Pirie turned, stuck his hands in his pockets and ambled across the road to a yard full of anchor chains.

Logan slumped against the roof of the car and smoked a

cigarette. He was grinding it out on the rusty paintwork when his mobile started ringing. He dug the phone out and grimaced: according to the display it was DI Steel. Probably wanting to know where the hell he was. He let it ring through to voicemail. She was back on thirty seconds later. Logan ignored it.

Down the street, Pirie stuck his head out of a gate and beckoned.

Logan hurried across the road. 'Well?'

'Sort of.' Pirie turned and pointed at one of the brand-new warehouses. It wasn't quite finished yet, the construction sign still up by the wire gates read: 'COMING SOON – RIGSPANTECH DOWNHOLE SERVICES'. Dark blue roof and beige walls, attached to a small office block that hadn't progressed beyond the raw breeze block and hollow window frames stage. No sign of life. 'According to my guy, there was a firm called Kostchey International Holdings Limited doing site security there till about a week ago. You wanna check it out, see if we can get a billing address?'

Logan did.

They abandoned the Fiat where it was and walked down the half-finished pavement in the blazing sunshine. This part of the road was quiet, just the occasional clang of metal on metal, or beep-beep-beep of a reversing forklift truck. A radio somewhere inside one of the yards, playing Northsound 2.

Pirie kicked an empty plastic bottle, sending it spinning down the dusty pavement. 'So . . . did you really get blown up?'

'That why you're helping me get back into Finnie's good books? Pity?' The further down the road they walked the newer the buildings got, until they were just partially constructed shells.

'Nope.' They'd caught up with the plastic bottle, and Pirie gave it another kick.

Logan's phone started ringing. Again.

'You going to answer that?'

'It'll be Steel, telling me I'm supposed to be in with Professional Standards.'

The ringing stopped, there was silence, and then it started again.

'It's kinda irritating.'

Logan pulled the thing out and switched it off. 'Happy now?'

One more kick and the bottle clattered against the fence surrounding RigSpanTech's almost-finished warehouse. A length of chain was looped through both sides of the gate, but the padlock wasn't shut.

Logan followed Pirie into the building site. They hadn't even started laying the road yet – everything was hard-packed dirt and rubble.

Pirie shaded his eyes against the sun, staring at the half-built office unit and the warehouse beyond. 'Look, over there – black BMW. Least we know someone's about.' He took two steps towards it, then stopped. Logan's pocket was making ringing noises again. 'Thought you switched that off?'

'I did. . .' And then Logan realized it wasn't his phone, it was the one Kravchenko had given him. He fumbled it out and checked the display: 'NUMBER WITHHELD'. His innards clenched. 'I have to take this.'

Pirie shrugged. 'Catch up when you're done then.' He wandered away, whistling *Scotland the Brave*, and leaving a cloud of pale yellow dust in his wake.

Logan punched the green button. 'Hello?'

67

'Aye, I thought as much.' It wasn't Kravchenko, it was Steel. *'What the hell do you think you're doing, screening out my calls? Where are you?'*

'Altens.'

'Altens? You're supposed to be getting bent over a desk by that knob-end Napier, no' swanning about in sodding Altens.'

'Got a lead on Kostchey International Holdings, I'm checking it out with Pirie.' He started walking again. The black BMW was parked at the far side of the unfinished office unit, beside a couple of pallets of breeze blocks and some pantiles. No sign of the driver.

No sign of Pirie either.

'They suspend you?'

'Are you kidding, I'm like the queen of sodding Teflon Town – nothing sticks to Detective Inspector Roberta Steel. But the bastards made me call the Warsaw police and tell them your mate Wiktorja was missing.'

Logan peered in through one of the office windows, or at least the hole where one would be fitted. Nothing but bags of cement and a mixer. 'Yeah?'

'She doesn't work there anymore.'

The doorway was a big open space, so he tried inside, his shoes scuffing on the gritty concrete floor. It was just a collection of empty rooms. 'I know.'

A flight of pre-cast stairs led up to the first floor. Logan climbed them and found more unfinished rooms: bare breeze block walls, gaping doorways, carefully piled boxes of building materials.

Where the hell was Pirie?

'What do you mean, you know?'

'She told me.'

A noise echoed up from downstairs.

'She told *you?'*

Logan peered down the hole where the stairs were, opened his mouth to shout hello, then swore very, very quietly. The person walking past on the ground floor – heading for the front of the office unit – was built like a rugby player, with angular features and hair that was receding at the front but a full-on mullet at the back. Kravchenko's henchman, Grigor.

Son of a rancid bitch.

It looked as if Pirie's informant was right; only Kostchey International Holdings Limited hadn't cleared out a week ago, they were still here.

'What do you mean she told you?'

Logan crept back out of sight of the stairwell. Straining his ears to follow Mr Mullet's progress on the floor below. It sounded as if he was heading for the front door.

'Hello?'

Logan whispered as loud as he dared, 'They're here!'

'They're. . .? What? Have you been drinking again?'

'I've just seen Kravchenko's thug go past downstairs.'

Logan followed him, one floor up, risking a peek out of the empty window frame at the end of the corridor. Grigor was standing just outside the building, a mobile phone clamped to his ear, talking in rapid Polish.

He was huge, and probably armed as well.

Bloody hell. Where was Pirie when you needed him? And then Logan got the nasty feeling he knew exactly where Pirie was – lying battered in a corner somewhere, both hands tied behind his back, waiting for a visit from Kravchenko and his Swiss Army knife.

Logan sneaked another peek over the window ledge. 'I think Pirie might be hurt.'

'That's all I need. Where is he?'

Outside, Grigor was facing away from the building, still on his mobile, staring out towards the chain-link fence.

Logan ducked down again. 'Haven't seen him since I got here. I'll go look—'

'No! You stay where you are, you hear me? I'll get a firearms team out there.'

'I've got an idea.'

'No, no ideas!'

Logan snuck back into the shadows, pulled his Airwave handset out of his pocket and clicked it on. The upper floor was almost symmetrical around the stairwell, blank offices on either side. He picked one at random – full of scaffolding poles, bags of cement, boxes of nails – and stuck the handset in the far corner, behind a stack of wooden two-by-fours.

'Are you listening to me?'

Logan crept out of the room and into the one opposite, pausing to grab a chunk of wood on the way. 'Right,' he said, flattening himself against the wall by the door, 'call me on my Airwave thing.'

'No chance. You want to get yourself killed? I'm no' helping.'

'Just call the bloody thing.'

'No.'

'Fine, I'll get Rennie to do it.'

There was a pause and some swearing, and then, *'OK, OK. But you better get Susan pregnant for this. . .'*

Through in the other room, Logan's Airwave handset started ringing: a high-pitched electronic warble, volume turned up full. He peered around the door frame. Come on, come on . . . Bingo. Grigor was charging up the stairs.

Logan ducked back, listening to the big man's footsteps on the concrete floor, then Grigor marched into the other office.

Trying not to make any sound at all, Logan inched his way out into the corridor, clutching the length of wood like a baseball bat.

Grigor was stalking across to the far corner, gun out, pointing at the sound of the ringing. When he got to the stack of two-by-fours he stopped, stood there for a moment, then peered into the corner.

Logan waited for him to reach for the handset, then tried to take the bastard's head off with the length of wood. It crashed into Grigor's skull, just above his left ear and the big man went sprawling. The gun flew out of his hand, clanging into a neat pile of scaffolding poles.

That should hold him. . .

Oh God, he was getting up again.

Grigor fought his way to his knees, and then to his feet. Logan smacked him in the head a second time, but he just staggered around, blood streaming from a three-inch gash in his forehead. *'Moje jaja! Pierdolony sukinsyn. . .'*

'What the hell are you made of?'

His face was all twisted up, teeth bared, hissing out obscenities in Polish as he scanned the floor for the gun. And then the big man lunged, going for the pile of poles.

Logan swung the two-by-four again: missed. Grigor wasn't just big, he was fast too. He was bent double throwing scaffolding poles left and right, hunting for the gun, his backside sticking up in the air. So Logan dropped the chunk of wood, took a run up, and did his best to kick the bastard's testicles into orbit. It wasn't quite as effective from the back, but it produced a high-pitched squeal. If in doubt – go for the balls.

Grigor collapsed face-first into the metal poles, one hand clutching his groin, the other still feeling for the gun.

Logan picked up a scaffolding coupler from the pile – like a pair of heavy-duty handcuffs held together with swivelling bolts – about the same weight as a bag of sugar. 'Hey, ugly!'

'Kurwa mać . . .' Grigor gave up on the gun and grabbed a length of scaffolding pole instead. He threw himself onto his back, swinging the pole hard and fast. It whistled past, a couple of inches from the end of Logan's nose, clanged against the breeze block wall and bounced out of Grigor's hand.

Logan jumped on him, grabbed him by the throat, and smashed the scaffolding coupler off his forehead. THUNK. The skin broke, and a fine spray of blood misted out into the sunny afternoon.

'You—' Logan hit him again, '—are—' And again, '—under —' One last time for luck, '—arrest!'

Logan sat back, breathing hard, the coupler heavy in his hand. Grigor wasn't moving anymore. The big man's head looked like a ruptured sausage, but at least he was still breathing.

Logan rolled him into the recovery position, then handcuffed his hands behind his back. And then lurched off into the corner to throw up.

68

'You still alive? Hello? What the hell's going on?' DI Steel's tinny voice rattled out of the phone as Logan slumped against the wall, breathing heavily. *'Hello? Are you dead?'*

'No.' He took out a fresh pair of latex gloves – struggled to pull them on over his trembling, blood-stained fingers – then bent down and picked up the gun. It was almost as heavy as the scaffolding coupler, but looked a lot more dangerous. Black, scuffed and functional. Logan pressed the release button and slid the magazine out of the handle. Eighteen slugs of dull metal with shiny brass casings. He slapped the magazine back in place and hauled the slide back to cock it. Then made sure the safety was on. Three settings: one white dot, one red dot, and three red dots. Logan went for the white dot, hoping that meant the thing wasn't going to suddenly go off at random and take some portion of his anatomy with it.

Just in case, he wasn't sticking it in the waistband of his trousers.

'Right, I'm going to find Pirie and Wiktorja.'

'Firearms team is on its way. Don't do anything stupid, OK?' He could hear her puffing and panting as she spoke, as if she was running or something.

Logan took the stairs back down to the ground floor.

'Thanks. Your confidence in me is really reassuring.'

'Hey, I'm no' the one let that bloody Polish tart into my house.'

Logan scowled at the phone. 'That "bloody Polish tart", is a missing police officer!'

'No she's not. You said you knew—'

'Wiktorja told me all about it, OK? They suspended her because of what happened when I was there. It wasn't her fault.'

The office unit had a single door at the back that opened out onto the warehouse structure. No more surprises. Logan snicked the safety catch from one white dot to one red dot. Then nudged the door open.

'Don't be a divvy.' There was the sound of a car engine starting on the other end of the phone, swiftly followed by the wail of a police siren. *'She wasn't suspended, she was fired. Two years ago, for taking backhanders from some German crime lord called Ehrlichmann.'*

Logan froze. 'What?'

'You heard: she's bent. And no' in the good way.'

'How can she be. . . But. . . No, she was there – Ehrlichmann's goons shot her!'

'I'm just telling you what her sergeant told me. She sabotaged a bunch of high-profile drug busts. Nearly went to prison for it.'

'But they *shot* her. . .'

A voice sounded behind him: 'What the hell are you doing?'

Logan spun around, the gun snapping up till it was inches away from DS Pirie's nose. 'What—'

'Ah, Jesus!' Pirie danced backwards, tripped over a drum of electrical cable and went crashing down onto his backside.

'You moron.' Logan lowered the gun. 'I could've killed you!'

'Fuck. . . Think I've just shat myself.' The detective sergeant stuck out a hand and Logan pulled him to his feet. Pirie's nose wrinkled. 'What smells of puke?'

'Where have you been?'

'What's going on? Hello?'

'It's Pirie, he's not dead.'

'Tell him no' to let you do anything stupid! He—' Logan hung up on her. Then switched the phone off so she couldn't call him back.

Pirie brushed cement dust from his backside. 'Where did you get the gun?'

'Big Polish bloke called Grigor, works for Kravchenko. I bashed his head in with a scaffolding coupler.'

Pirie's face went even paler than normal. 'Is he dead?'

Logan put a hand on the door. 'There's a firearms team on its way. You can stay here and wait for it, or you can come with me.' He pushed through into the warehouse.

The place was cavernous, just a big empty space with a freshly laid concrete floor. Piles of building equipment made little islands in the huge room, bathed in the sunlight that streamed in through a set of open roller doors.

'Ah, Detective Sergeant, what take you so long?' Kravchenko stepped out from behind a stack of dark orange I-beams, each one marked-up with chalk hieroglyphics. He was wearing a baggy linen suit and a white shirt. Even had a tie on. 'Did you get lost, yes?'

Logan pointed the gun right between the old man's eyes. 'Vadim Mikhailovitch Kravchenko, I am arresting you for the attempted murder of one Rory Simpson.'

'I see. . .' He smiled. 'You have gun. OTs-33 *Pernach*: Russian, sturdy, like machine gun. Is good choice, but not so accurate I am thinking.'

Logan took three steps forward. 'Face-down on the ground, hands behind your head, *now*!'

'You are forgetting something, yes?' He dragged Senior Constable Wiktorja Jaroszewicz out from behind the stack of I-beams. Her hands were tied behind her back, a livid bruise spreading a purple, green and yellow stain across her cheek. She was groaning and swearing behind a gag made of duct tape.

'I said, on the ground!'

Kravchenko frowned. 'You are not wanting to see her alive?' He pulled out a silvered automatic pistol, the kind they used in gangsta rap videos and pressed it against her stomach. 'Now we have the Mexican standoff. Put down your gun, or I will shoot her.'

Logan shrugged. 'And?'

Pirie tapped him on the shoulder: whispering, 'I really don't think this is a good idea.'

'Shut up, Pirie.'

'But I am serious, yes? I will shoot your woman.'

'Logan, I really think we should bugger off and wait for that backup!'

Logan marched further into the room, gun never leaving the dead centre of Kravchenko's face. 'She's not *my* woman, she's yours.'

'I don't—'

'Go on, shoot her.'

'Logan, what the hell are you playing at?'

Kravchenko frowned, head tilted to one side. 'This is the reverse psychology, yes? You pretend to want I shoot Senior Constable Jaroszewicz?'

'She's not a senior anything – they fired her two years ago, for taking bribes from a bunch of German mobsters.'

'I am not understand. . .'

'The pair of you played me for a right bloody idiot. Oh yeah, Wiktorja was looking for Gorzkiewicz, but not for the Polish police. And guess who found him for you – me, like an *idiot*. It wasn't your handler who tipped off Ehrlichmann, was it, Wiktorja? It was you.' He glared at her. 'What did you do, text them when you were in confession? That it? "Bless me Father, for I have sinned, oh and by the way, I'm selling out the stupid police officer from Aberdeen to my murdering bastard of a boss"?'

She shook her head, lank blonde hair whipping back and forth. Mumbling behind the gag.

'Bet you didn't expect to get shot. What, did they find out you were screwing Ehrlichmann over too? You weren't undercover, you were working for this . . . *prick*!'

'Logan, I really think we shouldn't be—'

'Shut up, Pirie.' Back to Kravchenko. 'She was the one told you how to find Rory Simpson, wasn't she? Where I was hiding him. All this bloody time, *using me*! So you know what, I'm calling your bluff.'

Pirie grabbed his sleeve. 'What the hell are you playing at? Don't—'

'Go ahead: shoot her.'

The old man shrugged. 'OK.'

And that's just what he did.

69

The gunshot echoed around the cavernous warehouse. Wiktorja stared down at the dot of black in the middle of her T-shirt as it spread out into a dark red stain. And then her legs gave way.

Kravchenko let go and she fell to the concrete floor, screaming behind the gag. Then he pointed his shiny gun at Logan. 'This is better?'

Pirie was swearing. 'Oh Jesus, oh fucking Jesus. . .'

Logan's mouth seemed to have stopped working. 'But . . . she . . . you. . .'

'Now we can get to business, yes?'

'You shot her!' Pirie pointed a shaky finger at the woman slowly bleeding out on the floor. 'SHE'S A POLICE OFFICER!'

'No. Detective Sergeant is right – she is not *policja* any more. She is interfering *kurwa*. She work for Ehrlichmann, try to find me for him.' Kravchenko smiled. 'But I find her first, no?'

The DS ran a hand through his ginger hair. 'You never said anything about killing her!'

Logan stared at Pirie. 'WHAT?'

'Why now you have conscience? You remember Lubosław Frankowski?'

Pirie fidgeted. 'That was an *accident*. Didn't know the silly sod would take all the whisky and pills at once, did I?' He turned to Logan. 'I swear to God, I was only trying to keep him quiet – buy him a heap of booze, keep his mind off stuff. He was going to call the station and tell them everything . . . I didn't have any choice.'

Logan stared at him. 'You're in on it? Are you *insane*?'

'This wasn't supposed to happen, OK? It was just meant to be a chat, see if you were on the team or not. Nobody was meant to get hurt, it—'

'Hurt? He's been blinding people, you moron! Setting up a drugs war! Not some piddling little turf dispute – HE'S GOT FUCKING MACHINE GUNS!'

'What was I supposed to do? He's paying thousands. *Thousands*. Bloody city's rolling in oil money, why shouldn't we get a slice, eh? Why shouldn't we—'

'You knew about this from the start, didn't you? You knew – you could have stopped it!'

'It's not like—'

Logan jabbed the gun into Pirie's ear. 'I GOT BLOWN UP BECAUSE OF YOU, YOU PIECE OF SHIT!'

Pirie backed away, hands up. 'I was just. . . It wasn't. . .' And then he turned and ran for it, bursting through the door and out into the office unit.

Kravchenko watched him go. 'Do not make worry, Grigor will catch him.'

Logan turned back. Wiktorja was lying on her side, knees curled up to her chest, dark red blood oozing out onto the concrete floor. She was shivering, moaning behind her gag. And it was all Logan's fault. 'She . . . wasn't working for you?'

Kravchenko leant back against the stack of I-beams, legs crossed at the ankle. 'This Pirie is weak man. Never have *jajca* to stand on own feet. Take money and do what is told.

Man who can be bought is weak – I buy him from your Hamish Mowat, maybe someone will buy him from me too? But man like you. . .' Kravchenko clicked his fingers. 'What is word for *"idealistyczny"*? . . . Ah: idealistic.'

Logan couldn't take his eyes off the expanding pool of blood. Feeling sick. 'We need to get her an ambulance.'

'Why you care? She is liar, yes? Make you into fool.'

Logan could barely hold the gun still. 'Get your arse on the floor, or I *will* shoot you.'

'You think I am too rough with her?' He nudged Wiktorja with his toe and she groaned. Her face was unbelievably pale, the bags under her eyes standing out dark purple. Kravchenko reached down and tore the duct tape gag from her mouth.

'Aaghh, Jesus. . .' Her lips were turning blue. 'Kill him. . .' She gritted her teeth. 'Kill him . . . *please*. . .'

'Why would Detective Sergeant kill me? I am his friend, but you . . . You use him to find me, I am thinking he does not like this.' He smiled at Logan. 'She pay man in Warsaw Police to tell her if anyone ask question about me. Is clever, yes?'

'You . . . you blinded . . . my father. You carved out his eyes!'

Kravchenko shrugged. 'I make blind many men. Maybe I make you blind too, before you die?'

She recoiled, trying to squirm away from him, hands still tied behind her back, but every motion made her cry out in pain.

Logan tightened his grip on the trigger. 'Get away from her. *Now!*'

Kravchenko reached into his pocket and pulled out the Swiss Army knife. 'When I am finish.' The little tin of lighter fluid was next.

'I'm not telling you again!'

Wiktorja stared at the knife's curving blade. 'Please no . . . Please! *Proszę*! *Proszę, nie zabijaj mnie!*'

Kravchenko grabbed a handful of her hair, pulling her face up. She screamed. Logan braced himself, aimed – and the door behind him flew open.

Something went BOOM and the old man ducked. Then the delicate pitter-patter of shot rained down on the concrete floor. 'Next one,' said a voice from the doorway, 'doesn't go into the ceiling.'

Thank God – the cavalry was here. . .

Only when Logan looked around, the guy standing in the doorway wasn't one of DI Steel's firearms team. He was massive, at least twenty stone, his face twisted with scar tissue – last seen working on an old Jaguar at Wee Hamish Mowat's place: Reuben. He'd ditched the overalls for a straining pink polo shirt, a pair of jumbo-sized jeans, and a sawn-off shotgun. Reuben lumbered into the room, fore-head glistening with sweat. And right behind him came a spotty youth with green hair, dragging a blood-smeared DS Pirie into the room.

Green-Hair dumped Pirie in the middle of the floor, then pulled out an old-fashioned revolver.

Pirie looked as if his nose had exploded, leaving a flat-tened, bloody flap above a swollen mouth. Voice slurred and lisping, 'Please don't kill me!'

Green-Hair kicked him. 'Shut up.'

Reuben looked Logan up and down. 'We're here for the Polish guy.'

Kravchenko picked himself up from the floor. Wiktorja's blood had stained one knee of his linen trousers, turning the cream material a dark raspberry. 'I am *not* Polish. I am from Ukraine.' He pointed his gun at them. 'And I am going nowhere.'

The kid with the green hair grabbed Pirie by the back of

the collar and hauled him to his knees. Then ground the revolver into the side of the Detective Sergeant's head. 'Put your fuckin' gun down or I kill the pig!'

Kravchenko sighed. 'We have already done the "who is make a bluff" talk.' The silvered automatic barked once. A small plume of blood burst from Pirie's stomach, a much bigger one spraying out of his back as the bullet tore straight through.

'SHIT!' Green-Hair let go and danced back, hands and feet high in the air. Pirie slumped back onto the concrete, screaming.

'Now is easier, yes? Now we—'

The fat man in the pink polo shirt said, 'Bugger this,' then shot Kravchenko in the chest with his shotgun.

70

The old man flew backwards, bounced off the stack of I-beams and crumpled to the floor, face-down in the pool of Wiktorja's blood.

The BOOM seemed to take forever to fade away.

Logan stared at Kravchenko's body, then back at the huge man in the pink polo shirt. 'You just—'

Reuben shook his head. 'No I didn't.' He glanced over his shoulder at his green-haired sidekick. 'That bastard Pirie still alive?'

The DS had stopped screaming, instead he was clutching onto the small hole in his stomach, face pale, mouth open, shallow breaths.

'Yeah, he's still alive.' Green-Hair kicked him again. 'Two-timing cock. Oh yeah, we know you been playin' both sides, Pirie; been followin' you for *days*, man. What you think Wee Hamish is gonnae do to you, eh? You're gonnae be pig food, you—'

'Jonny! Shut the fuck up, OK? We got a policeman present.' Then he smiled at Logan. 'Ignore him: this ain't got nothing to do with Mr Mowat. This is strictly personal.

Understand? Now Jonny and me are gonnae take Pirie and that Polish dickhead, and get out of your hair, OK?'

'What makes you think I'm going to just let you take them?'

Reuben turned the sawn-off shotgun until it was pointing at Logan's chest.

Logan looked down at the twin barrels. 'You've fired it twice already. No shells left.'

'You think?' The big man smiled. 'Jonny, you help Mr Pirie to his feet and see him out to the car, eh? We'll . . . ah . . . drop him off at the hospital on the way home.'

'Aye, right . . . hospital.' The green-haired youth hauled Pirie away by the armpits, leaving a smear of bright red on the concrete.

'Good boy.' The fat man lowered his shotgun, and pointed at Kravchenko's motionless body. 'Now, I'll just take that wee shite and—'

'No. You leave him where he is.'

A short laugh. 'I'm no' leaving any—'

Logan stepped forward and stuck the barrel of his gun in the middle of the fat man's forehead. 'Yes you are.'

Pause.

'Aye, fair enough.'

He waited till the door slammed shut, then hurried across the concrete to Wiktorja. She was pale, sweating, shivering, lying in an ever-expanding pool of her own blood. Logan dug out his phone, switched it back on and called for an ambulance, trying to figure out how long it had been since he'd spoken to DI Steel – how long it would be until the firearms team got here. Now that it was too sodding late for them to do anything. Maybe they'd be just in time to stop Reuben and his little green-haired friend from getting away with Pirie?

Drop him off at the hospital. Yeah, right.

But somehow Logan didn't care – the two-faced bastard deserved everything coming to him. Besides, Logan had more than enough to feel guilty about already. Whatever happened to Pirie was his own fault.

Wiktorja lay on her side, making little pedalling motions with her legs, smearing them round and round in the dark red slick. Logan picked up Kravchenko's Swiss Army knife, unfolded a serrated blade, then sawed through the cable-ties holding her wrists behind her back.

As soon as the plastic snapped she gritted her teeth and hissed out a stream of Polish obscenities. Her right arm – the one that used to be in a sling – made a disturbing sideways bow half way between her elbow and her wrist where Grigor had broken it. She clutched it to her chest.

'Are you OK?'

'You let . . . you let . . . him shoot me. . .' Each word squeezed out and painful.

'Why didn't you tell me?' He knelt beside her, cold blood soaking through the knees of his trousers. 'How could you be working for Ehrlichmann?'

She looked up at him. 'So I can find . . . Kravchenko . . . and . . . make him . . . pay. . .'

Logan had never seen anyone so pale in his life.

'You're going to be OK.'

Or maybe not.

She blinked a couple of times, as if trying to get the empty warehouse into focus. And then she saw the man lying next to her, his pale linen suit gradually turning dark red. Wiktorja screwed up her face and spat, but the bloody spittle didn't get that far, it just dribbled down her chin. 'I am . . . I am glad . . . you are dead . . . you old . . . bastard.'

Her left leg twitched in Kravchenko's direction. Trying to kick him. Not getting anywhere near. And then her head slumped forwards.

Logan checked for a pulse.

71

She was still alive, just, but if the ambulance didn't get here soon, she probably wouldn't be for long. Still, there was one thing he could do for her: Logan stood, walked over to Kravchenko's body, and kicked it in the ribs. *Hard*.

The old man groaned.

Logan stared at him. 'Oh you have got to be kidding. . .'

Kravchenko was trying to lever himself onto his side, the front of his baggy linen suit tattered from the shotgun blast, drenched in blood.

How the hell did he survive that?

Logan placed his foot against the old man's shoulder and shoved him over onto his back. Kravchenko's head hit the ground with a dull THUNK and he grunted.

Logan looked down at the ruined suit, the ripped shirt, all the holes from the shotgun pellets. And the guy was still moving. 'You're as bad as bloody Grigor!'

Kravchenko reached for his tattered chest with trembling hands, and fumbled with the buttons on his blood-soaked shirt. And that's when Logan saw the bulletproof vest. The old man coughed, then swore in Polish.

Logan reached into his pocket and pulled out Grigor's gun.

His latex gloves stuck to the handgrip, leaving bloody smears on the black barrel.

'Everyone thinks you're already dead.' He racked the slide back and a brass-jacketed 9mm bullet pinged out into the warm afternoon air, landing with a plop in the blood – sending out slow-motion ripples. 'Do you have any idea how much shite I've gone through, because of you?'

The old man rolled onto his side again, then struggled to his knees.

Logan kicked him between the shoulder blades, sending him crashing back to the ground.

'Thanks to you I've been blown up, shot at, I'm probably going to get fired, maybe sent to bloody prison. . .' He kicked the old man in the bullet-proof ribs. 'And I've started smoking again! You know how *stupid* that is? I don't even like the bloody things any more!'

Once more for luck, this time hard enough to hurt his own foot. Logan limped away, then back again, pointing the gun at Kravchenko's face. 'Right, first: the *Buckie Ballad*, where is it?'

'Go . . . make fuck with yourself.'

He jabbed the gun barrel up under Kravchenko's chin.

'Tell me where that fishing boat's going to unload the guns, or I'm going to blow your head off.'

The old man made a noise. It took Logan a moment to realize it was laughter. 'What the hell's so damn funny?'

'You are. Is big act. You are *policja*, you must to have rules. It make you weak.'

Logan took a step back. Kravchenko was right: there *were* rules.

'You know what? Fuck it.' Logan shot him in the chest.

Kravchenko slammed back into the concrete, mouth open on a silent scream, fingers scrabbling at the new shiny lump on the front of his bulletproof vest.

Logan watched him writhe. 'Hurts, doesn't it? Bet it's like being cracked in the ribs with a crowbar. Where's the *Buckie Ballad*?'

'Ffffuck . . . you . . . *kurwa*. . .'

'Want another go?'

Logan shot him again, this time in the stomach – right in the middle of the vest's abdominal panel. Kravchenko nearly folded in half, hissing in pain.

'You really think I'm going to let you bring a boatload of automatic weapons into my city?' He kicked the old man over onto his back and shot him in the ribs again. 'Where is it?'

'Aaaaaaagh! *Cholernik . . . Odpierdol się!*' Swearing, and groaning, and swearing some more.

'OK, fine. Let's make it more interesting.' Logan swung the gun around and blew a hole in the old bastard's leg. 'Now where's that bloody boat?'

Aftermath

I

CAULFLEG FARM, 35 MILES FROM ABERDEEN – FOUR HOURS LATER

'Now then,' Wee Hamish stepped into the barn, 'are we ready?'

A fat man in stained overalls hauled the metal door shut, locking out the sunny afternoon. He flipped a switch and the lights flickered on, just bare bulbs dangling from the ceiling, making the wet concrete floor glow.

Sties ran down either side of the building, full of big pink bodies, snouts poking through metal bars. It stank in here. A deep, savoury reek of raw sewage, sweat and terror. A dusty hint of dry straw bedding. The grunt and squeal of the pigs.

Hilary Brander looked at her husband. 'We're ready.'

'Good, good.' Wee Hamish held out a brand-new claw hammer. 'Well, there's no rush, so take your time. You want me and Reuben to wait outside?' He pointed at the fat man, who waved back, his face a deformed mass of scar tissue and patchy beard.

'No, no, you're OK.' She accepted the hammer and Wee Hamish nodded.

'Right, well, he's all ready for you.'

They'd laid out a couple of wooden pallets on a bed of straw in the middle of the concrete walkway. There was a man tied to the wood, spread-eagled. One side of his head was swollen and torn, covered in a red-brown mask of dried blood. He was big. Going bald at the front, the long hair at the back matted and glistening.

He mumbled something behind the gag, glaring at them with one eye as Hilary led Simon across the concrete floor, the scars where his eyes used to be hidden behind a pair of wraparound sunglasses.

Wee Hamish coughed. 'I'm sorry we couldn't get the other one. I'm afraid the police officer involved was. . . Well, never mind. I'm sure we can take care of that later.'

Hilary pressed the hammer into Simon's hand. 'He's all yours.'

Simon bared his teeth, feeling his way along the battered man's leg until he came to the knee.

The victim thrashed, jerking back and forth, but the ropes were nice and tight. He wasn't going anywhere.

Simon's first three goes with the hammer missed, thunking into the wooden pallets. The fourth clipped the edge of the man's leg, and the fifth crunched down on the back of his own hand. 'FUCK! FUCKING, FUCKING FUCK!' He hurled the hammer away and sat back on his haunches, sucking his knuckles.

'Are you OK, honey?'

'No I'm not O-fucking-K! I'm blind! I can't even *cripple* someone!'

Hilary stood, walked over to the hammer and picked it up. There were bits of straw stuck between the forks of the claw. She picked them free and let them fall to the floor. 'I'll do it.'

Wee Hamish laid a hand on her shoulder. 'It's all right, Hilary love, Reuben will take care of everything. Won't you Reuben?'

'Be my pleasure, Miss Brander.'

'You go inside and tell Mrs Williamson I said to give you a nice cup of tea.'

Hilary hefted the hammer in her hand. 'Thanks, but it should be one of the family. And Colin can't do it – not with the police watching him all the time. I owe it to Simon. . .'

The first blow was tentative. The second harder. The third strong enough to make the cartilage snap and the big man scream behind the gag. On and on, pounding away at the knee joint, spatters of blood flying as the noise got wetter and wetter. Hammering right down into the bone. Then it was time for knee number two.

She looked up. Wiped a hand across her face, trying to get rid of the little red drops on her cheeks and forehead, but probably just making a smeary mess.

Simon was smiling his bedroom smile, listening as the crunching started up again. She could see the bulge in his trousers. First time in years. . .

Tonight was going to be very special.

She grinned, then went to work on the big Pole's elbows.

Detective Sergeant Pirie screwed his eyes shut and tried to pretend he was somewhere else. *Anywhere* else. Anywhere other than lying on his side in an empty pig pen, drenched in his own blood. Handcuffed and gagged. Cold and shivering. Lapsing in and out of consciousness. Crying, and praying.

Then the sound of hammering stopped, and the big Polish guy was dragged away.

The barn door grated open.

Pirie could hear the pigs squealing as they fought over something. And then Reuben was back, his big scarred face twisted into a smile.

'Your turn.'

II

Grampian Police Force Headquarters – Monday

DI Steel was waiting for him outside DCI Finnie's office, lounging back against the wall, hands jammed deep into her armpits. She raised an eyebrow as Logan closed the door. 'Well, they going to throw the book at you?'

'Depends if the *Buckie Ballad* turns up where it's supposed to.' He grimaced and started down the corridor. 'There's still no sign of Kravchenko's thug, Grigor: ferries, bus stations, airports, nothing. Right now Finnie and Bain are in there fighting about who gets blamed for DS Pirie being bent. I've got a two o'clock with Professional Standards, so it'll probably end up being *my* fault.'

'Oh, come on, don't be such a grumpy monkey.' She slapped him on the back, then linked her arm in his. 'If you're nice to Aunty Roberta, she'll put in a good word for you.'

'Yeah, because that worked *so* well when they were looking for a new DI.'

'Don't start with that again.' She pushed open the door and they were in the stairwell. 'Anyway, you owe me for upsetting Susan with that paedophile thing. She's still sulking.'

Steel stopped him on the stairs, dug about in her pocket and came out with a little plastic specimen jar.

Logan groaned. 'Like things aren't bad enough?'

'Oh come on, it's the least you can do! Get your tattooed gothfriend to—'

'Inspector?' DI Beattie was coming up from the third floor, a cup of tea in one hand and a chocolate digestive in the other.

Steel didn't even turn around. 'What?'

'I think I've found out who stole the money from your swear tin!'

'Come on then, which thieving git's backside do I have to jam my foot up?'

Beattie cast a sneaky look left, then right. 'It was Detective Sergeant Pirie.'

Steel stood there, mouth hanging open. Then she slapped her cheeks, leaving her hands there for dramatic effect. 'Oh, my God, why didn't *I* think of that?'

'Well, don't be too hard on yourself, Inspector, it did take me—'

'You bloody idiot.' She shoved past Beattie and stomped down the stairs. 'Since it got out Pirie was taking backhanders, he's been blamed for everything. My money's gone missing? Blame Pirie. The milk's gone off? Blame Pirie. They promoted a bearded-sodding-halfwit to Detective Inspector? Blame Pirie.'

'But I—'

'You were a lousy DS and you're an even worse DI!'

She disappeared around the next flight of stairs, her voice echoing up from below. 'Lazarus, we're no' getting any younger here. Move your backside!'

He hurried after her, shrugging at a spluttering DI Beattie on the way past.

Logan caught up with the inspector in the corridor outside her office. She stopped with one hand on her door handle, and grinned. 'Think that's going to be my new hobby – winding Beattie up till he cries.'

She turned the handle and the door swung open behind her, which was why she couldn't see a startled-looking DC Rennie jumping up from behind her desk. He scrambled over to the window, pretending to be watching something outside as Steel turned round and sauntered into the room.

'What you doing here?'

Rennie went into a pantomime, 'Oh I didn't see you there . . .' act. 'I was . . . erm . . . looking for DS McRae. You know how they let Ricky Gilchrist out on psychiatric licence, coz he was only pretending to be Oedipus?'

'And?'

'Attacked a Polish barman last night, right in the middle of the pub. Managed to gouge one of the poor sod's eyes out with his thumb before the doormen dragged him off.'

'Wonderful – that's all I need.'

'Apparently, he was screaming about how the Polish were all rabid dogs, and how the police should never've let him go.'

'Aye,' said Steel, 'that's right, rub it in. Do you no' think Laz has got enough to worry about: half-dead Polish bint, a missing DS, escaped Polish henchman, and a blind paedophile who's suing our arses off.'

Logan collapsed into one of the visitor's chairs. 'I still don't know how Kravchenko found out we had Rory Simpson at your place. Wiktorja sure as hell didn't tell him.'

'Ah. . .' Rennie went brick red. 'Actually. . .' He coughed. 'That might've been my fault.'

'*What*?'

'Well . . . Pirie asked me what I was doing Thursday and I kind of . . . you know.'

'You told him.' Logan slumped even further down his chair, hands over his face. 'Oh for God's sake.'

'Sorry?'

Steel's voice was worryingly calm and level. 'Laz, do you have ten quid I can borrow?'

Logan peered out through his fingers. 'You told Pirie?'

'It wasn't my fault!'

'Someone lend me a tenner!'

Rennie dug a ten pound note from his pocket and handed it over. 'I really didn't mean to—'

Steel poked him in the chest. 'People nearly died! Rory Simpson got his eyes gouged out! You stupid, idiotic, half-wit, son-of-a-bitching, useless, bloody *tosser*!' That was just the warm up – once she got into her stride Rennie was subjected to a tidal wave of abuse. And then the rant came to a sudden and unexpected halt.

'Ten quid.' She turned her back on the constable and thrust the money she'd borrowed into Logan's hand. 'Stick that in the swear tin. And while you're at it. . .' She chucked the plastic specimen tub at him as well.

'But—'

'No buts.' DI Steel threw a finger in Rennie's direction. 'And *you* . . . you just think yourself lucky I'm skint!' She stormed out, slamming the door behind her.

'Bloody hell. . .' The constable slouched back against the desk. 'Is it just me, or is she getting worse?'

Logan didn't answer that, just sat there, turning the little tub over and over in his hands.

'Look, I'm really sorry about telling Pirie, OK?'

'What were you doing behind her desk?'

Rennie blushed. 'Ah, right . . . I sort of *borrowed* some money from the swear tin a couple of weeks ago. It was just a loan, I swear. I put it all back – you can count it if you like?'

'Beattie says Pirie stole it.'

'Oh. . .' Rennie chewed the inside of his cheek. 'Does that mean I can keep the cash? You know, if everyone thinks it was Pirie's fault?'

Logan just scowled at him.

'Right. No. Suppose not.'

More silence.

Rennie peered at the little plastic tub in Logan's hands. 'What's that?'

'She wants me to get Susan pregnant.'

'Really? Wow, hot lesbian gangbang for you then!'

'Just don't, OK? I'm not in the mood.'

'Don't see what all the fuss is about; just a wee bit of sperm.'

'It's . . . complicated.'

'Don't want to be a daddy, eh?'

Logan stuck the tub on the desk. 'Not particularly, no.'

Rennie pursed his lips for a minute. Then picked the container up. 'I'll do it.'

'What? No, she—'

'Oh, come on! Nearly got you killed: least I can do is wank in a cup.' He headed for the door, a spring in his step and a hand in his trousers. 'I'll show her who's a useless tosser.'

By the time Steel got back from wherever it was, Rennie had come and gone, leaving a slimy reminder in the bottom of the plastic tub. Not wanting to touch the thing, Logan had told him to put it on the windowsill in the sunshine to keep it warm.

Steel cracked the window open and stood there, staring at the little tub. 'Is this what I think it is?' She picked up the tub and squinted at the contents. 'Could you no' have managed a little more?'

'Look, forget about it. Chuck it in the bin, it's not—'

'No!' She clutched it too her chest. 'No, I'm no' being ungrateful, this is great. It's fine, honestly.' The inspector grabbed her jacket from the back of her chair. 'If anyone needs me, tell them to sod off, OK? I've got a baby to make.'

She hurried out. Then bustled back in again, planted a big smoky kiss on Logan's cheek, and said, 'Thank you.'

Logan watched her go, all happy with her counterfeit sperm. He tried to warn her, no one could say he didn't try. . .

He slumped back to the empty CID office. Screw Professional Standards, they could haul him over the coals tomorrow.

Someone had stuck a Post-it note on his computer screen. Yet another message from Dr Goulding about how he could help with some fictitious case.

Wee Hamish's bottle of thirty-year-old Knockdhu was exactly where Logan had left it, along with the glass he'd used to take Krystka Gorzałkowska's fingerprints when she was in hospital.

Maybe this wasn't such a good idea. Once you started accepting free booze, what came next?

He took the glass out of the evidence bag, tore the foil cap off the whisky with shaky fingers, and poured himself a stiff measure. It glowed like bottled fire.

Logan toasted Goulding's Post-it. 'Thin end of the wedge.' It went down smooth, hitting his stomach and spreading warm, sweet tendrils through his body, soothing out the tremors. Peat and alcohol making his breath tingle. It was good stuff. He finished the rest of the glass before someone came in and asked for a taste, then went onto the internet and found out how much a bottle of thirty-year-old Knockdhu was actually worth.

'Jesus. . .' It was a small fortune.

Really should phone Wee Hamish up and say thank you.

Only polite. Thanks for the hooringly expensive whisky: anything I can do in return?

Logan looked at the Post-it note. Or he could call Goulding, let the psychologist probe and prod away at his problems like a rotten tooth.

Wee Hamish or Goulding?

Whisky or toothache?

He pulled out his phone and made the call.

III

Her Majesty's Prison Craiginches – Two Weeks Later

The exercise yard is busy, even with the thin drizzle drifting down from a grey July sky. The outside world invisible behind high granite walls.

He folds his arms and leans back against the equipment locker, enjoying the fresh air. Five days stuck inside in solitary, just because someone accidentally got their hand trapped in one of the heavy cell doors. Six times.

Not his fault, is it? Not that they could prove anyway. No, he was real fucking careful about that. Two months for aggravated assault is quite enough, thanks.

Two months . . . God he could murder a joint.

Instead he settles in and watches the game.

It's supposed to be a football match – blues versus reds – but there are too many players, and half the buggers don't have a clue what they're doing. Bunch of Muppets. The score's twenty-three to fifty-two. That's coz no one wants to stay in goal, they all want to be strikers. Morons.

Don't understand the importance of taking one for the team. . .

He straightens up.

The Russian bloke's here – Russian, Polish, something like that – limping along with a face like a skelpt arse. Two weeks since that cop put a bullet in him, and he's already up and walking. That's one tough bastard.

Russians, eh?

Someone boots the ball out of play. It bounces a couple of times, then comes to rest at the Russian's feet. Should be a throw in, but the halfwits in blue and red all rush to see who can get to it first, hooting like fucking monkeys.

Right on cue.

Colin McLeod saunters across the scrappy grass behind the red team goal, looking dead casual, you know? Closing the gap.

The players hustle around the limping Russian, jockeying for position – 'Come on, pass the fuckin' thing!' / 'Gerroff!'/ 'Fuck you!' / 'Hey, it's my turn!' – obscuring Colin from view as he slides the shiv from his sleeve.

Nothing fancy, just a toothbrush, sharpened to a point on the floor of his cell. He rams it into the Russian's back. Three times in the kidneys, and twice in the throat.

The old man doesn't even cry out, just sinks to the ground with blood bubbling out of his mouth. Be dead in a minute. Now who's tough, eh?

Creepy Colin McLeod leans in and passes on the message he's spent the last five days practicing. Sounding it out in his cell every night until it's right.

'*Do widzenia,* you stupid Russian fuck.'

Goodbye.

And then the crowd yells and shouts its way back to the football pitch, taking Colin with it, leaving the old man's body to twitch and shudder, and finally lie still.

That's what happens when you fuck with Aberdeen.